HUNGER

CHRISTIE GOLDENWULFE

SISTER MOON PUBLISHING UMBRA

Printed in the United States of America

First Printing, June 2016

ISBN 978-0-9961197-2-6

Sister Moon Publishing
P.O. Box 739
Cedar Crest, NM 87008
www.sistermoonpublishing.com

Cover Illustration and design © 2016 by Christy Grandjean
Book design and production by Christy Grandjean

Edited by Nancy Cassidy, www.theredpencoach.com

For Kip. Thank you beautiful man, for being my Muse.

Acknowledgments

This is my first book, an immense labor of love with a hell of a lot of learning along the way. It would not have happened without the help of some awesome people.

For Sandra, thanks for cheering me on—and occasionally kicking my ass—when I felt like I was crazy for writing this. For my editor Nancy, for patiently correcting and instructing me in my writing, and for helping me to be a better writer. For my Alpha Readers: Hish (Sarah), Swifty (Jennifer), Aurora (Dana), and Moonie (Cecelia). Thank you for your love and enthusiasm. You helped me believe in my characters and their story.

For my little sister Cindy, who passed unexpectedly in the midst of writing my second draft. You would have been my greatest champion and my biggest critic. You would have loved this book. I miss you terribly and always.

And lastly for my fans who have watched me develop the Kierrn (the ancient name for my race of werewolves) over the years, and for supporting my art and other creative endeavors. Thanks for believing in me and for encouraging my crazy love of werewolves. You guys are the best.

PART ONE
THE HUNT

CHAPTER ONE
Monster

The motorcycle roared up the interstate in the moonlit darkness, recklessly careening through late-night traffic. The speedometer read 110 miles per hour as the rider sped northward through California's central valley with the police hot on his tail. Lights flashed through the night and sirens wailed in the darkness right behind him, goading him to go faster.

Kain Ulmer was having the time of his life.

The roar of the machine beneath him and the howl of the sirens faded against the scream of the wind past his ears, plastering his long hair to his skull and whipping it behind him. Thrilled by the chase, he urged the motorcycle to greater speeds and laughed into the wind.

The full moon rode high and pulsed in his veins, calling to the beast inside of him, filling him with exuberant energy. The chase had begun twenty miles back on I-5. He'd been headed northbound and doing ninety-five at the time with not a care in the world. He had stolen the bike earlier that night from a home in Burbank when the opportunity had presented itself. The theft had been discovered and reported quickly. A little *too* quickly for his liking, but oh well. What was life without a little dangerous fun? He hazarded a quick glance behind him and grinned fiercely. His pursuers were right on his ass.

Kain was no stranger to running. He'd spent most of his life running from one thing or another—usually women, jealous husbands, or the authorities. Running kept him free, and there was little he valued in life more than freedom. Nothing and no one would ever chain him down.

A cruiser sped up, attempting to pass him on the right. Kain leaned into the bike and cut the officer off, sending him sailing into the shoulder. Another officer followed him closely, right on his ass. A bridge came up in the darkness and he leaned in, passing dangerously close to the support pillars, never losing speed for a moment. The cruiser swerved back into the right-hand lane and nearly clipped another vehicle. Kain chuckled to himself. His friends should really be more careful.

Up ahead, two semis were paralleling one another and effectively blocking the two northbound lanes. Kain hit the throttle and shot between the trucks, sure of himself even when one trailer swayed toward the other. Once through, he sped far ahead of the semis while the officers jockeyed to move past the big rigs. Traffic was light at this time of the night, and ahead of the semis, the way was clear. After a moment he braked heavily, and the machine under him protested as the tires squealed on the pavement. Planting one boot, he pivoted the bike around and gunned the throttle with a whoop of laughter. The powerful engine roared and lurched forward, hurtling toward the oncoming semis like a rocket. He blazed past the trucks on the left hand shoulder, popping the bike into a half-wheelie as he passed the cops. The sound of braking tires shrieked behind him.

He stayed to the shoulder and slowed a bit, waiting for his friends to sort themselves out. They might choose to let him go at this point rather than continue such a dangerous chase, but he'd managed to piss them off pretty severely with his antics by now. They'd be determined to stop him. Sure enough, he spotted them in his mirrors, turning and tearing after him. Oncoming vehicles blared their horns at him, but he stayed well out of their way while he rode the shoulder. The officers were trained for this sort of thing and were skilled drivers. He had no problem leading them on a merry chase, but he had little desire for anyone else to get involved in his amusements. No sense in brining harm to innocent travelers.

It was time to take this show off the road.

He waited for a clear moment in traffic before he cruised across the lanes and skillfully pivoted the bike onto a convenient ranch exit. At the end of the off-ramp, he turned right and throttled the gas, barreling down the dark country road. Clouds scudded across the face of the moon, plunging the area into shadow, but his night vision was superb. There was nothing out here but fields and orchards in the middle central valley. This would be the perfect opportunity to escape, but there was no need to run off just yet. The moon's energy coursed through his body and he felt far too good to stop now. He wanted to play some more with his newfound friends.

He could see the flashing lights from the cruisers in his mirrors again, so he slowed and banked a hard left onto a dirt road and then a right, cruising into expansive, flowering orchards. He drove until the road came to a T, where he slowed to a stop and looked around. Orchards surrounded him, the neat rows of trees black and indistinct in the darkness. He cut the engine and silence enveloped him, except for the sound of wailing sirens growing closer. He dismounted, shifting the pack on his back as he checked his surroundings. He wouldn't try to hide the bike. It would be no fun if his friends couldn't find him, so he left the lights on and gave the machine a last, longing glance before he turned and headed into the darkness.

The sound of the cruisers increased as the darkness of the trees surrounded him. The clouds had thickened, shrouding the moon. Shadows lay deep under the trees here, and a low mist curled around the trunks. His senses were preternatural, however, and the night revealed itself to him.

He loped through the orchard, swinging his head this way and that as he caught different scents. The overpowering smell of the flowering trees, grass and other growing things; the old odor of a fox kill; scents of rabbits, mice, and the sharp musk of coyotes, the dusty scent of birds—nothing that shouldn't be there. The orchard was very large and it would take the officers time to coordinate a search. Likely, a chopper had been called to help with the pursuit, which meant he needed to stay alert. He would have to leave when it arrived, but for now he could still have some fun.

Kain strode to a remote part of the orchard and dropped his pack from his shoulders. He could hear the officers a long way off, though it was clear they were already spreading out to search. He had just a few moments, but it was enough. Besides his other…abilities, Kain had a few tricks up his sleeve. Kneeling, he pulled two items out of his pack—a small vial and a curved, silvery blade—and laid them on the ground in front of him. Then he lifted a necklace out from under his shirt by its woven leather cord, and cupped the fanged talisman in his hand.

The fang was old and big, fossilized and darkened with time, and capped with a carved antler tine. He'd worn the fang for a long time, relying on the talisman for a variety of quick spells such as the one he enacted now. He opened the vial and dabbed a tiny drop of pungent oil on the fang, murmuring guttural words over it. The carvings on the antler tine flared faintly, briefly, and the fossil warmed in his palm. Then he picked up the curved knife, pierced his palm with barely a flinch, and pressed the bleeding wound to the ground. He uttered a few more words and felt the earth take what he offered. Now, when he fled the scene, the earth would swallow his prints, his scent, and his spoor. None would be able to track him.

Chuckling in anticipation, he put the items back in his pack and began pulling off his clothes. Now for the best trick of all. He could hear the officers in the orchard now, searching for him. They would not expect what he was about to do. The misty night air had a chill to it that caressed him as he pulled off his boots and stuffed everything into the pack. Though temperature rarely affected his kind, the chill was welcome after the heat of the chase. The talisman was the only item he kept on. The strong, leather cord was long enough to accommodate his...other form.

Naked now, he stood and strode to a clear area between the trees. He flexed his muscles as he planted his feet and shook out his hip-length hair behind him, preparing himself. He could push this if he wanted, but he loved to savor this moment and he closed his eyes.

His lips parted slightly as he drew in several deep breaths, and he began to let go, opening the doors within him that were never quite shut, inviting the beast that lived within him forward. The beast was a dark well of power, and as it came into him, it filled his body with potent magic, bringing on the change. It started with a pressure within his body, then a crawling, and then a burning fire. He had long ago learned to temper the sensations and merely grunted in response as the first waves came.

His eyes always changed first, and they tingled and burned as they shifted. They would now be a chilling, icy blue ringed in red, terrifying to behold. His teeth lengthened into fangs; his already thick fingernails blackened and began to curve into claws. Fur rippled, then exploded over his skin with an intense itching as his bones lengthened and ground within his body. Muscles and sinews contracted and expanded with a delicious ache to adjust to his new bone structure, and his entire skull shifted with a painful pressure. His jaw lengthened, and his teeth continued to push themselves into huge fangs as he moaned into the night. His claws became talons as sharp and cruelly pointed as knives. He dug them into the earth when he doubled over onto all fours with a groan.

The whole process was accompanied by the sensation of a pleasure so intense it gave him an erection as his pelvis pushed out the bones for a tail, and his body finished its adjustments. He moaned and growled as his head completed the shift with a lingering burning sensation and he was left momentarily drained, panting and lying on the cool earth.

His body was now a hulking mass of muscle, bristling with black fur and a ridge of long, stiff hackles down his spine. His head was large and lupine in shape, but held enormous teeth far bigger than any natural wolf possessed. His limbs were thick with muscle, his body humanoid and bestial at the same time. When he rose and stood on two legs, he resembled nothing the men chasing him would have ever seen before, a creature out of nightmares. He was nearly eight feet tall and easily over four hundred pounds in this form, a monstrous beast made for the kill. Not human, not wolf, nor any other creature, but something… other.

The hidden moon called to him, and the Hunger welled up powerfully in him for a moment. It filled him with a deep desire for flesh and blood until he managed to quell the impulse with a growl. Though he could clearly smell humans in the area, he would not be satiating that need tonight. He had to be careful. The curse of his kind was always there, always ready to urge him to make a very bad decision, one that brought blood and death, and he had to be diligent not to let that happen. He only gave into the Hunger when he had no other choice, and when he did finally go hunting, he always chose fellow predators as prey. Murderers, rapists, thugs…they were all fair game. He never took the innocent.

Not after the last ones…

Shaking off the unpleasant memories, he stretched and flexed his limbs, muscle rippling under his fur as he moved. He twisted his head until there was a deep pop in his neck and then shook himself fully with a groan, his thick, black pelt throwing off stiff hairs and soft down into the air.

He took a moment to check where the humans were, questing with his nose and perking his ears to listen. They were closer now, yet still on the far end of the orchard, though fanning out quickly. He swiped his tongue over his nose and grinned wolfishly in anticipation. Time to play!

Throwing back his head, he opened his throat and let out a howl that thundered through the night, launching sleeping birds into the air with alarmed screeches.

The humans were warned.

He dropped to all fours and walked forward, his body making small adjustments for his his now quadruped stance. Satisfied, he bunched his legs and shot forward into the darkness. Running in this form was sheer bliss. There was nothing like the power and freedom of it, his claws digging into the soil, his powerful legs propelling him forward like pistons. The wolf in him wanted to run and keep running, far away from the humans, to celebrate the moon and make love to the night. But the human in him still wanted to have fun, and so he ran toward the policemen with incredible speed.

Flashlights swept the darkness and the acrid scents of gunpowder, oil, and metal filled the air. They had their guns out. No matter, guns weren't of any consequence to him…unless they held silver. His kind could survive most anything except that poisonous metal. He had toyed with the officers long enough to make them cautious about capturing him, and probably had them thinking he was a bit crazy and dangerous. He smiled to himself. You could call him that.

He came upon the first group of humans quickly, a pair of officers searching through a section of orchard. His howl must have unnerved them, for they had the scent of apprehension to them. The beams of their flashlights did little to dispel the thick darkness around the trees. Kain ran in low and fast, darting past their lights and eliciting alarmed shouts and even a shot. He could hear the crackle of radios and shouts from others as he sped away and he laughed, thoroughly enjoying himself.

He stopped in a dark spot across the orchard and listened, his ears perked. The officers he had buzzed were flustered, speaking angrily into their radios as they scanned the darkness. Clearly, they were truly frightened now by the huge animal they had seen, and the howl everyone had heard earlier. Kain growled softly in his throat, a wolfish chuckle, and moved off to a different part of the orchard.

Here he found one officer some distance from his partner. Inexperienced or stupid—either way he would soon learn not to stray from his friends. Kain circled around him, out of flashlight range. He was a young cadet only recently out of training, by the looks of him. Kain growled loudly, a sound that reverberated through the air and caused the trees around him to tremble. Nervously, the young officer aimed his gun and flashlight in the direction of the sound, and gasped when he saw Kain's eyes.

Snarling, Kain charged forward. The officer screamed until Kain reached him and cuffed him on the head. The kid went down like a sack of potatoes, dropping his flashlight and gun. Kain quickly grabbed him up and slung him over his shoulder, heading toward the road. They would find the kid later near his cruiser with one hell of a headache, but otherwise unharmed.

Back in the trees, he circled around again and listened intently, cupping his ears to hear things from far across the orchard. The officers were thoroughly spooked now, having heard the scream. The kid's partner was especially freaked out; he'd just found the flashlight and fully loaded gun on the ground with his partner nowhere to be seen. Radios crackled everywhere, full of orders and demands for information, mixed with rising fear.

The chaos was exhilarating. Kain took a moment to roll on the ground in satisfaction, rubbing the sweet scent of flowers and decay deep into his fur. Now he really wanted to mess with their heads.

Tongue lolling, he loped toward another group of four tightly knit men who were advancing slowly, deeper into the orchard. He circled around behind them and approached them as silently as possible, stepping lightly, easing his breathing. Carefully, he rose on two legs and spread his ape-like arms wide, huge jaws open and slavering, towering over the four men. Just when Kain sensed that one of the men could feel something horrible behind them, he bolted, the man's flashlight just brushing his fur.

The man swore loudly and trained his gun, his comrades flailing to follow suit, but Kain was not there. He came around low and fast, brushing past their backsides. They all jumped and turned, pointing their shaking flashlights all around them. Their radios squawked and they answered with obvious fear in their voices. There was something in the trees, and it wasn't a goddamned coyote.

Kain came in again, streaking past their lights, and someone shot at the night with an oath. Their radios shrieked out the voice of their commanding officer, but none of them paid any heed. Their instincts had kicked in, and though they were highly trained men, they knew they were being hunted—hunted by something they could not fathom. Kain howled again, bellowing into the night, and one of the officers pissed himself; the stink of urine carried on the air.

Kain breathed in their fear as he panted and circled them just outside the range of their lights. Terror permeated the air in a thick blanket radiating from the men.

The scent of prey. Human prey.

Saliva pooled in his jaws and he felt the Hunger take him then, consuming him in an instant. The dark beast inside surged and took over, blocking out his humanity, his reasoning, his compassion. Harmless fun turned now to serious hunting. The beast craved the taste of flesh and blood on his tongue. He growled in his chest, filled with aching desire and a ravenous craving for human meat. These men were now his.

He stalked forward, intent on the small knot of officers who were slowly retreating. He crept as close as he could, his lips rising in a silent snarl. He dove in and snatched the weakest of them— the one that had lost control of his bladder. The man screamed and Kain began running, dragging the man along by his leg. The other officers fired once before racing after them.

A bullet struck Kain's thigh, but he only grunted and continued to run into the dark of the orchard. The man screamed and squealed, and scrabbled at the earth with his bare hands to little avail. Blood, rich and intoxicating, filled Kain's mouth, but it wasn't enough to satiate the Hunger. He needed more.

The man's friends followed as fast as they could, and officers came quickly from other parts of the orchard, drawn by his screams. Kain was quicker and undeterred. His bestial mind knew only the Hunger, and would not give up its prize.

He finally stopped on the far side of the orchard and flung the man with a wrench of his head. The officer cried out and skidded several feet, thudding up against a tree and sending flower petals raining down over him. Kain was on him in an instant, pinning the man down so he couldn't move. He took a moment to survey his prize, teeth bared in his hunger while the man cowered under him. He could taste the man's fear across his tongue, and saliva spun from his lips. He opened his mouth wide, ready to rip out the man's throat, when his humanity came screaming back to battle at his instincts.

He paused with teeth inches from the man's up-flung hands and blinked. What the hell was he doing? He'd only meant to have some fun with the cops tonight, not actually hurt anyone, and it was definitely not his intent to give into the Hunger.

He growled and shrank back from the man, retreating to crouch in the shadows. The officer whimpered, cowering on the ground with his arms around this head. When death did not come, he lowered them slowly, staring terrified into the darkness. Kain turned his head in shame. What had he been thinking, testing himself like this? It had been too long since he had given in to the curse and made a kill. The Spring Equinox was only two weeks away and by then he would be forced to kill or face the consequences. With the moon full tonight, the risk of the Hunger taking over had been very high. He should have known that, but he had been too busy entertaining himself.

"Go." Kain's voice was more growl than real speech. The officer stared at him through the darkness, his eyes wide and obviously in shock. Kain snarled and roared at him, "Go now!" The officer scrambled to his feet, whimpering, and limped off into the orchard.

Kain paced on all fours for a moment, still shaking with the fierce call of the Hunger as he fought for control, cursing himself. Somehow, he always seemed to get into these situations, and someone always wound up hurt. He could never seem to resist that next bit of fun, that chance to test himself. It had gotten him into trouble more than once, and now he'd done it again. He growled softly, but stopped when he caught the faint sound of an approaching helicopter. He turned his head and perked his ears at the distant thrum. He could also hear the men retreating, ordered to evacuate the orchard. The cavalry was here, and that was definitely his cue to leave.

There were more lights now as additional units had arrived and every available light flooded the orchard. There were officers between him and where he had stashed his pack. He would have to be quick.

He started loping and built up speed, and by the time he was running past them, he was nothing but a blur. There were shouts and some shots, but nothing struck its mark and soon they were far behind him. His kind had the power to move incredibly fast, faster than any animal, and he put that speed on now, despite the burning wound in his thigh. He paused only briefly to gather his things, catching the strap of his backpack in his mouth, and he was running again, this time out of the orchards and northward into the fields. No cover there, but he was fast, and the clouds still obscured the moon. The chopper would be scanning the orchard first, anyway, and with the power of the spell he'd cast earlier with his talisman, they would never find him. Still, best to put as much distance as possible between himself and the chaos he had created before changing back to human.

The night opened up again to Kain as he sped through the darkness, but this time he was carried by his powerful body instead of the bike. Soon his regrets for the night were lost in the joy of running and he took delight in his bestial form once more. He never regretted what he was. In fact, he loved being a werewolf, and it suited him well. Except for the Hunger. Killing was never something he took lightly. He did what he had to, what the Hunger demanded of him every few months. It was the price he paid for his power and freedom.

The clouds shifted and the moon showed her face, cold light spilling across the land once more as he ran. He traveled through fields and orchards, past farms and ranches and barking dogs. He avoided towns of any size and slipped under freeways through drainage ditches and tunnels, bolting across smaller roads when he had to. Few people were out at this time of night, and he encountered no one except livestock and dogs.

After a while, he found himself in the middle of a large expanse of open brush and he slowed to a stop. He dropped the pack from his mouth and panted heavily, his breath steaming in the cool night air. After a moment, obeying her silent song, he turned his gaze up to the moon. Her light called to the wolf in him and sent a thrill down his spine, raising his hackles. He closed his eyes and savored her for a moment like a lover. Tonight could have gone badly, but he had prevailed. He was still alive and free, and the knowledge caused him to cavort for a moment before lifting his head to howl triumphantly.

Now he wanted a woman.

Flushed with excitement he sniffed the air until he realized what he was doing. He stopped, snorted, and shook his head. Now was not the time. The type of women he liked were easily found and getting one would be a simple matter. His kind exuded an animal-like sexuality that humans found irresistible, a power he could focus and intensify if he needed to, and his untamed good looks and natural charm made it easy for him to get whomever he wanted. Available or not, they came to him readily. But no, right now he needed to put far more distance between himself and his adventures. He also needed a car.

He picked up his pack again and continued on.

The moon hung low in the sky and dawn was a smudge of pale blue on the eastern horizon when he stopped once more. Daylight would come very soon now, and he could not risk being seen in this form. He had sped north, sticking to the fields and farmlands, and now he was somewhere west of Modesto, he figured, considering the lights of a large town to the east. By now, the sprawling farms and ranches had given way to trailers, smaller homesteads, and outbuildings. He should be able to find what he needed here. He trotted through the pre-dawn darkness with his tail held high, panting around the strap in his mouth as he explored some nearby buildings. Dogs barked until they caught his scent, then quieted and retreated in fear. *That's right Fido, better not mess with the big bad wolf.*

Snorting in good humor, he came around the front of an old, barn-like building off to the side of a large, fenced field. There were a few smaller buildings about, but no sign of a residence nearby. Sniffing around the entrance, he detected the scent of a car inside, though the two large doors were chained and padlocked. He set his pack down and reared up on two legs, took the chain between his hand-paws, and snapped it with a grunt. He swung the doors open and raised his ears at the sight before him. A 1968 Camaro RS SS, primer black, and obviously being refurbished by the owner.

Making a sound of appreciation, he dropped to all fours again and began circling the vehicle in excitement with his tail wagging. He inspected the tires and looked into the windows, checking the vehicle over. The leather upholstery was dusty, but still in good shape, and the instrument panel seemed to be intact. He didn't see any keys—not that it mattered; he could hotwire anything. The important thing was the condition of the engine, but checking that required shifting back to human form.

He sat on his haunches in front of the vehicle and began reforming his human self in his mind's eye, visualizing his human hands and face, his skin, hair, and body, but the wolf was still powerful from the moon and too excited by the night's run to give up so easily. Growling softly, he lied down. Putting his head between his forepaws, he forced the wolf to back down. The wildness in him fought for a moment, then reluctantly retreated and he tried the process again.

This time a tingling started, immediately followed by a feeling of energetic release, like hot water draining from a basin. He sighed as his face began to retreat into itself and his fur skittered back into his skin with a tickling sensation. His bones shifted again with a soft pop and grind in places, and his tail retreated back into his coccyx.

Within a couple of minutes, he'd regained his human form and lay naked and somewhat drained on the dusty floor of the barn. The price of ignoring the curse. He propped himself up on his hands and pulled into a sitting position. Had he made a kill tonight, as the Hunger had demanded, his transformation would be easy and effortless. Thankfully, he had not killed, trading remorse for a few moments of vulnerability. He reached for his pack and began wearily pulling on his clothes.

By the time he hauled on his boots, he was feeling more or less normal again. The bullet wound had completely healed without a trace, his body having pushed out the lead sometime during his run. The healing ability of his kind was astonishing, and such superficial wounds healed within hours, sometimes minutes. He finished arranging his pack and rose to his feet, taking a moment to dust himself off.

He tested the Camaro's door and found it unlocked. With a grin, he tossed his pack onto the seat, then opened the hood so he could take a look at the engine. Everything seemed to be intact, as far as he could tell. He checked all of the fluid levels and made sure everything was tight before closing the hood quietly. He prayed that the engine would actually start as he climbed back inside. There could be any number of things wrong with the car, but he didn't have time for more than a cursory inspection.

Life was a gamble anyway.

He was feeling for the panel under the steering wheel that would give him access to the wiring when he noticed the key in the ignition. He smiled wryly and sat back in the seat. He couldn't be that lucky. He absently touched his talisman and held his breath as he reached for the key and turned it. The starter grated, and he pumped the gas and muttered encouragement to the vehicle. The engine came to life with a sputter and then a throaty roar. He gave a shout of triumph and patted the dash, praising the car as the engine grumbled to wakefulness.

He let the car idle and climbed out to open the barn doors all the way. Though the sun had not yet risen, the moon perched on the western horizon and the eastern sky was much lighter. Early morning birds sang, and the scent of dawn lightened the air. Time to be gone.

After he got back in and situated himself, Kain put the car in gear and drove to the pavement, assessing the vehicle. The car rumbled in satisfaction, as if happy to be released from the barn. Once the wheels hit pavement he said a small prayer and stomped down on the gas pedal. The Camaro obliged him, jumping forward with a squeal of tires and a puff of blue smoke. Kain gave a whoop of laugher and shifted gears. Someone just lost themselves one hell of a car. He headed west and north, toward the Bay area and the setting moon, feeling immensely satisfied with himself. Now, if he could find a warm female body to claim for an evening or two, life would be utterly perfect.

Big bad wolf indeed.

CHAPTER TWO
Dragonfly

For days, the forests and mountains of Humboldt County had been under a pall of much needed March rain. The constant drizzle drenched the water-starved land and created a chill gloom that seemed to suffuse itself into the bones. Another storm had passed in the night, leaving the forest soaked and dripping as the sun began to rise, burning the veil of fog from the land. As the fog lifted, it revealed a world crisp and green, fragrant with a scent only a redwood forest can have—a mix of bay laurel, Douglas fir, rhododendrons, and the subtle spiciness of the redwood trees themselves, all washed clean by the rain and intensified by the warming sun. Birds sang and twittered in the canopy made by the towering arms of evergreens, joyous in their morning chorus.

The forest glowed in a riot of emerald and early morning gold as Autumn Sullivan jogged the last bit of trail toward her small cottage nestled among the tall trees. Stopping to catch her breath and cool down, she took in the view of her home and her heart swelled with the sight.

Plants and flowers grew in profusion, carefully tended by her hand. Insects stitched through the cool morning air and a few butterflies flitted among the early blooms, lending their color to the tranquil scene. Bisecting the little glade was a small stream, fed by a spring that emerged just up the hill, bubbling and laughing its way downward through the forest. Sword ferns crowded into any available space, greedy for any open patch not covered by the expansive arms of redwood, alder, and fir.

Perhaps Autumn's favorite part of the view was the cottage itself. It was small, yet the perfect size for her. It had two bedrooms, a loft, one bath, and a huge open room that was a wall of windows overlooking the garden where one could believe fairies should be found. Her home looked like a mix of old-world cottage and rustic, weathered cabin, which was exactly how her grandfather had planned it when he built it for her grandmother many years ago.

This was Autumn's home, the place she had grown up in, and now it all belonged to her. A beautiful sanctuary where she lived her life alone.

She was an only child. Her mother had died giving birth to her, and her father had passed four years later, leaving Oma to take care of her and raise her. Her mother had been Oma's only child as well, and since Opa died when Autumn was a little over a year old, it had just been the two of them. Oma had been her family, her world. She, too, had passed on some five years now, leaving Autumn alone, yet in some ways she was still here. Oma was in the cottage, in the garden, and in the stories she had told Autumn growing up of elves and gnomes, witches, trolls, forest-folk, and old German lore. She had taught Autumn so much, from gardening and herbalism, to cooking, sewing, and even how to repair various things around the house. Oma had lived well and loved life, exuding her own kind of magic into the world with her stories and laughter. Autumn felt blessed to have been raised by such a woman. She missed her greatly.

However, today was not a day for gloomy broodings. It was going to be a great day. With the years-long drought in California easing up a bit, the rivers and lakes were starting to fill and the land was abundant with the green of growing things once again. That meant tourism should begin booming any time now, and since the forecast called for a warm, sunny streak of weather, business might actually pick up at her shop.

Autumn had started toward her back porch when she spied a welcome sight. A dragonfly hovered around the recently bloomed dwarf irises near the stream. Autumn smiled, watching as it zipped around the ferns, hunting for breakfast. The dragonfly had been

Oma's symbol, one she had taught Autumn about through stories and lore. A creature of joy and light, of dreams and illusions, and considered good luck. It also meant that change was on the way. Good change.

Dragonfly was also the name of Autumn's coffee shop, the shop that she was surely going to be late getting to, if she didn't get a move on. Whistling now, she bid the dragonfly a good morning and hurried into the cottage to get ready for her day.

It was early afternoon when Autumn pulled her Subaru up to a stop in front of Dragonfly Coffee & Espresso in the little town of Myers Flat, California. Located on the east end of town along the famed Avenue of Giants—so-called for the groves of massive redwoods found along its route—Dragonfly was a cute, quaint cabin tucked back among a few redwood trees. The shop had opened its doors three years ago, and even though business was slow sometimes—OK, it was getting bad, but things would look up soon—and despite the fact she owed her soul to the bank, Dragonfly was still worth all the money, blood, sweat, and tears Autumn had put into it.

Her friend and employee, Marie, had opened the place at seven that morning to serve coffee and espresso to the tourists and locals alike. Dragonfly was already well known for its excellent espresso, and even the Java Hut in Redway couldn't make anything that came close to the roasted heaven that was their coffee. Dragonfly was the only place around to have free Wi-Fi, and also offered books, baubles, and local artwork in comfortable surroundings perfect for casual sipping.

Autumn drew in a deep breath of cool, fragrant air as she walked up the stairs onto the redwood deck that spanned the front of the shop, and stopped to survey the condition of her potted garden there. She dead-headed the pink dianthus, and checked the growth of her pansies and violas, noting that her primrose was flowering well, and her bleeding heart was starting to come up nicely. Satisfied, she sauntered through the front door, its stained glass dragonfly bidding her welcome.

"Afternoon, Autumn," Marie called from where she was measuring beans behind the coffee counter.

"Afternoon," Autumn called cheerily, looking around as she made her way into the store.

It was a lovely little shop, full of nooks and crannies that invited curiosity. Books and knickknacks loaded hardwood shelves dotted with little fairies and art glass, dragonflies, candles, and crystals. Chairs and tables were scattered around the dining room, colorful rugs blanketed the hardwood floors, and several windows overlooked the gardens planted under the spreading boughs of the three mature redwoods on the lot. There was even a wood-burning fireplace for those chilly days, which were plentiful in any season here, and the whole place smelled deliciously of coffee and chocolate.

"How has it been this morning?" she asked Marie, setting her things on the counter.

"Oh, you know." Marie shrugged, pouring the beans into the hopper on the grinder. "Carl and the guys were waiting when I got here, Carrie came in and bought a book…oh, and Afton actually came in off the mountain. Said he 'wanted to see what was so good about our Joe.' I guess he wasn't impressed. Said something about fancy piss water, and how his cowboy coffee was a better cup any day."

Autumn made a face, wrinkling her nose. "If he thinks boiling beans in a pot is better than our brew, he's been living up on that mountain for too long."

Marie shook her head and smiled. "Right? Some people have no taste at all. You want the usual?"

"Sure." Autumn smiled, and Marie went to work putting together her latte with honey, chatting about the slow morning, her sister's upcoming wedding, local news, her boyfriend Pete, and the awesome shoes she'd bought at the outlet mall in Eureka.

Autumn listened to her with half an ear, closing her eyes and relaxing into the afternoon, and reflected upon just how blessed she was. The world was hers. Life couldn't get any more perfect.

"Oh, by the way," Marie began with a sly tone, leaning over the counter as she handed her the wide cup filled with heavenly honeyed latte. "I met this guy the other day while I was at the outlets. He works at the leather store. He's like the manager or something. Anyway, he's 32, totally single, totally fine, and interested in you." She emphasized the 'you' with a poke to Autumn's shoulder.

Autumn groaned aloud, giving her an imploring look. "Maar-eeeee! You know I'm not interested."

"Auuut-uuum!" Marie mimicked her tone and pleading expression. "You need to go out. You have no life outside of this store and your place up there in the hills. You need to have some fun! You need to meet people!"

"I *do* meet people!" Autumn exclaimed defensively. "I meet people here. And I do have fun. I call it gardening, and painting… and pottery."

Marie pursed her lips for a moment, then leaned in closer with a serious look. "Autumn, you need to get laid."

Autumn spread her hands in front of her and shook her head. "No, I don't. I've been there, done that. After Ted…no, I'm done. No more relationships."

Marie narrowed her eyes slightly and gave Autumn a look. "It's called a fling. No relationship, just sex. It would do you a world of good. Max is hot with a capital H. I've got his number right here. You should call him, go have a drink, get out of lame-O Myers Flat for a few hours, and I don't mean retreating to your cabin." She wagged a finger.

Autumn gave her a level look. "I'm not going there, Mar. I know it's hard to believe, but a woman can live without sex. I am living proof. Now, if you'll excuse me," she said, shouldering her laptop bag and picking up her latte. "I need to go order some new inventory, and enjoy the sunshine."

Marie smiled wryly, crossing her arms. "You aren't a nun, Autumn. Just you wait, someday a major hottie is gonna come along, and then your little vow of celibacy will be over! You wait!"

Autumn rolled her eyes and made her way out to the deck where redwood tables and chairs dried in the afternoon sun. She settled into a chair opposite the parking area and leaned back for a moment, closing her eyes as the golden rays cascaded over her, warming the cool air. She didn't need anyone, truly she didn't. Yes, she did get a tad lonely at times; she could admit that to herself in the privacy of her own head. OK, more than a tad, sometimes, but all in all she enjoyed the privacy of her solitary little world. Besides, she had her best friend Cleo, and Marie, and all the local women who adored Dragonfly. They were her family when she needed company, her friends and confidants. Why did a girl need anything else?

Besides, men had only ever brought heartbreak to her life. After Ted, she'd made herself a solemn vow: never again would she open her heart to another man. Never again would she allow them in where they could do irreparable damage. Not even "just for sex." No more. Marie meant well, but Autumn would not be swayed. She would remain single until she was a happy, dried-out old crone.

Sighing heavily, she opened her Macbook and started it up, sipping at her latte gratefully. *Nope, men are trouble, and I'll be damned if I'll let another one back into my life.* Giving a satisfied nod, she set her cup aside and opened her inventory files, happily delving into her work. Her world was perfect, the sun was shining, and life was fine indeed.

The Camaro rumbled its way up US 101 toward Eureka, with Kain keeping a careful eye on his speed, driving just a tad over the limit. He wanted to open up the powerful V8 engine of the muscle car and see what she could do, but he needed to keep a low profile. Though his talisman was effective at hiding his back trail, it wasn't powerful enough to keep the owner from noticing their car was missing. Who knew when they would report it? It could be days, or mere hours, if they hadn't done so already. He would have to ditch the car eventually; it would become a liability before too long, but right now he was enjoying it far too much to think about letting it go.

He had just passed the exit for a town called Redway when he saw signs announcing the Avenue of Giants Scenic Highway. He had been through this area once before, many years ago, and remembered the route, a more leisurely—and likely less conspicuous—drive to Eureka than the busy 101. He took the exit, and slowed down to a relaxed pace on the two-lane highway through the forest.

He yawned lazily as the Camaro cruised through deep stands of redwoods, their tall branches blocking out most of the mid-afternoon sun. Rays of sunlight trickled through the giant trees and where they landed was an eruption of emerald. Beyond the scent of gas, oil, and exhaust from the car, Kain could smell the trees and foliage outside. The wolf in him leaped, wanting to hang his head out the window to get more of that glorious smell.

Humoring the beast, Kain rolled down the window and propped his arm on the door, smiling a little as the wind played with his long, wild hair. He felt wonderful, still high from the moon, the night, and the run. All he needed in life were fast rides, loose women, and loud music. Deciding music was what was missing, he reached over and turned on the old radio in the dash. He flipped around for a moment and found a Christian station, a Hispanic station or two, some top 40 bullshit, news radio—uninteresting crap. Finally he picked up a station from Eureka, blaring out an intense guitar solo from a circa late 1980's metal band. "Hair" bands they had called them. He chuckled softly to himself. He'd known these guys. He'd partied with them several times, and they did have some pretty wild hair. Those days were an intense and forever-altering time in his life, summing up who he had always been, even before there was such a thing as rock and roll.

He turned up the volume and winced at the hum emanating from the Camaro's old speakers. It was quickly drowned out by the heavy drumbeats and wail of the lead singer and Kain cranked it up further. He drove through the forest feeling fully alive and suffused with energy. He would stop tonight in Eureka and find some female company, he decided. The moon was waning now, but he would still be charged from its light for a few days. He needed to blow off some steam. He could deny the Hunger of the wolf, but he was a man and could not deny his hunger for women. He loved the game of seduction, the thrill of a night's conquest, to stir a woman's desires and sate her every appetite. He never left any of them wanting.

His thoughts shifted then. Memories sharp and vivid of decades past came flooding into his mind—people clawing for him, crying out for him as if only he could quench their thirst, only he could bring them the high that they needed, worshipping him as a god on the stage. The song ended, and as if conjured from his thoughts, a new song began to play. He recognized the chords immediately and with a snarl, he flipped the radio off before he could hear more. Those were days long gone, in the past, and that person was dead, never to return.

Brooding now, he drove through the forest and saw signs that he was approaching some place named Myers Flat. He was still a good fifty miles or so from Eureka, but the Camaro was getting low on gas and he needed to take a leak. Slowing, he crossed under the 101 and into the small town. A gas station was immediately to his left, followed by a small post office. On his right, there was a coffee place, followed by a private residence flanked by the 101. The Avenue curved to the right and continued into town. There was a closed restaurant, a quaint facade of worn-looking storefronts that were half boarded up, featuring a tie-dye t-shirt store and a little market. There was a rather nice looking bed and breakfast, a sign for a nursery and garden center, a local winery, a saloon, a closed garage, and finally a redwoods tourist attraction. That was the whole of the little town. Sighing, Kain turned around and headed back to the single gas station. Boring little town. No matter, this place was just a little blip on the map to wherever he was headed, and he was just getting gas, anyway.

He was just pulling into the gas station when a flash of fiery gold caught his eye at the flowery cafe tucked into the trees across the street from the station. There was a woman there, sitting on the redwood deck in a patch of sunlight. He watched her as he rolled to a stop at the pump. She sat in profile to him, her red-gold hair a glossy cascade over her shoulder, with an open laptop in front of her. Intrigued, he kept his eye on her as he shut off the engine and opened the door.

The world was a riot of scents as he got out and stretched. There were the overpowering odors of spilled gasoline and motor oil, old soda, fried food, tires, the garbage can next to the pump, stale cigarette butts, rancid beer, and laced underneath it all were the subtle scents of vineyards, river, and redwood forest. The breeze stirred as he moved to the back of the vehicle to get at the gas cap, bringing him a host of new fragrances. The strong, heady scent of good coffee, chocolate, flowers, rich soil, and flame-haired woman. He inhaled deeply. Definitely intriguing.

He walked to the pump and grabbed the hose from its cradle, keeping his eye on her as he inserted the nozzle into the car and began fueling. Gas fumes immediately overpowered his senses, and he made a face and stepped away from the vehicle to get her scent again. Watching her intently, he sifted her fragrance out of all the others and tasted it at the back of his throat. It was bright and fresh, alluring to his senses. Very interesting indeed.

Just then, as if sensing his interest, she looked up and over in his direction. Their eyes locked on one another...and the breath caught in Kain's throat.

Autumn was just putting in an order to one of her book suppliers when an odd itching sense niggled at the edge of her perceptions. She tried to ignore it at first, concentrating on her order, but it only became worse. Like she was being watched. Annoyed, she looked up and around, and her gaze collided with a dark form across the street. She stared back at him at first, so stunned by his presence that there was no room for thought, only the dark man at the gas station, returning her gaze from behind mirrored sunglasses.

She had vaguely heard the throaty rumble of an engine as it pulled into the station some moments before, but hadn't been interested enough to look up, and now she found she couldn't look away. He was so out of place in her world that she was mesmerized and oddly disoriented, as if she were somehow dreaming him there. He was long and lean, dressed in a snug-fitting black T-shirt and black leather pants, his long, long hair a wild fall of browns and sun-streaked bronze around his shoulders. He and his car were a shadow in an otherwise brightly lit world, and the intensity of his gaze seared and unsettled her even from a distance.

Trouble. Walking trouble, the kind that could hurt her badly. *Stay away!*

No problem there. A man like that was bad news, and she had absolutely no intention of getting any closer than this. However, he was staring at her so keenly that a small knot of worry began to form in her stomach. What was so damned interesting anyway?

A touch of surly anger was enough to bring her back to herself and she dismissed him with a sniff, turning back to her laptop. Her heart was racing, though, and she found it hard to see the webpage before her. The image of him had seemingly burned itself onto her eyes. What was wrong with her? He'd be gone in a moment and her day could return to normal. In a moment, he would be done fueling and he would get back in his car and leave. Any moment now…

Kain devoured the girl with his eyes, caught and unable to look away. Her gaze was on him, locked with his from across the street, and he felt a connection there unlike anything he had ever sensed before. As if he somehow knew her and that familiarity had him wanting more. He puzzled over his reaction to her as the gas level clicked off on the pump, announcing that the tank was full. He didn't normally go for her type. He liked blondes, for one, and she was definitely not blonde. He liked the ones he could easily pick up at the nightclubs and bars, the ones who were ready for sex and ready for him, the ones who were all too available to be his one night stand.

This woman, however, was young, probably in her mid-twenties, and she wore loose, flowing clothes in colors that perfectly complemented her hair and complexion: all roses and golds and shades of orange. He leaned against the car, folding his arms as she returned his stare with large, dark eyes. This was not an experienced woman; this was barely more than a girl— all flowers and innocence, one who likely lived in dreams and fantasy. Not the kind of woman he was drawn to at all.

But he was drawn to her, very much so. So drawn that he could not seem to look away, could not tear his gaze off her, and the wolf within him began to stir and awaken, lifting its head to stare out from behind his eyes with an intensity of its own. It was only when she suddenly frowned and turned away with a toss of her head, openly dismissing him as she returned her attention to her laptop, that Kain came back to himself, released from the spell. A slow smile spread over his lips and he chuckled softly. A challenge. She had thrown down the gauntlet of feigned disinterest, a signal he could not ignore.

Curiosity piqued, he definitely needed a closer look. A tingle of anticipation ran through him as he went about putting the hose back onto the pump. He trotted inside to lay down a few twenties on the counter. When he reemerged, she was still there, pretending to pay attention to her laptop. He whistled softly to himself. He would have his look, see what it was about her that had him so intrigued, and he would be on his way to find more appropriate prey.

Autumn held her breath as she heard the dark car start up with a roar. She stared fixedly at her laptop, willing herself not to look up. She listened intently and began to breathe a sigh of relief as she heard it leave the gas station, only to hear the rumble coming closer. Her head snapped up then, her eyes wide and heart hammering as she watched the black beast rumble into her parking lot, rolling slowly into the spot next to her green Subaru.

Oh no. Oh no, no, no, no! She panicked, eyes fixed and unable to look away as the car stopped and the rumbling engine abruptly died. The sense of being in a dream was back and the world seemed to slow down as the driver's side door opened and one leather boot appeared on the ground, and then the rest of his body rolled gracefully up out of the car. He was taller than she'd expected, at least a head taller than her five foot, six inches, and was even more stunning from this distance. Handsome hardly described the man. He was gorgeous, all primal, animal sex in an all too masculine body, and he looked like he knew it.

She couldn't look away from him, gawking as he closed the car door and stalked toward the front door of the shop with animal grace. His mirrored shades remained locked on her all the while. A small smile curved his sensual lips.

Dammit, Autumn, just breathe. The man's only getting coffee! She swallowed hard. He opened the door with a small jingle of bells and walked inside. She was being ridiculous, but she couldn't seem to get herself under control. What the hell was her problem, anyway? Men hit on her all the time, attractive men, and she turned them down all the time. No big deal. Perhaps she was overreacting, anyway. Perhaps all he really did want was some coffee. Why not? Who wants to drink gas station coffee?

Sure, and pigs could fly.

She tried futilely to lose herself in what she was doing, staring at the screen of her laptop for all she was worth, but not seeing a thing. All of her senses were tuned to the front door. When it opened again with a happy tinkle of bells, the force of his presence hit her like a wave, causing her breath to hitch in her throat. She forced herself to breathe, to remain calm and appear like she was really into what she was looking at, and not the least bit interested in him.

His energy was like a physical thing as he walked up to her, a paper to-go cup in his hand. He stopped just short of her, his presence demanding attention. Waiting for what he would do next, her senses hyper attuned to him, Autumn froze. When he spoke, she jumped.

"May I join you?" he asked, his voice a deep, amused rumble. Letting out her held breath, she finally conceded defeat and allowed her gaze to find him.

From afar, he was dark and mysterious, an anomaly in the world that piqued her curiosity. Up close, he was downright devastating to her senses.

Male. That was what hit her first. He was male in a way that was so undeniable that it was a statement of fact, and her entire female being reacted to it on a primal level. He was wild, exotic, and so excruciatingly handsome it was hard to look at him. He had taken his sunglasses off and returned her stare with an expression of amused satisfaction. His eyes made her breath catch. They were so blue it was like looking into twin sapphires, so dark and rich in color she wondered vaguely if they were contacts. His eyes were slightly almond shaped, turning downward at the corners, limned with thick, dark lashes and watching her from under slanting, brooding eyebrows. Intense eyes full of expression that held nothing back. The eyes of something wild, something animal.

The rest of his face was chiseled angles and smooth planes, his skin flawless velvet, his strong jaw and prominent chin shadowed by short stubble. His lips were simply sinful, utterly kissable, sensuously full, and curved in a wry smile that showed a hint of white teeth. He wore two double piercings of simple little silvery hoops in each of his ears, glinting against the darkness of his hair. All of it was framed in that spectacular, wild mane of tangled chocolate and bronze, contrasting against the black of his shirt and falling past his waist. She'd never seen a man with such long, gorgeous hair and her fingers itched to touch it, to see if was really his own and not somehow fake, though it certainly looked very real and natural. His shirt stretched across wide shoulders and a broad chest, and on top of it lay some sort of tribal leather necklace bearing what looked to be a long, black stone. Or was it a tooth of some kind? The shirt tucked into the waist of black leather pants that displayed his long legs nicely, and her eyes were drawn to the bulge of his crotch.

Autumn blinked and dragged her eyes back up to his face, inhaling a ragged breath of air spiced with the scent of coffee, leather, and male, and tried to get a hold of herself.

"Uh…" She coughed when the sound came out as a squeak. "Um, yeah, I suppose. Sit anywhere you want."

The stranger broke into a wide grin that gave her cause to have a heart attack all over again. His smile was amazing, full of long, bright teeth, his canine teeth longer still at the edge of his mouth. It was dazzling, feral, and added to his potent animal attractiveness.

"Thank you," he said, his voice rich and sinfully masculine, like black coffee spiked with whiskey. Heat pooled in her belly at the sound.

Autumn tried to ignore her reaction to him and returned her attention to her laptop, but it seemed to be a useless ruse. The stranger settled himself into the chair opposite her, the leather of his pants creaking in a most distracting way. Autumn squirmed in her seat, cleared her throat, and tried to make it clear her attention was on her business.

"I hope I'm not bothering you," he said after a moment. Autumn glanced up, her eyes meeting electric blue, the clash like a lightning bolt that caught her breath. Forcing her eyes back to the screen she made herself take a deep breath and tapped at the keys randomly, hoping it was convincing, hoping he would get the hint. He simply watched her for a moment with a maddening, sensual half-smile, then sighed and looked around him.

"Beautiful forest you have here. I've never seen anything like it."

Autumn made a small "um-hmm" sound without looking up, still desperately pretending to be interested in her work. He was staring at her again. She couldn't help herself, when he remained silent, she flicked her eyes up at him briefly. Again she was caught off guard by his slow, sensual grin. Dammit!

Oh, why don't you just tell him to go away? she fumed at herself. Because a part of her *was* really interested, very much so, and was whispering all sorts of fascinating, shocking things about this man. Her body seemed to be in perfect agreement. Here was walking sex seated across from her, making his interest in her clear, and certain parts of her that hadn't seen anything but plastic in a long time were getting fired up and ready for the real thing.

"I'm sorry, did you need help with something?" she asked politely. Hopefully, being direct would be a better approach to the situation. He regarded her and leaned back casually in the chair, lightly shrugged his broad shoulders, and took a sip from his cup.

"Just enjoying the coffee."

She stared at him a moment, torn between disgust and intrigue.

"My name is Kain. Kain Ulmer," he continued, inclining his head slightly, causing his mane to shift around his shoulders. Autumn's belly tightened at the unbidden thought of all that hair falling around her from above as his naked body covered hers. She swallowed hard.

Kain? What kind of name was that? Not that she would expect anything normal like Bob, or Rick, or Mike from a man that looked like he did, but *Kain*?

It was simply too much. She had to get rid of him. Now.

Summoning up the last of her resolve and the shreds of her dignity, she drew herself up and politely as possible said, "Well, *Kain*, I'm sorry, but I have a lot of work to do—" She was cut off when he chuckled; a deep, thoroughly sexy sound down in his chest, and a lance of heat spiked from her stomach to her groin and back, flushing her with unaccustomed lust. It made her uncomfortable, her reaction to the man. *He* made her uncomfortable, with his sinful good looks and confidant arrogance. He had her on edge, affecting her like no one else ever had before, and the bastard *knew* it! He knew it! And he was enjoying her discomfort in his presence, a perfect stranger. This was not good. Not good at all.

"You'd like me to leave? I haven't even gotten your name in return," he said with a slightly arched eyebrow. Autumn crossed her arms and leveled a look at him. Not a chance.

Kain watched her with a hunger that he hoped didn't show too much on his face. Up close, she was even more enticing than what he had seen from afar. Her face was heart shaped, her delicate chin matched her dainty, pert nose, all framed by that fall of long, fire-gold waves. Her lips held his gaze, lusciously curved and dimpled at the corners, her lower lip succulent and pouting and he bit back a growl at the thought of suckling it. Her eyes were captivating, large and beguiling, framed by long, dark lashes, with slender eyebrows arching over them. Her eyes were the color of smoke and warm, dark cognac in crystal, burning with fire and intelligence.

Her neck was slender, curving down to where her arms crossed over generous breasts, thrusting them up ever so slightly under her Bohemian, flowery top, and Kain's mouth watered at the sight. Her legs were lovely, clad in form-fitting leggings and crossed at the knee, her foot tapping lightly in irritation. Her hips were wide, her waist narrow, and Kain nearly groaned, imagining those legs wrapped around him.

She was all curves and buxom temptation, certainly no petite waif but a classic beauty fully-figured and formed; the kind of woman who was considered the epitome of femininity in the days of his youth. Up close, her scent was richer and more complex, delicately laced with notes of sweet pear and warm amber, a hint of jasmine and vanilla, and her heady, feminine musk was a dusky note under it all. He breathed her in deeply and savored the scent of her. Oh yes, this was definitely more than casual interest now. This was full-blown attraction.

"Sorry to disappoint," she said, still managing to hold his gaze, "but you'd best get on your horse and keep riding. I'm not interested."

She was certainly blunt and full of fire. He liked that a lot. He gave into the urge to test her further, to see how susceptible she was to his power. He held her gaze for a moment more, then with exaggerated care set his cup down and leaned toward her slowly, his mouth curving in a sensual smile. She swallowed and leaned away from him, but Kain held her with his gaze. With a little mental nudge, he amped up his supernatural power to allure and bathed her in it. He watched as her eyes became dreamy and her lips parted on a sigh. Oh yes, highly susceptible. He could easily have her if he wanted. God, was he tempted…

Aching need emptied her head of everything except for him. She needed him, wanted his long, lean form stretched on top of her, wanted his lips devouring hers, her hands tangled in his wild mane. She wanted her senses filled with every part of him. Her lips actually parted and began to pucker for the searing kiss his lips promised as he leaned farther toward her. She was utterly unable to think of anything else but the overwhelming need to be his.

Just then, her knight in shining armor rode in and saved the day, clattering into the parking lot in her aging steed, a Volvo that had seen far better days. Autumn blinked, released from the strange spell, and got to her feet in a cloud of indignation. She had no idea what had just happened, but whatever it was, it was *not* OK with her. He had somehow manipulated her. Kain sighed and leaned back, looking away as if conceding defeat, all to the sound of Phish being played far too loud.

"Hey, Autumn." Cleo waved from her car, shouting over the music just before she turned the car off.

Kain's gaze flew to Autumn, his face brightening with triumph, and she groaned.

"Autumn," he murmured, looking her up and down like a caress. She sat back down on the edge of her chair, angrily returning his gaze.

Cleo bounced her way up onto the porch, and her thick, dark eyebrows rose all the way up to her short black curls as she caught sight of Kain. She wore a black T-shirt with the words "Bitch, I'm Fabulous" in rhinestones on the front, accompanied by a tie-dyed scarf tied around her hair, patchwork corduroy pants, wildly colored socks, and sturdy sandals. The cloyingly rich scent of patchouli and a certain herb filled the air around her.

"Well, hello tall, dark, and gorgeous! Who do we have here, Auttie?" she asked breathily with a huge smile, looking Kain up and down. He flashed that dazzling smile back at her and Cleo beamed at him, her hands on her hips.

"No one. He's just leaving," Autumn said, glaring at him and making her displeasure clear.

"Hi, I'm Cleopatra, but everyone calls me Cleo," she said brightly in her smoke-roughened alto, extending her hand far forward and practically pouncing on Kain. Autumn rolled her eyes in disgust.

"Cleo, lovely to meet you. I'm Kain," he rumbled back, taking her hand with a small inclination of his head. Cleo made an appreciative sound in her throat.

"Kain, huh?" she said, eagerly pulling up a chair. "Well, I can tell you are *definitely* not from around here. Where are you from? Are you just passing through?" Kain chuckled and sipped his coffee with a grin.

Marie took that moment to quit spying and came outside to join them.

"Hi, Cleo." She smiled as she approached, then turned to Kain. "Do you need anything else, Mr…?"

"Hey, Mar. Oh, his name's Kain," Cleo said, waving in his direction. "Hey, have a seat. We're just hanging out with Auttie's mystery man here."

Autumn groaned aloud and plopped her head onto the table. He was never going to leave now, and these two would happily lap up his attention. Enough was enough.

"Well, it's been fun, but I really need to get some work done," she said, getting briskly to her feet and snapping her laptop closed.

"Oh, come now, Auttie. It's a nice day," Cleo protested as Autumn shoved her laptop into her bag and shouldered it.

"Correction, my dear, it *was* a nice day," she said, pinning Kain with a glare. He watched her with an amused smile that sent a delicious shiver through her.

"My apologies for disturbing you," he said and Autumn snorted, rolling her eyes as she turned toward the door. "It was good to meet you…Autumn."

The sound of her name on his lips almost caused her to trip and she all but raced for the safety of the shop, his smile following her.

Kain's eyes stayed on the door even as Autumn's friend Cleo began chattering again, joined by the barista from inside. Both were attractive in their own way, but they were of no interest. Some baffling part of him was completely drawn to Autumn. She had filled his senses and his attention completely. The other women might as well not even exist, and that wasn't like him at all. He adored women, all women, regardless of their age, body type, or temperament, and he adored being adored by them. But right now, all of his attention was for the one who had just left. Her intoxicating scent still lingered in the air.

He considered the situation as her friends prattled on. Much as she intrigued him with the challenge she presented, and much as he was attracted to her, he had no business pursuing someone like her. His morals may be loose but at least they were in place. There was better, more suitable prey out there for him this evening. He'd gotten his look, and she'd made her position clear. Time to go.

Cleo was asking him questions again, and with effort, he brought his attention back to the women.

"I'm terribly sorry, ladies, but I really must get back on the road," he said with a slow grin. "It truly has been a pleasure."

Cleo sat back in her chair with a quirky, amused smile. "Bummer. Well, it was good to meet you, handsome."

"Likewise." Kain chuckled as he donned his mirrored sunglasses and got to his feet.

"Come back and visit us again," the younger brunette said. "Best coffee in Humboldt County."

Kain nodded to the two women with a grin as he slipped past them, both pairs of eyes devouring him. He got back into the Camaro and started it with a rumble, and then a roar as he applied the gas, favoring the two women with his feral grin once more. They were all smiles as he backed out of the parking lot and he forced himself to turn the wheel, to drive away, to leave this place, and leave *her* behind. He growled as he gripped the steering wheel and stomped on the gas, baring his teeth as he drove away.

Autumn watched him leave from the safety of the window. The black muscle car rumbled out of the parking lot and roared onto the Avenue of Giants, headed north and west toward Eureka. She let out the breath she'd been holding and leaned her forehead against the glass. He was gone, thank goodness. Her day could get back to normal now, filled with her shop, coffee, and friends. No men, no complications, just her perfect life.

Still, she couldn't explain the sudden sense of longing he had left in his wake.

CHAPTER THREE
A Second Look

Kain drummed his fingers restlessly on the steering wheel as he continued his drive down the Avenue of Giants. He could feel the moon approaching again, still full enough to affect him, and knew it contributed to his agitation. But this was much more than the moon's influence. He rubbed the back of his neck and grimaced, huffing out a breath. What had happened back there? Sure, he had been strongly attracted to women in the past, but not in such an immediate and visceral way, and certainly not to one like her—young, innocent, and earthy. He could not get her face out of his head, and the ghost of her scent lingered in his nose.

He growled and slammed a fist against the roof of the car, denting the metal with his agitation. He needed to be gone from here, to put distance between himself and last night. He needed to start thinking about satisfying the Hunger again. He didn't have time to be taking an interest in challenging young women he had no business being attracted to.

The farther he got away from Myers Flat, however, the deeper his agitation became until he finally pulled into a shady picnic area overlooking the river and slammed to a stop. He bolted out of the car and paced quickly up and down through the trees, breathing in the fragrant, clean air to calm himself. What the hell was wrong with him? He snarled, the inhuman sound vibrating out of him in his frustration and he felt his nails burst into claws. What was it about this girl that was driving him insane?

"She's not for you!" he hissed at himself, clenching his fists until his palms bled.

The wolf in him was fully awake and anxious. The creature wanted her as well, and with an uncharacteristic intensity Kain hadn't experienced before. That worried him. Whenever he chose an evening's conquest, the wolf usually expressed a mild to moderate interest and went along for the ride, so to speak, fueling his animal potency, but not interfering. Even on a full moon, when the wolf was at its strongest, Kain never lost control of himself.

Yet now he could feel the wolf's powerful desire for her quake through him, making it hard for him to contain the beast inside. The wolf wanted to see her again and smell her, wanted to be close to her, to press their body to hers. The man wanted to run, to be gone, and to forget about this. But his instinct was more powerful than he could deal with, more powerful than reason or logic could dispel. He waged a short battle within himself, fighting his inner wolf, but the beast was too strong with the moon just a day past full. They would see her again, they would smell her again, and they would be close to her again. Anything else would cause the creature to be wild. He had other plans tonight, plans that involved a woman, and not the one the wolf was so eager for. He needed to keep the beast under control or things could get dangerous for any would-be bedmate, but he sensed the wolf would not cooperate until he'd had his way.

Fine. He growled, pushing a hand into his hair. He would find where she lived and get another good look at her and the wolf in him would see that she was not what he wanted, that she was an innocent girl, and he could be on his way. He would maintain fierce self-control, he warned the wolf, and if it got out of hand, he would leave immediately. The wolf in him gave a violent but controlled burst of excitement and Kain trembled in response, then sighed gustily in resignation.

"I've got to be crazy," he grumbled, and returned to the car. Despite all of his caution, however, he found he was filled with anticipation at the coming hunt. He would be seeing Autumn again tonight, and the thought of it was exhilarating. He started the car and revved the Camaro's engine until it roared like a dragon, the wolf surging through him. He grinned at the sound and growled deeply in his chest. Tonight would be a good night to hunt.

"That's not the kind of man I want," Autumn said, gesturing with the flowerpot in her hand. "I want to be wined and dined, taken on dates…you know, gentlemanly stuff. A guy like that probably doesn't even have a job, is probably an alcoholic, a womanizer, and an abuser. I bet he smokes and does drugs, too."

Cleo and Marie sat outside with Autumn in the warm sunshine, watching as she busied herself with repotting. The two had not stopped since *he* left, prattling like a couple of horny teenagers to one another about the handsome stranger until Autumn was about to explode with irritation.

"Yeah, but you can bet the sex is *amazing*," Cleo said with a wink and Autumn rolled her eyes with a groan. "The man had an ass like a twenty dollar mule." She mimed the taut roundness with her hands.

"And those leather pants! My God!" Marie breathed, fanning her face. Autumn scowled at them both with disgust.

"Aw come on, sweet. Admit it, the guy was smokin' hot." Cleo grinned as Autumn continued filling the pot with a sigh.

Marie chuckled and rolled her eyes. "It's not like he's going to return to haunt you or something,"

Autumn's lips twitched as she set the pot down. "All right! He was…interesting, OK?" she said casually and kept at her work, gently pressing a young plant into the new soil inside the pot.

Cleo's face broke into her customary quirky grin. "Interesting, eh? My dear, that man was panty-moistening."

Marie sniggered, and Autumn's lips quirked up at that. "OK, so he was panty-moistening hot. Satisfied?"

Cleo gave her an amused, appraising look. "Ahhh, so you *are* a straight woman after all."

"Now, really," she said, suppressing a grin as she faced them both with her hand on her hip. "Just because I find a handsome man attractive does *not* mean I want to sleep with him." She wagged the spade at Cleo. "It simply means I am a straight woman who can appreciate a good-looking man. That's it, and that's all."

"Uh huh." Cleo crossed her arms over her chest and raised an eyebrow. "Sure, hun, but I've never seen one get under your skin so badly. Look at you, all surly and pouty now."

Autumn pursed her lips and mock scowled at Cleo, then erupted into a laugh. He really *had* gotten to her, hadn't he? Cleo and Marie grinned as she gathered them both in a hug and kissed Cleo on the cheek. She adored her friends, and she simply could not remain mad or sad around them for long.

She chuckled, letting them go. "Yes, he was hot. He was *amazingly* hot. It bothered me he was so hot, OK? I just had no idea how to handle it."

Cleo waggled her dark eyebrows at her "Well, it's good to know you're not a nun."

Autumn tsked and swatted at her with her spade, showering them all with dirt. After a moment of surprise, they all erupted into gales of laughter in the sunshine.

Though Kain was more than eager to get back to Myers Flat, it was still mid afternoon and he wanted to wait for nightfall to begin his hunt. Predators had to be patient if they ever wanted to make a kill and it was no different here, so he practiced that patience all afternoon long, taking his time to make his way back. Though he never needed much sleep, he napped in the Camaro under the deep shade of the redwoods, trying to envision the last woman he slept with—a sultry brunette with a smoldering gaze and fantastic breasts. No matter how hard he tried, though, his vision would change, and it would be *her* eyes he saw, *her* lips and shapely body, what she might look like when she smiled, and especially what her nimble hands could do to his body.

Unable to bear his heated thoughts he finally roused himself and continued on. He found a small grocery store and stopped for a package of red meat. He really hated the cold, processed, dead meat that tasted like chemicals and plastic wrap that the stores offered, but he didn't have the time to hunt tonight. He was after prey of a different sort.

He drove on, considering his plans as he chewed on the cold steak. Finding her should be easy enough. Myers Flat was a very small town, and her scent at that shop had been strong, which meant she spent a lot of time there. He should be able to find a trail from the coffee shop to her house without much difficulty. All he had to do was wait for dark, shift, get her scent, and track her down. The thought of hunting her made him smile, cold blood dripping down his chin and arm. The steak helped, but he would need to find fresh meat soon. The Spring Equinox was only fifteen days away, and the Hunger would be at its worst by then. He would have to make a kill. A human kill, which meant he needed to be gone from here as soon as possible to find suitable prey.

No matter. He would be on the road again later that night, anyway. Perhaps he would make his way to Portland instead and see what he could find there. He hadn't been to Portland in a long while, and he could hunt easily in the city. There were a few women that he was sure would love to see him again…and a few that would love to kill him, come to think of it.

Kain grinned and hummed cheerfully to himself, absently tapping the steering wheel as he neared Myers Flat. He kept alert for possible places to stash the Camaro and begin his shift. There, that would do. A dirt road took off to his left, heading deeper into the forest. He took it, causing the Camaro's tires to squeal in protest at the abrupt turn, and he slowed as soon as he hit dirt. He drove through the trees, crossing under the 101 again and deeper into the forest until he felt comfortable that he would not be seen or disturbed, and stopped.

The last of the sunlight gilded the very tops of the giant trees as he got out and breathed in the rich, clean scents of the forest around him. Twilight would be setting in soon. Eager for the change now, he sat and removed his boots so that his bare feet could sink into the cool, loamy soil. He flexed his toes, enjoying the sensation. That was better.

Senses alert, he began to walk around the area, filling himself with the thousands of scents the forest presented to him. Humans had no idea of the world around them they were missing with their feeble noses. Enjoying himself, feeling very much alive, he stood and let his head fall back and closed his eyes. No, he would not change what he was for the world. He would never, ever want to be human again. Before the change, he had not truly known what it was to be alive. What life could be as a werewolf.

The howl started softly, rising from his throat like a prayer, and after a moment, it grew until it filled the world. He sang his satisfaction out to the forest, his voice a strange mix of human and wolf, at once airy and booming, a sound no mere human could make. Unlike most of his brethren, howling fulfilled something deep within him, a song to express his joy, anger, frustration, or sadness, whatever he was feeling. For other werewolves, they howled only to instill fear into their prey. Their howls evoked a primal terror, pulling a deep, ancient instinct from humans to flee when they heard those howls in the night. Fear flavored the blood of their prey and was far more satisfying to the Hunger.

He had known long ago that he was subtly unlike the others of his kind and was considered an outcast for it. His maker, Alessia, said it was why she had chosen him. She said she knew he would be different somehow; his wolf a little wilder, a little less of a beast than the others, his human side more in control and balanced with his wolf. He enjoyed being both wolf and man, both instinctual and reasoning. The others were ruled by their appetites, slaves to their instincts and their powers, often times barely in control of themselves. If it weren't for their inherent abilities to confuse the minds and senses of humans, the world would have known about his kind long ago.

He let the howl die away, echoing little in the dark forest. The trees and soil absorbed most sounds, but he knew his howl had carried anyway—not that it mattered. The song was for himself and not meant for anyone else's ears. He let his head fall again and opened his eyes, breathing deeply. Shadows came quickly here, and though it was not quite twilight, it was plenty dark enough to begin.

He eagerly began to pull off his clothes, whistling a little, and stashed them in his pack until he stood naked in the half-light. The chill air was delicious on his skin, and he stilled and centered himself in preparation. He called the wolf to him, and the wolf came eagerly, filling him with the same blissful, burning, itching ache he longed for. The shift was lengthy this time, and pleasurable as he contained it and stretched it out within himself. He wanted to feel everything tonight.

He was taken with pain and arousal as his bones ground and shifted, his muscles bunching. He longed for Autumn even as he resisted the fantasy, imagining her hands stroking his changing body, and he groaned aloud as fur rippled out of his skin. His mouth and nose pushed into a muzzle, his teeth aching with a desire to bite her as he imagined thrusting inside of her again and again. The shift was ecstasy, the sweetest pain and euphoric pleasure. What he could make her feel…

He snorted and shook his head as his human mind reasserted itself and pushed back his lustful thoughts. He was here to dispel this silly infatuation, not encourage it, and though sex while shifting was an erotic fantasy of his, it wasn't something he would ever attempt with a human. He growled at himself as his body finished its adjustments, joints popping into place, his extremities caught with a lingering burn. He promised his inner wolf that he would find someone suitable for them farther down the road, someone they could take their passion out on. The wolf only snorted in response.

When he finished shifting, he laid on the ground and waited a few moments to recover from the change. Once he felt better, he got to his feet and paced around for a bit. He flexed his muscles, worked his jaw, swiveled his ears, lashed his tail, and finally stretched his back with a small pop. Satisfied that the change was complete, he checked the Camaro over and pissed on the tires, then grabbed his pack and stashed it in a nearby tree. That way if anyone found the Camaro, he would at least have his pack.

Sensing the impending moon, he gave himself a thorough shake, luxuriating in the rising energy as it tingled along his spine and raised his hackles. He chuffed and snorted, kicking the ground with his hind feet in a surly display until his human self managed the calm the wolf down. *Not tonight, wolf. Remember, I am in charge,* he whispered to the creature and the wolf grumbled, settling down again.

Finally ready, he set off at an easy trot through the night. He got the scent of the 101 freeway and began paralleling the road along the ridge, keeping to the trees as he broke into a run. His desire and unease were soon forgotten in the magic of his wolfish body, the rising moon, and the scents and sounds of the forest as he neared civilization. He smelled humans and all their strange odors well before he began to see lights through the trees.

He perked his ears when he came to a rise that overlooked the little town, and stopped to get his bearings. The coffee shop was on the east end of town, where the Avenue of Giants crossed under US 101 again. That would be the place to pick up her scent. He continued on until he stood in the shadows of the trees on the other side of freeway, not far from the coffee shop. He scented the air, trying to detect her. *Ah, there she is.* He narrowed his eyes in pleasure and took a moment to savor her bright, womanly fragrance, intermingled with the scent of her car. She had come past here not all that long ago, headed south on the Avenue. He had no way of knowing where she was going, but assumed she was headed home.

He dashed back into the forest again, following the Avenue this time as he kept the scent of her car in his nose. He could tell from the thickness of her trail that this was a route she drove at least once a day. That was a good sign he was on the right track. He followed her for a few miles and then abruptly lost her scent. Backtracking he found that she'd turned off onto a dirt road on the other side of the Avenue. He made sure there were no cars around and dashed across the road and down the private drive. There was a closed gate across the road with a sign that read "Private Property – No Trespassing." Her scent was thicker here. This must be her territory.

He leaped the gate and trotted down the road in the twilight to where a small bridge spanned the river. The bridge looked to be old but in good repair, and he hurried across it to the darkness of the trees on the other side. The road wound up the hillside and the forest thinned some, redwoods giving way to fir and alder. It topped a rise and followed a ridge line for a ways before dipping back down again where redwoods appeared once more.

He was moving farther into the deepening forest when he stopped short, his senses picking up on a shift of energies. He was entering…something. There was some sort of power here he didn't immediately recognize, and he hesitated as he tested the flavor of it. It was strong and wild, deep and ancient under his paws, yet it lay dormant. There was a node here, a strong one, and not currently warded as far as he could tell. Fascinating. He continued on, taking note of the wealth of power under his feet.

A path took off from the dirt road, and he stopped when his nose encountered her track. Her scent came up and met him like perfume to his nose, setting his tail wagging. He came back to himself and cursed, making his tail stop and fall. *Easy wolf,* he soothed the creature and thoroughly explored her scent again. The track was recent, and she had been barefoot at the time. The thought of her bare feet padding through the ferns here made him smile. Few humans allowed themselves to feel the earth under their feet anymore, to be connected to their world in even that small way. The fact that she did this made him wonder what else she did in the privacy of her territory. He cursed again and snorted, shaking his head in irritation. He really needed to stop such lascivious thoughts. It didn't help anything.

Her trail led away from the road and into the forest. Intrigued, he followed it, moving at an easy pace. The moon had yet to rise and the forest was dark, but his night vision outlined all of the details of the world in subtle shades and hues. His vision was enhanced by his sense of smell as he trotted along. He followed her scent as it wound its way down into a small valley in the hills where ancient redwoods grew, their trunks huge, their tops scraping the sky. Her scent was everywhere, as were little signs of her.

Here was the trunk of a redwood that had chunks of quartz and other stones embedded in the cracks of the bark. There, a spiral of rocks artfully arranged according to size and color. Among the ancient roots of an uprooted tree were crystals and stones, the antler of a black-tailed deer, and bells hanging from the roots. The zing of silver in his senses caused him to pause and investigate an old silver butter knife hanging from a tree, along with old keys and other odds and ends. A strange work of art perhaps. Chimes, crystals, and bells hung from the branches of various other trees and other such curiosities were hidden everywhere. *Nature altars. Interesting.* He spied the odd displays and collections all around him, strange and intriguing, and her scent touched it all.

He could detect no others save for the local wildlife. This was her territory, and whether anyone else lived here with her, he would find out soon enough. The possibility of her being mated to another caused a deep growl to well up in his chest and Kain reached out and soothed his wolf again. His dearly hoped she was with someone—a boyfriend, a lover, maybe a husband—then he could walk away in good conscious, wolf be damned.

He continued on, hurrying his pace in the need to see her again. Soon lights glimmered through the trees and he broke into a trot, slowing again when the forest gave way to an open area. There, a house nestled against a hill, giant redwoods towering over it. He stopped and sniffed deeply for a time, scenting for a dog or other noisome animal. There were faint scents of a cat, but that did not bother him. Cats were of no concern, and even if one of the little devils decided to try him, they were quick and easy prey to his wolf self.

Deciding it was OK, he prowled slowly into the area. A small stone bridge spanned the little brook that meandered through the glade. She had set a carved pole on the other side of the little bridge, adorned with rocks and crystals, a marker of some sort, and beyond that was a lush garden that surrounded the quaint little house. Kain's gaze, however, fixed on the windows of the house that looked out over the garden, for there she stood, looking out into her domain. She could not see him, as he was still well in the shadows. She drew him to her as if she were a siren, singing to him and calling him near. He slunk through the darkness, careful to keep out of sight as he neared the porch, and angled himself so that he could watch her without being seen.

Autumn had spent the day concentrating on things other than the mysterious stranger. She had done inventory with Cleo once Marie had left, and tidied up the store. They cleaned the shelves, prattled about gossip, and avoided the topic of a certain attractive man. They talked somberly for a while about the shop, that business was slow and the last of Oma's inheritance was running out. Few customers came in these days, and they bought little more than coffee and a pastry. It was just enough to see to the day-to-day expenses, but her business loan still loomed, threatening like a gallows, and the bank wouldn't honor another extension. She was running out of options.

"It's the economy," Cleo had said as she gripped Autumn's hand across the table. "It'll pick up. Times are tough for everyone, hun, but Dragonfly will make it. It will, and it will see you into your golden years when you're a dried up old crone." Cleo laughed, teasing out Autumn's smile.

The day waned, getting too late for the coffee crowd, and they closed up the shop. Autumn promised Cleo they would get together soon, but she needed her alone time tonight. Of course Cleo understood, kissing her on the head and giving her a big, patchouli scented hug, and a lingering, concerned look.

"No funks, young lady," she chided, wagging her finger at her. "Go home, take a bath, meditate, eat some food, and relax. Forget about everything. It will all be here when you come in tomorrow." She smiled and Autumn sighed. What would she do without her Cleo?"

I promise, Mama Bear," she said with a small smile and pecked her on the cheek. "You get some rest too. Don't get too baked." Cleo waggled her absurd eyebrows and Autumn chuckled.

"Night's just starting, princess! See you tomorrow, my sweet." And with that, she flounced off to her Volvo, waving out the window as she rattled out of the parking lot, leaving Autumn alone with herself, and her thoughts.

She drove home in the gathering darkness of twilight, determined not to let her worries get to her tonight. Her business was in danger of folding, and yet now that she was alone, her thoughts kept returning to those sapphire eyes, that arrogant grin, that wild mane of hair…what the sound of his voice alone had done to her.

It's apparent where my priorities are today. She grumbled and blew out a frustrated breath. She turned into her long driveway and crossed the bridge, winding up over the hill and down into her own private redwood sanctuary. She parked in her usual spot in front of the garage set next to the cottage. Home at last.

She entered the quiet of her home and dropped her keys and purse on the nearest stand, then leaned back against the door with a deep sigh. Why couldn't she seem to get Kain out of her head? Damn the man for intruding into her world and making her question her convictions. She didn't need any man. Life was so much less complicated without them…and so much lonelier. She sighed and pushed herself away from the door.

Her thoughts turned to Ted, her ex-husband by three years now. Her last relationship. They had been so good in the beginning, and so in love…or so she had thought. They had met their freshman year of college and married after a year of being together. Their marriage had lasted a little over three years, and it had been good for awhile. Yet as the burgeoning dream of Dragonfly began to take her attention, their relationship began to falter. They had grown distant, and Ted began spending more time at his job in Eureka. Autumn hadn't confronted him; she had simply given him his space. She was too busy building her business, anyway. When he told her he was leaving her for a co-worker and moving to the Bay area, she had stared at him in dumbfounded disbelief.

Three years of marriage undone in an instant. But now… it seemed as if their split had been inevitable. She could never seem to be fully present in a relationship, and somehow none of the men had ever been truly right. Eventually each relationship crumbled. She was the one who usually left, needing her space, or time to figure things out. It seemed fitting that this time, the guy had left her, instead.

There was movement as a huge, long-haired ginger cat uncurled himself from his perch and stretched daintily, yawning as he did, big copper eyes blinking at her. He jumped down from his ledge overlooking the great room and slunk over to her, fluffy tail in the air, and paused on his way for another long stretch. Autumn smiled and banished her gloomy thoughts. She toed off her shoes with a grateful sigh. She was home, in her sanctuary where everything was all right.

"Hey there, my big boy," Autumn cooed as the cat came up to her, trilling contentedly while he wound around her legs. She scooped up the big cat in a hug, his copper eyes slitted happily. "How's mama's cuddly boy?" she asked, rubbing her nose against his. He made a "Prrap!" at her and butted his head up under her chin. Her Toby was all the man she needed in her life.

She endeavored to forget all about Ted, and especially about Kain, as she cooed to her cat and set him down. He promptly trotted toward the kitchen, his tail like a flag, meowing loudly for dinner. She went about her nightly routine, opening a small can of cat food for Toby, then began putting together her own dinner, her usual vegetarian fair. Tonight it would be sautéed kale with cherry tomatoes, perhaps some hummus with gluten-free pita chips, and maybe some chocolate for dessert. Oh, and of course the best part, wine.

She opened up a new bottle right away, a delicious 2004 pinot noir from the winery in town that she'd been saving for something special. Tonight she needed to banish her blues, and she deserved a little treat. What better occasion than that? She let the wine breathe for a moment, then poured herself a glass and savored the fruity vintage.

She continued her dinner preparations, humming softly and sipping her wine as she worked. Deciding she needed some good music, she paused in her cooking to set up her iPod in its speaker dock. She smiled and thought of her Oma again as she set the player to shuffle and Norah Jones began to sing. Oma had always loved to put on some of her favorite music in the evenings and together they would dance and laugh in the great room until they were exhausted and all cares pushed away. On a whim, Autumn decided to light a fire in the hearth as well. Oma had also loved her evening fires.

Autumn sighed happily as the hearth began crackling merrily and she went back to preparing dinner. She was perfectly capable of providing herself a nice dinner, having some good wine, and listening to good music—all of those "romantic" things the world seemed to think a single woman couldn't enjoy by herself.

Then there were his eyes again, burning in her mind, uninvited. Wicked and wild and full of seduction, such a deep blue a woman could drown in them. Gritting her teeth, she began chopping kale firmly. She would not think of him. Yet, since she'd laid eyes on him, he seemed to remain at the back of her mind, his mesmerizing eyes peering through her thoughts, a seductive grin on his too-sensual lips.

She made it through cooking her dinner and then sat at the table, mechanically eating her food and barely tasting it. Dammit, why couldn't she get him out of her head? He had been crass, and annoying, and had delighted in the uncomfortable embarrassment he had caused her to endure. Plus, he was a stranger, a stranger that had been all too familiar with her.

It pissed her off.

It had made her, well, feel alive again.

She cursed as her fork full of food, forgotten and hovering near her mouth while she brooded, landed with a wet plop all down her front.

"Oh for goodness sakes," she hissed, throwing the fork down and spreading her arms to assess the damage. Sautéed kale and tomato juice had left a streak down her blouse. Sighing defeat, she got up, put away her leftovers, and went to get changed.

The house was hot from her cooking and the fire in the hearth, so she changed into her favorite dark blue yoga camisole with a moon batik design and a pair of boy shorts. She padded barefoot back into the kitchen, finished her dishes, drained her wineglass, refilled it, and brooded over the sink some more. *How dare he?*

How dare he...what? Find her attractive? The man only wanted one thing from her. But then again, was that such a bad thing? For someone to want her in such a way? She thought about that as she swirled the wine in her glass. No harm done, really. He was gone now and she'd never see him again, so what did it matter? Maybe it wasn't such a bad thing, to be desired, and by a man like that.

"It's not like I invited him home." She snorted and took another drink.

She chewed at her bottom lip and wandered into the great room, unconsciously digging her toes into the thick rug there. She decided to open the screen door to the night air, and a soft, cold breeze caressed her bare legs and arms as she tilted her glass to her lips again. Besides Ted, she'd had few lovers in the past, though men had pursued her all her life. None, however, had ever stirred in her a desire like Kain's simple stare, not even Ted. With Ted, desire had come slow and warm, over time as they became best friends and fell for one another. With Kain, lust had been instant, searing through her body and scorching her senses.

He had stared at her as if all he wanted to do was taste her. Men had stared at her before, but not in the heated, hungry, animal sort of way that caused her body to instantly react. Not like Kain had. The comfortable buzz from the wine dulled her senses now, and desire flowed through her warmly as she thought of his toothy, wicked grin, those kissable lips curved and inviting. Feeling flushed from the drink and her thoughts, her cheeks heated, she tossed the rest of her wine back and set the glass aside.

Dear God, to be kissed by lips like those! She sighed, allowing herself to imagine it, and then imagined those lips on other places. Gooseflesh rose on her skin and she thought of his hands, so masculine and strong, with wide palms and long, thick fingers. Oh, what those hands could do to her. She closed her eyes and sighed as she imagined what his touch must be like. What the sensation of his fingers trailing against her skin, his hands twining in her hair, his palms kneading her flesh would be.

One of her favorite songs came on then, and it was one that spoke of sensual delights, weaving a beat she could not resist. She began to move to it as she imagined him, imagined those lips on her skin, on her mouth, and she let her hands flow over herself as her hips swayed. Her hands found her hair, bound earlier while cooking, and she undid it, allowing the silky mass to caress her bare shoulders.

The music entranced her, her tipsy thoughts wrapping her in a passionate spell of her own making. She moved as the music demanded—without thought, flowing and erotic, feeling incredibly feminine and sexy at the thought of him. She wondered what he tasted like, could imagine his intimate scent and taste of his skin and she undulated in a circle, weaving her hips around. She was caught up in the music, in the dance and her own arousal, oblivious to the rest of the world around her.

Kain bit back a groan of desire as he watched her from the safety of the shadows. She stood in a large room on a thick carpet, her feet bare, while she drank wine and stared into the night. Her hair was pinned up on her head, a few loose strands touching her bare neck, and the temptress wore practically nothing. The tiny camisole she wore molded itself enticingly to her lovely breasts; her nipples puckered against the fabric in a way that made his groin tighten. The shirt was slightly rucked up at the bottom, exposing a bit of her soft belly, and he swallowed hard at the sight of the jewel dangling from her pierced navel. He bit back a low growl as his gaze traveled downward to what could barely be called shorts, exposing every bit of her shapely, slender calves and plump thighs.

She stood before a door that was open to the porch and the night with the screen in place, allowing her scent to escape. He narrowed his eyes as a faint breeze brought it to him. He detected no others here, just the tang of cat, and old scents of her friend Cleo. It was apparent she lived alone. His eyes snapped back to her again as she moved in the room, setting aside her wineglass to stand in the middle of the large rug, looking out at the night. Music played from inside the room, sensual and vaguely erotic.

He watched in fascination as she closed her eyes and breathed deeply, swaying softly at first to the beat of the music, then slowly gyrating her hips as the lyrics began. He was captivated, watching her undulate to the rhythm, sinuously moving her hips, belly, and arms with her eyes closed. Her hands moved up and unbound her hair, letting it fall like silken fire around her. The song was one made for seduction, for inspiring desire and she moved to it, drawn up in the music. A woman began to sing, adding her seductive voice to the heady beat, and the scent of arousal from Autumn hit Kain like a sledgehammer. He could not look away, could think of nothing else except his hunger for her as he watched her movements through the screen.

She danced in a way that was more than mere dancing. Her hands began to rove over her body, and the intoxicating scent of her heat rolled off her. Unaware of anything but her, he moved out of the shadows and onto her porch. He panted in excitement, tasting her scent across his tongue as she wove the music around her. Her hands pressed against her undulating body, sliding up across her groin, belly, and breasts and into her mass of hair as she twisted and turned, writhed and arched before him.

The hunger was on him, urging him to take her, to taste her, to consume her in a very carnal way. But it was not blood this hunger asked for. It was her, all of her, every secret, intimate part. He was ready for her, so aroused he could do nothing but pant as the music continued its erotic beat. Sweat began to bead on her skin, rich with her scent, and her tongue darted out to lick her upper lip. Her hands moved to her breasts, cupping them in her hands, and her mouth parted as she touched herself through her shirt. Her fingers skated across the tight peaks of her nipples under the fabric, and her breath hitched in her throat.

He crept closer, so consumed with need that he was neither wolf nor man, but a creature of raw lust and appetite. His desire forced itself into a low growl in his chest as he bunched his muscles to leap, to bring her down, to make her his, when the music wound to a stop.

Autumn whipped around at the sound that came from the porch. She caught a glimpse of some large, dark shape as it bolted into the night. Panting from her erotic thoughts, she stared wide-eyed at the door, then made herself move to quickly turn on the porch light. Nothing there that shouldn't be, yet a heavy musk hung in the air and she had distinctly heard a growl. An animal had been here, watching her. It might have been a bear, but something in her told her it wasn't.

Alarmed and shaken, she quickly closed the door and engaged the dead bolt—something she never did—and switched off the light. She backed into the room, then jumped as the next song on the playlist came on. She hurried to the counter and turned the player off, then thought it would be a good idea to secure the house. She walked to all the window and doors, shutting and locking them and turning off the lights. When she was done, she returned to the great room and stared out at the darkness again. The night was pitch and still as it always was, with moonbeams just starting to slant through the darkness.

It was just an animal. Surely, it was only a bear, and she'd never had problems with them before. She knew how to be bear-safe. Besides, it had run off, obviously spooked away. Whatever it had been. She should be more worried about herself and what she had just experienced. She had *never* danced like that before! And the thoughts she'd been entertaining…that wasn't like her at all. And yet she was still tipsy and so miserably turned on, aroused by thoughts of a man she would never see again and had absolutely zero business thinking about.

Her cheeks flamed red as she went about turning the last of the lights out and banked the fire for the night. She had obviously drunk more wine than she'd thought. Maybe she just needed to go to bed. Perhaps she could forget about him in the oblivion of sleep…she hoped.

"Autumn, you need to get laid," she mumbled miserably to herself as she went to go brush her teeth.

And admitting that just sucked.

Kain ran. He streaked through the night blindly, his feet carrying him where they would. He ran, because if he did not run he would turn right around and take Autumn any way he could. He was out of control, so he set his body to running until he felt some semblance of sanity settle back over him. Soon he was miles away at the top of a peak, reaching a point where the forest cleared enough to give a view of the endless surrounding hills. Here he stopped, panting hard, though he continued to pace out of sheer necessity.

The moon had crested the horizon and bathed him now in her cold light as he paced. He whined between pants, trembling with unspent rage and lust. The moon sang through him and added to his agitation. His muscles burned with the exertion of his run, but his loins burned hotter still. He needed to find his release, but he wasn't going to get it, and the frustration of that fueled his rage. He turned his head to the sky and roared out a screaming howl that carried for miles.

Aggravated and full of the moon's siren song, the wolf in him was ready to bolt into the night again, intent on taking his rage out on the first creature he came across. Instead, the human part of him wrested control from the beast with the strength of his willpower, reining him in and soothing the wolf until his wild urges subsided.

He breathed deeply for a few moments as he paced, completely unsettled. He didn't know what was going on here, why he was so bewitched by this girl. It made no sense to him. Sure, she was beautiful, but no more so than any of the many, many others he'd bedded in the past. He vaguely wondered if he were under some kind of spell, but dismissed the idea out of hand. He would have sensed such a thing. He growled to himself, the sound like a rumbling machine in the quiet night. She was all wrong for him. She was too innocent. He would only hurt her. But his wolf was nearly frantic for her, and his own attraction to her was too strong. He felt helpless against his instincts, and he knew only one thing.

He would have her.

Oh yes, he would have her, but he would give her a fighting chance in this, he decided. She would come to him, not he to her. No cheating, no magic, just pure seduction. He would give her every opportunity to deny him. When she surrendered, her downfall would be her own, and his conscience would be clean. The wolf was impatient, but he was not, and he was a master of his control. Patience was what was needed here with a girl—no, woman—like her. To win this little game he would have to weave her passion carefully into a fine, hot flame that she could not deny. She would surrender to him completely, and when she did, he would take of her fully, and brand himself to her core. Then he would leave, as he must, as he always did. He would break her heart, but she would never forget him.

Resigned to his fate, he grumbled and licked his muzzle, calculating. The Hunger would be a factor, but if he made enough animal kills, he could conceivably stave it off until she was his. It shouldn't take more than a few days to thoroughly seduce her and win her over. He was a master of the art, and she would be unable to deny him.

Still planning, he got his bearings and headed back the way he came, anticipating tomorrow.

CHAPTER FOUR
The Hunt Begins

Morning light invaded Autumn's senses, slowly dragging her from her exhausted oblivion. It had been a long night, her body tense, and her dreams strange and chaotic. She had finally managed to fall into a deep and dreamless sleep sometime after the first hints of dawn blushed the sky. Now the sun was up and golden light streamed through the forest outside the glass doors of her bedroom as she stretched carefully. She ached all over as if every muscle had been clenched all night. Her blankets lay tangled around her, and her head felt like it had been hit with a sledgehammer. She had definitely drunk too much wine, and what the hell had she been dreaming? What time was it anyway?

Rolling over gingerly, she checked her clock with one bleary eye and cursed softly at the time. Then she picked up her cordless phone and saw the multiple missed calls from the shop. *Fuck.* She had promised she would cover part of the shift for her second employee, Tanya, who had an appointment with the dentist this morning. She must have turned her ringer and alarm off sometime last night in her drunken haze, hoping to get some sleep.

Groaning, she sat up slowly, then swung her legs over the side of the bed and took a moment to hold her aching head. When she felt like she could open both eyes, she called the shop.

"Dragonfly coffee, Tanya speaking."

"Hey, Tawn, it's Autumn," she croaked out, wincing at the gravel in her voice and the pain it sent shooting through her head. "

Autumn, are you OK?" Tanya asked with concern. Autumn stifled a groan and closed her eyes against the damnably bright sunlight outside.

"God, I am so sorry, sweetie. I overslept," Autumn apologized groggily and pushed a hand delicately through her sleep-tangled hair. It felt like every hair follicle was screaming.

"Did you have a bad night? Are you sick?"

"Yes, and no," Autumn sighed, rubbing the back of her neck. "I drank a little too much wine, and had some bad dreams, that's all."

"Sorry to hear that," Tanya said apologetically, "but could you get here as soon as you can? I need to leave in twenty minutes."

Guess she wouldn't be showering today. Autumn sighed quietly to herself. She desperately needed the hot water to help her recover.

"Yeah, I'll be right there."

"Thanks Autumn, I appreciate it," Tanya said gratefully. "I'll be ready to leave when you get here."

"No problem. See you soon."

Great. No shower, not even an initial coffee. She had just enough time to quickly wash her face and brush her teeth, throw on some clothes, and run out the door. Not to mention she was exhausted, hung over, and had a migraine splitting her skull.

It was going to be one of those days.

Hunting was a game of wits, patience, and a level of skill that could only be honed with time and experience. Good hunters needed to be crafty and devious, and know their prey well. Hunting humans required a much more cunning and clever mind than hunting animals did, whether he was hunting criminals to satisfy the Hunger, or women to satisfy his other urges. Hunting was hunting, whether death was involved or not, and Kain prided himself on his skills.

He could Compel her with his powers. It was an ability every werewolf had. It made their prey biddable, if they chose to use it. A subtle suggestion in a certain tone, a look into the eyes, a push of willpower, and weak-willed humans would do anything for them. Autumn was susceptible to his powers, but such means were beneath him when it came to seduction.

Hunting Autumn would be tricky and would require patience, yet he was growing short on time. Still, his strange need for her overrode any reservations he might have had about the Hunger or the coming Equinox. He would have her, and it would be well before he had to make a kill. Then he would be on his way to begin a hunt of a different sort.

Patience meant he had to stay in the area for as long as it took to seduce her and bring her down, a few days at the most. That meant he needed a place to stay, a reason to be there, and some essentials—a few props for the stage he was about to set.

He headed to Eureka early, intent on his mission.

Finding clothing that fit his six-foot, four-inch frame but that were also to his taste was often a huge headache for Kain, but to his delight he found a shop in Eureka that not only catered to big and tall, but had exactly what he was looking for. Based on her reaction to his leather, he also calculated that Autumn would appreciate certain clothing on him more than others, and he shopped with an eye toward what he felt she would like. He bought a couple of pairs of worn-looking jeans, another pair of supple, black leather pants, a leather jacket, a few T-shirts, a couple of silk shirts, and another pair of black, leather biker boots. Underwear he didn't bother with…ever.

A quick stop at a local grocery store took care of the few sundries he would need, including a couple more steaks to keep him fueled and his wolf at bay. On his way back to town, he noticed a small pawnshop and saw a Fender six-string acoustic propped in the window. Something about the sight of the guitar made him stop, and he went in to look at it. It was nothing all that special, but he stared at it for several minutes, considering. He hadn't held a guitar in many, many years, and despite the old memories the instrument brought to the surface, his fingers yearned for those strings. With a small curse he bought it, memories be damned. He was a sentimental old fool, but it would be an easy tool to lure his prey. Women loved musicians, he knew that fact well.

On his way back to Myers Flat, he took note of a junk yard in Rio Dell where he could stash the Camaro. He would return to it in a bit, but first he had to rent a room. In Myers Flat he had seen a sign for cabins for rent pointing to the south end of town, near the river. A few short blocks from the coffee shop were the Redwood Roost cabins, which would do nicely. They were small, individual rental cabins nestled among a grove of redwoods that lined the river's edge. He rented the cabin for several days, unloaded his purchases, and then left to return to the junk yard in Rio Dell.

At the junk yard, he talked to the owner, an older gentleman in coveralls, who showed Kain just what he needed: An older model Harley that the owner had been tinkering with on the side. It was worn around the edges, but otherwise in good condition and it ran well enough. Using his powers of charm and Compulsion, Kain asked if he could rent the bike for a few days. He explained that he was out vacationing and wanted to check out the area on a bike since the weather was so nice. Lulled by the Compulsion, the older man didn't see anything wrong with that, and agreed to rent him the bike and to park the Camaro. He would keep it covered and parked out behind the yard until Kain came back for it, and no, he wouldn't tell a soul about him or the car. Satisfied, Kain left the vehicle to the old man and headed back to Myers Flat on the Harley.

All of his preparations were made. It was early afternoon, about the same time as he had met her yesterday. He hoped she

would be there. He was impatient to see her as he roared toward town, anticipation singing through him.

Oh yes, it's definitely one of those days. Autumn sighed as the last of a large busload of tourists left the shop, chatting loudly with one another in German. It had been busy since she arrived, just in time for Tanya to dash out the door with a quick wave. It was also Marie's day off and she would *not* call her friend in. Marie worked hard enough for her as it was. She just had to suck it up and deal with it. Autumn had messed up several drinks in her tired haste to serve the crowd all by herself, her head pounding with an ache that three shots of espresso and two Excedrin couldn't dispel. She appreciated the business, but why did it have to be *this* morning?

She was disheveled, hastily dressed and un-showered, beyond tired, and now the espresso machine was acting up again. She really needed to buy a new one, but that would be a large purchase that she just didn't have the money for, so she kept putting up with the cheap model and its constant hiccups. Normally a sharp bang with a hand to the side of it would do the trick, but no matter how much she hit it right now (admittedly a little harder than she should) it still wasn't budging. There was a clog in there or, something, and she didn't have the patience to try and work it out right then. It looked like she would be serving drip coffee for the rest of the day.

I'm just…working too hard. She sighed as she looked around at the mess left from the morning rush—the coffee grounds, scattered beans, spilled milk and water all over the counters, supplies scattered about, and a pile of dishes waiting to be washed. She really needed to hire another employee to take some of the burden from her, but Marie and Tanya were all she could afford. There were two shifts a day, her employees trading off, but Autumn was here every day but Sunday when she closed the shop. *The joys of running your own business,* she thought ruefully and rubbed tiredly at her temple.

No use feeling sorry for herself. There was the afternoon lull now, and a lot of work to be done still. Heaving a sigh, she grabbed a washrag and began cleaning up the coffee prep area.

Kain dismounted from the Harley where he parked it next to a green Subaru in the parking lot. *Her* car, he could tell by the smell, and he breathed deeply. She was here. He stretched fully, arching his back and shaking out his long, unruly mane. There were no other cars in the dirt parking lot at the moment, which meant he likely had her to himself. Perfect.

He had prepared well for the hunt. The stage was set, all was ready. He had been anticipating this moment for ages it seemed, and all of his senses were attuned to the door set with a round, stained glass window depicting a dragonfly. The scent of coffee, redwoods, and woman were strong in the air. He gripped the handle as if in slow motion, opened the door with a small jingle of bells, and there she was.

Her back was to him as he entered, busy behind the counter. Her hair was pulled up into a messy ponytail, loose strands falling out of the tie that held it. She wore a plain white T-shirt and a pair of jeans, and she was washing dishes. He stepped up to the counter slowly, his boots noisy on the hardwood, and grinned. *Let the game begin.*

Autumn sighed as she heard the bells of the door jingle merrily, announcing another customer. *Can I at least get the dishes done before the next barrage?* She grimaced irritably. No, she was grateful for the business, she chided herself. "Wear a smile and put on an attitude of gratitude," her Oma would always say. Oma would be appalled at her behavior today, tired or not tired, hangover and aching libido or not. *Get it together, Autumn.* She waved a soapy hand behind her "Be with you in a minute," she managed as cheerfully as she could. She finished rinsing out her dish, snatched up a dry dishtowel to wipe her hands, pasted on a smile, and turned.

And let the towel drop limply to the floor.

"Hello again, Autumn," he said softly, standing at the register with his hands resting on the counter. Words failed her, as did thought. Here he was again, with that damnable, sensual half-smile playing at his lips. She gaped stupidly at him, and her body flushed with heat as his deep blue eyes stared into her. He was wearing a white T-shirt this time and a plain, black leather jacket. His mane tangled around his shoulders, falling wildly down his back. She inhaled sharply, breathing in the scent of leather, male, and spice, mingled with spilled coffee and the tang of cleaner.

"You!" she managed to breathe out, her eyes narrowing. "What are *you* doing here?" His smile became amused.

"This is a coffee shop, is it not?" he said, arching a slanted eyebrow. "I simply wanted some coffee."

She bristled at him, that he was even here, standing at her counter, teasing her and feeding her bullshit while some other treacherous part of her was breaking out the champagne and party poppers in celebration of his return.

"Why are you here? I watched you leave yesterday in that… car of yours." *That incredibly sexy, devil of a car.* "You should be long gone, so *why* are you here?" she demanded.

"That 'car' broke down just down the road," he said casually with a small shrug. "So, I had to rent a vehicle and a place to stay here in town for a few days while it's being fixed. While here I will need coffee, and this is the only real place in this town to get any. It's that simple." He smiled.

Autumn stared at him in disbelief. Did he really expect her to believe that? Really? *And do I have any choice?* She had no way to know if he was lying or not, but she wasn't stupid, and she hadn't imagined his intentions toward her yesterday. His story was all too coincidental and convenient, yet she simply couldn't call the cops or throw him out; he had done nothing, really, to merit that. So here he was, and she had to deal with him. Again. There wasn't enough coffee and Excedrin in the world for this.

Suddenly she was too exhausted to argue and she closed her eyes and sighed, defeated.

"All I have right now is drip coffee," she said tiredly as she opened her eyes again, resting her hand on her hip. "Espresso machine is busted."

Kain raised an eyebrow, the corner of his lips lifting to show just a hint of teeth.

"Busted you say? Mind if I take a look?"

Autumn looked at him warily and folded her arms across her chest. He looked sincere enough, harmless even, if a beast could ever be considered harmless.

"I have a lot of experience," he smiled, blinking slowly at her, the picture of innocence. She was just sure he did. *All kinds of experience,* a part of her thought wistfully and she shook her head.

With a deep sigh, she ran a hand over her hair to get the errant strands out of her face and then waved it at the infuriating machine. "Fine, if you think you can help. I doubt you can do more damage to it than I already have."

He smiled wide, showing perfectly white teeth and Autumn inwardly groaned as he took his leather jacket off and came around the counter. She stepped back to let him pass in the narrow space and clenched her eyes shut as he brushed past her. She was hit with his warm, masculine scent and she had to swallow hard against the fire that leaped in her belly. No man should smell that good. She opened her eyes to find him much too close to her as he examined the machine. She could not resist the temptation to look her fill.

His broad shoulders stretched the white T-shirt across his back, and his long arms were toned with lean muscle. His tangled mane was even more amazing from behind, thick with dark under layers of chocolate and chestnut, streaked with incredible bronze and caramel highlights, the longest tips lightest in color. It fell in long, unruly layers across his shoulders and down his back, the tips brushing over his ass, an ass clad in snug-fitting black jeans. Her eyes caught there, drawn by the way the material creased under those curves, and a small, dreamy breath hitched in her throat.

She came to herself again when he pulled the machine away from the wall and she dragged her eyes from him, shaking herself mentally as she sucked in a deep breath. What was wrong with her?

"I assume you cleaned everything properly and discharged the steam, right?" he asked over his shoulder and she cleared her throat, nodding.

"Yeah, all the usual procedures. It was working fine and now it just…stopped. The pump isn't working or something," she said, firmly crossing her arms over her chest and stepped to the side so she could watch him work.

He grunted noncommittally and turned the machine, checking it over while she chewed at her lower lip. She watched his hair slide across his shoulders as he shifted, checking the inputs.

"Well, you see here, this water line is cracked," he said, motioning her closer with his fingers. He shifted so she could get in to see and she shivered when he brushed against her with his body. His head was close to hers while he showed her the water line. There was indeed a small crack where he had pulled it out from under and behind the counter.

"I will bet that's your problem." His breath puffed against her face, smelling faintly of mint. He pulled away to let her get a good look at it. She just stared stupidly at the plastic tube and her senses screamed at the heat of him so close to her, his masculine scent enveloping her. Gritting her teeth, she drew back and stepped hastily away from him and the machine, crossing her arms quickly across her traitorously peaked nipples.

"Well, great." Served her for buying a lesser priced model. "I don't think I want to ask where the water has been going."

He chuckled, smiling sympathetically. "No, you probably don't. But let's find out anyway."

He crouched down and opened the cabinet doors underneath the espresso machine and pulled out bags of beans, filters, and boxes of miscellaneous supplies, then leaned in, feeling around.

"It's a little damp, but not as wet as it should be," he said and sat back again, peering into the space. He rubbed his hands on his ass, pulling her gaze there again. Her mouth went dry at his words and she jerked her eyes away, cursing mentally as he began putting the supplies back.

Kain stood with a sigh, closing the cabinet doors. He leaned against the counter with his hip, crossing his arms over his chest and raised an eyebrow at her. "I don't suppose this place has a basement?"

She stared blankly at him, distracted by the display of his folded arms, his biceps bulging against the fabric of his short sleeves.

"Autumn," he said deeply. The sound of his voice speaking her name brought her back to herself with a flush.

"What?" she asked softly, and was disgusted at her own tone. What was she, fifteen?

He smiled, showing a hint of teeth. "I asked if this place had a basement. It could be where your water is going."

Autumn inhaled a shaky breath and expelled it hard, scratching her head as she gathered her wits. God, she was tired, and he was altogether too sexy and distracting. She just couldn't take anymore of this today.

"Um, yeah, I do, but look," she sighed, closing her eyes briefly, "thanks for your help, but if that is really what's going on there's nothing you can do about it. It's not your problem."

Kain raised an eyebrow, keeping his pose. "Are you sure? It wouldn't be a problem to just take a look."

Autumn pursed her lips and hugged her arms tighter to her chest. "Mm-hmm, no need. I'll have a professional come and take a look down there. Thanks for your help."

He shrugged his shoulders and shoved off from the counter with his hip. "Suit yourself. I just wish I could be more help."

"You've helped enough, really." She smiled tiredly as he pushed the espresso machine back against the wall and then she backed away as he strolled toward her, his lips curled up at one corner of his mouth. She bumped up against the back counter and stood her ground, giving him plenty of room to slip by.

"I'm glad to be of help," he rumbled, stopping a touch away from her and inclining his head. She was sure he was going to do something, like touch her, or even try to kiss her as he stood towering over her, his expression unreadable, and she held her breath.

His lips parted as if to say something and he hesitated, smiling instead. "I hope you get some rest." He reached out to lightly, briefly squeeze her shoulder. She froze at the contact, but he was already moving past her and around the counter, gathering his jacket.

She stared mutely at him, the heat from his touch lancing through her. She knew she should say something as he shrugged his jacket on, the scent of leather-clad man wafting past her nose again.

"Thanks…again," she managed to blurt out, her butt still firmly to the back counter, her arms crossed tightly against the all too visible signs of her arousal.

"You're welcome Autumn." He said her name again in his wonderfully sexy, masculine voice and she trembled slightly, hugging herself firmly. His electric blue eyes stared deeply into hers as he said, "You'll see me again." A promise. He gave her a slow, feral, sexy grin once more, then turned and walked out of her shop.

Autumn released the breath she was holding just as soon as the bells on the door tinkled. She slumped against the counter, putting her head in her hands before letting them fall limply to her sides. *I am in trouble. Big, big trouble,* she sighed. The scent of him still lingered in the air.

She waited until she heard the bike roar out of the parking lot before she found the will to move, surveying the disaster her life had become. She wondered if she had somehow asked for this by defiantly waving her flag of celibacy in the face of the Powers That Be. Surely, they had a sick sense of humor to send this man to test her. Something about the man turned her into a brainless sex kitten when he was around. She didn't understand it, and she didn't like it. She felt defenseless against him. Her anger and her resolve were the only weapons she had, and when she was tired like this, she didn't even have those.

Well, so be it. If he was going to be around for the next few days, she would simply ignore him…and if he became a problem, she would ban him from her shop. She would be sure to be well rested and in full control of herself when she saw him again. Her libido be damned, she would *not* succumb to this man! Resolved, she began cleaning up once more, determined to be the one in control. She would be cool, and clear-headed, and he would not affect her again. Two could play this game.

She finished the last couple of hours of her shift with renewed energy, then closed the shop as evening began to creep among the pines. She turned out the lights and locked the doors behind her, eager to get home to a well-deserved shower and a warm bed.

CHAPTER FIVE
House Call

Kain waited for night again, anticipating the hunt. This night, though, he was going for his usual fare. A hot-blooded deer, full of fear and adrenaline that would appease the hunger of the beast inside. The wolf in him was still restless with energy, the waning full moon still potent in him and he was eager to be on with it, but the man tempered instinct with patience once again. The cabin that he rented was close to a portion of Humboldt State Park, just across the river via a footbridge. After dark, he would have the place to himself and shouldn't run into anyone. Just to be sure, though, he set off as the sun was setting and, crossing the footbridge, he worked his way deep into the forest, enjoying himself thoroughly.

When it was dark enough, he stripped off his clothes and stashed them in the hollow trunk of a redwood tree. He shifted quickly, his thoughts on the gnawing need of Hunger inside of him. Deer were thick around here like fleas on a dog, having no natural predators save for the odd coyote. Cars also took their toll, but not enough to thin their herds. They were incautious creatures, tamed by the locals' handouts. This would be pathetically easy.

He marked the spot where he stashed his clothes and then set off, his nose to the ground as he sifted through the scents. Fresh tracks were everywhere, and after only a short while he came upon a trio of black-tailed deer browsing in the moonlit darkness. They sensed him immediately, since he had no need for stealth. Not when he was so much faster than they were. They bolted, tails in the air, and Kain tore after them. They split up quickly, but Kain had made his choice, a doe with slight limp from an old wound. She would be the easiest.

She fled, and he pursued her, effortlessly keeping pace with her as she twisted, leaped, and dodged through the dark woods. Kain herded the doe uphill, away from the river and knew when the precise time to end it. She was winded, beginning to falter, and a slight stumble in her gait had Kain leaping onto her back. He rolled with her and sank his fangs into her neck, holding onto her with teeth and talons as she thrashed, making windy noises of fear in her throat. Hot blood sprayed against his face and poured into his mouth as he clung to her, his claws ripping her deeply as he avoided her flailing hooves. Her fight did not last long and she slowed quickly under his weight and her injuries. She lay panting underneath him as her blood gushed out between his teeth.

Her death was intimate to him, sensual almost, and he thanked her mentally as she twitched and shuddered, her life flowing out of her. With a sharp and powerful jerk of his head, Kain ripped her neck out, her meat shredding in his jaws and he swallowed her life greedily. Power suddenly flowed through him, electric and intense, and the Hunger took him. He lost control, tearing into the deer with teeth and claws, swallowing huge chunks of meat and blood until he became woozy and drunk with it.

Sated finally, he dragged himself away and lay in the ferns and sorrel, his belly huge with meat and his fur wet with blood. He felt drunk, high, and incredibly good as he always did after a kill. The power of a life taken vibrated through him, and he lost his lethargy quickly. He needed to run.

Leaving the rest of the carcass there for the forest scavengers, he broke into a run. There was no question where he was headed. He felt too good not to see her. He ran, faster than ever, feeling alive and charged, briefly replenished in his power. He longed to share this with her, this wild joy. Using his nose, he made his way through the forest. The forest was largely untouched by man on this side of the river, and he found few signs of humans. He reached her land quickly. Once there he slowed, marking the area with his scent to warn others that she belonged to him, and him alone. He sauntered through her territory, luxuriating in the power of the node there as he lazily scented the area, marking here and there as he went. His tail even waved lazily behind him and he let it, happy to show the world how good he felt.

The lights were off at her place. He expected that she had gone to bed early, as tired as she had seemed earlier that day. He went about sniffing the area thoroughly but found nothing amiss, then padded up onto the porch and peered into the windows. All was quiet in the main area of the house, and he prowled over to the far side of the porch silently. There she was.

He peered in through the glass door of her bedroom and saw her asleep in her bed, the covers crumpled at her feet as she sprawled all over the queen size mattress. He grumbled in his throat and paced in front of her windows a moment, warring with himself. His wolf was powerful after the kill and still strong from the moon, and he couldn't stand the glass between them no matter what the human part of him cautioned. He had to smell her, to see her. Kain knew he couldn't win against his wolf in this, so he yielded the fight for now. Besides, what harm could a little look do? She was asleep, and if she woke up…well, he could always Compel her.

He released the change and melted back into his human form as quickly as he could. His dark fur was tickling back into his skin as he grasped the handle to the door and found it unlocked. A bad habit of hers. *All sorts of intruders might waltz right in.*

He stepped into her bedroom on silent, bare feet. She twitched, mumbling something and he froze halfway to her bed. He waited a moment but she did not stir again. She was not awake, just dreaming, and obviously deeply asleep. He relaxed and watched her, idly licking blood off his hands and arms as he did so, and took a full look at her nicely displayed body.

She only wore panties and a small T-shirt, her hair fanning out around her head. She was beautiful, and Kain unabashedly raked her body with his gaze. He imagined what he would do to her when she finally surrendered to him, all the tantalizing ways he would tease and pleasure her. She would scream his name, he promised himself. He would hear it again and again.

She shifted in her sleep and mumbled something, pulling Kain from his lustful thoughts. He came closer, standing next to the bed now as he watched her. She flinched, and moaned out what sounded like a soft "No." He cocked his head at her. Was she was having a nightmare? She was deeply asleep, but her breathing had become faster and she twitched, jerking her head.

It was really beyond stupid of him to be here, risking so much, he realized with a frown. Sure, he could Compel her if she awoke; convince her she was dreaming, but what if she resisted? Though she was susceptible to his power, it was still entirely possible for her to resist his Compulsion, especially if she felt threatened. It could ruin everything. Still, he was fascinated by her, and the distress she seemed to be in during her nightmare. He reached out and gently laid his hand on her out-flung palm, surprising himself, and watched as she breathed out softly in her sleep. Her fingers curled around his and she stilled, her expression softening, her breathing deepening again. He stared at her fingers curled slightly around his and an unnamed feeling stole through him. Protectiveness? Or something else?

Leaning over he used his willpower to reach out to her, subtly altering his voice to command. "Sleep deeply and do not dream. Do not waken until dawn."

He watched her face for a few moments more, then gently removed his hand from hers, and backed away from the bed carefully. She should sleep like the dead now, until dawn at least. But what had she been dreaming that upset her so? And, more importantly, why did he care? Unsettled, he made sure she was still sleeping soundly and went to explore her house.

Autumn dreamed of darkness in her woods. Something was there in the pitch black of the forest, something that was purely evil. Something blacker than night that she couldn't see, and the thing wanted her, wanted to hurt her. It had been looking for her for a long time. She dreamed she sat huddled in her room against the wall, the house dark and cold. Her cat Toby lay in pieces on the porch just outside her bedroom door, torn apart by something unfathomable. Terror gripped her as the glass door swung inward silently on its own, though she could see nothing on the other side. She felt it, though, the horrible creature coming, just on the other side of the door. She knew it would do terrible things to her, and she nearly sobbed in fear.

Suddenly there was another presence there, powerful and commanding. A huge, black wolf stepped into the room, its blue eyes blazing as it faced the door. A low rumble issued from its throat.

She knew the wolf, had always known him. He was her protector. She felt the menace retreat, withdrawing back into the darkness once more. The wolf stayed where it was, watching the night. In the way of dreams, things shifted then, calm spreading through her mind at the wolf's presence. She began to dream normally with all the strange randomness of the dream world, but one thing stayed in her mind: The black wolf standing at the door, keeping back the night.

Kain roamed through her small house quietly, taking his time to sniff out the place. Since he was here, he might as well investigate and see what useful information he could find about her. Everything was tidy and well taken care of, the rooms stuffed full of curiosities and color. It seemed in every room and in every nook and cranny there were little signs of Autumn. Fairies, glass things, bits of wood and bone, feathers, crystals, sculptures, artworks, pottery, and various knick-knacks of all kinds were tucked in every available space. Plants were abundant, and there were several bookcases filled with books. The second bedroom seemed to serve not only as a guest room, but also as a sewing room and small office as well.

Kain couldn't help but smile as he poked around, noting all of her little touches. The place was so much hers he ceased to wonder why she obviously spent so much time here. This was her sanctuary, her world. He noticed the wood floors were strewn with colorful rugs while he padded around, softening his steps as he entered the large room of the house. He smelled the scent of paints and clay, old cooking, incense, a wood fireplace, flowers and plants, and then the sudden sharp scent of pissed off cat.

He whirled around and cursed as he saw the thing on a chair. The cat was huge to begin with, but sitting there crouched and puffed up it looked giant. Its ears were pinned to its head, and its eyes were hellish and round. Kain froze as the thing hissed softly then uttered a low growl, a menacing sound that meant it would launch itself in a moment. That would wake Autumn for sure. Though the wolf in him wanted to kill it before it could make more noise, Kain was sure she cherished the pet and so he reached out to it with his powers, locking eyes with the little beast.

He had been taught long ago that the Allure of his kind, the ability of a werewolf to seduce and draw people to themselves, also worked on animals. A little trick few of his kind actually knew, or cared to know. Kain had this power in spades, and he used it now on the cat. The cat resisted his Allure at first, but then he felt its fear melt away under his gaze and its fur settled again. After a moment, the cat jumped down from the chair and was immediately around his legs, rubbing and purring.

Kain sighed and pinched the bridge of his nose as the cat sat before him and looked up at him adoringly. Next, he was going to be writing poetry and braiding flowers into his hair, and he had to wonder if this was really worth putting himself through all of this for the sake of a woman. He looked down at the cat that was now rolling around on the floor in front of him. He sighed and bent down to give its fluffy belly a scratch.

"Well, big guy, what do you think of her?" he whispered softly and the cat made a small noise of happiness, peering up at him with blissfully slitted eyes.

Kain grunted and shook his head as he stood. The cat followed, tail high, as he made his way back to the bedroom, and Kain stopped in the doorway to watch her. He had his answer. He would do what it took to have this woman, to have all of her and then some. He would move mountains for her surrender, to lay with her, to touch her, to drink in her scent and touch her skin. He didn't understand it at all.

Sighing, he walked to the glass door and looked out at the dark forest, her domain, as the cat twined around his ankles. The night was quiet, and he was lulled by her fragrance and the sound of her soft, regular breathing. The scents of the night forest trickled in through the partially open door. With a sigh, he lowered himself to the wood floor and curled up, looking out into the forest. He mulled it over as the peace of the place washed over him and the cat curled up against him, purring contentedly.

He had a better idea of who Autumn was now, and he now knew the best approach to take with her. He would have to gentle himself a little bit more, but that was OK. It was all a ruse to bring her to him anyway, and he would be his wild and carefree self again after he had her and went on his way. He continued to calculate and plan as the night wore on, and Autumn slept peacefully mere feet away.

In her dreams, the black wolf lay at her door, her protector, and she slept deeply and peacefully all night. When she awoke in the morning to sunlight spilling into her room, she was surprised to see the glass door open and swinging gently in the cool morning breeze.

Thankfully, Autumn was scheduled again for the later shift that day. After the day she'd had yesterday, she felt overdue for a little TLC. She roused herself, donned her yoga pants, a sweatshirt, and tennis shoes, and went for a run in her woods. Thoughts of her dreams and of her day yesterday ran through her head as she jogged her familiar trails, snaking their way through her forested property. Her normally perfect world was taking on a note of the surreal, and it was ever since *he* had decided to poke his nose into it, stirring things up, and messing with her head. And what was with those dreams last night with the wolf? She shook her head and decided to concentrate on her breathing, clearing her mind. She didn't want to think about anything right now. She just wanted some peace.

It was another sunny morning, and her forest was full of bird song and golden shafts of light as she ran. Steller's jays screamed at one another in a rhododendron bush, nuthatches twittered, and chipmunks and squirrels darted through the woods before her. The air was clean and cool as she breathed in and out, mentally following her breath. Her world was perfect, and Opa and Oma had ensured it would be that way, even after they passed. They had set aside a trust just for the land, and it stated clearly in their will that the land could never be sold, but must always remain in the family. As if Autumn would ever consider selling any part of this land to the many and various interested buyers who had continually hounded Oma, and who now hounded her.

Her heart was tied to this land; it was a part of her. She knew every tree here, every bend in the trail, every creature that lived here. She had grown up in this forest, running barefoot along these very trails. She had played in the trees, pretending to be a deer or a fairy as she ran through the ferns. Oma would call after her about wearing shoes and ruining her clothes, but never scolded her for long. She always allowed Autumn to be as free and creative as she wanted to be. Autumn had always hated shoes, but they were a necessary evil in the world, especially when jogging. She so loved instead to feel the cool earth beneath her feet, savoring all the textures and temperatures, feeling connected to the earth.

She began to slow as she approached her favorite part of the forest. Here there was a circular growth of redwoods, a cathedral group, located at the heart of the little valley. She circled the ring of older trees and panted from her run, trailing her fingers along their trunks. She remembered when she was young she had named all of them and had built a little den in the hollow of one of the trees gutted by an ancient fire. She smiled at herself, silently naming them again as she made her way around the ring, feeling much more herself. They were her sentinels, guarding the forest from any who would intrude. They made a pact that way, her and her trees, and she could always find sanctuary here.

She continued on, the trail weaving more northerly now and into a denser part of the forest. The brush was thicker here with deadwood scattered about the area. She had considered having this part of the woods cleared a bit, to remove a lot of the tangle, but she could not do that to any part of her forest. She wanted things to stay as they were, natural and wild, not tamed by her hand. So she dealt with the thicket and ran through it as she always did, concentrating on her breathing.

Something made her come to a stop on the other side of the thicket and she looked around, panting, wondering what was amiss. Things looked as they always did, yet a vague sense of unease stole through her. She turned about, eyes searching the area, and landed on the trail behind her as it disappeared into the thicket. Late morning light was scattered all around but did not pierce through those shadows very well. She watched the trail for movement. Her breathing calmed and she listened, but all was absolutely silent—no birds, no creatures scurrying in the underbrush, no sound at all but her own heartbeat and breath. The hairs rose along her nape and she took a step backward, her sense of unease mounting.

You're just being silly, she told herself. If there was something or someone in there, she would see movement. The thicket wasn't *that* thick. She saw no hint of danger, and yet her senses were warning her of something.

Something not good.

She waited for several moments, holding her breath, ready to flee at the slightest movement or noise, but nothing happened. Then slowly the sensation faded, a bird chirped, and then another, and soon the thicket was just the thicket again: A jumbled area of brushes and branches, undergrowth and fallen trees. Breathing out a huge sigh, she chided herself for being jumpy because of her nightmare and set out running again. Still, some panicky little animal part of her made her pick up the pace until she was around a bend and into a sunny patch of trees and sword ferns.

That had just been weird. It had certainly never happened before. She always felt perfectly safe in her forest. She was just off-kilter because of Kain, she decided. Something about him had set her world askew and made her unsure of herself. Damnable man. She hoped like hell he wouldn't be there when she went to the shop today. She didn't want any more of his distractions.

She finished her run and cooled down in her garden as she wandered about checking on everything. Oma had kept the garden in beautiful condition all the years of her life, cultivating it, growing it, and tending to it lovingly. She used native and deer-resistant species, loathing to put up any kind of fence to keep the deer and little critters out so that it was a part of the larger forest. She taught Autumn everything she knew about growing things, about herbs and their uses, and Autumn had learned well, cultivating a bright green thumb. Now it was hers, and she loved nothing better than spending time here when the weather permitted.

Satisfied that everything was in good shape she hurried inside, eager for a shower and some coffee.

HungerHunger 81

Autumn pampered herself the rest of the morning, doing her yoga, drinking her fresh juice for breakfast, and taking her time in the shower and with her grooming. She decided that she needed to look good today. Looking good went a long way to feeling confident, and she needed all the confidence she could get right now.

She had a taste for the Bohemian chic, with gauzy tunics and colorful skirts, flowered dresses, old lace, leather, crocheted pieces, the hand made, and the antique, and she pulled it off well, she thought. She dressed carefully in a brown knitted boho tunic with a dropped point hem, black leggings, and tall brown suede boots with a slight heel. She completed the look with a long necklace of antique beads, and around her wrists were leather cuffs inset with turquoise. Casual enough to be work friendly, but flirty enough to catch the eye. And not any specific eye, just, you know, people.

She regarded herself in the mirror for a few moments, looking herself over critically. She had never minded the fact that she was a 130 pound, curvy size ten, and even though in the world of magazine models she might be considered "plump," she didn't look at herself that way. Sure, she didn't have that desirable Grand Canyon gap between her thighs, and maybe her muscles weren't visible and her belly was a little poochy, but she didn't mind. Besides, she did work out and her diet was healthy, and she knew she wasn't overweight. She was what most described as "buxom," with her mother's hourglass figure. She had a long, narrow waist, wide hips, and plump but firm thighs.

She eyed her breasts, pushing them up a bit in her black underwire bra. They were definitely one of her best features, decent size Cs that weren't too big or too small, she thought, and turned to look at her butt. It was a little on the round side, but at least it wasn't flabby. She wasn't some model, but she could sure pull off cute, she decided, and smiled at herself in the mirror as she smoothed her tunic.

She had to stop being a silly, hormonal teenager about Kain; she chided herself as she grabbed her things. She was a grown woman and she had been with her share of men. OK, not a huge pile of them, but enough that she wasn't some tittering ninny every time an attractive face came along.

Firm in her resolve, she drove to the shop with her chin held high and her back straight. confident and relaxed, yet when she pulled into the parking lot she gripped the steering wheel and grimaced. He was already here, sitting out on the redwood deck with Cleo and Marie, all of them chatting and smiling amiably as she parked. She made sure her eyes were unreadable behind her brown-tinted sunglasses, and breathing in a sigh of resignation, grabbed her purse, and got out of the car. *Dignity, Autumn*, she told herself. *Dignity and strength. You can do this. You can be around this man today.*

Drawing herself up proudly she forced herself to step up onto the deck, ignoring him as she smiled at Cleo and Marie who greeted her with a genial, "Good morning."

"Morning girls," she replied as cheerfully and normally as she could, focusing on their smiling faces. She was determined not to look at him, but his sheer presence was like a magnetic force, compelling, not to be ignored. He simply sat there, waiting.

"Autumn, you didn't tell us that our mystery man came back," Cleo admonished her, making a swatting motion at her with her hand. "Kain was just telling us how his car broke down and he's stuck here for a few days, the poor man."

"Yeah, we were just talking about that. And you," Marie piped in with a sly grin, and that was all it took for her ire to simmer to the surface. What, exactly, had they been telling him? She shot a look at him, a caustic remark on her tongue, but it died as her gaze found him.

He sat back casually in one of the redwood deck chairs, one of his long legs propped up on his knee at the ankle. He wore a rich blue, button-up silk shirt with the top two buttons undone and the sleeves rolled up at the wrists. The color matched the blue fire in his eyes. The shirt was untucked over a pair of worn-looking, loose-fitting blue jeans, and he wore the same black biker boots. He had obviously showered, and he had shaved a bit, tidying up his scruff. He wore his now brushed out mane tied back at the temples, a few unruly strands hanging down around his face. He looked so casual, yet that seductive brush of predator was still there, languid and relaxed.

He just smiled at her mildly as he brought a paper cup of coffee to his lips, his eyes never leaving hers. He didn't say a thing.

Autumn was vaguely aware that Marie was still chattering on. "Oh by the way, the repair man called. He said he won't be able to get out to fix the machine until Monday, and the contractor will be here later today to look at the basement. It sucks that we can't do espresso, but do you want some coffee anyway? Autumn?"

There, she had done it again. Allowed the damnable man to distract her with his mere presence while important things were forgotten around her. He didn't even have to do anything, just sit there, and look at her with those eyes. She wanted to claw them out.

"I need some coffee," she grumbled, and Kain chose that moment to shift and get to his feet in a slow, graceful motion.

"I really must be going ladies," he said, and her friends made disappointed sounds.

Autumn tilted her head at him slightly. "You're leaving?" she asked, perplexed. Kain only gave her a small smile.

"He's been here since opening. I'm sure he's tired of us prattling hens," Cleo chuckled and Autumn looked at her, then back to him. Seriously?

He reached into his back pocket and pulled out a business card. "I don't have a cell phone, but this is where I am staying if I can help you with anything," he said as he held it out to her. She stared up at him and then at the card, hesitating a moment before reaching out for it. "I'm in cabin B3." His eyes were steady as his fingers brushed hers. She caught her breath, unable to think of anything to say.

He smiled at her, his eyes lingering on her a moment before he turned to her friends. "Ladies," he said with a nod, and then turned and casually walked to his bike.

Autumn stared after him, her fingers curled around the card. Was he for real? He was really just going to leave the moment she got there? *The nerve!* She fumed, crushing the card in her palm.

They all watched him get on his bike and start it up, smiling at them as he backed out and left the parking lot slowly, and drove out of sight toward the other side of town.

Cleo was regarding her with a look of fascination as Autumn turned back to her friends, the sound of his bike receding in the distance.

"What?" she asked, looking between them.

"Ooooh, girl. You *are* in trouble," Cleo said, shaking her head and giving her a sympathetic grin.

"I think he likes you," Marie said slyly. "I mean, he didn't say it so much, but he asked about you."

Autumn blinked at her. "And just what did he want to know?"

"Oh come on, Autumn," Cleo said, rolling her eyes a bit. "We didn't give him your social security number."

"He wanted to know if you had a boyfriend." Marie giggled and Autumn's temper flared up about ten notches.

"What?" She nearly exploded at the same moment that Cleo thumped Marie on the arm.

"No he did not. Mar's just fucking with you."

Autumn just stared at them incredulously.

"OK, you need a time out and some coffee," Cleo said, stepping between them, and guided her toward the door, "and we need to have a little talk, I think."

Autumn allowed her friend to sooth her ire, taking deep mental breaths as they went inside. She was glad that Cleo was here, because she really did need her best friend right now. Obviously, she wasn't doing a great job of sorting this out on her own.

Cleo waited while Autumn made herself a mug of coffee while Marie excused herself to finish her chores. Coffee made, they headed out onto the sunny porch again, settling themselves at a table. Autumn loosened her shoulders as the first sips of hot, dark coffee began coursing through her, calming her temper and allowing her to relax.

"So, what has gotten into you?" Cleo asked, leaning across the table and staring intently at her friend.

Autumn sighed and wrapped her hands around her coffee mug, staring at it. Cleo was going to make her admit it. She pursed her lips and shrugged a shoulder lightly, then took a deep breath and let it out with a sigh.

"I...can't seem to deal...with the current situation," she hedged, not exactly sure what the problem was with herself. Cleo sat back and regarded her for a long moment as Autumn toyed with her mug.

"This is the first time you've been attracted to someone in a while. Really attracted, isn't it?" she asked and Autumn lifted her eyes to her, nodding slightly. Cleo curved her lips into a lopsided grin and reached across the table to take Autumn's hand.

"This isn't a bad thing," she assured her, gripping her hand. "It isn't a crime to be attracted to someone."

Autumn looked at her and shook her head. "But I don't want to go there, Cleo. It's making me crazy. *He's* making me crazy. Being attracted means that he can get at me. I don't like it."

"He makes you feel vulnerable," she stated and Autumn sighed deeply.

"Very much so."

Cleo considered Autumn for a moment and pursed her lips. "I know Ted hurt you pretty badly. You've been wounded and shut down all these years. I understand that. But why does your heart have to be involved? It's just sex, honey. That's all. It really isn't complicated." Cleo gave her hand a squeeze at her miserable expression. "And if anyone needs to get laid, my dear, you certainly do."

Autumn smiled a little and Cleo grinned, patting her hand. But she simply did not agree. That man did all sorts of crazy things to her inside, things she didn't trust.

"You know me, Cleo. I've never been able to just…sleep with someone and have it mean nothing. I'm just not wired that way." She shook her head. "I don't think I could do it."

Cleo nodded sympathetically, knowing her friend well. "Sorry, but I seriously doubt Kain is the boyfriend type, let alone the marrying type," she joked gently and Autumn chuckled, then sobered again.

"That's my problem," she sighed. "I simply have no idea how to handle this. I'm not an idiot…the man wants me. But if I were to," she swallowed, "have sex with him, I'm deathly afraid it will break my heart. Again. No Cleo," she shook her head. "I just need to stay away from this one."

Cleo sighed and sat back in her chair, regarding her friend. "I know honey, but he's sniffing around. You're going to have to buck up and give him the news, and mean it. Don't lead him on."

Autumn nodded. Cleo was right. She needed to nip this in the bud, not ignore it. Much as a secret part of her really enjoyed his attentions, she needed to make it clear to him that she wasn't available. She didn't trust her heart not to get involved.

"OK, Mama Bear. Whether or not he's really stuck here in town, I will make it clear that I'm done. I'm flattered, but it just isn't going to happen. The end."

Cleo smiled gently at her and nodded. "It sucks honey. It really does. But you'll get over this, and someday you will find a man that turns you on, makes you smile, and will cherish your beautiful heart. You deserve no less."

Autumn nodded, smiling wanly at her friend. Yes, that was what she had always wanted, what she had been holding out for. Beautiful man or no, she would not entertain this. She would march right over there and tell him to leave her alone, and if he couldn't do that, well, then the cops would get involved. She had to assert her boundaries and respect herself.

She simply needed more in a man then what Kain offered.

CHAPTER SIX
A Walk In The Woods

It was a few hours later when Autumn pulled into the Redwood Roost cabins and looked around for B3. She decided she wouldn't do this immediately lest she appear too desperate to get rid of him, so she had chatted with Cleo and Marie for a bit while they enjoyed the sunshine. Cleo had to leave soon after, telling Autumn that she had to head to Santa Rosa and wouldn't be back until Monday, but to call her and tell her how it went. Marie had left as well, since her shift was over, but she also wanted details.

Autumn had busied herself with business around the shop for a while, waiting for the repairman to get there and have a look in the basement. There had indeed been some flooding, he said, but the damage wasn't severe. He worked at removing what water was there, and set some fans to finish drying it out. Repairing the espresso machine and the water line would have to wait for the technician, who wasn't coming until Monday. Once that business was taken care of, she closed the shop and set off to find Kain, determined to be done with this.

She parked near the office and got out of her car. There was a map of the cabins on a nearby post. She checked the map and located B3, down near the edge of the cabin property, close to the footbridge and the river. She decided to walk to give herself time to think over how she was going to handle telling him that she wasn't interested. Swallowing, she squared her shoulders and set off down the path.

She noticed as she walked that there were few cabins rented out. Things had been almost unnaturally slow for business this winter, likely due to the ongoing drought, and the locals had begun feeling the financial pinch. It was apparent everywhere as businesses in the area that had long been around had suddenly closed shop, and tourism had slowed to a crawl. It was bad news for an area that relied upon those tourist dollars. Unless you were an illegal marijuana farmer, you were tightening your belt. She just hoped that the economy picked up soon. She didn't know how Dragonfly would survive without steady business.

Lost in her thoughts, she didn't realize what she was hearing until she came around a cluster of trees near the B section. Someone was singing and expertly plucking out a haunting tune on an acoustic guitar. She would swear it was coming from a radio if she didn't have a niggling suspicion of exactly where the tune was coming from. Her suspicions were confirmed as she approached the little rental cabin, but she wasn't prepared for the sight that met her.

Kain sat on the little covered porch out front of the cabin. He was leaning back in a chair and playing the guitar as if he never knew a day when it wasn't in his hands. His bare feet perched on the rough-cut railing, and he was wearing the same clothes she'd seen him in earlier that day, all shades of blue that accented his caramel brown hair and dark features nicely.

He seemed to be deeply caught up in what he was doing, his eyes closed as he sang, and he plucked and strummed the strings of his guitar flawlessly. Autumn was taken aback, watching him from where she stood half concealed by a tree. The performance was so perfect she would think that it was another ploy to woo her, except that he couldn't know she was there. Besides, there was something incredibly sincere and heartfelt in his singing. He seemed unaware of anything around him.

Not only was he astoundingly good at playing, but the song was captivating, heartbreaking even, and his voice was unlike any other she had heard before. A baritone of no small talent. The expression on his face as he sang made her breath catch in her throat. She was fascinated by his hands and fingers on the strings—so light and precise that it was mesmerizing to watch him play. The tune was very haunting, speaking of love and regret and she held her breath to listen.

He hadn't intended to play this particular song. He had never intended to play it again, but he had come back to the rental and decided to pass the time playing the guitar. He'd even looked forward to it. He had tuned the six string and messed around with some chords, then broke into a rock ballad he had written long ago. It felt good to play again, damned good, even if it was just for himself. He had moved easily into a couple of melodic pieces as memories began flooding him, memories of the past and another life.

Then there were the memories of Carley, and the song he had written for her but never finished. He hadn't wanted to play the blasted song but his fingers found the tune anyway, his voice the melody. He had loved her, in his own way. He had betrayed her. She was a high point of regret in his life and he sang for the memory, allowing the old wound some release. He rarely bothered with the past, or with regrets, but there was something about being here, about being around Autumn, that opened that part of him.

He was lost in his thoughts, lost in the music, and he sang his regret.

Autumn watched him breathlessly, unable to comprehend the man, and realizing she knew absolutely nothing about him. He was all ego and swagger, seduction and danger, and yet here he was expressing a depth of soul she could hardly fathom. She desperately wanted to believe what she was witnessing was an act, for if it was she could hate him for it. But something in her knew it wasn't. There was pain here, and deep feeling. It called to her, and it was even more alluring than all his exotic good looks and seductive charm. She had no idea what to do with it.

The song ended with a light strum and he took a deep breath, his head bent, hands stilled upon the strings. Then he lifted his eyes to hers across the open space between them and she gasped, catching an emotion there for just a fleeting moment. Just as quickly, it was gone, replaced by a languid smile.

"Hello, Autumn," was all he said, and for once, she couldn't get irritated at him. Her defenses had been cracked by what she had just seen. She had no idea what to feel.

He dropped his eyes to the guitar again and strummed a random tune, obviously waiting for her to make a move. Straightening her back, she decided to get it over with and just go to him.

His fingers toyed with the strings as he watched her approach, his expression unreadable. She stopped a few feet away and they regarded each other as Kain strummed the guitar lightly.

"Did you need help with something?" he asked, his gaze on her as his fingers deftly plucked out a quick, melodic tumble. She stared at him, her mouth parted slightly as she tried to figure out what to say. She couldn't just say, *"Oh, hey, I've been thinking, and you're nothing but bad news for me so you need to go away now. 'K thanks, bye."* No, not after what she had just seen and heard.

"I just…" she began lamely, gesturing. "I had no idea you were a musician. You're very talented," she finished softly, folding her arms. "Your song was beautiful."

Kain smiled slightly and then stilled his hand.

"Thank you," he said, inclining his head a little as he set the guitar aside. "Many years of practice."

She bit her lip and rubbed a hand against her arm. "Were you ever a professional? You really should be. You're incredibly good."

An emotion crossed his face then and he got to his feet, stepped off the porch, and prowled toward her. She stared at him, her mouth falling open at his sudden intensity, and her feet were rooted to the ground as he advanced. He stopped just short of her and stared into her eyes, his expression tense but unnamable. They stayed that way for a moment, eyes searching one another. Autumn opened her mouth to say something, anything, when he suddenly said, "Walk with me."

She blinked up at him, taken aback. "Walk with you? Where?"

Kain stepped back, his expression softening into a smile.

"Here." He gestured at the forest. "There are trails. Show me this forest of yours."

Autumn continued to stare at him, surprised and a bit wary. He wanted to go for a walk and have her show him the forest? She was intrigued by his request, but why should she trust him? She wasn't a naive teenager; he might be hoping to lure her away into the forest where he could force himself on her. Yet he looked so sincere, and she was interested despite her caution.

Kain gave her a gentle smile, folding his arms lightly. "I absolutely understand your hesitation. I promise I mean you no harm, Autumn. All I want is to walk with you. That's all."

Autumn eyed him skeptically, considering. She did have pepper spray in her bag, and her cell phone actually worked this close to town. She could even text Cleo right now and tell her what she was doing, and if she didn't hear from her in fifteen minutes…no, bad plan. Cleo was on her way south and didn't need to worry about her. Autumn chewed her bottom lip as she considered and Kain watched her placidly, waiting. It was incredibly stupid, and she would hear about it later from Cleo, but what the hell. Her curiosity was eating her.

"Sure, I guess," she said slowly and he grinned. "But I am warning you now, I have pepper spray and I claw like a cat."

Kain chuckled at that and nodded his head. "Warning taken. I promise, no funny business." He returned to the porch and put the guitar inside the door, then shut and locked the little cabin while she waited.

"Shall we then?" he asked, strolling up to her with that animal grace. She looked down at his bare feet and back up to him.

"Aren't you going to put on shoes?"

He gave a small shrug. "I hate shoes."

Autumn gaped for half a second, then made a small sound and broke into a wide smile, surprised by him all over again. Kain's face lit up at her smile and he grinned down at her, his eyes sparkling with pleasure. She could see subtle laugh lines around his eyes and wondered faintly, around the thundering of her heart, just how old he was. Damn, the man had a smile that could melt butter.

Autumn coughed and looked away from him to compose herself, gesturing toward the trail. "All right then, after you."

They didn't speak for several long moments as they began walking toward the footbridge that crossed the river. Late afternoon sunlight streamed through the breaks in the redwood canopy above, dappling the world around them in gold. Autumn was painfully aware of the man strolling next to her. His bare feet padded quietly across the ground while they politely kept their distance. She couldn't believe she was doing this. Wasn't she supposed to be giving him the boot? Yet here she was, casually strolling through the forest with him, wondering what was going to come next.

"So you must have questions about me I imagine," he said, breaking the silence with his deep voice. Gooseflesh ran along her arm at the sound of his masculine baritone. He was looking at her with a raised eyebrow and she returned his gaze, blinking in surprise.

"Go ahead and ask." He smiled reassuringly.

She stared at him a moment more, seeing the sincerity in his eyes. OK then.

She considered, then asked, "Where did you learn to sing and play like that?"

A small smile curved his lips and he leaned toward her as he said, "Vienna Boys' Choir." Laughter twinkled in his eyes and she frowned, giving him a skeptical look.

"I'm only kidding." He chuckled, lifting his hands in surrender. "My mother was a stage actress long ago. I was taught to sing by my mother, and then by a voice coach employed by the theater. A stage hand taught me the guitar and I've played ever since."

Autumn stared at him openmouthed. She waited, but he didn't go on and she was dying of curiosity now.

"Did you ever play professionally?"

He shrugged. "I worked for the theater for a little while. Worked as a stagehand and call boy, did some backup in the chorus from time to time, but in the end, it wasn't for me. No, I was never a professional anything. I've sort of been a…jack of all trades my whole life."

She stared at him in fascination. "So is that what you do for a living? Odd jobs and such?"

"You could say that."

She narrowed her eyes at him and opened her mouth for another question. "Ah ah, I've answered several of your questions," he said, cutting her off. "Now it's my turn."

Oh. Well, that was fair, she supposed. But did she really want to tell him anything? What if he was just fishing for information so he could get closer? Then again, he had just shared personal information about himself. It would be rude not to answer at least some of his questions in kind.

He looked over at her, his expression curious. "So you work at a coffee shop. What else do you do?"

She hesitated a moment, then lifted her chin with some pride. "Correction, I *own* a coffee shop."

Kain looked surprised. "You own the cafe?"

Autumn's spine stiffened, her brow furrowing at his incredulous tone. "Is that so hard to believe?"

Kain's lips quirked into an amused grin. "Only because of your youth. You're what, twenty-five? Twenty-six?"

Autumn lifted her chin again and folded her arms across her chest, eyeing him warily as they began crossing the footbridge. "I'm twenty-six…and I have a Masters degree in small business."

Kain nodded appreciatively and put his hands behind his back as he walked. "That's quite an accomplishment at your age. You should be proud of yourself."

Another smile twitched at Autumn's lips, secretly preening over his praise though she endeavored not to show it. "I am, thank you. It was—*is*—a lot of hard work."

"But well worth it I hope?" he asked with a gentle smile. Autumn looked down at her feet and grinned, blushing a little, and nodded.

"It is," she said simply, giving him her full smile as she tilted her head up and looked over at him. Kain grinned unabashedly at her and Autumn felt her heart skip a beat. She looked away quickly, almost melting on the spot at his gorgeous smile.

They lapsed into silence then as they finished crossing the bridge and entered the forest on the other side of the river where shadows and dappled light enveloped them once again.

"What about family? Do you have any?" he asked and Autumn bit her lip and turned her head away, looking off into the forest.

"Not anymore," she said after a moment, looking down at her feet. Oh, that wasn't fair! She had asked him general questions, not personal details. But he was looking at her with such honest question in his eyes when she looked back up at him that she decided it couldn't hurt to continue. Everyone around here knew the story anyway.

"My parents died when I was young," she said with a deep sigh, watching the path in front of her feet with arms folded. "My father's family couldn't take me in so I went to live with my grandmother here in Myers Flat. She died about five years ago.

So, no, I don't have any family. None that I would consider such anyway."

Kain nodded and hesitated for a moment before he spoke. "I never had much family either. My mother passed when I was fifteen, and I never knew my father. The only family I ever knew was the theater troupe. I left there shortly after my mother died."

Autumn looked up at him with her mouth slightly open. Well, they had that in common then; they had both lost their parents at a young age.

"I'm sorry to hear that," she said, and meant it. She knew how lonely it was to be without family. Kain only nodded his head and gave her a small smile.

Careful Autumn, she admonished herself. *He's starting to get to you.* But she was even more curious about him now.

"No wife? Kids? Extended family then?" she asked before she could stop herself and she cursed inwardly as he chuckled deeply and gave her that slow, seductive grin.

"No, Autumn. It's just me."

She looked down quickly lest her blush give her away. Of course, the man was a veritable lone wolf. She easily believed he had no attachments, no wife or girlfriend, just a free man who could do what he wanted, where he wanted, and with whomever he wanted. She was pretty sure this was not a man that allowed anything, or anyone, tie him down.

And you would just be flavor of the week, her inner reason cautioned, but she was intrigued despite herself. Dangerous, fascinating, seductive, charming man. She should stay far away from him until he left, but she couldn't help herself. She wanted to know more.

They walked in silence for a moment as they began to enter the thick of the forest. The shadows lay deep and emerald here and the trees swallowed the sound of civilization so that they were the only two people in the world.

"What about you?" he asked casually, looking over at her. "Other family? Children? Relationships?"

She met his eyes and her inner voice cautioned her again, but he had been truthful with her, and she had asked the question first. She shook her head slightly and sighed, turning her head to look down the trail.

"String of bad relationships, married once. Divorced once, and no kids except for my cat. Happily single," she said firmly, refusing to look at him.

Kain made a noncommittal noise and said nothing, but Autumn swore she could sense the pleasure coming off him at her answer.

They continued on for a bit longer while Autumn composed herself, looking off into the forest and banishing her thoughts.

"So tell me, what do you like to do?" Kain asked, looking at her again with a small smile.

Autumn drew a deep breath and considered the question. "Well, I love to listen to music, I love to garden, to create things with my hands…sewing and pottery and such. I also love to read, and cook, though I cook vegetarian," she admitted, looking up at him from the corner of her eye.

"Vegetarian, huh. Why does that not surprise me?" he asked, smiling at her, and Autumn felt herself blushing. Was she so easy to figure out?

By now, they had entered a large, ancient grove of redwoods, the giant sentinels silent around them. They both stopped, stilled by the power of the old, old trees.

Autumn stepped away from him, drawn to a huge trunk of the oldest of the trees. She placed a hand against the rough bark, looking far up into the branches, and felt awed yet again by the giant trees. She had such love for these ancient beings, felt an almost sacred connection to them, and she folded herself against the bark for a long moment.

She was aware that Kain was watching her, having crouched down to wait. Attracted by his gaze she turned to look at him let out a shuddering breath. He appeared so at ease there in the shadows and sparse sunlight with his bare feet perched in the soil. His eyes were bright and hooded as he watched her. His shaggy mane fell all around him and caught soft rays of sunlight, glowing with copper and bronze highlights against the blue silk of his shirt. One of his silver earrings glinted in the cascading light, and she sighed softly. Had she ever seen a more beautiful man?

She had to look away from him, blushing. A woman could get used to that intense stare.

Oh, Autumn, she sighed to herself, *you are in a whole heap of trouble.*

Kain watched her from his crouched position as she communed with the giant tree. He was so captivated by her, and their walk so far had been torture as he resisted touching her. Or dragging her to him and kissing her thoroughly. He was utterly delighted by her smiles, her glances, her curiosity, and her natural charm. He had kept his composure, however, and kept his distance.

He watched her looking far up into the canopy, studying her expression of pure love for the old trees. So few people in the world had a true reverence for nature. The wolf in him longed for wild places, savored them, relished the wilderness like a lover. The others of his kind had little interest in nature. They saw animals as beneath their notice or as sport, and the wilderness only useful as a hunting ground. Mostly they preferred the cities where human prey was plentiful. He had no love for the majority of his own kind, leaving him a loner even among his fellow monsters.

Nature child, wild, fey creature of the forest she was as she leaned into the bark. She enchanted him, fascinated him like no woman had in a long time. He nearly howled with wanting her, but he was a patient predator. Even now, his claws were beginning to sink into her, and soon his teeth would find their mark and bring her down.

"They're some of the tallest and oldest living trees in the world, you know," she said as she approached him, looking up briefly and gesturing to the trees. "In fact the tallest tree in the world right now is one of these coastal redwoods. They only grow along a small band of California and Oregon's coast. That's because they thrive on the rain and fog that comes in off the ocean. They need a very specific environment to survive."

Kain smiled casually at her as he got to his feet, charmed by her love for the trees, and filled with longing to draw her close and taste her lips. She stopped just out of arms reach and tilted her head at him, giving him a shy smile. "You probably think I'm silly, don't you. Tree-hugging hippie-chick and all that."

His warm smile was reassuring as he stepped toward her. "Not at all. You seem to be many things, but silly is not one of them."

Her lips parted and her expression became soft, her large eyes speaking volumes. Kain was pleased at her reaction. It was a very good sign. He turned slightly and held out his arm to her, an easy smile on his face.

"Ready to move on?" he asked and she swallowed, looking up at him. When she took his arm, a shiver ran down his side and he practically growled at the contact. He laid his other hand on hers possessively as they began walking again, now arm in arm.

"So…" they both began at the same time, earning a small laugh from Autumn. Kain grinned at the sound, realizing this was the first time he had heard her laugh.

"You go ahead," he said, drinking in her smile again.

"Well, I was going to ask you what your interests are, since you asked mine," she said with a chuckle, looking up at him.

"My interests, huh?" he mused, returning her gaze and she looked away, still smiling. "Well…life interests me, as does truly living it. I believe life was made for adventure, and experiences.

For seeing, touching, and tasting with all of your senses, not just living in a cubicle pushing an endless boulder uphill for a paycheck. So, I enjoy traveling, sightseeing, trying new food, meeting new people, trying my hand at various trades… I make a living out of my life." He shrugged, and Autumn stared up at him with fascinated, wide eyes.

They came upon a stream trickling through the trees, its banks covered in green watercress and ferns, small flowers and sorrel. Kain let his arm slip from her hand and went to it, crouching down to trail his fingers in the flow, his face thoughtful.

"Life interests me, so this stream interests me," he said, letting the cool water flow over his hand. "I see its movement, the life it supports, and I wonder where it comes from, where it goes." He looked up at her, his eyes twinkling. "Life intrigues me in all of its forms."

Autumn watched him in rapt fascination, completely taken aback by the man. One minute he was pinning her with that come-hither-and-taste-me gaze, and the next he was practically spouting poetry, a man who respected and revered life. He couldn't possibly be for real, yet here he was in his bare feet and denim crouching in front of a stream. Was he playing with her? The thought evaporated from her mind as he lifted his hand and licked the water from his fingertips.

Oh my. Heat seared through her at the sight. He got to his feet, sucking the last finger dry as he walked back to her, his eyes full of mischief.

"I have an interest in all things beautiful."

His eyes locked on hers as he walked by her, headed back the way they came. Autumn stared after him, dumbfounded and so full of aching that it left her empty headed and rooted to the ground.

"Are you coming?" he asked, turning around to walk backward so he could watch her. She shuddered, coming back to herself with a shaky breath. Good heavens she was never going to survive him being here. He only chuckled and turned around, his mane bouncing around his broad shoulders as he sauntered away. Autumn forced herself to breathe, closing her eyes to ground and compose herself for a moment.

Get a grip, woman. He isn't what you want, remember?

Breathing deeply she opened her eyes and followed after him, watching the way he walked. It was truly hard to remember her convictions as she watched the movement of his perfect ass, the tips of his hair brushing back and forth across the denim. He cast her looks over his shoulder, smiling in a way that caused her stomach to flutter and yet made her suspicious all at the same time.

He moved quickly, disappearing around a bend in the trail and she blinked. "Kain?" She hurried to catch up, but as she rounded the bend, he was nowhere to be seen. She stopped, turning in a circle and looked around the forest. He had simply disappeared.

"Up here," he called, and Autumn turned to see him crouched on the top of an old, giant redwood stump, smiling down at her. "You need to come up here and see this."

"What?" she asked, examining the stump warily. "How did you get up there?"

"I climbed." He shrugged and motioned for her. "Come around the back. It's easier that way."

She regarded him warily as she left the path, her boots sinking into the soft, cool fodder of the forest floor as she climbed to get behind the stump. It was less steep here, she saw, yet the stump was still much taller than she was. Kain looked down at her and crouched, offering his hand with a gamin smile. She hesitated, unsure, and looked up and met his eyes.

"Trust me," he said softly, his eyes dark and sparkling.

"But I'm in heels." She laughed lamely, looking down at her feet. "I might slip, and I'll definitely ruin these."

"So take them off." Kain shrugged, and Autumn stared up at him for a moment. She wandered her own patch of the forest bare foot most of the time anyway. What did she have to lose?

She smiled up at him and threw up her hands in mock defeat with a sigh. "OK, what the hell," she said and leaned against the tree to remove her boots. Kain chuckled and watched from above her until her shoes and socks were off. She wiggled her bare toes in the moist layer of needles around the base of the stump, savoring the sensation.

"Come on, take my hand," he said, and extended his hand to her again. Autumn dropped her shoes and bag next to the tree and took a deep breath, reaching out to him, and his hand closed strongly around hers. His strength was unexpected as he pulled her up the stump, and her toes dug easily into the deep fissures of the bark. She gasped as he took her under her arms and pulled her the rest of the way up next to him. He kept his arms around her and gazed down at her, his eyes soft with desire, his lips curled into his sexy half-smile. She could not look away and felt herself flush with heated arousal at the sensation of his body pressed so closely to hers. His scent enveloped her, invading her senses and she breathed softly, her lips parting as she drowned in his eyes.

They stayed that way for a long moment, Kain's eyes roving all over her face while he held her possessively. Her arms were pressed up against his chest and she swallowed hard at the feel of the heat of his skin through the silk of his shirt, her fingertips just brushing some of his chest hair peeking through the unbuttoned top. Autumn willed herself to stay very still. She sensed that any encouraging movement on her part would send them tumbling over the edge, and not of the redwood stump.

After a moment, he chuckled deeply, sexily, and moved, sliding around behind her, his head close to hers.

"There," he said softly, still holding her close around the waist. "Look at that."

She had no idea what he was talking about, and then he motioned out at the forest and she looked, breathless.

They were high up, affording them an amazing view of the forest surrounding them. Late afternoon light streamed in through the branches overhead, landing on leaf and bark, and caused the forest to glow with unearthly emerald light against the dusky blues of the farther depths. Faint sparkles of sunlight on the river glittered through the deep green in the distance. It was truly as if they were the only two people in the world and Autumn sighed, acutely aware of his body against hers.

"The world goes on forever," he murmured next to her ear, his stubble scratching lightly against her jaw, and she shivered.

"There are more amazing places out there than you could ever know, could ever see in one life. There is beauty in unexpected places, and in unexpected forms," he said, and her breath snagged on a little sigh, caught up in his spell.

What the hell am I going to do? She closed her eyes for a moment, leaning against the hard warmth of his body. She couldn't just give in to the man; she would surely live to regret it. But God help her, she wanted to!

He was too tempting, intrigued her too much, and the man would only leave as soon as he had had his way. She had to protect her heart, but it had been so long since she had known a man's touch that she felt like a woman starved.

She opened her eyes again and savored their contact as they stood that way for a time. Kain made no move, just kept his arms around her waist, holding her lightly against him. His chin just brushed the top of her head. She knew that if she wanted to escape he would let her go instantly, but she felt dazed, intoxicated by his masculine scent, his heat, and his closeness. She was all too aware of the unmistakable hardness just barely brushing her backside and she screamed at herself not to press back against it. Just then, the sounds of other hikers began to reach them and the spell was broken.

"Come on," Kain said, disengaging himself from her and drawing her around. He smiled at her, then simply leaped off the side of the stump. Gasping, she hurried over and saw him crouched there on the ground, a good ten feet below. He smiled up at her and got easily to his feet while she stared at him openmouthed. How did he do that without breaking his damned leg?

"Don't try that," he warned, circling around to the back of the trunk again and held his arms out to her. She raised an eyebrow at him, daunted by how high up she was.

"What do you want me to do, jump into your arms?" she laughed nervously and he answered with an easy grin.

"Get over the side. I'll help you down."

She gulped. It was the only way off this thing and she nodded at him. Having grown up in this forest, she was used to climbing stumps and trees, but none this tall. Gingerly she got down and swung her legs over the side, digging her toes into the bark once again, and took her time to lower herself. When she was low enough, he gripped her hips, causing her to freeze.

"Let go," he said softly. Autumn stared back at him with wide eyes, unsure. He only smiled gently up at her, his strong hands around her. "Let go, Autumn," he said again and she held her breath. What choice did she have?

She let go, pushing off from the bark with a squeak of alarm and he caught her up in his arms. She gasped and wrapped her arms around his neck automatically as he stepped back, steadying himself. He chuckled, holding her as if she weighed nothing and their eyes met. Electricity danced between them, hot and full of need. She was so sure he was going to kiss her then that she closed her eyes, her lips beginning to form a pucker when he suddenly bent and set her on her feet, then let her go. She stumbled and stared at him in disbelief, completely taken by surprise. He only gave her a sexy half-grin and began to walk away around the stump, whistling softly. The bastard!

She snatched up her shoes and bag and went after him, ready to give him a piece of her mind, but a group of hikers appeared on the trail just then, noisy with chatter. Their eyes followed Kain as he passed them by. She bit back her ire and gave the group a tight smile as she hurried to catch up to the man.

"What was that all about?" she hissed when she reached his elbow. He only looked down at her with a questioning look on his face.

"What was what about?" he asked casually, quirking an amused eyebrow at her and indignation flashed in her eyes.

Oh the insufferable ass! She seethed internally. He was being so wonderful, and now he was going to tease her again and make her feel like an idiot by making her admit that he'd gotten to her? That she had actually *wanted* to kiss him? No fucking chance! He'd had his opportunity to kiss her back there at the stump. He would get no others. Cheeks flaming, she stomped past him, walking quickly and furiously down the trail. He would not make a fool of her again.

He chuckled and caught up to her easily, grabbing her around the waist and spun her around. His lips were on hers before she knew what was happening, hard and hungry, possessive as he pressed her to him. She melted before she could make herself resist, clinging to him and leaning into him, a desperate little noise escaping her throat as he slid his lips firmly over hers. He growled against her mouth and pushed a hand into her hair, fisting it gently, his other arm circled around her waist.

It seemed to last a small eternity, and all thought fled from her mind. There was only this man's mouth on hers, her body molded to his, and aching arousal like molten fire through her whole body. She parted her lips instinctively, inviting him in, but all at once, he seemed to come to himself. Slowly he let her go and pulled away from the kiss. He breathed heavily against her lips for a moment, his mouth parted and his eyes languid with craving.

He hadn't meant to do that, but he'd just not been able to resist teasing her about the desire so blatant in her eyes, desire she tried to deny. When she stomped off so furiously he could no longer contain himself. She was begging to be kissed, and he could not stop himself from it.

Her lips were all they promised; sweet and sensual and made for being thoroughly ravished. He was barely able to stop himself from tasting her fully, when she had parted her lips to him so innocently. She was alluring, her lips and body asking for more, but he made himself stop. He dared not take any more than this from her right now and it nearly tore a snarl from his throat as he forced himself to end the kiss, to pull his mouth away from hers.

She stared up at him in a daze, her tantalizing lips slightly parted, her lower lip puffed out from his kiss, her tresses mussed from his grip.

"Forgive me," he said softly as he smoothed the back of her hair and then trailed his fingers lightly against her face. He forced himself to release her completely, lest he grab her again, and backed away, unable to tear his eyes from hers. She continued to stare at him for a moment more with unfocused eyes, and then she dragged in a huge, shuddering breath and turned away from him.

Autumn closed her eyes. The throbbing ache of arousal pounding through her with her heartbeat, and coherent thought came back slowly as she willed her body to calm down. When she opened her eyes and turned, he was still standing there with his long legs spread and his lean form loose and ready, looking at her. A smile began to spread across his lips, his eyes dangerous and seductive. She backed away from him, needing the distance from him or she was going to do something incredibly stupid, like launch herself into his arms.

Well, you asked for it, dummy, she berated herself angrily, a*nd now look what happened. He kissed you like you wanted, and what did it prove? Only that you are in way, waaay over your head here.* She could barely handle his kiss, and it was the most mind blowing, seductive kiss she'd ever had. It was over far too soon, leaving her wanting him even more. She needed to get away from him and get her head back on.

Kain bent and politely offered her shoes and bag and stepped back as she took them. He placed his hands behind his back as they began walking again, giving her space. When she sneaked glances at him, though, he wore such a self-satisfied smile that she almost wanted to smack it off his face. However, even her temper did nothing for the miserable ache in her and the painful awareness of him as they finished their walk in silence and arrived back at his cabin.

She walked away from him, avoiding his eyes as she found a convenient boulder and sat to put her shoes back on. He leaned against the post of the little porch, his arms crossed as he considered her.

"You know you never did tell me why you came over here today," he remarked casually. She looked up at him with wide eyes from the curtains of her hair, her lips slightly parted, and his mouth quirked into an amused smile.

"Oh, um…" she faltered, clearing her throat and looked away as she finished tugging on her boot. She continued stalling as she put the other boot on and got to her feet, brushing at her pant legs. "Yes, I…forgot to ask you something."

Kain raised an eyebrow at her, still smiling in amusement. "Oh?"

"Yeah, so I was wondering…" She looked at him and smiled sheepishly, her cheeks heating, "how's your car doing?"

Kain chuckled, giving her a slow grin that showed his teeth and set her heartbeat racing. "You came over here to ask me that?"

Autumn simply smiled at him and bit her lower lip, nodding as she rubbed absently at her arm. *Good one, Autumn,* she admonished herself sarcastically. Well, honestly, it was the best she could come up with on the fly, and she couldn't tell him the real reason she had come here. Not now. Not after that kiss.

He watched her with an amused expression for a moment, then shrugged casually.

"They're waiting on a part to come in from the Bay area, since this is an older, classic vehicle they don't make parts for anymore. It actually has to be tooled and shipped, and then they have to finish the repairs. A couple more days they told me."

Autumn shifted and looked up at him again, nodding in relief. "Oh. Well, that's…good. I guess you'll be around until then?" she winced at the hopeful tone in her voice and wished the ground could just swallow her up when he chuckled softly.

"Yes, I suppose I will."

Autumn shifted lamely, feeling like an idiot. "Good. OK." She shouldered her bag, looking around her as she tried to figure out how to make her escape.

"Are you working tomorrow?" he asked and she glanced up at him again. He waited, and she shifted her feet nervously, shaking her head.

"Uh…no," she said, clearing her throat. "It'll be Sunday and the shop is closed."

Sundays were her one day off a week. Which meant she wouldn't be seeing him. *That's a good thing…right?* She had no answer. Her lips still burned with his unexpected kiss and she looked away self consciously, confused and unsure how to feel.

"Come with me tomorrow," he said suddenly, and she looked up at him in surprise.

"Where are you going?" she asked warily, folding her arms.

He shrugged a shoulder lightly. "For a ride. Sightseeing. Come with me."

She regarded him cautiously as she considered his request. She should tell him no—no way, absolutely not—and her mouth opened to do so but she faltered. Her mind whirled with what he was offering. She had planned to work on her vegetable garden tomorrow and ready it for spring planting next month. The boxes needed tilling and fertilizing, and she needed to get her early lettuces and peas into the ground. Or she could spend the whole day with him. On his bike. Which meant she would be on the back of it, touching him closely. For the entire day.

Perhaps he might kiss her again.

She shouldn't. There were a million reasons why she should say no and stick to her guns, to firmly tell him she wasn't interested and mean it. But as she stood there looking at him leaning casually against the post with all of his sinful good looks and his eyes smoldering, waiting for her reply, she knew there was no way in hell she was saying no.

"All right." She nodded, and he grinned, giving her a triumphant, sexy smile full of white teeth. *Oh, Autumn, what the hell did you just do?*

"Very good. Meet me here in the morning, say seven-ish. Wear something sturdy and warm. The wind can really chafe you," he said, clearly pleased.

"Tomorrow morning then," she said, smiling nervously, trembling a little as she began backing away.

He merely nodded at her and rumbled, "Tomorrow." His eyes lingered on her, intent and languid with satisfaction.

Her belly tightened and, giving him a hasty wave, she turned and all but ran back to her car. *Ooooh, why did I just agree to that? Why couldn't I have told him to go away already?* she lamented as she fled. Because she didn't want him to go away, she admitted miserably. She was captivated by him, intrigued, and horribly turned on. He surprised her, and despite her caution, she *wanted* to go with him. Because she longed to see what came next.

She wanted to know more about him. She wanted to spend every available minute with him and unravel his mysteries. She never had adventures in her life and always played it safe, doing the "responsible" thing. Going with him would be reckless, and probably dangerous. They could get into an accident, or worse, he could be planning to take advantage of her. But after their walk, she just didn't feel like that was his intent. He plainly wanted to seduce her. *And doing a damned fine job of it,* she sighed.

She thought of his kiss again, and just the memory of it almost had her knees buckling as she unlocked her car. Yep, she was in a whole heap of trouble with a capital T.

But she was loving every minute of the ride so far.

CHAPTER SEVEN
Excursion

It was another beautiful sunny morning as Autumn pulled into the parking lot at the rental cabins. Morning sun gilded the air and filled it with the fresh scent of redwood forest and river. She had hardly been able to sleep last night, and she had woken that morning feeling giddy with excitement at what today would bring.

As she got ready, she decided finally that she deserved to throw caution to the wind for once and enjoy life for a little while. She had certainly been working hard enough lately. It didn't mean she had to sleep with him, it just meant she was giving herself permission to be the center of his attention for a day. It gave her a purely feminine thrill. Besides, the forecast was calling for a warmer than usual March day full of sunshine and she hadn't gone sightseeing in a long time. She deserved this, and she was resolved to enjoy herself and not apologize for it.

Autumn smiled to herself at the sight that greeted her as she parked and turned off her car. Kain was outside, crouching down as he checked his bike over and she took an unabashed, appreciative look while she gathered her coffee and things and got out of her car.

He wore black jeans today, snugly fitting at the crotch and pulled over his black leather boots. His T-shirt was black and he wore the same leather jacket as the other day, simple and unadorned. His hair was pulled back into a long braid, a few errant strands falling around his face. The effect was sexy as hell. He looked up and gave her his gorgeous smile as she approached, sipping her coffee.

She hoped she was dressed appropriately enough. She had never been on a motorcycle before. She wore boot-cut jeans with a dragonfly embroidered on the leg, a wide beaded belt, and a pair of brown faux leather boots with a short heel. She wore a rose colored, form-fitting lady tee emblazoned with sparkly rhinestones, the front tucked behind her belt buckle, and over that was a short brown suede jacket she'd scored at a thrift store recently. She had braided her hair to either side of her head and tied a brown and pink patterned scarf around it. A pair of pink-tinted sunglasses perched on her nose. She thought the outfit was cute, suitably biker enough without having to be a leather queen. Besides, she just really didn't do black.

She walked toward him and Kain's eyes raked her over appreciatively as he got to his feet and wiped his hands on his jeans. She inhaled a nervous breath as she returned his smile, steadying herself. *Just allow this, Autumn. No fears, just…be here.*

"Good morning," he said, taking a few slow steps toward her. "How did you sleep?"

She smiled up at him as he reached out to her and ran his hand down her jacketed arm. Her eyes dipped to his hand but she didn't pull away. She simply shrugged and met his eyes again.

"I slept fine," she said, then smiled coyly and laughed a little. "Actually, I was a little restless. I've never been on a bike before."

He grinned at her, his eyes roving over her face and he chuckled softly. "Ah, a new experience then. Good. I'm glad I can offer you one."

All sorts of new experiences, she was sure. She hid her blush behind another sip of coffee. He gave her shoulder a squeeze and then let his hand fall away. Autumn wished her shoulders were bare to feel his touch.

"Well, I think we're ready here. Are you good to go?" he asked and she had to swallow fast, wiping at her mouth with the back of her hand.

"Uh, yeah, I guess so." She smiled shyly, her stomach full of butterflies as he smiled and moved to the bike. *Here we go.*

She walked her coffee cup to a nearby trashcan while he mounted the bike. He got his balance, kicked back the stand, and donned his sunglasses as she approached. She was nervous as he held out his hand to her, his gaze hidden behind the mirrored shades.

"Come on, Autumn. Get on behind me."

She went to him, taking his hand briefly, breathlessly, before sliding onto the bike behind him. The seat had her sitting a bit higher than he was, and she drew in a shuddering breath at the feel of her thighs pressed to his hips. She was all too aware of how her crotch pressed so intimately against his ass. In fact, her whole body was pinned to him by the back of the seat. To be straddling him this way, even though it was necessary for her to ride, sent heat flushing through her whole body. She trembled and lightly put her hands to his sides.

His chuckle was deep and sensual as he moved to kick the bike into life. "Better hold on tighter than that," he said, and she slid her arms around him as the machine started up with a roar. Sound and vibration engulfed her, and the bike rumbled under her in a startling and not too unpleasant way. It would take some getting used to, but with her arms around this man and her body pressed close to him, she doubted she would be aware of much else.

They started out slow, Kain allowing Autumn time to get her balance and equilibrium with the bike. He felt incredibly possessive of her and utterly alive with her body pressed to his, the wind beginning to stir as they picked up speed and began making their way out of town. Once they turned onto the Avenue of Giants, Kain hit the throttle and Autumn's arms tightened further around him. He grinned, opening up the bike as his inner wolf howled with the joy of the wind in his face and the woman at his back.

They headed west out of town toward Eureka, Kain keeping an easy pace, and the morning unfolded around them. Sunlight slanted through the tall trees in splashes of emerald and gold. They crossed over a tall bridge that spanned the Eel River, and Kain took a left, leaving the Avenue and heading deeper into the forest.

He felt incredibly satisfied with the world as he felt her relax behind him, imagining the expression on her face as they cruised smoothly through the morning. This was simple, pure joy to show her this, to let her taste the freedom that was his life. He wove them through switchbacks as the road began ascending, climbing up one of the peaks and hills around the area. He had chosen this route well, mapping it out last night. He would show her things today that, even though she lived here, had grown up here, she had never seen before. Not fully. Not in this way.

They crested the summit and he felt her breathe in at the view. The Pacific Ocean spread out against the horizon, and the mountains and hills of Humboldt County stretched off in emerald swaths to the north and south. He slowed but did not stop as they both took it in, the air crisp and crystal clear, and affording them unparalleled views. He grinned as they began their descent and she shifted behind him, leaning into him again as gravity pulled them downward, the bike banking in the sharp turns. They descended into shadows and sunlight and viridescent hues again as the forest took them in, filling the air with clean, woody scents.

The road continued to curve as they made their way down to the ocean. The dense redwood forest gave way to more deciduous forest and scrubland, and finally grassy foothills dotted with California cypress. The tang of ocean was in the wind. At last, the road leveled out and opened up, and there was the Pacific, curving away toward the north and south. Kain opened up the throttle again and grinned as Autumn wrapped her arms around his waist, her laughter on the wind.

The road paralleled the ocean for just a little while, then curved sharply to the north toward Eureka. It wove through foothills and valleys until they finally cruised into the Eel River basin where the river emptied into the sea. There were farms and fields here as well as mills and lumberyards. The scent of lumber and agriculture was heady in the air, a mixture of earth and alfalfa, fruit trees and produce, garlic, roots, hay, livestock, and even marijuana. He wished she could smell the world the way that he did. It made the average and everyday smells into a veritable tapestry of interwoven notes and chords. It added to the pleasure of his life immeasurably.

They headed on, cruising onto the 101 again and into Eureka, threading through early afternoon traffic.

Autumn was struck with wonder at the feeling of being on this bike with this man. She felt so free and alive with the wind caressing her, the sky so open and wide, and the world around them animated and full of life. She had never known how sheltered and safe she really was in a car until now. How strapped down and removed from the world she normally was, surrounded by glass and molded aluminum and plastic, with the air never really allowed to touch her. She felt somehow cheated by it. On the bike with him, she was a part of the world they moved through, fully alive. Sure, it was dangerous, to be on the back of this bike without seat belts or a helmet, but she felt utterly safe with Kain, and he handled the bike expertly.

They cruised into Eureka, and Autumn felt a jumble of feelings after their incredible ride, overwhelmed by them. She had not felt this alive in, well, perhaps ever. As they sat in traffic she felt right seated behind this gorgeous man, her hands possessively at his waist again. Yes, possessively, she thought at the stares of people around them, because for today he was hers to enjoy. She was sure people didn't see a man of his caliber every day, a dark, dangerous, wild thing on an equally wild machine, and with someone like her perched on the back.

The lights changed, and they continued to weave deftly through town until the 101 opened up again, meandering past Arcata and other suburbs, through more fields and farms, RV parks and neighborhoods until it began to parallel the ocean closely.

They stopped in Trinidad to order a couple of sandwiches to go from a local shop and then rumbled into town, making their way through the streets until they came to a parking area for the local beach. Kain parked the bike smoothly and Autumn breathed deeply, ready for a break. While she did yoga almost every day and ran a few times a week, there were muscles being used to stay on the bike that she hadn't been aware that she had.

Kain toed down the stand and let Autumn dismount first, smiling as she groaned.

"Oh, I am not used to this." She giggled, stretching her arms way over her head and arching her back as Kain dismounted, swinging his long leg over the saddle easily. She watched him appreciatively as he grabbed the sandwiches and a couple of other things from the saddlebags, then he turned to her with an easy smile and held out his hand.

She gave him a winsome smile and took his hand easily, her small fingers curling around his, and he rubbed his thumb along hers as they began navigating a short dune to get to the beach.

Trinidad beach was a small, somewhat sheltered cove, arching in a crescent shape with rocky outcroppings and a small island where a few pines grew. Kain pulled Autumn along after him, his hand keeping a tight hold of hers as he helped her manage the trail. They made their way down the dune and hit the open sand, stopping there to take in the area.

There were a few people here and there on the beach, playing or walking, digging in the sand, throwing Frisbees. Children laughed and frolicked at the water's cold edge, and a lone person was kayaking farther out in the cove. Sea birds whirled above them in the breeze and, grinning, Autumn held onto him and tugged at her boots, eager to feel the sand in her toes. Kain chuckled and waited for her to finish, then handed her the packages and it was his turn to hold onto her while he took off his boots. She wrapped an arm around his waist to help steady him.

His feet free, he accepted the packages back from her and they grabbed their shoes. Without hesitation, she took him by the hand and led him down the beach. They found a good place just a bit down the strand where a few jutting boulders created a small area where they could leave their things. They put down their shoes and their lunches and removed their jackets. Then, with a shout of laughter, Autumn went running toward the water, pulling the scarf from around her head as she did.

Kain smiled, captivated by her joy, enraptured by it. She was a creature of sunlight and innocence who had yet to be corrupted by the weariness of the world. There was still a childlike goodness to her that called to him, her light to his darkness.

She frolicked at the edge of the shore as he strolled after her. He grinned when the cold waves found her toes and she danced away with a yelp, the hem of her pants now wet. She turned to look at him and he forgot to breathe. She smiled so prettily at him, and her eyes were merry behind her pink-tinted glasses. The wind caught her colorful scarf and swirled it around her, and the sun on her head blazed through her hair as the wind tossed her braids. Her smile did things to him, bewitched him, tugged at his own lips until he was smiling openly back at her as he strolled to her across the sand.

As he came closer her grin turned mischievous, and she turned away from him toward the ocean. Kain quirked an eyebrow, wondering what she was up to. When he was almost to her she bent, laughing, and scooped up a handful of salt water and tossed it his way, then she took off shrieking across the sand.

Kain was shocked for all of a moment as the cold sprinkles of water landed on his face and front, and the sly little sprite was giggling and running from him down the beach. He launched after her immediately with a happy growl, running low at her. She yelped and began running away from the water, then as he lunged for her, she quickly darted left toward the ocean again and squealed as the water splashed up her pant legs. He laughed and went after her, allowing her to gain a little bit of ground. She breathlessly looked over her shoulder with a bright smile as she headed back into the sand, and then he leaped to bring her down.

He caught up to her effortlessly and grabbed her up around the waist, swinging her around and around while she screamed happily, then he dragged her down and rolled them until she was pinned under him, breathless and giggling. Triumphant he growled, smiling down at her. His eyes devoured her face, captivated by everything about her. The bits of sand on her cheek, sunlit wisps of her hair licking across her features in the wind, her eyes bright with sunlight and humor behind her pink sunglasses, softening now with desire. Her infectious smile faded as her expression became wondrous and flushed with open wanting.

There was no coherent thought as he closed his eyes and bent his head to hers. He brushed his lips across hers, groaning as he came to instant, painful hardness. She yielded immediately, softening to him while her hands came up slowly to lightly cup his rough cheeks, savoring him. He fought for control as he deepened the kiss, slanting his mouth over hers with the sweetest of friction, touching the seam of her lips with the tip of his tongue before pulling back a little, then laying soft kisses on her mouth that she accepted eagerly.

His erection lay against her thigh and he ground it against her instinctively, growling in his throat at the intense pleasure of her body under his. He had to stop or he would take her right now, out here in the open, in public, in front of God and the great blue sky and every person out here. He was trembling imperceptibly with need and restraint when he stopped himself and pulled his lips from hers, their breaths mingling. He nuzzled her, rubbing his nose against her own for a moment before pulling his head back to regard her.

Her eyes were shadowed by her lashes, her gaze vaguely unfocused, and her hands still cupped his face as she stared up at him through her pink shades. He kissed her palm before staring deeply into her sexy, dazed eyes, her succulent pout slowly turning into a smile again. With a groan, he lifted himself off her and in one graceful motion rolled to his feet, spraying her with sand, and walked away a few feet. He removed his sunglasses and scrubbed his face with his hands, willing himself to be calm, to back down from the desire that howled through him with the voice of his wolf.

Autumn sat up and watched him a moment, knowing he was struggling with himself. Just as she was struggling with herself. Never in her life had she been so turned on by a single kiss. Her whole body was painfully aware of him and the promise that he had pressed against her thigh.

And what a promise it is. She breathed deeply and willed herself to calm down. They were playing with potent fire here and she knew it, yet she had never wanted that fire so much before in her life. She wanted *his* fire, his passion united with hers, passion he so easily awakened in her. *And what happens when he leaves you?* An angry little voice demanded and she sobered, not wanting to think about it. She would not think about that until she had had the rest of her day with him.

Determined to hold on to her happy mood she got to her feet and went to him, putting her arm in his, and savoring the feeling as she smiled up at him. He looked down at her and returned her smile, touching her fingers.

"Forgive me...again," he said almost sheepishly and she shrugged a shoulder.

"It's OK, these things happen," she replied easily. He laughed at that, and he bent to kiss the top of her head. She grinned, and he began leading them back to their things. "How about those sandwiches now?"

They made a little impromptu picnic near the rocks, bare toes peeking happily through the sand, and, to her delight, Kain produced a small bottle of sweet red wine. He uncorked it with a pocketknife corkscrew and she laughed when he pulled out a couple of slightly crumpled Dixie cups.

"I'm all class, baby." He chuckled as he poured them wine, then, setting the bottle aside, he turned to her with his little cup raised, his smile sweet and genuine.

"To life," he toasted, and Autumn grinned, toasting back.

"*L'chaim*," she said and tossed it back. He laughed around his cup, almost snorting it.

"L'chaim?" he asked after swallowing and she stared at him incredulously.

"You've never seen Fiddler on the Roof? And you worked in theater?" she laughed, and then sang the verse, toasting her Dixie cup. Understanding, he laughed out loud. She'd gotten him on that one. Oh, she was working her magic on him, and even though he knew he was getting too close to her, he didn't give a damn. She was pure, unfiltered joy. He hadn't felt this good in a long time.

They finished the wine and their sandwiches, making small talk in the sand with the sun high in the sky and the cool, salty wind brushing lightly around them. After they finished they gathered their trash, jackets, and their shoes and, holding hands once more, made their way back to the parking lot.

They helped each other to clean the sand off their feet and clothing, laughing as they brushed at one another, and put their shoes back on. Ready to ride once more she easily mounted behind him. This time she slid her arms up under his jacket to wrap them around his waist and pressed herself against his back as he started the bike. Kain stilled a moment, taking in the sheer pleasure of her arms around him, her hands briefly caressing his ribs, and he rumbled in his chest with animal pleasure. He backed the bike out of the parking spot and they were off again, both of them suffused with such lightheartedness that the rest of the world melted away, their awareness for one another only.

They traveled the rest of the afternoon, continuing north on the 101 as it wound along the coast until they turned off at the Klamath River and began following Route 169 southward again toward Willow Creek. While the magic of the day seemed eternal, the spring sun did not last and soon began to set as they took Route 299 back toward Eureka and Myers Flat. Though Kain knew Autumn was beginning to tire and the air was getting cold, he did not want this day to end. He cursed the setting sun silently as they climbed a last mountain pass.

When they reached the summit, Kain followed his instinct and turned the bike off the pavement and onto a dirt road where it ended at an amazing overlook. The ocean spread out before them once more, the setting sun a molten ball of golden light on the horizon as it sank off the edge of the world. He parked the bike and turned it off, staying where he was as they both took in the view. Autumn sighed deeply behind him, and he felt her lay her head on his back, squeezing him with her arms as they watched the ocean and the dying light. He caressed her arms, sliding his hand up to find where hers rested flat against his chest and his gaze was drawn to the side as he imagined what she was thinking.

He was loath to end this day, would rather extend it far into the long hours of the night loving her passionately, but his timing had to be impeccable in this. Not tonight, but tomorrow…oh, tomorrow. He would lay down his Ace, because his desire for her was becoming more than he could bear. He would have her, and if not he would fly fast and far from here, from her, and try to forget all about her.

No, he snarled inwardly. *I will not lose this game!* Her desire was too hot, too full of need for him for her to deny him once he laid his cards down. He would trust in that, and would trust that her hunger for him would be undeniable, especially after today.

They stayed that way for a long moment as the sunset slowly changed from honey-gold to a burnished orange over the waves, neither daring to speak lest they break the spell they had woven around themselves. Finally, Kain gave her hand a final squeeze and shifted, starting the bike again. They continued on, descending toward the lights of Eureka as the sun burned out into fiery orange, then red, then just a purple smudge against the ocean.

Wanting to prolong the inevitable, he decided that they should have dinner in Eureka. They were both hungry again, and he would not be denied one ounce of time with her today. He had noted a diner along the 101 on the south end of town when they had driven through earlier. He headed there and parked the bike outside. He shut off the engine and stilled as Autumn laid herself against his back again, boldly running her hands against his chest in a way that made him almost want to purr. She needed to stop that or there would be no tomorrow, there would be tonight!

He grabbed one of her hands and kissed her palm, squeezing it as he said, "I don't know about you, but I'm starving."

Autumn sighed and let him go, sliding her hands around his sides as she leaned back. She should be alarmed about being so familiar with him, and about the things her heart and body were feeling, but she just couldn't seem to care right now. She craved touching him, and she would take what she could get.

He waited for her to dismount and she stepped away as he dropped the kickstand, appreciating the view as he swung his leg over the saddle. He had such long legs, and she admired them clad in those snug-fitting jeans. Her belly tightened at the thought of peeling those off him and tasting his flat belly and she had to give herself a mental shake as he held his hand out to her.

"Shall we?" he grinned and she nodded, taking his hand and following him into the diner.

They sat at a booth across from one another. Kain ordered a huge stack of pancakes and sausages, while Autumn ordered a baked potato and side salad. They talked about small things until their food arrived, and she laughed at the towering mound of pancakes set before him.

"There's no way you're eating all that," she said as he dumped maple syrup all over the pile. His grin was mischievous as he brought his fingers to his lips and licked the syrup off. Heat bloomed in her belly and everything tingled with intense arousal at the sight of him licking his own fingers, and she blushed.

"Watch me." He grinned, stabbed a fork full, then shoved the dripping, gooey mess in his mouth. He chuckled at her, teasing her as he made a show of eating the sticky meal, deliberately licking the food from his fork, sliding his fingers through the syrup, and sucking them slowly while she squirmed in her seat and picked at her food.

Autumn watched him with a small, shuddering sigh, knowing she should be irked at his teasing, but she was just too fascinated. The man was walking sensuality on all levels. Even the way he ate and drank was carnal and seductive. Never in her life had she been turned on by someone eating, until now. His eyes were on her while he ate his meal and she only poked at her potato and salad. She guessed she just wasn't very hungry... For food at least.

She had to admit it. She wanted to sleep with him. Badly. So badly, the desire was painful, and she was a little afraid of it. But that small, too cautious part of her screamed against giving in. She was already getting too attached to him. She didn't want today to end and she couldn't wait for what might happen tomorrow, but the reality was he wasn't staying. He wasn't stuck here forever, and he would head on his way once his car was fixed. Sex or no sex, he would leave, and she wouldn't see him again.

Sobered by the dose of reality she sighed and ate a bit of her food. That wasn't today, though. Wasn't right now. Right now, he was here, and she was here, she reminded herself. She would enjoy his presence in her life, however brief it may be. She smiled and looked up at him, laughing a little. He was just running the last sausage through a dribble of syrup, and she shook her head.

"You really just ate that whole plate. I'm impressed." She smiled as he popped the last morsel into his mouth, grinning at her as he chewed. He swallowed the bite, then wiped his mouth with a napkin and leaned back, tucking his hands behind his head.

"Told you. I have a healthy appetite," he said and Autumn swallowed, shaking her head a little. He ate like a horse, but from what she could tell (and feel, from letting her hands roam a bit today) he had little body fat. She reached for her water and took a long drink, suddenly thirsty. Damn, the man was a walking sensual temptation on every level.

He was watching her with an utterly satisfied, lazy expression on his face and Autumn blushed again, making herself eat another bite of her own food.

"Will you be working tomorrow?" he asked and she nodded, taking another sip of water.

"I have the early shift again. Have to meet up with the repair man," she said, sighing. She looked up at him and smiled a little, her fingers toying with the syrup decanter.

"Thanks for helping me with that, by the way. Sorry I was so…surly."

Kain grinned at her and leaned forward to put his elbows on the table, his fingers finding her hands.

"Don't worry about it. We all have bad days," he said, his palms rubbing the backs of her hands that were still holding the syrup. She swallowed hard and smiled up into his eyes, which were warm and lazy. She let her hands drift into his, palm to palm, and they curled their fingers around one another on the table.

The spell was broken as the waitress came with the check, smiling at them, and asked how long they had been dating. "Not long," Kain said at the same time Autumn said, "Oh, we're not dating." She blushed and Kain gave her that sensual smile. The waitress chuckled and placed the check on the table.

"Well, good luck to you two," she said, smiling at them. "No rush on the check; whenever you're ready."

Kain thanked her as she walked away and he turned back to Autumn. She felt herself still blushing as he chuckled softly, then he lifted her hand and placed a kiss on her knuckles.

"We should get going. You have an early morning," he rumbled, running his thumb across the top of her hand and she nodded, unable to speak. He squeezed her hands and let go, getting up to pay the check.

Autumn breathed a heavy sigh and let her head fall into her hands. She wanted more of him; she wanted all of him, everything he offered…she just couldn't do it. She was a fool, and worse she was letting him think he had a chance. She desperately wanted the man, but she was terrified of everything she was feeling. He would only break her already too battered heart and she could not bear that, no matter what her libido was demanding. She couldn't do this to either of them.

He returned and smiled at her, sending shivers down her body as he lightly stroked her arm with his fingers.

"Are you ready to go?" he asked and she drew in a deep breath, then smiled and nodded up at him. She couldn't resist taking his hand again as he helped her out of the booth and lead her out of the restaurant, possessive. However, this time when she mounted the bike behind him she kept herself away from him as much as she could, touching him only as much as she had to and holding onto him only enough to balance.

Kain noticed the change in her and frowned a little, his wolf not liking it. She had withdrawn from him again and removed her energy from his. He grumbled softly to himself as he started the bike and guided it onto the 101 again. She was just afraid, that's all. Her hunger for him was still very much there, she was just pulling it back because their day was coming to an end. He understood that, but he didn't have to like it. He was tempted briefly to speed up and get a little dangerous with the bike just so she would cling to him once more. He controlled himself, though, and allowed her some space. Tomorrow it wouldn't matter. Tomorrow would tell all.

The last of their ride back to Myers Flat in the darkness was uneventful, and soon they were pulling into the Redwood Roost cabins where Kain stopped the bike next to her Subaru. He killed the engine and she dismounted politely, stepping away as he situated the bike and got off it. They stood staring at one another in the darkness for a few moments, then Kain took a step toward her. She tensed, looking away, and Kain frowned.

So that's how it was going to be? Not even a good night kiss? He clenched his jaw as she looked up at him and smiled tightly, putting her hands in her back pockets.

"Did you have a good time?" he asked, managing to keep his tone even. She nodded and kept her distance, scuffing her boot a little.

"I did, thank you. That was…amazing," she said sincerely with a smile and it soothed him a little, but he was still not happy. He wanted her in his arms; he wanted to kiss her again, to taste her and touch her and breathe her gasps of pleasure into his mouth. A deep rumble began in his chest, so subtle it was barely audible and he clenched his hands against his wolf.

"Well, you're welcome. I'm glad you enjoyed your first bike ride," he rumbled out and she backed up a step, nodding.

"I should really get going. It's late," she said and it was his turn to nod stiffly, battling the wolf in him. He was glad it was dark and she couldn't see his eyes well. They were tingling and he was sure they had changed color.

"Have a good night, Autumn. I will see you tomorrow," he all but growled out and she smiled a little, pulling her keys out of her pocket.

"Good night, Kain. Sleep well," she said, and turning, went to her car.

His gaze followed her hungrily, his claws sliding out of his nail beds while he growled deep in his chest. His wolf had enjoyed her affections today, and now that she had withdrawn them, it was driving his beast wild. He closed his eyes as she started her car, then the headlights bathed him briefly as he turned and walked back to his cabin. He would run tonight. He would run and mark his territory, and make sure the world knew that Autumn belonged to him.

Her taillights turned and faded as she left and he began removing his clothes as he strode past his cabin, angrily tearing them from his body. He would not be denied. She would surrender and be his, or he simply didn't know what he would do.

He shoved down his pants and kicked them aside, fur already sprouting along his shoulders and back, and he began running. *Tomorrow,* he panted. *It has to be tomorrow.* He needed her far too much after today. He ran, exploding with rage into his bestial form, and galloped into the deep darkness of the forest.

CHAPTER EIGHT
Ultimatum

He prowled her territory in the darkness, intent in his mission. Tonight he made her territory his as he ran her trails, calling upon powers he rarely needed to use. When he had been changed, his maker, Alessia, had gifted him not only with her changing bite, but had bequeathed to him all of her knowledge and power. Spells and ancient magic others would kill to possess sat safely inside of his head, a library of coveted knowledge. He rarely needed to use that power, save for the odd small spell, or to activate his talisman. His Allure and Compulsion were usually all that he needed to get out of trouble. Spells also called attention and the bigger the spell, the bigger the spotlight, so he used them sparingly.

Tonight, though, he would make sure that she was protected. Weaving an ancient magic that tied the land to him he moved along, stopping every so often to lift his leg and urinate, growling ancient words as he did so. He wove a barrier between her land and the outside world, feeling it snap into focus as he pissed the last marker. He turned and scented the air, feeling outward with other senses as well. He could now sense everything within the barrier, the area attuned to his very being. He could sense the depth and breadth of the power here and it nearly took his breath away. How no other magical being had come across it by now, he didn't know. Such power was a highly sought after prize and should be protected. He would be sure to lay more potent spells here before he left, ensuring Autumn's safety.

For now, this spell was enough. He would know who came and went, where every warm-blooded creature was, and if anything threatened this space. Satisfied, he swiped his long tongue across his muzzle and panted heavily. He had a sense of her now, and knew she was asleep in her bedroom. He snarled, snapping at the air with his desire to go to her, to touch her, and to be touched by her. Yet his human side held him in control and he turned his paws away, out of her territory and back to the forest.

The wolf didn't have to like it. He made a guttural roar of frustration and impatience as he launched himself back into the night. He would run fast and hard, and continue running until dawn touched the sky. It was all he could do for now.

Autumn dreamed of the wolf again, sitting in her doorway, watching her as she slept. The wolf entered her room, and when she did not wake, he climbed onto her bed and lay next to her. She felt his heat, the weight of him on the bed, his massive head next to hers. She dreamed she awoke and looked into his intense blue eyes. Wild, ancient eyes, full of intelligence and mysteries, and stars glowed within their unfathomable depths. His gaze was mesmerizing, compelling, and as she sat up, he rose with her until she knelt before him on her bed.

The wolf sat on his haunches, eyes locked onto hers. He was a magnificent creature, regal even as he sat among her rumpled bedding. Autumn felt almost reverent in his presence. As if she knelt before a wild god of some sort. He had a message for her, she suddenly knew, yet she could not understand him. The wolf lowered his head, his shining eyes willing her to understand something. She felt she almost understood. She stilled her breath and strained to hear something faint in the air.

Like the rolling of thunder, she suddenly heard loudly in her head, "Awaken."

Autumn shot up in bed, flailing for a moment as her alarm shrieked loudly. She looked around blearily as the dream faded and reality set in. There was no wolf here, only her cat Toby glaring at her in annoyance from his spot on the bed.

Sighing, she leaned over and silenced the alarm in irritation, then tiredly swung her legs over the edge of her bed.

Monday morning, and back to business as usual.

Not only was she having these weird as hell wolf dreams, but it had been a wretched night to begin with. She had come home, despondent and horribly alone, but knowing she had done the right thing. She had gone listlessly through her evening routine and fallen into bed, only to lay there replaying the day in her head. Beautiful day. Beautiful man. He had kissed her again, and it had nearly broken her defenses. She'd shed a few frustrated tears over that kiss.

God, she was tired.

Sighing and running a hand through her tousled hair, she rose and went into the bathroom. She took a long, hot shower, leaning her head against the tile and letting the hot water pour over her until she could have a semblance of a thought again. What an utter mess she was. She had had her fun and now she had to face the man today and pretend it never happened. Had to act like she was utterly immune to him and his charms, that the things they had shared yesterday meant nothing, and that she wasn't an aching, miserable mess because of him.

Sighing deeply she forced herself to finish her shower and tiredly went through the rest of her morning routine before work, her mind far away, still on the back of his bike.

At least you get to see him again, a small hopeful voice said and she sighed, cheering a little. There was that. One more day of his gaze, one more day of his sensual smiles, one more day of his voice and faint scent hovering around in the air. But for how much longer?

She forced herself to clear her mind and stop thinking as she dressed casually in a pair of well-loved jeans, her favorite pair of Vans, and a clean Dragonfly Coffee and Espresso T-shirt. She pulled her hair up in a simple ponytail, and left it at that. No frills today. No more leading him on. She'd done enough damage already.

Feeling somewhat better, she grabbed her things and hopped in her car, focusing on her breathing to keep her mind from straying to unpleasant thoughts as she drove to the shop. A cold front had moved in overnight and a low bank of fog hung in the chill air, shrouding the world in gray. It was still early so the parking lot was unsurprisingly empty as she pulled up in the gloom. Not that she had been expecting anyone to be there, but she still bit back a little sigh of loneliness as she parked her car, went inside, and began her preparations for the day.

It turned out to be a slow morning as the fog persisted, lending a chill dampness to the air. There were few customers, just some of the regulars, so Autumn busied herself with doing a thorough inventory. At least she attempted to. A part of her attention was always on the door, her ears listening for the sound of a motorcycle. After she counted the boxes of coffee filters for the fourth time, she finally gave an exasperated sigh and threw down her clipboard. Where the hell was he?

A jingle of the bells at the door had her head whipping up so fast she banged it on the bottom of the counter she had been crouching under.

"Sonovabitch!" she yelped, rubbing the top of her head as she rose and squinted at her best friend.

"Oh, honey, are you OK?" Cleo asked around a big box in her hands. Her arms were covered in bright rainbow arm warmers today, and she had on rainbow leggings to match. Cleo set the box down on the counter and gave her a concerned look as Autumn rubbed at her bump.

"Yeah." Autumn winced, the spot tender but not bleeding. "You just surprised me. I was expecting someone."

Cleo looked at her with a quirked eyebrow, appraising her, and shoved the box to the side. "Uh huh. And just what were you up to yesterday, missy?" she asked, leveling an accusing finger at her. "Did you sleep with him?"

Autumn glared at her and crossed her arms lightly. "Please. I certainly did not."

"Uh huh," Cleo said, her gaze shrewd. "But you were with him weren't you?" She wagged her finger in Autumn's face. "You didn't call me and that makes you suspect. Don't lie to me. I have the nose of a hound dog."

"You *are* a hound dog," Autumn grumbled and rolled her eyes at Cleo's look. "OK, yes, I was with him. All right? But we didn't have sex," she said, throwing up her hands. "Happy?"

"Not in the least. Details. Spill," Cleo said, pulling up a seat at the counter. "And you might as well give me a dark black while you're at it. I was hanging out with Ron last night."

"Oh ho! So who's the one pointing fingers here?" Autumn grinned, moving to pour her friend a cup.

"Nuh uh. Don't try to get out of this," Cleo warned, "Tell me what you were doing with Kain."

Autumn sighed and, admitting defeat, poured herself another cup as well and began telling Cleo about one of the best days of her life.

"He kissed you? Twice?" Cleo gasped, lifting her chin from where it had been propped on her palm. Autumn nodded, her cheeks heating in embarrassment.

"It's not like I meant for it to happen. But it just…happened. God, what was I thinking Cleo?" she moaned, dropping her face into her hands.

"You were thinking a hot man wanted to kiss you?" Cleo offered helpfully and Autumn lifted her head to scowl at her.

Cleo laughed "Look, I'm all for you having a hot shag, sweet pea. It would be good for you. But," she said, holding up a finger, "can you do it without falling for him? Can you just let it be sex?"

Autumn gave her a morose look and wiped a hand over her face, shaking her head. "I've been asking myself that same question all day, quite honestly."

Cleo considered her friend, tapping her finger against her lips.

"Did he say when that car of his was getting fixed?" she asked, and Autumn shook her head, fiddling with her coffee cup.

"He said a few more days…he didn't really know for sure."

Cleo grunted, watching her for a moment, then reached across the counter and cupped Autumn's face in her hands, smiling at her affectionately.

"Listen to me, sweet pea. Don't do something that you'll regret, OK? I'd say just go with your gut on this. You're a grown woman and it's your decision alone to make, just make the best choice for you. And don't let Kain pressure you into anything, OK?"

"OK. Thanks, Mama Bear," Autumn said, leaning far over the counter to give her a kiss on the cheek. Cleo smiled and gripped her hand briefly, then let it go and gave it a pat.

"Oh! So I brought my latest creation to show off." She beamed, reaching into the box and pulled out her work of art proudly.

Autumn stared at the thing, shaking her head and chuckling at Cleo's creation. It was made out of an old lamp, or at least she thought it was, but it was hard to tell from all the junk glued to the thing. Small toys and bottle caps, plastic utensils, Christmas light bulbs, crucifixes, beads, and even a doll's head were all stuck together in a surprisingly artful way. What wasn't covered in junk was painted in bright colors. It was colorful, garish, trashy, and so very Cleo.

"I love it." Autumn smiled and Cleo looked it over proudly.

"I call it 'Walking with Jesus.' I'm gonna take it over to that gallery in Fortuna. Lynn has been asking to see more of my work."

Autumn smiled and shook her head again as Cleo stuffed it carefully back in its box. "It really is something. She should be proud to have it."

"Thanks, love," Cleo replied, picking the box up again, and gave Autumn a warmhearted smile.

"Good luck with your piece," Autumn said and Cleo waggled her eyebrows, smiling as she headed for the door. She paused just before opening it, her lips pursed as if considering something, and turned back to her friend.

"Sometimes," she hesitated, and then seemed to decide to say what was on her mind, meeting Autumn's eyes, "Sometimes it's good to give things a chance, you know? Take care, love. See you later." She smiled, and Autumn blew her a kiss as she left out the door.

Autumn turned, leaning back against the counter and blew out a long breath. Cleo's words rang in her head. *Sometimes you just have to give things a chance.* She chewed at her lower lip and stared into space, her belly fluttering with something unnamed. *Give things a chance...you know?* She drew in a deep breath and checked the clock on the wall. It was almost noon now. Where was he?

Clenching her eyes shut she scrubbed her face in her hands and blew out a heavy sigh, then wiped her hands on her jeans as she looked around. *Just keep busy,* she told herself. *Just do something, keep your mind occupied, and he'll eventually show up.*

She hoped.

It was almost two by the time Tanya showed up for her shift and by then Autumn was beside herself. He knew she was working this morning, so why hadn't he come? Was he angry with her about how she had left him last night? Had something happened? Had he left already…without saying good-bye? She just didn't know, but she needed to find out. Badly.

As soon as Tanya walked in the door, Autumn turned things over to her with a quick apology that she had an errand to run, and practically ran to her car. She tried not to speed as she drove the short distance to the cabins, yet got there in record time. What if he was gone? What if something had happened to him?

And what if he had gotten his car back?

She pulled into the parking lot with a knot in her stomach.

He was there, under the hood of that beast of a car as she came to a stop, unable to tear her eyes from the sleek matte black vehicle and all that it meant.

Kain leaned back from the engine and gave her a curious look, grabbing a rag and wiping his hands as she turned off her car. Autumn breathed out at the sight of him. He wore a tight black T-shirt again today, the fabric stretched over his broad chest, showing off his sculpted arms. He was wearing blue jeans, and those same black biker boots. She got out and he smiled slowly at her, working the grease and dirt off his fingers while she approached him, too many things racing through her mind.

"Hello, Autumn," he said with a small smile, looking her over. She stopped well away from him, folding her arms protectively against her sudden nervousness.

"I see you have your car back," she said lamely, meeting his deep blue gaze.

"Yes, they called here this morning. Finally got her sorted out." He finished removing his tools and he dropped the hood with a bang. Autumn couldn't think of what to say.

"I'm sorry I didn't come in for my coffee. I've been busy dealing with returning the bike and picking up the car," he said casually as he gathered his things. He gave her a small apologetic smile as he strode past her and went inside the cabin, leaving the door open. She approached the door, drawn to him, her head awhirl with all of the implications. He was leaving.

She was surprised to see the place was tidy. The small one bedroom cabin was equipped with a small table, another chair, a TV, and queen-sized bed…the standard hotel arrangement. He had made the bed and his things were neatly set on a chair to one side. She heard him in the bathroom washing up and she stared at the made bed, imagining him sleeping there.

What in the hell was she going to do now? He would leave; he had no reason to stay here now. Unless she asked him to stay, and she didn't kid herself as to what that would mean. It was either that, or watch him drive off, taking all of his seduction, danger, and mystery out of her life forever. Or she could allow this; allow herself this taste of him, this time with him, however short it may be.

Sometimes you just gotta give things a chance, you know?

He came out of the bathroom, wiping his hands and face on a towel, minus his shirt, and her world turned on its ear. Her mouth fell open at the sight of him and she gaped at him stupidly. He was beautiful to behold, primal in his half-naked maleness. His wide shoulders were strong-looking, his arms sleekly toned with muscle and dusted with hair. His broad chest tapered into his flat belly, coarse hair spreading across his chest and all the way down into the waist of his jeans in a way that made her knees weak. His jeans hung loosely around his hips, unbuttoned but still zipped, revealing a darker trail of hair that started at his navel and dipped so enticingly below the waistband.

She dragged her eyes back up at his face and found him staring back at her with desire in his sapphire eyes, watching her heatedly.

He prowled to her, and she felt herself unable to move. If he touched her half-naked as he was she would be lost, but her feet seemed to have grown roots. She was lost anyway as he came to her, his long wild hair falling around his face and shoulders in a way that made her want to take all of it in her hands and pull him to her. His eyes were intent as he stopped and stared down at her, his gaze roving all over her face while she stared up at him, breathless.

He reached up a hand and trailed his knuckles against her face gently, his sensual lips parted. She was mesmerized, captivated by him and unable to think.

"I'm leaving. Checking out tomorrow," he said softly and she drew in a breath, searching his eyes. The moment of truth. He didn't need to say any more, they both knew what he had just laid between them.

She stared into his gorgeous face, taking him in, her heart racing. Take this chance, or lose him forever. Time seemed to stand still as they both stood there, eyes locked, while fate turned. His eyes softened and he stared deeply into her. His warm hand cupped her cheek, caressing her face with his thumb. She closed her eyes, breathing out a shuddering sigh as she surrendered. She didn't care anymore. All she knew was that she wanted him like she had never wanted anyone else in her life. She was a fool, but she could no more stand against her desire any longer than she could lift a mountain.

"Stay," she said simply, looking up at him with an open expression. He smiled at her slowly, genuinely, and pulled her against him.

"Do you mean it, Autumn? There's no taking this back," he rumbled, nuzzling the top of her head. She trembled against him and simply nodded, unable to speak.

She was nestled up against his bare chest, pressed lightly against the heat of his body and Autumn felt herself shake at the contact. He smelled like man, and leather, good earth, sandalwood, and some subtle musk that drove her senses wild. His body hair tickled against her cheek, and the leather cord of his necklace pressed into her skin. Her hands lay against his chest and she strongly resisted the urge to nuzzle him back, to start kissing him and tasting his skin right now. Not yet. She had committed, but she needed some time.

She pulled herself away from him with a shaky breath and looked up at him, his expression heated and full of desire.

"Come to my place tomorrow…for dinner," she managed to say, knowing full well she was inviting him for far more than that. He grinned at her and touched her face again, gently cupping her chin and running the pad of his thumb lightly across her lips. Her eyelashes fluttered down, concealing her eyes and she almost let her tongue slip out to taste his finger. She needed to go before things got out of hand here. She wasn't ready for this. Not yet.

As if sensing her thoughts he let his hands drop to her shoulders, caressing her lightly before letting them fall away. He took a couple of steps back and nodded his head at her.

"What time should I be there?" he asked and she looked up at him again for a long moment, then breathed deeply and pushed a hand into her hair, looking away.

"How about seven? I'll cook. I take it you want some sort of manly kind of meal," she said, looking back at him with a wry smile.

He nodded with an amused grin. "I'm a meat and potatoes kind of man."

And pancakes with syrup, Autumn thought and blushed. Oh, she really did need to go.

"OK. I can do that," she said with a small smile and he chuckled softly.

"Do you have something I can write on?" she asked, "I'll give you directions to my place."

Kain smiled to himself, mentally tracing his path to her door while he searched for something to write on, recalling the scent of her trails, the sight of her home. She had asked him to stay, invited him to her home. He could howl with the joy of it, and could nearly taste her on his tongue. He came up with a small note pad and a pen from a nearby drawer and handed them to her. She took them lightly with a shy smile and moved to the small table, then began to write the directions down. Kain moved up behind her, unable to stop himself from needing to be close to her, to breathe in her scent.

She finished writing and turned to him, gasping softly at finding him so close. Holding his gaze, she lifted the bit of paper to him and he took it without looking at it, devouring her with his eyes. They stared at each other, both struggling with need for a few moments, then Autumn inhaled deeply and backed away a step.

"So, seven then," she said and he nodded, unable to help himself from stepping toward her.

She continued to back away, her eyes flitting away with nervousness. "OK then," she said, then stopped and looked up at him. "I'll see you tomorrow…Kain."

He stilled at his name on her lips and his spread into a slow, wide smile.

"Tomorrow," he said, and she nodded, turning to go. She reached the door, then looked at him over her shoulder, dazzling him with a warm smile before she fled to her car.

Kain shook with the need to go after her but he held himself in check. He felt glorious, savagely happy as he stood in the doorway and watched her leave. He had to bide his time just a little bit more, just until tomorrow and she would be his. He was so close to it he trembled.

Growling happily in his throat, he walked out into the yard and looked up at the sky, letting his head fall back and his eyes close as he breathed in the cool air of the redwood forest. At last, he would have her. He felt like he had waited eons for this. She was surrendering to him, and when he finally tasted her she would fall completely, and at long last, his hunger would be sated.

CHAPTER NINE
Surrender

Waiting was the purest form of hell, Autumn decided. Waiting was anticipation, but it also left room for the doubts that niggled at her. Autumn had never moved so fast with anyone before in her life. She had dated Ted for several weeks before they slept together for the first time, and it had been months before she allowed him to come to her cottage to meet Oma. She was always such a cautious and practical girl, but Kain seemed to bring out something in her she had never experienced before. She felt vibrant, fully alive, and a tad reckless when it came to him. She felt things she didn't think were inside of her.

She couldn't believe she'd invited him, a near stranger, to her home.

Oh well, no use fretting about her decision any longer. As Oma would say, she had made her bed, now she had to lie in it. With him. In all sorts of tantalizing positions that her overactive imagination was coming up with.

OK, maybe the anticipation wasn't the worst thing.

She tried to concentrate on other things as she cleaned every inch of her home that evening, but her mind was in overdrive, especially after being pressed against his naked chest, and she knew she'd been too long without sex.

It had been a little over three years since she had last had it, to be precise. She'd not been with a man since she divorced Ted, and even then, the last six months of their marriage had been sexless, distant, and strained. Little did she know he had been nailing his co-worker behind her back while she'd been opening her shop.

She tossed her head as she scrubbed her toilet and blew a strand of hair out of her face angrily. She would not think about that now. She did not want to think about the past, or anything that might come. She wanted to be here, now, to enjoy this while it was hers. She would pay for it later, but she was beyond caring. She wanted this, she wanted Kain, and she would take what she could get of him.

At least she was sure to have one amazing night she would never forget.

She finished cleaning late that evening and fell exhausted into bed. For once since he had sauntered into her life she slept deeply and did not dream, waking in the morning intensely aware of what the day meant.

Autumn went to work and was glad that she'd taken the early shift again. It would give her a few hours to go into town to shop for what she needed for dinner. Despite being slow again, work flew by, and thankfully, Kain did not make an appearance. She didn't think she could handle seeing him before tonight. She might just do something stupid like jump on him, dinner be damned. When Tanya got there, Autumn asked her if she would cover her shift for the next day. Tanya agreed and Autumn thanked her profusely, telling her that she had an appointment she had completely forgotten about. She felt a little bad about lying about her true reasons, but she didn't want loose tongues wagging. Not yet.

She drove to Eureka to buy groceries and a few other essentials, her mind racing as she made a mental list. Shopping was an adventure as she tried to think of something to cook for him. She ended up with a thick steak oozing blood in its package, a cut she was sure he would just love. For herself, she planned on cooking her favorite recipe, eggplant parmesan, though how she would possibly be able to eat with her stomach in knots she didn't know.

High gray clouds were scudding quickly across the sky from the ocean as she finished her shopping and headed back home. The weather had shifted and rain was moving in again. There was a chance for thunderstorms this evening, which would actually suit her just fine. A stormy night might be quite fitting for what was to come.

It was five o'clock by the time she got back home, the time fleeting by too quickly, and she rushed into her kitchen and began putting her groceries away. There was still so much to do! Once that was done, she moved to the bathroom and took a quick shower, making sure she was fully clean and smooth from head to toe. Her grooming finished, she pinned her hair up and wrapped an old robe around herself as she went to the kitchen to prepare dinner.

She got out her ingredients and set to work chopping, slicing, and sautéing. She'd always loved to cook, and Oma had taught her everything she knew from an early age. There was a joy to cooking that reminded her of creating a work of art. One had to understand the methods of preparing and cooking ingredients, the balance of flavors, what enhanced and what would ruin a dish. It was something akin to a magic spell, and Autumn enjoyed it greatly.

The meat was difficult for her, cold and slimy in her hands as she rubbed salt and herbs into the cold, wet muscle. However, she found as she set it to broiling that her mouth was watering at the smell. She tried to ignore it, thinking instead of her own delicious eggplant. She prepared a peppercorn sauce to go over the broiled meat and tender oven potatoes. It was after six-thirty when she finally stepped back from the stove, allowing the sauces to simmer and the cooked meat to marinate in its own juices under a hot plate. Time to get dressed.

She went to her bedroom and began rifling through her clothes, torn as to what she should wear for him tonight. Something suitably feminine but also easy to remove.

It was a while before she decided on a pretty, pink, high-low chiffon dress with a layered, dropped point handkerchief hem, and a lovely embellished bodice. It was strapless and would leave her shoulders and neck bare, something she was sure he would appreciate. She debated wearing a pair of cute pink heels to go with the dress, but then recalled Kain's penchant for being barefoot. The same way she enjoyed being barefoot. Why bother with heels when they just hurt to wear anyway? It's not as if they would be leaving the house. Instead, she donned a couple of toe rings and called it good.

After a bit of fussing with her hair she decided to simply allow it to fall naturally in its long, loose waves around her face. She could put it up in some way, but it would just get mussed later. Besides, she felt that Kain might enjoy her hair being unbound and touchable.

When it came to her makeup, she decided on making her eyes just a little smoky and mysterious, but not enough to overdo it. She added some light foundation and just a hint of rose gloss on her lips, just enough for effect but not enough that it would get all over everything.

When she was done, she looked herself over in the mirror. She looked utterly feminine, and a bit seductive. The dress showed off her bare legs and shoulders nicely, her loose hair and smoky makeup adding intrigue and a touch of wildness to her look. *Damn, I look smoking hot.* She smiled at herself and smoothed her dress with her hands, turning this way and that. She had to admit she'd done a good job. Kain was sure to be pleased.

She checked the time and gave a little yelp. It was just about seven. He'd be here soon. She buzzed around the house, lighting candles here and there and started a fire in the fireplace. Dusk had fallen and the sky had darkened considerably. The wind sighed through the forest outside as she finished her preparations. She was just lighting the last candle when she perked at the sound of a growling engine pulling up outside. Her mouth went dry and she stepped toward the door, unconsciously running her hands through her fiery mane and smoothing her dress. *Here we go.*

His knock on her door caused her to jump, and she resisted running over and flinging the door open just to see him. Carefully she padded over, her skirt swishing around her, soft music coming from the stereo. She had carefully selected the music tonight, a mix of some of her favorites that were sure to set the mood. She held her breath as she slowly opened the door, then exhaled a trembling sigh at the sight of him.

He was like a wild, Pagan sex god come to visit her in the night. He wore a black silk shirt, the top few buttons undone, exposing just a touch of hair. The shirt tucked into black leather pants that were laced at the crotch and belted with a studded belt, she noticed with wide eyes. He was also wearing the leather jacket again, and a leather pack of some kind was slung over one shoulder. He held a bottle of wine, his hair whipping around him in the wind, and he gave her a slow, sensuous, wicked smile.

Kain drank in the sight of her hungrily. She looked amazing. She was feminine and seductive in her pink dress, showing off her luscious curves and shapely legs for him. He noticed her bare feet and had to suppress a lusty growl. It made his groin tighten, that his Fae temptress would think of such a detail for him. Her lovely shoulders and throat were exposed, her breasts thrust up and bound behind the strapless pink fairy dress, and her hair was a tumbled mass of red-gold waves. He growled appreciatively, eyes roving all over her as she stared at him wide-eyed.

"Something smells good," he murmured, stepping closer to her. She was a bouquet of scents tonight from the subtle flowery fragrance of her toiletries, to the savory scents of cooking and wood-smoke that clung to her, and underneath it all was her own unique amber-pear-woman scent. He wanted to drag her to him right there just so he could smell her over completely, but he resisted and offered her the bottle of wine instead.

Autumn blinked, tearing her eyes from his and looked at the gift.

"I promise, no Dixie cups this time," Kain said with a wry smile. She blinked again, then blushed prettily up at him and took the bottle with a small laugh.

"I suppose glasses will have to do, though they aren't as classy." She smiled and he chuckled deeply in response, enjoying her blush.

"Come on in," she said warmly and he stepped into her home. His eyes followed her as she turned and padded her way into the kitchen.

"So did you have any trouble finding the place?" she asked as he closed the door behind him firmly. *Mine.* He mentally marked his territory and set down his pack.

Kain turned and looked around, taking in her domain for the first time as an invited guest instead of an intruder. "No problem. Your directions were superb," he said, smiling to himself. He hadn't even looked at her directions.

Her cat looked up at Kain from his chair, his big eyes blinking at him. Kain crouched down and wiggled his fingers, whispering to the cat. With a cooing rumble, the cat got to his feet, stretched luxuriously for a long moment, then finally jumped down and ambled over to him with his huge tail in the air. Autumn noticed and gasped, rushing over just as the cat rubbed against Kain's fingers.

"Be careful, he can be mean with new people..." she warned, but the words died on her tongue. The cat loved all over Kain, twining against his legs and rubbing against his hands with happy purrs and trills, his copper eyes slitted with kitty pleasure. Kain stroked the cat, scratching through his orange fur and murmuring to him.

"He seems happy to me," Kain said, looking up at her from his crouch. Autumn's mouth was slightly open, her eyebrows raised as Kain got to his feet again. They watched for a moment as the cat rolled around on the floor in front of him.

"That is really bizarre." Autumn bent down and scooped the huge feline up. He purred against her and butted his head up under her chin.

"I've never seen him act that way with anyone," she said, and stared at Kain as she scratched through the cat's fur. Kain merely shrugged and smiled innocently, thrusting his hands in his pockets. Eyeing him suspiciously, she took the cat back to a room and Kain heard her say "Be good. Mama will get you in the morning." A door closed.

When she came back into the room, she stopped, regarding him for a moment as if trying to decipher his secrets.

"Well, I'm glad that cat likes someone," she said finally with a small laugh, and gave him a soft smile as she entered the kitchen again.

"Go ahead and make yourself comfortable," she said as she began rifling through her kitchen drawers. "Mi casa es su casa and all that." She chuckled, snatching a corkscrew out of the drawer in triumph.

Kain grinned, drawn to her as she moved about in the kitchen.

She had set the corkscrew aside and was busy stirring and tasting sauces as he came up behind her, the air thick with rich scents, hers the richest of all. She froze and he made a low sound in this throat as he trailed his fingers along her arm.

"I don't know about you," he murmured, "but I'm hungry."

Autumn braced herself against the stove at his intimate touch and shivered.

"Yes, hungry," she said, sliding away from him to get out the dishes. "But food first."

He chuckled, a throaty purr at her back.

She turned around halfway, plates in her hands and shot him a look. "Go, quit distracting me. Out of my kitchen," she said and he raised an eyebrow at her.

"Your wish is my command," he said with a smile, bowing to her, and she giggled as he wandered out to the great room again.

Kain roamed the large, open room as she plated the food, noticing the candles and little touches. He wandered to the fireplace, eyeing the plush couch angled in front of it. It was deep and wide, well cushioned with a soft, velvety fabric in a passionate, dark purple color. There were many pillows of different textures and shapes, and a few throw blankets draped over the end. He smiled to himself as he ran a hand against the fabric of the couch, calculating. His boots sank into the plush carpet the couch sat on and he suddenly wanted to feel that softness, to gauge it. He took off his jacket and tossed it to one side, then sat to remove his boots. Once his feet were bare, he set his boots aside and sank his toes into the rug. He stretched his legs out, warming them by the fire as he tested the depth and softness of the couch. Yes, very nice. This would do well.

He watched her from the couch as she bustled about in the kitchen, setting up the table with a happy air. He could smell the meat she had cooked, and his mouth watered. It would be good to eat before he sated his hunger. Finally, she brought in steaming plates and set them down on the table, looking up at him with a coy smile and announced that dinner was served.

Autumn knew she had cooked well as she watched Kain savor every bite of the rib eye. She was fascinated by his mouth, how it worked as he chewed, and by the juice that dripped from the meat. She sipped her wine and her stomach growled hungrily. Though she loved eggplant, it was just not satisfying to her tonight, so she picked at her meal unconsciously while she studied the man across from her.

Kain returned her gaze as he ate, glancing at her barely touched food. He swallowed his mouthful and drank a bit of wine.

"This is really, really good. Are you sure you don't want some?" he asked, licking his finger. Autumn's mouth watered at the suggestion but she shook her head.

"No… I don't like meat," she murmured, but her stomach was telling her other things. What was wrong with her?

Kain raised an eyebrow at her and cut a piece from the steak, skewering it on his fork and holding it out toward her. "Are you sure? What's not to like about this?"

Autumn swallowed, watching as juice dripped from the pink center of the morsel. "I…it's a life, and the way the animals are treated…" she said, trailing away as Kain pinned her with an animal stare.

"We are animals ourselves. All life is connected in the circle of birth, killing, and eating, feeding the cycle. Human beings are no better than wolves, and wolves are no better than the animals they hunt," he said, licking the meat off the fork, watching her as he chewed. "It's all about the cycle."

She stared at him, breathless as she tried to drum up her arguments, "But…human beings are enlightened creatures. We can be above the cycle. Above the killing." She watched him cut another piece.

"Ah, but we aren't, are we? We're animals with fancy clothes and nice cars. When it comes down to it, you would eat the meat if you were starving, and you would love it. It is in your basic nature to hunt, kill…and eat."

He held out the fork to her again and Autumn was entranced, her stomach constricting painfully at the sight of the bloody juice on his plate and the pink morsel he was offering to her. She wanted to be repulsed. She wanted to be disgusted. She wanted to remember all those poor animals and how they were treated, how they died, but somehow she could think of none of that. She only knew her hunger for what he was offering.

She leaned toward him across the table as he brought the fork to her lips. The first taste of the meat was like a shock on her tongue and her body reacted. It was like life itself, and she suddenly felt ravenous for it. She closed her eyes as she chewed, savoring the flavors and her stomach clenched its hunger. What in the world had she been missing?

Kain watched her, enraptured as she ate the small bit of meat. It was the most erotic thing he had ever seen, knowing that what he had given her was something forbidden in her own little world. She opened her eyes slowly, her pink tongue sliding out to lick her lips and Kain could not tear his eyes away from her. He cut another piece, offering it to her again and she took it without hesitation, savoring the bite. He was hard for her as he fed her and she ate hungrily, devouring what was left of the steak. She savored each bite, chewing methodically and swallowing with care. When the plate was clean she sat back, licking her lips, and drew the wineglass to her mouth, their gazes locked.

Lightning flashed outside, the wind shrieking around the jambs as they gazed at each other with parted lips, lust sizzling between them.

"I ate all your food," Autumn said softly with an abashed chuckle, blushing. Kain shifted in his seat, his erection uncomfortably bound by his pants.

"Clearly you…desired it," he said with a small smile, leaning back in his chair to watch her taste the wine. She blushed prettily and turned away, looking at her own plate again.

She had no idea what had just happened, but for some reason she found that she felt good. Alive. Primal. And although she couldn't believe she had eaten most of his steak, she only felt distant chagrin about it, as if it had been the most natural thing in the world. She found she was still hungry, but she no longer had any desire for the eggplant. She was hungry for other things now.

"Why don't you go ahead and make yourself comfortable while I clean up?" she asked, setting her glass down and picking up her plate, careful to avoid his eyes.

Kain grinned seductively, staying seated as she came over to his side of the table and bent over him to get his dishes. He ran a finger down her ribs, brushing the feather light material of her dress and she shuddered, sliding away from him quickly and back into the kitchen.

She heard him chuckle as she went to the sink, and Autumn watched him out of the corner of her eye. He rose and went to the fireplace where he added another log and stoked the fire back to life. She avoided looking at him while she took care of the dishes, scraping the leftovers into containers and rinsing the remainder off into the sink. Outside the wind howled and thunder rumbled, accompanied by occasional flashes of lightning up in the clouds.

"Looks like it's going to be a wild night," she commented from the kitchen and blushed immediately to Kain's chuckle.

"Yes, I suppose it is," he said and she shook her head, her cheeks heated. When was she going to stop saying stupid things?

She finished putting the dishes in the machine and started it, then she wiped her hands on a dishtowel and turned out the light to find him lounging back on the couch, one arm propped on his bent leg, staring at her like a large predator. She stayed where she was, her mouth dry at his feral, hungry gaze. She found she could not go to him, suddenly caught with a flash of nerves.

She fidgeted nervously, pacing around the room and checking on the candles. She was all too aware of Kain's wolfish gaze, following her.

"Tell me," he said, his voice low and soft, "when was the last time, Autumn?"

She froze, going pale at his question and she swallowed hard. "The...the last time for what?" she asked stupidly as she turned her head to him, eyes wide, knowing full well what he was asking. He grinned slowly at her, that damnable sexy, feral smile that devastated her, and she felt her knees go weak.

"When was the last time you were with a man?" he asked, capturing her with his eyes and she could not look away.

Lightning lit the room just then and thunder boomed, causing her to jump slightly. Kain continued to stare at her in a way that made thinking impossible; his long form nestled in her couch, his crotch plain for her to see. Her eyes lingered there for a moment and she clearly saw the outline of his erection inside his pants, bulging against the leather. She tore her eyes from it to meet his gaze again, breathing hard. He smiled wickedly, and suddenly the power flickered and died, throwing them into fire-lit darkness.

Autumn blinked and turned, wandering to the glass doors where she looked out into the dark forest, pressing her palms to the glass. The wind howled through the trees, thrashing them as rain began to come down, driving against the window. Lightning flickered in the clouds overhead, illuminating the forest in subtle flashes.

"Redwood branch must have come down on a power line," she said absently, looking out into the darkness. Rain streaked against the glass door under her palms.

She heard Kain rise from the couch but did not dare to turn and look at him. He approached her, his bare feet padding softly on the thick rug, and a moment later she felt his heat on her back. She swallowed hard, her heartbeat thudding in her chest as he lightly touched her bare shoulders with his fingertips.

"I want to know, Autumn. When were you last touched?" he murmured softly, curling his fingers around her shoulders. Autumn caught her breath, holding very still. He drew closer and moved her hair away from her shoulder with a light touch. He bent his head to her and she felt his breath on her neck, a strand of his hair brushing against her arm, his hands warm on her skin.

"When did you last feel a man's hands upon you? When were you last pleasured?" he asked, his hot breath in her ear. Lightning flashed again outside, illuminating the forest beyond.

Autumn could not think, though something in her was screaming about the danger of finally giving in to this man. That the surrender would cost her more than she cared to give. It did not matter a moment later when he pressed his mouth to her ear and whispered softly "When?"

Her knees nearly gave out when his teeth raked lightly and unexpectedly across her skin and she gasped, her nipples hardening painfully under her bodice.

"When was it?" he asked against her neck, nuzzling her, his stubble rasping over her skin. He pressed his lips against the place where he had bit her and moved to her ear again. "Or can you not remember?"

Autumn almost sobbed as his tongue flicked out to trace the shell of her ear lightly while his hands skimmed along her arms, leaving goose flesh in their wake. His hands continued their exploration, gliding over her bodice now, caressing her belly through the stiff fabric, and lower, stroking down her hips to her thighs. His fingers trailed through the petals of her skirt and Autumn's breath hitched in her throat as he drew his hands up and back. He briefly palmed her ass, groaning, and kissed her neck before tracing the line of her pulse with his tongue.

The Hunger sang through Kain at the taste of her skin and the feel of her soft curves in his hands. The change called to him and he felt his eyes tingle as they shifted to icy blue with his desire. He wanted her intensely, so intensely he could easily lose himself to the animal within as he ground himself lightly against her sweet ass with a hiss. *No no, wolf*, he admonished himself as he pushed the beast back, *she is not yours, and you will behave. I am in control.* He felt the wolf subside and his eyes stopped tingling as they returned to their normal color.

He trailed his fingers against her face then, tracing her features. Her lashes fanned her cheeks, her lips slightly parted. He cupped her cheek in his palm and caressed her soft skin with his thumb. The scent of her arousal filled his senses. He touched her, drinking her in, savoring her the way she had savored the taste of meat after so long without it. She was ready. Ready at last to give him what he wanted, to give in to what she wanted, and to do so fully.

With one hand on her hip, he held her against him and, gripping her jaw, turned her face toward his. He could hear her heart pounding as his breath fanned against her lips. He prolonged the agony, rubbing his nose against hers, his breath hot on her lips until she was trembling in his arms. He touched his lips to hers lightly, briefly, and pulled away again, teasing her with it. He waited for her to open her eyes, and she gazed at him with such ardent desire that he couldn't wait any longer.

He bent his head and brought his mouth to hers, inhaling sharply at the contact. It was like the lightning that sizzled outside, scorching and electric between them, shocking him down to his toes. He held her there with his hand against her jaw, her back to his front, and kissed her hard. His lips slid across her sweet mouth, demanding, hungry, needing more. His tongue glided across the seam of her mouth and she whimpered. A soft growl of triumph rumbled in Kain's chest as she parted her lips and his tongue slid deep, claiming her fully at last.

Kain pulled away from her then, only to turn her in his arms and crush her to him. His mouth descended upon hers once more, and this time he held nothing back. His kiss was demanding, unyielding, and full of long-denied hunger for the woman in his arms.

Autumn slid her hands against his jaw and into his hair, uttering a little noise of distress, and clutched his long mane to pull him closer. He met her with a growl, and moved his hands to grip her head and hold her still while he sealed his mouth over hers and kissed her hard. He drew the breath out of her hungrily until she could no longer breathe without him, then he thrust his tongue deeply into her mouth with a long groan. He felt her legs buckle slightly with the force of his kiss and he held onto her while he swept his tongue against hers, gliding in and out until they were both breathless.

He suckled her lower lip briefly before pulling away, panting, his heart racing as he looked down at her. She stared up at him in a daze, her hands tangled in his hair, her body trembling. He grinned a slow, wolfish grin full of teeth. He would do all he knew to free the wild thing he sensed inside of her tonight, to unleash all of her passion fully and completely. He would feed on it with all of the hunger for her he'd been holding on to since the moment he saw her.

This night, his little fey temptress would howl like a wolf.

CHAPTER TEN
Night Fire

The rain continued to pour down outside and lightning flickered through the stormy night, eerily illuminating the forest before plunging it into darkness once more. Thunder roared with the lightning and the wind moaned through the tall trees, battering the rain against the windows and creating a wild cacophony. The storm was a perfect accompaniment to the erotic passion that seared through Autumn as Kain continued to kiss her.

He kissed like an expert, rubbing his sensual lips against hers with sweet, agonizing friction, stroking his tongue against hers with practiced skill. He held her still with his hand palming the back of her head, his other arm encircling her waist. She was thankful for the support since it seemed like her trembling legs might give out at any moment. She clung to him desperately, her hands entwined in his long mane, breathless and shaking with desire.

She returned his kisses with all the passion she had for him in her, which seemed endless. They kissed with abandon, passionately trading breaths and small noises of pleasure. Their erotic exchange seemed to go on and on, and soon she needed more. She pulled her hands from his hair and slid them against the silk of his shirt while he continued to kiss her. Her trembling fingers found his buttons and began to undo them.

He pulled his lips away from hers and gazed down at her with a lazy smile, watching while she unbuttoned his shirt. His hands stroked down her back and sides as she popped the last button and impatiently pulled the tails from under his waistband. Parting the silk, she pressed her face to his chest and nuzzled his chest hair with a little sigh. Autumn had never understood the appeal of a clean-shaven male body. A man with body hair made her feel all the more feminine.

She placed worshipful kisses on his chest and collarbone as she slid her hands up under his open shirt and explored the silky texture of his skin and the shape of his body. He, too, was trembling a little, she found, and it sent a delicious thrill through her, realizing that she was also affecting him deeply.

She kissed him for a few moments more, her tongue darting out to taste the salt of his skin. When she licked one of his flat, dark nipples, his body jerked and he made a rough, impatient sound. He gripped her jaw and turned her face up to his to take her mouth again in a hard and savage kiss.

Autumn melted against him, whimpering against his lips at the feel of his erection pressed against her and his bare chest under her palms. His tongue darted in and out of her mouth, flickering against hers, and there were simply too many clothes between them. She needed to feel all of him. Now. Apparently, he felt the same. He broke the kiss with a frustrated snarl and felt along her bodice, looking for how to remove it. Finally, he stopped, stared into her with wild, heated eyes, and took a step back from her.

"Take it off," he growled softly, deeply, and a sizzling flutter of molten heat suffused through her.

Mouth dry, she reached behind her and found the hidden zipper to the dress. His eyes glittered ferally as she tugged the zipper down and, breathlessly, she let the dress fall to the floor.

Kain stared at her openmouthed while she stood shyly before him, gooseflesh rising all over her body at his savage gaze. Her breasts felt swollen and heavy, her nipples hard, aching, and the way Kain was looking at them made the breath hitch in her throat.

"Christ, woman," he gritted out, his voice rough with strain as his gaze roved all over her. Autumn felt his stare as if it were a blowtorch, igniting her until she couldn't stand the heat of it a moment more. She made a small sound of need and that was all it took. Instantly he was on her, pressing himself up against her with a hiss of breath, and used his hands and body to guide her backward to the couch. She fell gently onto the cushions and he followed her down, kneeling between her thighs as he covered her with his body and kissed her deeply again.

The feel of his bare chest against her aching nipples was searingly erotic, and Autumn whimpered, needing more. He ran a hand into her hair and gripped her lightly, pulling her head to the side, exposing the delicate flesh of her neck. He nuzzled her pulse, gently abrading her skin with his scruff, and then tasted her with a long swipe of his tongue.

Autumn moaned softly and wrapped her legs around his hips, pushing her hands into his long mane that fell around them. He held her still with his gentle grip, licking and kissing her neck, then his teeth were on her again, nibbling and biting her sensitive skin. Autumn gasped, gooseflesh rising all over her body. Her nipples tightened against his chest painfully with need. The sensation of his bite was doing crazy things to her and she felt flushed and chilled at the same time. She had been nibbled on and playfully bitten before by past lovers, but not in the carnal way Kain was using his mouth on her. It drew out something primal in her, sending her to new heights of arousal. He locked his teeth onto her neck and she whimpered, shivering as he swirled his tongue around her flesh with a growl.

He continued to lick and nibble at her neck, nipping here and there, finding all of her most sensitive spots with his tongue and teeth. He nibbled just under her ear and Autumn squirmed under him, trembling as he flicked his tongue against the tender area. He bit down then with a growl and held, suckling her skin gently between his teeth. He ground his leather-bound erection against her panties and the sensation was too much. Her thighs tightened around his hips and she arched against him, uttering a surprised little "Oh!" Her toes curled and her body shuddered, relief flooding through her in a gentle wave. Kain chuckled darkly as he laved her once more with his tongue before releasing her hair with a caress.

"That's one," he murmured, smiling smugly down at her dazed expression.

He brought his lips to hers again and kissed her lazily, then slid his hands down to cup her breasts with a possessive growl. Autumn arched into his touch with a grateful sigh. His hands were hot on her skin, rubbing his palms against the hard pearls of her nipples while he ran the tip of his tongue along her bottom lip. He lifted his head and she stared up at him in a daze with her mouth parted.

She slid her hands across his shoulders, grasping at the open collar of his shirt to pull it down. She needed to feel him, all of him. Kain happily obliged her, lifting himself away from her to tear the shirt off, and then he was covering her again, skin to skin.

The contact was utterly erotic. Autumn wrapped herself around him and he met her in a kiss and cupped her breasts again. She whimpered, and he smiled against her mouth with a small chuckle and kept on kissing her, licking along her lips before plunging deep with his tongue again. She dug her nails into his back with her impatience, needing his mouth on other areas. He growled out a chuckle and slid down to do her bidding. He nuzzled between her breasts, kissing her there, his stubble rough on her skin. His thumbs brushed across her nipples and she panted softly, pressing her head back into the cushions.

She was aching, her nipples hard and ripe with need. His hot mouth finally descended upon one, tearing a cry from her throat as he drew it in and suckled. He worked his tongue against the sensitive nub and raked his teeth over it, then pulled it deeper into his mouth with a hard suck. She arched up against him and clutched at his head while he growled around his prize. He continued working her with his tongue, pinching and rolling the other nipple between his fingers.

Releasing her with a final, wet suck, he then trailed his tongue across her skin and rolled her other succulent peak into his mouth with a curl of his tongue. Autumn moaned aloud, trembling from the sensations of his mouth. She was ready and aching for him, wet and hot with her need, but Kain did not relent. He suckled her into a fever pitch that had her panting, pulsing with electric heat. Her body shuddered with an impatient yearning to be touched elsewhere, and *now*. But just like he took his time with his kisses, he prolonged her exquisite agony with his hot mouth, suckling, nipping, and licking her tender nipples until she felt ready to scream.

He chuckled darkly when she gripped his hair and pulled his head away from her overworked peaks, almost frantic with her desire.

"Easy, woman." He grinned at her, then began kissing his way downward with his hair brushing all along her skin. Autumn breathed out a grateful sigh.

He paused at her navel piercing, licking and tugging at the sparkling jewel with his teeth, growling playfully while Autumn giggled. He took a moment more to worship her belly, then he moved lower, placing soft kisses on her skin until he reached her panties.

He nuzzled against the slip of silk and breathed deeply with a low growl. Autumn knew she was thoroughly soaked, and she was embarrassed for a moment until he looked up at her from under his eyebrows with that feral, seductive gaze and smiled slowly. Her breath hitched in her throat in anticipation.

He pulled himself away from her and sat back. looking her over as he caressed her thighs.

"You are exquisite," he murmured, and trailed his fingers across her hips and along the lacy pink waistband. Autumn gasped and squirmed at the ticklish sensation. Kain chuckled softly and ran his finger under the tiny band. His eyes flicked to hers, filled with heated promise as two of his fingers found their way along the inner edge of the scrap of lace and brushed against her mound. Autumn whimpered, biting her lower lip, and waited breathlessly. She gasped and he watched her as his fingers dipped under her panties and parted her dampened folds. He began sliding his fingers back and forth through the slick wetness and she moaned, her eyelids fluttering closed.

He slid his fingers down and Autumn cried out when he pushed them into her hot, wet opening. He growled as she clenched around them. She mewled and arched from the couch at the sensation, gripping the cushions while he worked his fingers inside of her. He curled his fingers to stroke her G-spot and she whimpered, tossing her head against the cushions. She opened her eyes again, meeting his smoldering gaze. He watched her as he withdrew his fingers and found her clit, slicking her own juices over it as he rubbed gently.

He pulled his fingers out of her panties then, and made sure she was watching as he brought them to his lips and sucked the taste of her off them. A hint as to what was going to come next. Autumn parted her lips and shuddered as he closed his eyes and savored her taste a moment, then looked back down at her as he slowly pulled his fingers out of his mouth. She was so aroused that she felt her heartbeat pulsing in her sex and wondered if she might come from his gaze alone.

His lips curved in a wicked smile, and he kept his eyes locked on hers while he dragged the scrap of lacy silk down her legs slowly. She trembled as it came off and she was finally bare to him. He caressed her thighs and took a moment to look her over hungrily then, licking his lips. Reaching out, he stroked his fingers over her wiry auburn curls almost reverently.

He looked up at her from under his eyebrows with a growl. "I've been dying to taste you, Autumn," he said deeply and spread her thighs wide. Autumn quaked with anticipation.

He dropped down with an eager rumble and positioned himself, sliding his shoulders up under her thighs and gripped her hips in his hands. Autumn held her breath as he nuzzled her wetness with an appreciative purr, then laved her with a long stroke of his tongue.

Autumn groaned and gripped at the cushions of the couch as he lapped at her, finding her clit and expertly attending it, tonguing it and suckling it, then licking the hot, wet length of her over and over again while he made small sounds of pleasure in his throat. Waves of erotic sensation rolled through her as he took his time, unhurried in his task. She writhed on the couch and he held her still by her hips while he lapped and suckled and licked. Soon her breathing became panting, her thighs trembling. The pleasure intensified, climbing to a peak. Kain flicked her clitoris over and over with the tip of his tongue, driving her closer to the edge. She tightened and he snarled into her heat. Her thighs clenched around his head, and finally she arched against him with a cry as her orgasm ripped through her in an intense wave of ecstasy.

Kain kept his grip on her, growling deep in his throat as she came. His tongue continued to work at her engorged clit until her thighs clamped down around his ears once more, wailing as she orgasmed a second time. He continued gently licking at her as she began to relax and go limp, breathing hard, and he lifted his head and pulled away from her.

She watched him lazily with her head turned into her hair, panting as he positioned her thighs around his hips again.

"That's three." His eyes smoldered as he wiped his mouth on his arm.

He got to his feet then, standing over her, eyes locked on hers as he unbuckled his belt. She watched him for just a moment, then she sat up, put her hands on his, and looked up into his face. He stilled, looking down at her with a hungry gaze. She put her face to his belly, kissing the hair there and gently moved his hands away. He looked down at her in aroused fascination while she tugged free the laces of the leather pants, exposing him inch by inch.

Autumn breathed in his intoxicating scent of leather and heated male musk as she parted the leather and pushed it away and down—unsurprised and pleased to see that he wore no underwear—exposing his dark nest of hair and the veined base of his manhood. Breathlessly she reached into the leather and pulled him out. The full, hard length of him came free with a little bounce, and she gasped in appreciation. She slid her hands to cup his ass under the leather and closed her eyes, letting out a little trembling breath as she nuzzled against his rough pubic hair. His straining erection rested against her cheek and she savored the hot scent of his primal maleness. She pulled away slightly and regarded his erection, the crown reddened and taught with arousal. Precum beaded at the slit. He was thick and long, curving upward, and she felt a nervous tickle in her belly at the thought of him inside of her. She wasn't sure she could take him.

She reached out and gripped him at the base, her fingers barely curling around the velvet thickness. She darted out her tongue, licking the bead of moisture from his tip. He hissed and thrust his hands into her hair as she swirled her tongue around the silken crown, sucking lightly on it. Just as he had savored her, she savored him, his taste of musky salt tinged with leather, and she slid his silken hardness into her mouth. *Tit for tat.* He groaned breathlessly as she withdrew and took him in again.

Kain kept his hands on her head as she worked her mouth up and down on him, growling in his chest as his hips began moving in rhythm with her. She sensed the subtle trembling in his thighs and the tightening of his lower belly as she sucked and teased him. She loved doing this to him, pleasing him this way. She felt a sense of smug satisfaction as his breath hitched in his throat and his hips bucked, his hands tightening their grip.

With a snarl, he suddenly pulled away from her mouth and stepped back. He had his eyes clenched shut and his hands fisted at his sides, and Autumn looked at him in dismay, wondering what she had done wrong. He seemed to be waging a silent battle with himself, however, and she watched as he kept his eyes closed and took deep, steadying breaths.

Finally, he opened his eyes, and Autumn gasped softly. His eyes were wild, glittering in the firelight, and she would swear they were almost a different color. Lighter somehow. Then with slow deliberation, he shoved his leather pants the rest of the way down his long legs until he was standing before her, utterly naked save for the fanged necklace that hung down his chest. He stood staring at her dangerously with his legs slightly spread, his shoulders squared, and his delicious cock jutting out in front of him. Lighting illuminated him for a moment and Autumn could barely breathe. He was savagely beautiful, wild and untamed standing there. His mane cascaded all around him, and he was so utterly, devastatingly magnificent in his naked glory that Autumn was in awe.

"Lay back and grip the back of the couch," he ordered in a deceptively soft voice and Autumn swallowed, doing as he asked. She lifted her hands behind her to clutch the back edge of the couch. "Keep your hands there, don't move them."

She felt almost delirious as he knelt in front of her once more, his eyes on hers as he spread her thighs wide. Gripping his erection in one hand, he rubbed the taught head between her folds with a sharp inhalation, moistening the tip with her slick wetness. Autumn moaned, arching against him, so ready she could weep with wanting him inside of her.

"Keep your eyes on me," he commanded. Autumn licked her lips and did so, trembling with anticipation. He fed her the first few inches of himself, breath hissing between his teeth as he did and she bucked, her head tossing against the cushions with a loud moan. His size burned inside of her almost unpleasantly, stretching her wide. She was tight from so long without sex, and he was so damned big! There was no way this was going to work. She met his eyes again and he thrust in another inch before her muscles clamped around him, stopping him from going farther. She mewled in desperation.

"Relax, Autumn," he growled through his teeth, pushing against her, but her inner muscles resisted the intrusion and clenched against his size.

"I'm trying!" She panted desperately.

He snarled and pulled her up to him, bending so he could lock his mouth onto a nipple. She moaned and arched against him while he pushed forward, gaining another inch before her body resisted him again. He growled against her breast and suckled her deep but her body still wouldn't relent and she thrashed her head.

He released her nipple and looked up at her from below his eyebrows. "Can you take more?" he asked huskily and she whimpered, shaking her head.

"I... I don't know..." She panted and trembled, unsure. Growling in his throat, he took her thighs from around his waist and propped her calves onto his shoulders, exposing her and opening her wide.

He bent over her then and thrust into her ruthlessly, causing her to buck and cry out as he forced himself deeper, pushing past her defenses with an animal snarl until he was finally, firmly seated in her to the hilt. She had taken him fully.

"Fuck, Autumn..." he breathed, his head bent with her ankles next to his ears. She panted and he repositioned her legs to let them slide past his shoulders while he stretched over her, muscles rippling. He propped himself up and bent his head to her, claiming her lips again in a heated kiss. He slid his hands up to hers, then pulled them down next to her head and twined their fingers, pinning her to the cushions by them. He stayed where he was for a moment, occupying her, claiming her, his forehead to hers as they breathed together.

After a moment he ground deeply against her and she gasped, his heavy breath against her mouth as he withdrew a little, then drove deep again. Their lips met again and Kain tongued her deeply as he moved slowly in her at first, taking his time.

He clenched her hands in his and licked her lips while she shuddered and arched beneath him. She whimpered his name and Kain groaned, pressing his face into her neck. Then, tossing his head back, he rose above her, his face taut with lust as he began thrusting deliciously into her. Waves of pleasure pulsed through Autumn and she leaned up to him, licking and kissing his neck as he strained, the curtains of his hair swinging around them with his motions. He moaned and snarled, clutching her hands as he bent into her, his face in her neck again, and thrust faster now. Autumn whimpered, feeling her climax coming again. Her open mouth was against his neck, panting against his skin as she rocked with him. She instinctively nipped him, urging him to go faster, to send her over the edge…

Kain cursed and began to thrust wildly, pounding into her, his breath shuddering near her ear until he flung his head back and came with a roar. His cock pulsed forcefully inside of her and filled her with liquid heat. She whispered nonsense against his shoulder while he strained with his orgasm, and he dropped his forehead to hers and ground against her one more time. It was enough. Stars exploded behind her eyes as she came hard, wailing his name as she convulsed around him. He growled in her ear as she shuddered, gasping as her body gave one last spasm and at last began to relax. Kain stiffened with one final pulse of his own inside of her and fell against her, spent.

They panted together, covered in sweat from the heat of the fire and their passions. She accepted him, holding him as he laid limply against her, his face in her neck, his cock still throbbing inside of her with his heartbeat.

Autumn stroked his damp mane from his face, overwhelmed by him. She had never experienced such passion before, and she had no idea what to do with it. She wanted this moment never to end; the two of them entwined and momentarily sated, Kain still inside of her, wonderfully relaxed and blissful. No yesterday, no tomorrow, only this perfect moment. Too soon, though, he stirred, and kissing her softly he pulled out from her with a small groan. He stood then, and Autumn gasped as he gathered her into his arms and picked her up.

"That's four. I'm not done with you yet." He smiled down at her seductively, and a shiver went through her, making her ready again almost instantly. Sweet heaven but he was like a drug to her, and she couldn't seem to get enough of him. She was glad he seemed to feel the same way about her.

She wrapped her arms around his neck as he carried her to her bedroom. "Why are you counting?" she asked softly.

Kain smiled down at her. "I'm counting the number of orgasms you're going to have tonight," he said casually as they entered her room where a few candles flickered softly in the darkness. "A dozen should do I think."

"A d-dozen?" she stammered with wide eyes as he laid her gently against her pillows. He gave her a wicked look full of promise and pulled the covers down beneath her until she lay on the sheets, then he got on his hands and knees and prowled up the bed to her. He grinned wolfishly as he knelt over her, bathing her with his body heat.

"I'm afraid you won't be getting much sleep tonight," he growled, showing her his teeth and Autumn blinked up at him with parted lips.

Heavens. He nudged her thighs apart and settled himself between them, then bent his head to nuzzle against her neck. *Is he serious?*

Oh, he's quite serious. He bit her neck again and pressed his erection against her sex with a satisfied growl. She couldn't believe the man's stamina. He'd just had an orgasm and he didn't even seem to be tired, let alone flaccid! He kissed her heatedly and Autumn whimpered into his mouth. This was certainly shaping up to be the best night of her life.

Sex with Autumn had been everything Kain had hoped. Unlike his usual bedmates she was sweet and a little bit shy, gentle and yet curious, open to his guidance, and he sensed in her a deep passion he had yet to tap fully. He had been with so many women in his life he could no longer count or remember them all, women of all shapes and sizes, but never before had one turned him on so thoroughly. When she had so sweetly sucked his cock he had nearly lost it, his wolf rising in response and he'd had to stop her. When he came inside of her, it had been euphoric. Nearly sublime. She was like candy to his wolfish appetites. He simply couldn't get enough of her.

One of his hands glided down her body to stroke her thigh, then around to palm her behind. A wicked thought occurred to him, and he licked her lips lasciviously.

"Turn over," he growled against her mouth and lifted off her. She obeyed breathlessly, rolling onto her stomach and propped herself up on her elbows. He settled himself over her again and kissed along her shoulders, raking her with his teeth here and there. She instinctively dropped her head down when he brushed her hair aside and then she gasped as he bit the nape of her neck with a growl.

Mine! Kain snarled to himself and licked his bite, then began moving down her spine with his lips and tongue. He knelt back from her as he came to her bottom and palmed the twin cheeks roughly. She had an amazing ass, plump and round, and she squeaked when he bent and bit a cheek with a deep growl.

She twisted to look back at him then and he gave her such a wicked look that her eyes widened. He gripped her hips and roughly jerked her up onto her knees, and before she could ask what he was up to, he spread her cheeks with his hands and pressed his face into her.

"Oh!" Her breath came out in a forceful exclamation as he thrust his tongue inside of her hot, wet core with a muffled groan. He began to work his tongue in and out of her rhythmically, gripping her ass firmly with his hands as he kept her opened wide to him. She mewled, pressing back against his tongue, and Kain growled in pleasure.

He took his time, savoring her taste, relishing her slightest reaction. He'd fantasized about doing this to her, had jerked off a few times thinking about it, and the reality of it made him painfully hard again. Relinquishing a cheek, he slid his hand up under her and found her clit. His fingers began stroking it in time with the thrusting and lapping of his tongue and she moaned loudly. Her sheath was silken against his tongue, sweet and divine as honey, and he let out a long groan of satisfaction. She was panting, her thighs trembling when he suddenly stopped and pulled away to Autumn's dismayed cry.

"You're not getting off that easily." He chuckled darkly. Autumn turned her head to look at him in distress. He patted her rump reassuringly and moved to kneel between her legs with a feral grin. He caressed her hips with his palms as he pressed the length of his erection to her wet mound with a growl.

Autumn's eyes fluttered down and she arched like a cat. "Oh yes, please." She whimpered, tossing her head and thrusting back against him. Kain growled in his throat, pleased by her begging.

"What was that?" he asked as he slid a hand under her to trace his fingers lazily against her labia. He brushed against her damp hairs teasingly while he ground himself lightly against her cleft again.

Autumn made a small sound of distress and squirmed as his fingers grazed too lightly over her clit.

"Kain, please," she begged with a toss of her head. Kain grinned at her words and withdrew his hand to grip her hips tightly as he pressed himself firmly into her.

"Please what?" he asked casually, grinding against her and she bucked, mewling in distress.

"Please, I need you!"

Oh yes, Kain growled with savage pleasure and took himself in hand, his cock twitching with impatience. "Autumn are you begging me to fuck you?" he asked with a rumble and rubbed the head of it against her wet folds. He was so aroused by her that he worried he might not have enough control to keep himself from coming at her words alone.

"Yes!" she wailed desperately.

Kain hissed with the need to be inside her. "Say it, Autumn," he growled deeply, finding her opening with his swollen glans and stilled himself there, inside of her with just the tip.

Autumn pressed back against him and tossed her head, looking back at him with her eyes full of pleading. "Please, Kain," she whimpered, "I need you. Please…" She swallowed, seemingly unwilling to say it, but her need finally won out over her pride.

"Please fuck me."

Kain drew in a deep breath at her words, at the look in her eyes, and something in him howled in triumph. He emitted a guttural oath and shoved into her roughly, filling her unmercifully and completely, and Autumn arched back with a cry. She gripped the sheets tightly as her inner muscles clenched around his size. He groaned and gripped her ass tightly with both hands as he withdrew and thrust into her again.

Kain had never been so full of need to fuck someone in his life. He was only vaguely aware that his wolf was in full participation with him, mounting her as well as they thrust again and again. He bent over her and reached forward to grab her mane, twisting it around his fist. Gently but firmly he pulled her head back and held her still while he drove into her from behind. Dominating her. Claiming her completely.

Autumn moaned and clawed at the bed like an animal as Kain pumped her hard. The headboard knocked against the wall in time with his powerful thrusts. His eyes burned with the change, and he growled in savage arousal as she bucked and cried out underneath him.

The change flowed over him uncontrollably and he didn't know if he was human or wolf as he mated with her. He felt burning in his appendages as his claws slid from his fingertips and his toes dug into the mattress with a faint ripping sound. His face pushed into a half muzzle full of sharp teeth while he rode her. His tail slid from his pelvis and black fur rippled down his back. He moaned softly, the change coursing over him with intense waves of pleasure. Autumn writhed and snarled under him, overtaken with the animal power that poured out of him and into her with his changes.

She gripped the sheets with a cry and her sheath pulsed around him, then she arched back and wailed out her orgasm as he continued to thrust into her. She was just coming down when she rose with another wave, howling and clawing like a wild beast.

Kain growled inhumanly and released her hair, then gripped her hips to pound into her deeply, quickly, frenzied and lost with his own need. Some small part of him desperately fought for control against the changes coursing over him, causing him to be stuck halfway between beast and man. He grunted like an animal as he moved with her, bent over and slavering with the need to bite her while she trembled and tightened around him with her orgasms. Her third one was more than he could take and he lunged for her shoulder. His teeth found their mark and sunk into her flesh. Her blood was like sugar on his tongue.

She cried out at his bite and Kain snarled, holding onto her with his teeth while he rode her. Finally he let her go, rearing back from her as he pounded against her with powerful thrusts. His own orgasm pulsed through him then and he fought hard against howling out with his wolf voice as he spilled into her and arched back, gripping her hips to his pelvis. The sound came out as a strangled moan to match her desperate panting cry. It lasted for several long moments, the intense release into her, and he almost swooned with it. He was beginning to come down when a surprising second orgasm rushed through him, as strong as the first, and Kain groaned in ecstasy.

Finally, slowly, they both came down from the intense fiery power that poured through both of them, panting and shuddering. When at last he swam out from the sparkling darkness of release, Kain realized he was still changed, bent over her and deep inside. And he was stuck. Literally stuck, his penis swollen inside of her in the way of wolves. His body still pulsed with pleasure and small changes while his form fought between the two states of wolf and man.

They both panted hard as Kain desperately wrestled with the wolf, unable to get control. He was exhausted from fighting the creature within and from the power of their mating. He needed to calm down, needed more time. He panicked slightly as she began to stir under him.

He reached out to her strongly with his powers, asserting his will as he bent to her ear and used his Compulsion to take control. "Don't turn around Autumn. Sleep. You are tired, you must sleep," he murmured around too-long teeth, doing all that he could to keep his voice human and the edge of panic from it. She made a small noise under him and he felt the power overcome her, lulling her as his voice mesmerized her senses.

Finally, he felt her relax completely, asleep under him as he struggled with the wolf inside. After a few moments bent over her prone form he finally felt the power seep away and out of him, taking the changes with it. He withdrew himself from her with a small tug and sat back on his knees, panting, his head bent as the last of the fur rippled back into his skin. He was finally spent and once more in control of his body.

However, he felt anything but in control as he looked up at Autumn's lovely form. Her hips and perfectly round ass jutted up at him invitingly, her shapely legs spread, and her fiery hair was tousled around her head as she slept peacefully. He had tied with her, like a wolf, and that certainly had never happened to him before. Not with his mistress, not with other female werewolves, not with any other woman. He had also bitten her on her shoulder, and though the wound wasn't that bad and only bled a little, it was a reminder. He had gotten out of control. He had hurt her. He trembled as he gently swung his legs over the bed and rose, attempting not to disturb her.

He went to the glass door of her bedroom and opened it softly. Rain still drizzled outside in the darkness as he stepped out into the chill air and closed the door gently behind him. He needed to run, and he needed to think.

The rain misted over him in a cold shower, clearing his head as he padded naked through her garden and out into the dark forest. He was treading on very dangerous ground here with Autumn. She had a power over him he didn't understand. A power over the wolf that he had never experienced before. The wolf wanted her in a way it had no other, not even his mistress, the one who had changed him those many years ago. No previous lover had ever affected him like this, and it scared him, deeply.

He should leave. He began to trot through the damp darkness. The cold rain washed down his skin and trickled through his hair, cooling his overheated body. He'd had his way, he should just leave while she was there sleeping. Things were too dangerous with the Spring Equinox a mere week away now and the Hunger so close…and the way she affected him. She so easily brought out the animal in him, and she made him want her with her barest glance, her smallest smile, her mere existence. He sighed and stopped, pressing his back up against a tree and lifted his face to the rain. Now that he had had her, he wanted more. It was not enough, this small taste of her. It was not nearly enough, and that was what scared him the most. He groaned out his frustration and pressed his hands to his face for a moment, then let his head fall to rake his hands through his wet mane.

I need to just go. End it now while she's sleeping. He turned and looked back toward her house in the darkness. *It'll be easy. Just go back there, get your shit, and get the fuck out of here. It'll be a clean break. You have to do it. You owe her that much.* He made up his mind as he began to lope his way back to the cottage. It would be better for both of them.

He entered through the door of the great room silently, tracking in rain that dripped from his naked body across the rug. He gathered his things quietly, and all the while, the wolf in him battled against his will. He stalked to the bathroom and used one of her towels to dry himself off, willing himself not to look at her, not to go to the bedroom to see her one last time. *I should at least cover her.* He found himself drifting down the hallway, drawn toward her. It was too cold tonight. She was only human, and she might catch a chill. He went to the darkened bedroom, scrubbing the towel through his unruly hair and stopped when he saw her. His night vision picked her out from the candlelit darkness perfectly.

She had rolled over, her body turned toward him and her face was peaceful in sleep. His body stirred in reaction, but it was his heart that leaped at the sight of her. He wanted to touch her, to cradle and hold her while she slept, to simply be near her. The reaction was completely unexpected, and warning bells went off in his head. His reason screamed at him to leave, but he was helpless against her. He drew closer to the bed until he was standing over her, griping the towel in his hands.

Leave her, he growled to himself, but he was riveted, trembling now with torment. He was well and thoroughly bewitched by her. A small, soft whine escaped his lips, his wolf rioting inside against him.

He sat gently on the edge of the bed and contemplated the towel in his hands as if it could tell him something. He had always had excellent control of himself and his wolf in the past. Perhaps...perhaps he just needed to keep an even tighter leash on himself, not get so carried away. He would leave, of that, there could be no argument, but he needn't rush right off, really. If he kept control, he could linger a little longer. One more day, and one more night with her. That was all he would allow himself. Perhaps then, he could sate his overwhelming hunger for her.

The wolf in him backed off at this and he breathed a sigh, closing his eyes in resignation. So be it, but losing control wasn't going to happen again. *You will watch and nothing more, wolf. If you so much as sniff her yourself we'll leave immediately, got it?* There was no response from his animal self at that and he shook his head slowly. What had he gotten himself into?

Autumn made a little noise in her sleep and he turned to her, a small smile curving his lips. She was so lovely, and now that he had allowed himself more time with her he felt the strong urge to hold her close. He pulled the duvet up and over them as he slid in next to her. Autumn stirred and mumbled and he smiled, pulling her close so that the lengths of their bodies were pressed together, face to face. She woke a little as he studied her face, tracing her features with his fingers, and she blinked at him sleepily.

"Where did you go?" she mumbled and he smiled softly at her.

"I took a shower," he said, trailing his fingers against her cheek and she closed her eyes with a small smile.

"Oh," was all she said, and she drifted into sleep again. A deep contentment stole over Kain and he laid his arm over her and twined his legs with hers. He kissed her forehead softly and buried his free hand in her hair with a deep sigh. He did not understand what was at work here, but she was still his…at least, for a little while longer.

CHAPTER ELEVEN
Revelations

Entwined in Kain's arms, Autumn dreamed.

She stood in the perpetual twilight of the deep forest, surrounded by the trunks of tall trees and gnarled roots, ferns, and undergrowth. The black wolf was there, his dense, dark coat grizzled and shaggy, his striking, otherworldly eyes intelligent and wild. He was not alone this time and he turned his head to another wolf that stepped out of the shadows.

She was massive for a female, not much taller than the black wolf but heavier. She was bigger than any dog Autumn had ever seen, and her short, thickly-furred ears sat atop a wide, massive head. Her jaws were heavier than the black wolf, and she was stocky, thicker in the shoulders, and shorter in the leg than he was. She was a powerful creature, made for subduing prey with sheer strength where the black was made for the long run, for wearing prey down. Her fur was a striking mix of cream and tan, her ears and hackles a lovely red-gold down her back. Her pale gold eyes burned with starlight as she stared into Autumn.

A thrill stole through her as she stared into the wolf's dark-rimmed, enigmatic eyes and the black wolf turned his azure gaze to Autumn again as well. There was communication, wordless, yet she felt it all through her body. It is time.

The she wolf stepped toward her, eyes intent, her head lowered. Autumn trembled with trepidation, yet she took a step toward the large creature, inexorably drawn. The wolf was a beautiful beast, her movements graceful for a creature her size, and fear seeped away from Autumn as she approached her. She stopped just short of the wolf and a sensation passed through her, raising all the hairs on her body. Kismet. Fate, as if she was always meant to be here, as if this was always meant to happen. The dream seemed so real, the wolf vivid and tangible before her, and she trembled again with anticipation.

The wolf pulled her lips back from her massive teeth and bunched her muscles, and as she sprang Autumn opened her arms to welcome the wolf at last.

Soft morning light was just beginning to suffuse the world with pale hues, dimly lighting the forest outside the glass doors of Autumn's bedroom when Kain awoke slowly. He cracked open his eyes and breathed deeply into her hair, smiling to himself as her scent filled him. He was holding her, spooning her naked form closely from behind, his arms wrapped possessively around her. He felt wonderfully sated for the moment, sleepy and spent.

He had made good on his promise to her, taking her again several times during that night, riding her hard and fast, capturing her cries of passion in his mouth. He had scrounged in her kitchen and brought back cheese and fruit, feeding her and building up her strength before he took her again. She was as insatiable as he was, yet she was only human, and he had wrung the final, twelfth orgasm from her exhausted body with his hands. They had both finally fallen into a blissfully sated sleep only a few hours ago.

He was gloriously content and sleepy, her naked body warm in his arms. So, what had awakened him? A small sensation tickled his senses, like someone running their fingers delicately along his spine. Suddenly alert, he looked up and out into the still shadowy forest, tuning his senses to the wards he had placed around her property.

Something had tripped them. Something had intruded, and the feel of it set all of his hairs on end. Something was very wrong.

He quietly slipped from the bed, careful to not wake Autumn, and moved on silent bare feet into the great room. He paused to look out the doors, still not seeing anything in the dim morning light, but all of his hackles were on end. He quietly opened the door and slipped out onto the porch with his senses attuned sharply to the world. He smelled the air and caught nothing but the usual scents of her home, but the wolf in him was tingling up his spine. A low growl rumbled in his throat.

Sure that Autumn was sleeping, all of his awareness focused on the beacon calling to him, he trotted off into the woods.

Autumn woke with a small jerk and a soft gasp and raised her head to blink at the pale light outside. Kain was no longer holding her, and she looked around, sensing something was amiss. A moment later, she heard the door in the great room open and a breath of cool air stole through the house. She sat up and looked about sleepily. It was really early. *Why isn't he still in bed?* she worried, coming to full wakefulness. *Is he leaving already?* She climbed out of bed and quietly went to see what he was up to.

She saw him on the back porch, staring off into the woods, deliciously nude. He was breathtaking to behold, and she quietly admired the view of his naked body for a moment. She recalled bits of last night with a tight tingle in her belly and a blush. With Kain, she had done things and acted in a way that she never had with anyone else. He made her wanton, called to some wild part of her she only vaguely knew of and didn't understand at all. With him, all her inhibitions went right out the window.

They hadn't even used protection, she recalled with a small frown. A reckless choice she should be horrified about, yet she felt oddly detached about it. She should be furious that he hadn't used a condom, but she couldn't be angry with him when she hadn't stopped him either. She'd been far too hungry for him, and the feel of him naked and raw inside of her had been unbelievable… besides, she'd been on the pill since she was seventeen. She wouldn't worry too much about it. What was done was done, so she might as well enjoy it now.

She was exhausted and ached all over with a delicious soreness. She would have some bruises from their rough play, but she wasn't ashamed. She would happily do it all again, especially if he would just come back to bed. She was about to call to him but something made her stop, and she watched him in silence.

He seemed very intent, almost unnaturally still in the morning quiet, and stared alertly out into the forest. She was starting to wonder if something was wrong when suddenly he leaped off the porch and went jogging into the woods, barefoot and buck-naked. What the hell? Why was he gallivanting off into the damned trees instead of staying in bed with her?

Insanely curious, and a touch concerned, she dashed into her bedroom and hastily threw on sweat pants and a sweatshirt. Slipping on a pair of tennis shoes, she ran out the door after him.

Kain trotted through the morning mist with a sense of foreboding. He had set his wards so that animals would not trigger them, but anything else would. She lived in a remote area, and nothing should have activated his mystical perimeter, but his senses were on high alert and the wolf's instincts warned of danger.

He leaped up onto a fallen long and crouched there, sniffing the air intently. The air was still; dampened with mist and fog from last night's storm and the scents were many and tangled. Yet the faint trace of blood was on the air, oozing through the sword ferns like the mist. Snarling, he leaped off the log and ran in a slight crouch, low to the ground, keeping the scent in his nostrils.

Finding the source of the scent was not hard at all, and when he came upon it, the sight brought him to a dead stop.

Autumn watched Kain from as close as she dared, running lightly after him, ducking and hiding when he stopped. He seemed like he was on a mission of some sort, and she was keenly curious and altogether baffled at the same time.

He leaped up on a log with the grace of a wild animal, and she stared in fascination with a tingling at the back of her neck as he sniffed at the air. What in the world was he doing? After a moment, he leaped off the log and started running, hunched over and low to the ground. She was truly concerned now.

She followed as silently as possible, which was easy thanks to the now damp, spongy soil of the forest. Thank goodness she ran several times a week. She'd surely give herself away with panting or tripping over something by now if she hadn't kept in shape, and she could also kind of keep up with him. He was so damned fast!

He stopped again and stood tall, still as a statue, and Autumn took cover behind an old tree stump where she crouched down and watched.

Rage and shock boiled inside of Kain at the sight before him. It was a dog. Or at least parts of one. The big canine had been torn apart, its body ripped in half and strewn across the ground. Its entrails and organs were scattered about, its blood and offal a dark stain on the earth around its remains. Its head was speared prominently above the carnage on a jutting branch of a fallen log. A grisly scene, but that was not what made the beast in Kain rise now. The dog's jaws had been propped open, its face frozen in a snarl of death, and in its teeth was a small picture of Autumn.

Kain approached, trembling as horrified rage surged through his body, jolting through him like cold spears as he pulled the photo from its jaws. It was a recent shot taken from perhaps a few yards away from her. She was wearing the same outfit she had when they had taken their walk that day in the redwoods, not two days ago. She was at her shop, her head turned as if speaking to someone, smiling kindly.

Kain looked around sharply, his lips rising off his teeth as he crumpled the photo in his hand. Only then did he see the message left for him. There, on the ground, its pale loops of intestines had been arranged to form a word: "HER." Kain stared at the message, his blood roaring in his head. The area reeked of the dead dog's blood and offal, but even more potent was the shit the killer had left among the entrails. There was no other scent like that.

It was an *Eater*. And it wanted him to know it was after Autumn.

Autumn crept forward a little closer. Kain appeared to have found whatever had interested him. He seemed transfixed, and stiff as if frozen. Something in Autumn caused her to stop then, some sort of instinct she couldn't name, and a crawling sense of danger raised the fine hairs on her scalp and arms.

Leave now, a voice whispered in her. *Run. Get back to the house.* But she stayed where she was. She was concerned for Kain and wanted desperately to know what had him so transfixed. Suddenly the uneasy feeling mounted and became an overwhelming urge to flee, shooting up her spine and pounding in her head with the message *RUN!*, but she found herself rooted in place, staring wide-eyed as Kain began to…change.

It all happened very quickly, but for Autumn time seemed to slow down as he began to transform. He suddenly grew in all directions, becoming taller, wider, thicker. His sleek muscles bunched and bulked out, his feet and legs growing, stretching, elongating, his heels jutting up and back, a pink snake slithering out of his sacrum, all so quickly it was difficult to follow. As he grew his skin darkened, and then a wave of black fur exploded all over him, covering him in seconds while his body continued the transformation.

Autumn was rooted to the ground, gaping with mind-numbing fear, unable to do anything but shake uncontrollably.

Her breath came in tiny gasps, and she stared in horror at the thing that now stood where Kain had been a moment ago. The thing he had become. A loud rumble came from the Kain-thing, and it was so deep and primal that it shook her bones and flashed white-hot terror through her.

Suddenly it stepped back and flung its head up in the air, ape-like arms swung wide, and a sound blasted from it that filled the world so loudly it stung Autumn's ears. It was an inhuman scream that drew out into a roaring howl, shaking the ground with its intensity. Autumn sobbed, and the roar abruptly ended as it snapped its massive head around to look directly at her, unholy ice blue eyes ablaze.

Cold terror flashed through Autumn like an icy dagger and, crying in fear, she bolted. She ran blindly and clumsily, crashing through the forest to save her life. Quickly she was bowled over and brought to the ground with a scream under the weight and heat and intense musk of the thing, and she thought herself a heartbeat from death.

Instead, she was picked up and the world zipped past while she tried to breathe around sheer panic, caught in bands of steel and black fur, incredible heat, and wild musk. *Ohgodohgodohgod,* she panicked inside of her head, sure that any second now she was going to be torn apart by teeth and claws. But instead of a grisly end, they were back at the cottage before her brain could catch up and she was being set gently on her carpet inside. Then the monster stepped away from her and prowled back to the sliding glass door.

She scrambled away as quickly as her trembling limbs would take her, panting and whimpering, and came up against the couch. She huddled there, staring with fear-wide eyes as the black beast closed the doors and locked them. Growing smaller and pinker by the moment he turned with a snarl and slapped a paw/hand on her kitchen counter, leaving something there, then strode to the bedroom. When he emerged again some moments later, he was once more Kain, though his eyes were still that of the beast…the werewolf.

He didn't spare a glance for her cowering form as he went through the house, locking doors and windows, double-checking that they were secure before he picked up his pack and strode into the kitchen where he tossed it angrily on the counter.

"Why did you follow me? Why did you have to fucking follow me?" he snarled at her and began rummaging through her spice cabinet and started tossing bottles of herbs and spices onto the counter.

Autumn was still in the tight grip of fear, staring at him wide-eyed, wanting to run, afraid to look away. An answer was impossible.

"Goddammit, a fucking Eater!" He laughed harshly, pawing through his pack until he came up with a small mortar and pestle that he slammed down next to the jars. "How could I be so fucking careless?"

He continued to mutter to himself and withdrew a few more items from the pack, then began sorting and sifting bits of spice and herb into the mortar. He uncorked a few glass vials from his own supply and tossed in unidentifiable bits of this and that. Autumn crept up backward onto the couch, making a ball of herself in the corner; sure he would kill her at any moment.

He turned his head to her as he began grinding the mixture together with the pestle. His features were now mostly human but his still too-bright eyes pinned her against the couch. "I'm the least of your worries now. I want you to listen to me and listen carefully. Your life depends on it. Are you listening?"

Autumn only stared at him wide-eyed and managed the smallest of nods.

"Good. There is something hunting you, and it isn't me. I don't know why it wants you, but it wants you, Autumn. It left a pretty fucking clear message for me out there," he said, and tossed what looked like a crumpled photograph in her direction.

It landed on the carpet near her. Despite her fear, she reached out trembling fingers for it and unfolded it.

She stared at the photo, uncomprehending as he continued. "This...thing can assume the shape of any living thing close to its size, but that is not its true form. It can come at you as your neighbor, your best friend, a dog...it can mimic these things precisely. You will never see it coming. Trust no one," he emphasized, and she looked up and met his gaze with fear-wide eyes. "Understand? Trust no one!"

He turned back to the pestle and added a stream of liquid from one of his vials. "In a moment you are going to run from here and keep running. I am going to try to distract it and disable it enough to allow you to escape, but this thing is damned near impossible to stop. It will come for you and keep coming until I can kill it. If I can kill it. Until then you keep running, do you hear? Do not call your friends, do not call the police. This thing is incredibly clever and will know you will try to find a safe haven. Don't. Just keep running until I catch up to you."

She stared stupidly at him in near panic, pretty sure she was starting to hyperventilate. *I'm dreaming. I've got to be dreaming. All those nights of nightmares and dreams about wolves have caught up to me and I'm having a doozy now. Maybe I got drunk, or stoned, or hit my head or something and I'm imagining all of this.* Yet details of the room were painfully clear to her, and she felt perfectly awake.

She gasped as Kain grabbed a knife from his pack and without blinking, sliced his palm. Muttering softly he let his blood fall into the mortar, then finished mixing the concoction. Autumn shrank even farther into herself and watched with wide eyes while he lifted his hand and long, black claws pushed from his nail beds. He dipped one talon into the mixture, then murmuring what sounded like growls and snarls, he closed his eyes and began scratching precise symbols into his chest.

Autumn stared at him, horrified, as blood welled from his cuts and blackened with the mixture. He was insane. He was a werewolf. She must be the one who was insane. She felt a hysterical giggle rise up in her throat, watching him do whatever it was he was doing, but it froze within her as new terror stole through her.

Something was watching her from the porch.

Shaking from terror, her breath coming in painful gasps, she slowly turned her head to look at it. It almost defied description save that it was tall, and black, and seemed to be made up of teeth and talons, spindly arms and legs, and two tiny, glowing eyes. It looked nothing like any animal or creature she had ever seen, and a high scream tore its way out of her throat.

Kain's eyes flew open to see the Eater on her porch, looking directly at Autumn. Quickly he roared out the last of the incantation and smeared the rest of the potion on his chest. He felt the symbols scratched into his skin burn with icy fire as the spell flared into life. He leaped the counter, then, and called forth his beast. His change came on powerfully like lightning, fueled by his need to protect her. He turned to Autumn who was still screaming, bunched up into a ball of terror against the couch.

"Autumn, *run!*" he roared and the change ripped over him, through him, the sigils burning in his skin. Bunching his powerful muscles he crashed through her window and into the Eater eagerly awaiting him with open jaws.

PART TWO
HUNTED

CHAPTER TWELVE
The Devil You Know

Autumn ran, terror fueling her flight as she bolted for the front door, the deafening sounds of inhuman battle lending speed to her legs. She managed to grab her keys from the bowl near the door and flung it open, sprinting, and nearly falling in her haste to get to her car. She whimpered, fumbling at her lock while unnatural roars, screams, howls, and shrieks tore through the normally quiet forest around her. The ground shook for a moment with a sound like trees being ripped from the earth and she sobbed as she flung her door open and managed to get in, her hands trembling as she started the vehicle.

She didn't look to see what was happening as she hit the gas. Gravel spat out from her tires and she drove as fast as possible, sure that at any moment one hideous thing or another was going jump in front of her car. She careened along her drive and crossed her bridge, then hit the Avenue of Giants with a squeal of sliding tires, almost losing control of the vehicle, and stomped on the gas. She was in a blind panic, not knowing or caring where she was going as long as it was away from her home.

She sobbed as she made it into town, and thought briefly about running to the safety of her shop where Tanya would be working. But what if the Kain-monster couldn't defeat that other nightmare? And if it was indeed after her, then she'd be putting her friends in danger. Wouldn't it still come after her no matter where she went? If this was all really happening, she couldn't put her friends, or anyone else, in danger. She simply didn't know what else to do.

She turned at the last moment and sped onto the onramp for 101 westbound toward Eureka. *Autumn you need to wake up very soon,* she whimpered, wiping tears from her eyes, and gripping the steering wheel with white knuckles she raced away from her home.

Kain ripped into the Eater, fueled by a furious need to protect Autumn. They rolled through her garden, slashing at one another with wicked claws, and tore each other's flesh with their fangs and powerful bites. The Eater was stronger than he was, however, and it was lightning fast. It also healed so quickly that Kain's brutal lashes with claws and teeth did little to slow it down, so he drove at it with his fury instead, not giving it an inch as he kept attacking. He could feel the marks he had made burning on his chest under the fur, and every time the Eater struck him, it roared with pain. The spell would reflect any of his pain back onto the attacker twofold, and it was the barest edge against the thing he could manage. It would cost him later. Such magic always had a price.

The Eater roared as Kain managed to get his fangs around something solid, it's deceptively slender arm. He bit down and wrenched his head sharply to the side. He tasted its rancid blood in his mouth and he almost gagged, but continued tearing the flesh in his jaws. The Eater roared and managed to get its hind legs between itself and Kain, and with a mighty kick sent Kain flying into a tree with a crunch, leaving long tears down his belly. It was on him again in an instant. An unnatural laughing noise escaped its throat as it bore down on him, ripping at him with its talons even as it screamed in agony from the spell. Kain snarled and sank his claws into it, forcing himself to move, to roll the thing under him, biting at anything he could get his teeth on.

They tussled again on the ground, tearing up great gouts of earth as they roared and bit and slashed at one another. Blood and spittle and fur flew, and Kain was starting to take more punishment than even his strong, resilient beast body could endure. The Eater was healing lightning fast and kept on coming at him. Its strength, speed, and stamina were beyond anything Kain had encountered before, and even with his spell he knew he was outmatched.

He needed a different tactic.

Calling up his reserves of strength, he got his legs under him and leaped away. On all fours he ran for all he was worth into the forest, trusting that the Eater was so enraged it would come after him. He could feel it right on his tail and gaining. He snarled, pushing himself to run as fast as he ever had before. It was not easy in this forest, thick as it was, and they bounded and leaped, ducked and wove around fallen trees and thick tangles of branches and brush. It stayed right on his tail, never wavering, and he felt its fetid breath on his haunches. *Just a little farther,* he panted, his paws flying over the ground. *Just a little farther, close now.*

He caught a glimpse of her cottage through the trees and he banked hard toward the right, where he had seen something before on his patrols of her property, something that might help him. His turn was all the Eater needed, though, and it reached out a long arm and swiped his back legs out from under him. Kain flipped and tumbled end over end and smashed into a redwood, white-hot pain searing through him as he yelped aloud. The Eater was on him in an instant, cackling maniacally again as it thrust all of its talons into his belly and tore him open. Kain screamed and swiped at it with his claws, but the creature simply caught his arm and deftly broke it at the elbow, then dealt him a blow across his face with a crunch of bone. Kain howled in pain and the creature perched on top of him shriek-howled mockingly, seemingly ignoring not only its own pain but also the pain caused by the spell. It cackled breathlessly as it looked down at him. Its beady, white eyes were mad and piercing.

"Mine-mine-mine-mine," it seemed to say, chattering its needle teeth at him. "Run-run, she cannot run. Mine-mine, mine to eat!" It laughed, swiping its teeth with a long tongue.

Kain was dizzy with pain. One eye was bloodied and useless from the blow to his face. His arm was broken, his belly was ripped open, and one of his legs was numb at the hip. He was simply injured in too many ways. He let his head fall to the side, his breath coming sharp and labored. He couldn't let this thing kill her. Not her. He had to do something.

Something glittered near him in the dark forest soil like a beacon and he focused his good eye on it. It was the handle of a butter knife. He thanked the moon and all the powers of creation for the gift. It had been what he was aiming for, and somehow, he had managed to crash into the very tree he had seen it in.

With a roar of fury, Kain swiped up the knife, and using all of his faltering strength, he jammed the blade deep into the creature's eye. There was the strong scent of ozone and the Eater reared back, shrieking in pain, scrabbling at its face with its claws. It stumbled away from him, screaming inhumanly as it writhed and tore at its face. It shook its head furiously, then snapped its ruined gaze to him and screamed out a deafening roar of rage. Then, with an anguished howl, it dashed swiftly away into the forest and disappeared.

Kain panted as he watched the creature flee, then rolled clumsily to his side and into a sitting position. He should go after it, but although his body was healing, he had taken a great deal of damage and pursuit wasn't an option. He snarled and heaved himself to his hind feet in a haze of pain. Holding his innards in with his unbroken arm, the other hanging limply to the side, he began making his way back to her house. He needed to heal, right now. He needed to find Autumn before the Eater could recover and resume its hunt.

He stumbled through the wreckage of her once beautiful garden and up onto her porch where glass and wood from her doors was scattered about. Growling, he ignored the glass and limped into her house, dripping blood, and went to the kitchen where his pack still lay on the counter. It was difficult to manipulate with one large, clawed hand, but he finally managed to find the vial he was looking for inside of his pack. He regarded the contents with his good eye, panting around his pain.

It was about two ounces of nondescript, clear liquid. It was a potion, costly and time consuming to make, but damned handy for when he needed to heal fast. He was just glad that he had some of it left. Unscrewing the cap was the biggest challenge, but with some pained and annoyed snarling, he gently used his claws and teeth to remove it. Once open, he downed the entire contents in one gulp.

Power, intoxicating in its strength, flowed up from the earth and into him, bright and searing with the pain of sudden and fast healing. He roared in agony and smashed back against her refrigerator, sending magnets and notes scattering. He crumpled to her kitchen floor, holding onto himself as his body healed rapidly and began shifting him back into his human form. The forced shift was a side effect of the potion, and though at times unwelcome, it was one he would gladly take right now.

Once it was over, he lay naked and spent for a moment, his mind churning as he gathered his strength. He needed to find Autumn. But first, he needed to wash the stink of the Eater off him.

He showered quickly, scrubbing himself as thoroughly as possible to get the all the blood and filth off. Where had she run to? He could track the scent of her vehicle only so far, but it would be lost once she hit the main roads, especially if she had gotten on 101. How would he track her then? He scrubbed shampoo through his tangled hair, worrying, when suddenly a gentle sensation came to him. He closed his eyes and felt for it. A direction, a beacon, somewhere north and west of here, calling him softly. He stopped, going still as a stone, his eyes opening wide as a flutter of realization tingled in his stomach. Impossible.

Quickly he finished cleaning his hair and, not even bothering to grab a towel, turned off the water and hurried from the bathroom to her bedroom. The bed was unmade, rumpled from last night and reeking of them both. He crawled over the bed, sniffing it deeply, running the scents across the back of his tongue as he moved. Desire flooded him at the richness of her scent, at the smell of their lovemaking, and there, just a speck or two of her blood on the sheets. He had bitten her, he recalled, and his heart leapt. Last night in the throes of intense passion, he had bitten her with wolf teeth. Enough to draw some blood. It wouldn't change her, as that was a different and very special kind of bite, but this…this was something else.

His eyes widened as the implications of the bite hit him. Impossible. Or was it? He bent and breathed her scent deeply from where she had been sleeping. Too tangled with his scent to tell, but his pulse quickened, regardless. He needed to know. He had to find her. Now.

Urgently he went to his pack and pulled on some clothes over his still damp body, then stuffed his feet into his boots. Grabbing his things, he hurried to the Camaro and tossed everything onto the seat next to him, then he started the car with a roar. He would follow her beacon and find her, and then he would know. His stomach trembling, he backed out and tore out of her driveway and down the road leading to the pavement, hot on her trail.

Rational thought began creeping in again as Autumn neared Eureka. She was still terrified but she was beginning to think clearly again, and she ran the events over in her head as reality unfolded around her. It was a beautiful morning, the world rain-washed and clear in the watercolor light of dawn. Rising fog snaked through the tops of the trees, breaking up here and there to show a glimpse of crystal blue sky beyond. Everything had that familiar, wonderful scent of damp forest and earth, and all of it was so vivid and real that there was no way she was dreaming, or had been.

That had really just happened, all of it, and she was now on the run from something she didn't at all understand, but knew she had seen. And the man she was pretty sure she had been falling in love with was a werewolf. A goddamned honest-to-God werewolf! She trembled and sobbed a little, her eyes blurring with tears as the reality of it hit home. What was she going to do now? She had not grabbed her purse or cell phone when she ran blindly from her home, and all she was wearing was just a sweatshirt, sweatpants, and tennis shoes. No underwear, no bra, no socks, no change of clothes or toiletries. No purse, which meant no credit cards or cash. Even though her Subaru was fairly economical and had 3/4 of a full tank, she would eventually run out of gas if she kept running. And if she was going to run, where was she going to run to?

Trembling with adrenaline she slowed as she came into town, her hands gripping her steering wheel as her mind raced. She should find a police officer and…tell him what, exactly? That a creature out of some horror movie was chasing her, and that her lover was a werewolf? Right, and she would end up in jail or a psych ward. But at least she would be safe…unless this creature that Kain had said could assume the form of anyone came for her, disguised as an officer or nurse. Then she would be dead for sure, torn apart by its wicked talons.

But what if Kain had been lying about it being after her? She breathed deeply, attempting to calm herself as the light changed to green and she mechanically kept driving. Perhaps, but what reason would he have to lie? She had just watched him turn into a fucking monster. What did he have to gain by lying to her about the motives of a terrible creature she had seen standing on her porch with her own two eyes? Unless he wanted her for himself, to kill as he pleased?

She shuddered and uttered a little sob, wiping at her tears. What if it were true? He had been a werewolf all along, after all. Suppose he just wanted to fuck with her head, then fuck her literally before eating her? Who knew what his real motives were? Just what did she really know about who he was anyway? Ohhh, she was in a world of trouble, either way she looked at it. He told her he would find her. And what then? Would he enjoy the chase before the kill?

She almost rear-ended someone stopped at a light and she slammed on her breaks, just avoiding hitting them. Shaking, her heart racing, she pulled off the road into the parking lot of a bank and parked. She needed to calm down and think. She let herself breathe, staring blankly out her windshield at the morning traffic as she followed her breath in and out. When her heart rate slowed again, she thought about her situation with a clearer head. She recalled the photograph. Why would he suddenly have a photograph of her? Where did he get it from? He had tossed it at her when he told her that this…thing was after her. It had been a recent photo of her in the shop, taken at a time when she knew for a fact he hadn't been there. And there had been blood on it. She shuddered, staring out her windshield at familiar sights. Traffic, people going into the bank, a bicyclist pedaling past. A normal day for the rest of the world.

She gulped in a breath, let it out again, her mind in a whirl. She needed to find a pay phone, if such things existed any more. She needed to call someone, anyone, because she needed help and didn't know what to do. She needed to talk to Cleo.

Not knowing what else to do she got back on the road and drove on, searching as best she could for anything that looked like a pay phone. Such things had become obsolete, however, and she couldn't seem to find one. She was just about ready to find a random stranger and ask to use their cell phone when she came across an abandoned gas station on the north end of town. It was tucked back among some trees and overgrown with weeds, but there was a pay phone. She had no idea if the thing would even still work, but she had to try it. Pulling into the lot, she parked her car and got out. Looking cautiously around her, she approached the old pay phone.

Hands trembling, she picked up the receiver and was amazed and relieved to hear a dial tone. "Oh thank God," she whispered, but then realized she had no change. She ran back to her car and rifled around inside of it for a few moments, coming up with a small handful of change. She had no idea what pay phones cost, but she would sell her soul to the devil to be able to make a call. Running back to the pay phone she readied her change, her fingers hovering over the number keys and her mind completely drew a blank. For the life of her, she couldn't recall Cleo's number.

Oh, you have got to be kidding me. She searched her memory for the number. But these days who ever remembered anyone's number anymore? You simply tapped on a name in your cell phone and the phone dialed it for you. Add that to the fact that she was still strung out on fear and adrenaline, and recalling the number became impossible. But she desperately needed to talk to Cleo, to figure out what she should do!

Perhaps they still have directory assistance or something, she thought, looking the pay phone over. The phone book was long gone, and the cable it had been on dangled under the phone box uselessly. She bit her lip, looking around for any labels or signs to help her but those too were worn off. Why the hell is this thing even fucking still working? She slammed the receiver back on its cradle.

Well, then call the shop, dummy. She groaned. She knew *that* number well enough. She would have Tanya get Cleo's number for her. She had just picked up the receiver again when the sound of squealing tires and a rumbling engine entering the lot caused her to go pale. She turned around, and her trembling hands dropped the phone as the Camaro slammed to a stop next to her car. Kain rose out of it and stormed toward her, advancing quickly, his face a thundercloud.

Monster, and a pissed off one at that! She backed away along the boarded up frontage of the station, her eyes darting and heart pounding, looking for a way to escape. But there was nowhere to run and she knew she couldn't out run him. She just hoped she could struggle enough so someone passing by might be alerted before he could kill her.

Kain slowed as he came nearer, his head lowered, stalking her. Fear. He smelled it in the air strongly and she backed away from him with wild eyes full of terror. He had driven like a mad man toward her beacon, breaking every law there was to get to her. Luck was again on his side and he had met no police, no accident in his flight, and only managed to piss off a lot of drivers. She was here, unharmed yet terrified of him. He needed to touch her desperately.

"S-stay away from me," she stammered out, putting a hand out in front of her as she continued to back away. His lips rose off his teeth in a predatory smile as he continued to stalk her, backing her up into a corner.

"Don't run from me, Autumn," he growled, and her eyes widened as she bumped up against the wall. Realizing he had her cornered, she made to bolt, but he moved in fast, boxing her in with his arms braced on the walls to either side of her. He snarled a warning in his throat. She was panicked; her eyes wide, her breath hard and fast with her hands up between them. She stank of fear, emanating it like a fog, but he needed to know if what he suspected was true.

He leaned closer to her and she whimpered, shrinking away as much as possible. He breathed her in deeply, sniffing close to her face and hair, scenting for confirmation. He caught it, and his heart leaped in his chest. Oh Christ, it was true! He closed his eyes and dropped his head down, unable to breathe for a moment with the realization. She smelled of him of course, practically reeked of the scent of their lovemaking last night, but what he smelled on her now was something different.

Her scent had changed fundamentally and now mixed with his own to create a new fragrance any werewolf would know and understand. He had marked her last night. His wolf had claimed her as their own. The bite he had left on her would be like a sign to all others, and it had joined them partially in a mate bond.

But such a thing wasn't possible with a human. He lifted his head to look at her. He had never heard of it before, and in fact, knew it should not be possible. It only happened between two werewolves, and rarely at that. Yet here it was, unmistakable, and he knew Autumn was human. She bore no other scent.

Oh what have you done, wolf? He was both dismayed and awed at the same time as she cowered against the wall. She was terrified of him and it gutted him right to his core. He needed to feel her and know she was safe. He needed to touch her and breathe deeply of her changed scent that marked her as his. He leaned forward and dropped a hand to grasp her arm gently and she flinched, turning her face away from him with a whimper.

"I promise you, Autumn, I won't hurt you. I will never hurt you," he said softly, gently, and lifted his fingers to brush them against her tear-stained face. She flinched again, but after a moment her eyes found him, regarding him warily.

"I promise," he said, trailing his hand to her shoulder to caress her reassuringly.

"H-how," she squeaked out, "How do I know you aren't th-that…thing? Y-you said it could be anyone…" Her eyes grew large and he smiled. *Good girl, using your head.* A strong surge of protectiveness and possession came over him then and he stared into her wide, fearful eyes.

He gripped her shoulders so she couldn't escape and bent his head, crushing his mouth to hers with a sharp intake of breath. His heart soared with her new scent in his nose. She resisted, stiffening against him in distress. He growled against her mouth and wrapped his arms around her, holding her tightly to him, kissing her deeply.

She fought him, resisting, her fisted hands up between them while she pulled her head as far back away from him as she could get. He howled inside at her resistance, agonized by it, nearly unable to bear it when suddenly she yielded the tiniest bit by softening in his arms and turning her head slightly to his. Relief flooded him and he smiled against her lips. It was a small victory, but it was enough.

Autumn resisted him with all of her might, terrified, recalling the beast he had changed into before her eyes not once, but twice. *Monster! Demon!* her mind screamed and she struggled, resisting his kiss. But then his taste was in her mouth, so familiar by now, and his scent was in her nose and memories of last night flooded her and she felt her treacherous body soften. Fear began turning slowly to yearning, caution to need.

Thankfully, he chose that moment to pull his lips away from hers and drew his head back with a shaky little breath, then eased his tight hold of her to stroke her hair.

"That is how you will always know me," he said roughly, staring into her eyes for a long moment. She stared back at him, trembling with a mixture of fear and yearning.

His eyes searched hers as he continued to stroke her soothingly. "Trust me that I mean you no harm, Autumn. Yes I am a...werewolf." He smiled ruefully, darkly, "But I have no desire to hurt you, only to keep you safe. You have my word on that. Do you trust me?"

She stared up at him with her heart thundering, and her body shaking with too much adrenaline and fear. Did she trust him? Was he kidding? But what real choice did she have? She had no idea what else to do or where to go. He obviously knew about this thing, knew what it was capable of, and he apparently knew how to sense it. She was running blind, without so much as a weapon or anyone to rely on. She knew now that contacting Cleo or anyone else was out of the question. She could not put anyone in danger from the thing that was after her, or from the man, the beast, that held her now.

She nodded slowly up at him and he smiled at her gently, leaning to place a kiss on the top of her head before pulling her close.

"I will keep you safe, I promise," he murmured into her hair and she gave one last violent tremble then stilled, softening against him with a sigh.

Better the devil you know than the one you don't.

CHAPTER THIRTEEN
On The Road

They drove east on 299, headed toward Redding in a stolen car. He had left her Subaru there at the gas station. The police would be quick to respond to an APB on her car once it was discovered she was missing, and better they find it in Eureka where it would be impounded safely. He needed to make their trail hard to follow, and to do that he needed to ditch the Camaro. Pity, because he had gotten pretty attached to the dark, growly machine. It suited him well.

They drove now in an inconspicuous gray Toyota Camry that had been conveniently parked out in the back of a small cluster of businesses in Arcata. Stealing the older vehicle had been easy, and Kain hadn't had a choice but to leave the Camaro parked out in the business lot to be discovered.

Before they had left the station, he had done something he'd never done before. He'd taken his fanged talisman from around his neck and put it over hers, growling out words of power as he did so. She'd stared at him, then lifted the fang to look at it.

"Don't take it off," he growled, "It will keep you hidden. Safe."

She'd looked skeptical for a moment but then nodded her assent, and he'd felt marginally better. He had no idea what the talisman would do for her, really, since he couldn't properly attune it to her, but he knew it made her feel safer. And seeing something so personal of his falling between the swell of her breasts made him growl with possession. It was another reminder of his mark on her. He prayed it would keep her safe.

They drove toward Reno, cutting across country on back roads until they could get out of California. He knew the moment they had left the abandoned station where they were headed. He needed to keep Autumn safe and figure out what was going on, and to do that he needed to call on an old friend. So he headed east, toward the desert, his mouth set in a grim line. It would be a long drive, and he would have to play it cool with the stolen car, but he would get them there as quickly as possible.

Time was beginning to run out for him. The Spring Equinox now less than a week away, and he would have to make a human kill. He could feel the Hunger there under the surface, crawling like a junkie's need for his next hit. He could hold it off a few days more, but it would soon become too demanding to ignore. And if he did not make a kill, the price he would have to pay for it would be more than he could withstand. No, he would have her safe by then and he could hunt as he needed. He would do what he had to, he would sate the Hunger, and then he would return to her. After that, he would figure out what to do about their situation.

They continued in silence and Kain kept his eyes on the road, trying not to look at her. She was huddled in the passenger seat with her knees drawn up to her chest and her arms wrapped around them. She was turned away from him and facing the window. He gripped the steering wheel to keep from reaching out to her in his need to touch her. She needed space. She had gone along with him only because she didn't know what else to do and he knew it. He understood it. But her distance from him now was like a blade through the center of him, bitter and biting. And it pissed him off.

He brooded as he drove, still unable to believe this turn of events. In a matter of days, his simple life had all of a sudden gone to hell. He hadn't needed any of this. He had just been looking for a little fun and a lot of sex, but instead he had been blown away by a girl he would never have seriously considered bedding before. She did things to him that he simply could not understand and had never dealt with. She was bewitching with her innocence, beguiling with her smallest smile. She made him weak in the knees, for fuck's sake, and *that* certainly never happened to Kain Ulmer.

He cursed his wolf internally again and breathed deeply, taking in her new scent that made something in his stomach tremble. Why her? And goddammit *how*? It wasn't possible. He searched his memory, digging up what he knew of the mate bond.

Alessia had taught him of it once. He had wanted to make her his mate those many long years ago and hadn't understood why he couldn't. He recalled her words clearly.

"Silly boy, the human part of you does not choose your mate, if you are so lucky to have such a thing happen," she had chided, lazily running her fingers over his naked body. "It is the beasts who choose. Wolf to wolf, they know one another, they choose one another. You cannot make such a thing happen."

He had stared at her in fascination, her exotic eyes far away with some memory. "Wolf to wolf," he said, turning her face to his. "So we cannot choose whom we mate with. And never with humans?" he'd asked and she had stretched herself on top of him, her seductive eyes glowing.

"No," she said, her eyes moving over his face lazily. "A wolf cannot mate with a human. They are too weak, their spirits too fragile. We use them for our pleasures, for our prey, but never take them as mates. Wolf to wolf, beast to beast. It is the only way the bond ever happens."

With all of the partners he had been with his wolf had never chosen anyone. Yet, he wasn't wrong here. His wolf had marked Autumn. He knew it like he knew his own face, and she was fully human. She reeked of human, yet there was his mark on her. Even among his kind, mate bonds were rare, and something almost all yearned for. To have your soul bonded with another, to share your long, dark life with a companion at your side. It also lessened the effects of the Hunger, and it was said that those who were mate bonded could share in kills, share in the fulfillment that came with the death of their prey. They could sense one another, might even share emotions and possibly thoughts.

He sensed Autumn now, but only in so much that he had an awareness of where she was. He had no idea what she was thinking or feeling, only what her scent told him. Their bond was incomplete, he could sense it. Being human, she didn't have a wolf, so how could she ever mark him back? It seemed to be a one-sided bond, but how was that possible, either?

He pondered what it meant and concluded that he simply didn't know what was going on here. There were too many factors in all of this that he didn't understand and had never heard of. There was only one person in the world who would likely know the answers, and he had to think long and hard before he chose that route. Until then he would find out what he could on his own.

Sighing deeply he decided to just let it be. Things were as they were, and nothing could be done but remain alert and get her to his friend and, hopefully, to safety.

Autumn was awake for a while, staring blankly out the window as the green world passed them by. She didn't know where they were going and didn't have the strength to ask. She'd been taken from her home and she had no idea what lay before her. She had to put her trust in a…man…she shouldn't trust, and didn't know. Not really. Her life was in his hands, and his hands could just as well kill her as the thing that was after her.

She sighed deeply and closed her eyes. She didn't have a choice, in any of this. Her life was slipping past her as the miles rolled by, disappearing into the emerald hues of her beloved forest. She had nothing to hold onto now, only him. She couldn't even talk to her best friend and tell her she loved her, that she was OK, and that she would be home as soon as she could. If she ever went home again. Cleo would worry, would know that Kain was involved in her disappearance. She would ride the police about finding her. She was sure Cleo would take care of her home and poor Toby, but what would happen to her shop? Would the bank foreclose on it? Would she lose everything?

Tears slipped from under her lashes and she wept silently for the life being left behind her, maybe forever, in the redwoods.

Beside her, Kain gripped the steering wheel hard and ground his teeth together, using every ounce of will to leave her be and let her grieve. He knew she wept, and he couldn't stand her sadness. He howled inside with it, knowing he had brought this all upon her. At every turn in his life, he brought grief and pain to those around him. It was why he never got attached. It was a part of his own personal code he lived by. And yet here it was again, another life destroyed, either by his claws or by his actions. If had just kept driving that day...

He damned his wolf to hell and back and tried his best to ignore the torrent of self-loathing and bitterness running through him. Growling, he turned up the radio, which had been on low volume, and after some searching came up with a loud classic rock station out of Eureka. Kain turned it up, soothing himself with heavy guitar riffs and rhythmic drum beats, drowning out the small sounds of her grief.

After a while, fatigue finally claimed Autumn. She was exhausted from their night of intense sex, having had little sleep, and the events of this morning had left her utterly drained. Lulled by the subtle vibration of the car she slipped into dreaming, and not even the music blaring from the speakers could keep her awake.

She was running, running swiftly through the green of the forest on four sure feet. The feeling was glorious, amazing, and the feel of the wind whipping past her face and along her body was like a caress. She flew effortlessly with long strides and powerful bunching of muscles, her paws barely touching the ground. The wind had scents to it she had never even imagined in all her life, rich and seductive, and she opened her mouth to let them slide across her tongue. Oh, and wasn't that delicious as well? The wind across her tongue was amazing, and had a wonderful cooling effect on her whole body. She had never imagined such a thing!

She felt strong, vibrant, and fully aware of herself, delighted as her paws hit the ground rhythmically, sinking claws deep into the soil and launching her ahead, faster and faster. After a moment, she became aware of something attached to her rump like a weight, streaming out behind her and keeping her body well balanced as she ran.

Amazed, she turned her head back and caught a glimpse of a tail floating behind her and she barked out a laugh, leaping high over a fallen log. A tail! What a wondrous thing! She twisted and turned through the forest, leaping and bounding, running and not tiring in the least. She was a creature made for this, and she cavorted with wild abandon through the woods.

Then he was there, speeding up from the rear to run full length alongside her. His blue eyes were slitted as he ran, and he gave her a mischievous sidelong glance. She growled at his challenge and put on speed, sprinting faster, and he lowered his head and pursued her. They raced through the forest, mouths open in toothy, fanged grins, snapping at one another mockingly as they leaped and dodged around fallen logs and branches and shoved at one another with their shoulders.

With a sly grin, she quickly sped ahead of him and let her tail buffet his face, then she darted to the right while he skittered to correct himself and he leaped after her with a happy snarl. She dashed behind a thick tangle of brush and tensed, waiting for half a second while he caught up, but instead of coming around the bush after her like she thought he would, he pounced over the top of it and bowled into her.

They crashed into the brush, rolling and snapping, snarling playfully as they tussled. Finally, he got the better of her and rolled her onto her back and stood over her triumphantly. She snapped at him, kicking at him with her paws. He laughed at her, using the height of his long, lean legs to keep her teeth from him. Then he bent down and began licking her all over her face and she felt her tail wag in delight, swishing through the leaves under her. She returned his kisses, emitting little squeaks as she licked his mouth and muzzle with splayed ears.

He leaped away from her and landed in a bow, tail waving lazily as he beamed at her with an open maw. Growling, she rolled to her feet and leaped after him as he darted away, the chase joined once more.

Autumn woke slowly, awareness coming to her like a fog lifting. For a moment she was confused, her body strange to her, and she didn't know where she was. Rocky hills swept by outside the window, sunlight glinting off a side mirror, and she realized she was in a car, curled up in the seat. The forest of her dreams receded, and memory came flooding back in. She groaned, uncurling herself, her entire body stiff and sore.

She looked around blearily and then over at Kain, squinting against the sunlight. He looked back at her, his eyes hidden behind those mirrored sunglasses, and gave her a small smile. She stared at him in a sleepy haze, trying to wake up and clear her mind. He looked so harmless and human driving the car, dressed in a black T-shirt and blue jeans, and damn her if he still wasn't as attractive to her as he ever was. He was dangerous, he wasn't even human, but right now he looked like nothing more than a sinfully gorgeous man.

A wolf in sheep's clothing.

She turned away and sighed, closing her eyes as memories of the last few days tried to invade her mind, unwanted. She needed to think about their situation now and what to do, not recall the taste of his skin or the feel of him inside of her. She didn't want to remember any of it. She doubted she'd ever be able to forget.

Firmly brushing those thoughts away, she yawned and stretched some more, easing her cramped muscles. What was up with that dream? It had seemed so real, so tangible, as if she really had been a wolf. It was just a dream, though, she told herself, yet the feelings it had awakened stayed with her. The feeling of running…

She recalled that when she was younger she would dream of herself as an animal, but it was never clear what that animal was, and the dreams had stopped when she hit puberty. Perhaps it had something to do with Kain. He was a werewolf after all, but she was dreaming about wolves, not werewolves. Still, they had started shortly after he had arrived.

Not wanting to think about that either, she breathed deeply and ended up yawning again before she took a look around. They must be on the other side of the Sierra's by now since the land was much more arid and open. How long had she been asleep? She looked at the time and was a little astonished. She had been sleeping for almost six hours now. Not surprising, she supposed, given all that had happened this morning…and the all-night sex marathon they'd had last night. It seemed ages ago now, but her body still ached with subtle bruises and strained muscles, and something on her shoulder burned.

"I hope you slept well," Kain rumbled from the driver's side as she rubbed at her shoulder, "We should be hitting Reno soon. We'll stop and get some food."

Her stomach growled at the suggestion and she was suddenly aware of how hungry she was. And she needed to use the bathroom. She nodded but didn't say anything, still not ready to talk to him, and looked back out the window instead.

She was aware of hands tightening on the steering wheel but she chose to ignore it.

They drove for a little while longer and finally entered the outskirts of Reno. She stayed silent, not looking at him as they drove, and she could feel how tense he was. She knew he wanted to talk to her, but she still needed space from him while she tried to sort it all out in her head.

He finally pulled over into a popular fast food chain and looked over at her. "Does this work for you? Will they have something you want?"

She only shrugged and nodded without comment and he frowned, growling a little as he parked the car. They got out of the car and, sighing, she followed him into the restaurant. He stopped her when she went to enter the women's bathroom, and she flashed him an annoyed look. Did he really need to hover over her like this? She knew he was protecting her, but really. He grumbled and gave her a pointed look, then held the door open with an arm over her while he lifted his head and breathed deeply. Autumn felt heat rise in her cheeks and looked around in embarrassment. No one was looking at them, thankfully, but she was still mortified. Apparently satisfied by whatever he smelled he grunted, nodding for her to enter.

Shaking her head, she ducked into the bathroom and went in to do her business.

When she was through, they went to the counter to order their food. Kain ordered half a dozen burgers, plain, two orders of fries, chicken tenders, and a milkshake. The employee behind the counter gave him a bored look and asked if that was all. Autumn stared at him incredulously but he only gave her a small, amused smile and asked what she wanted to order. Did he really just order all that food for himself?

Autumn looked at the menu, repulsed by the choices, yet she was as hungry as a bear. They had salads, or what passed for as salads here, but she didn't want those. Perversely she wanted their biggest burger, stacked with cheese and bacon and three meat patties. She practically drooled thinking about it, smelling the cooking meat in the back. Instead, she ordered a chicken wrap sans the chicken and a bottled water. Kain raised his eyebrow at her as she placed her order.

"That's all you want?" he asked and she looked up at him and shrugged.

"You've got to be hungrier than that," he said skeptically, but she just addressed the employee with a, "That will be all, thank you."

He made a soft grumble as he laid down cash for their order and took their number. She went to stand against the wall as they waited, folding her arms over her chest. He followed her and she avoided looking at him, so he stood away from her and scanned the restaurant with a scowl.

When the food came, he grabbed the tray and strolled past her without looking at her. She sighed and followed him, and they sat down in a booth near the windows. Autumn kept her gaze averted as they tucked into the meal, yet she watched out of the corner of her eye as he began devouring his stack of burgers while she nibbled at her vegetarian wrap. She felt starved, but couldn't seem to eat more than a bite or two. What was wrong with her? She told her body that it wanted this food, needed it, and that she had no desire for the burgers Kain was stuffing in his face.

As if sensing her thoughts, he unwrapped a burger and set it on top of its wrapper, then slid it across the table to her. She looked at it, then up at him with a questioning look. He didn't answer, just nodded at the burger and turned his attention back to his meal.

Autumn stared at the hamburger before her, plain and unadorned, just a patty of meat between two slightly mangled buns. She should find it repugnant, willed herself to be disgusted, but she just couldn't. She was just too damned hungry and she plain didn't want what she was eating.

Heaving an annoyed sigh, she put down her wrap and picked up the burger. She willed herself one more time to put it down and not eat it, but she just didn't have the strength. She took a bite…and it was wonderful! She began eating it greedily, feeling like she was starving and couldn't eat it fast enough. She finished it quickly, wiping her hands together as she chewed with a full mouth and then stopped, aware that he was watching her. She looked up to see his face poised above his burger with a look of sheer amusement on it.

Autumn blushed, aghast with herself, and looked away in embarrassment until he started making a noise. She looked back to see him shaking with silent laughter, his face turning red with it, and she started to bristle in anger but stopped. Well, she deserved it didn't she, wolfing it down like that? She was sure that had been something to see and she couldn't help herself. She gave an abashed chuckle and shook her head, wadding up the wrapper ruefully. What was wrong with her?

Kain set down his burger and did his best to compose himself, wiping his mouth with a napkin while he bit back his humor with a polite cough. He didn't say anything, just slid the last hamburger to her, and went about eating his fries.

Autumn looked at the burger and up at him, wondering if he was trying to mock her. She had just embarrassed herself and now he was giving her another? She wanted to refuse it, but she still felt like she was starving. The first had been so good, and Kain seemed to be politely ignoring her. Sighing in resignation, she picked it up but forced herself to eat slower this time no matter how good it was. It was a cheap fast food burger, so why was it so appealing? Why did it taste so amazing to her? She just didn't understand this change in her, and she figured it must have something to do with him.

"Others…like me," he said, keeping his eyes on his fries as he munched them, "we all have rather large appetites and need to eat quite a lot. Our metabolisms are very high," he explained, and Autumn finished the burger and looked at him, feeling her curiosity stirring.

"So that's why you can eat so much and stay…well…fit?" she asked despite herself and he found her with his eyes, smiling a little in triumph.

"Yes," he nodded, "and our bodies are strong, and healthy. Always. It's part of…what happens."

She stared at him in fascination, wanting to know more, and yet not. She was just sure there were things she didn't want to know about his kind, and yet here he was, a creature out of myth and legend. A creature of death and darkness all of those myths said, but still he was something magical in the world, and he was being candid with her now.

Careful, a cautious voice whispered. *You can know too much, and he could kill you for that.*

But he just didn't seem all that menacing at the moment as he dunked a chicken strip into barbecue sauce and looked at her inquiringly, obviously waiting for her to ask her questions.

She opened her mouth and began to ask another question, but what came out was, "Why me?"

Kain stopped with his next bite almost to his mouth and looked at her in surprise.

"I mean, why did you stop that day? Why did you single me out?" she asked, needing to know and not knowing why.

He blinked at her and then sat back, regarding her as he licked his fingers. He didn't answer her for a long moment, just watched her as she waited. She began to feel self-conscious and she looked away, frowning, and started gathering the trash together. "Look, I shouldn't have—"

"I'm not sure why you want to know, Autumn, but I'll tell you."

She looked up at him and he smiled faintly, shrugging his shoulders. "I may be something…else, but I am also a man. You intrigued me that day. You were a challenge, and perhaps that is what drew me to you. But there was something about you that hooked me, and I couldn't deny it so I went for you. I really can't explain it any more than that."

She stared at him with her mouth slightly open, unsure what she had expected to hear. He spread his hands then and said, "Look, it's neither here nor there at this point, isn't it. There are other more important things to worry about, like getting you safe. Agreed?"

She narrowed her eyes slightly and nodded. Agreed. It was a pointless question anyway, and she had no idea why she'd asked it. Besides, he had just said it plainly. He was a man, and she had piqued his interest. She could have told him no and sent him packing like she had wanted to do at first, so maybe she had asked for it in some way. Yes, he had seduced her, but she was the one that invited him into her home, into her bed. She was as much to blame for all of this as he was.

Annoyed with herself she continued to gather the trash together while he crammed the last two chicken strips into his mouth and she went to throw the trash away. She owned her fault in all of this, and she must never forget for even a moment that he wasn't just a man, he was a werewolf. She drilled that into her head until it was rock solid, then she followed him out the door and to the car.

Werewolf, she reminded herself firmly as she got in and buckled up. *Werewolf,* she fumed as he donned his glasses again and started the engine. He likely killed and ate people, she reminded herself as she steadfastly looked forward and refused to look at him at all. She could not afford to think of him in any other way. Werewolf. Monster.

Firm in her resolve she turned her face to the window and determinedly ignored him.

Kain knew he had done it again, somehow pissed her off and she was back to ignoring him. Her distance annoyed him, and though he couldn't blame her for being scared and confused, he just couldn't understand her mood. He sighed as he made his way to the interstate, shaking his head. He had answered her question as loosely as possible so as to not insult her, or give her too much of the truth, and yet she had immediately slammed her walls up again. He doubted that as long as he may live, and it might be a very long time, that he would ever really understand women.

They got onto the interstate headed east and Kain turned up the radio again rather than suffer her silence. They traveled several hours that way, driving through the long vistas of the desert as the day waned and the sun began to set behind them. Autumn kept her face to her window, or straight ahead of her. Occasionally he would catch her humming along to a song but as soon as she caught herself doing it, she would stop. He realized he would love to hear her sing, and wondered if she did while she was alone in her car.

The sun had set to a dark russet glow against an indigo sky on the western horizon. Around them, the empty desert was dark save for the traffic on the interstate, and a sky full of brilliant stars. They had lost the latest radio station and Kain was getting bored, tired of the silence between them. She needed to know certain things. She needed to understand what she was a part of now. He would omit certain key points that she didn't need to know about, but she had to be told. He flipped the radio off and they drove in complete silence while she tried to avoid looking at him.

"Perhaps there are things you would rather not know about me and my kind," he said, keeping his eyes forward as he drove. "But the reality is that you are being hunted, Autumn, by something even I know little about. It wasn't my intent for you to have anything to do with my world, but for some reason you were forced into it and there are things you need to know…whether you want to or not."

Autumn looked at him then, her eyes wide in the dim light. Kain glanced at her and then back to the road again. "Listen to me, because your life depends on what I'm about to tell you about the world around you. You need to understand just how little you know about reality, and about the dangers that are out there. Your world is not as it seems."

CHAPTER FOURTEEN
Bitten

Autumn lay curled up in the uncomfortable hotel bed, fully clothed and under the blanket. She was exhausted, it was two in the morning, but she couldn't sleep, so she absently clutched his talisman and stared at the far wall. The details about what Kain had revealed to her whirled through her head, terrifying her and shattering her conceptions about the world. Werewolves were real, and so were other...things. Horrible things, none of them nice.

He had told her about the creature after her, called an "Eater." He explained that it had once been a werewolf that became addicted to killing people, humans, and that it got some sort of power off doing so. It killed so many people that it became incredibly powerful and went insane. But it was clever, and deceptive, with a cunning instinct for hunting its human prey. It was able to assume the form of anyone it saw, and could assume the form of animals as well. He told her he'd barely been able to injure it enough to escape it since it was far faster and stronger than he was, it never tired, and it healed almost instantly. And it had targeted her for reasons he said he couldn't understand.

He told her of other creatures that could mimic humans but weren't, alien beings that could capture your mind and lure you to them, then they would drag you away and feed off you until you died and you would never know you were dead. He told her of shadows and fogs that could consume you whole if you entered them, spirits that could possess your body and cause you to do horrible things, real live witches that cast spells and charms with blood magic, and indescribable beings that lived in ancient woods. All of them fed on or used humans in some way.

She had sat in silence for a little bit after that, stricken. Was there nothing good in the world? Did everything eat something else, "feeding the cycle" as he had said? Was it really all death and darkness? Then she had turned to him in fear and had asked him if all werewolves killed people. He had told her no, only the bad ones. As if that were supposed to be comforting. He told her that he only killed animals when he had to, to satisfy that wolf side of himself, and assured her that he was one of the "good" werewolves.

And then he began describing to her what it was like, being a werewolf. She had felt her fear begin to slip away into fascination as he talked about his senses and abilities. He could smell things from miles away, hear conversations across an entire building, and see things so sharply he could spot a penny on the ground from across a parking lot. All while still in his human skin. He was strong, and fast, and could endure for great lengths, and he healed very quickly.

He'd told her about the shift, and she had asked if it hurt. He said somewhat, but more it was physical sensation, an intense feeling that was both pleasure and pain. He said he could shift at will and had control over it, something that took some time to master. She'd asked how long it had taken him and he'd simply hedged and said "A while." She took note of that but decided not to press the issue of his past for now.

He continued, saying that nothing could kill a werewolf except beheading or pure silver. Silver chased the beast in them away and cancelled out their ability to heal, and if left inside of a non-lethal wound it poisoned their blood until they died from the toxicity, sometimes within hours. He told her silver, to his senses, had a sheen to it, a glow almost, and an odor similar to rain before a thunderstorm. Every werewolf could sense it nearby and they instinctively avoided it.

By then she was fascinated and asked if the part about the moon were true.

"It is to a certain degree," he'd said, looking out at the waning moon just above the horizon now. "We're not forced to shift on full moons per se, but they do have a pull on us. It calls us strongly, and on that night, we become far more…primal. When you are newly changed, it can make your beast rise, and cause you to shift. After a while, you learn to control it, even ignore it if your willpower is strong enough, but it has an effect on us all. Most will run, some will hunt, others resist and spend themselves on… other…carnal delights that night," he'd said, looking at her with that heated, seductive smile. She'd looked away hastily, her body reacting to him.

She was still aroused by him, she admitted to herself as she lay in the room staring into the darkness. Despite everything he still turned her on, and so easily with one heated glance. And that was possibly more terrifying than all his tales of dark and horrible things.

He'd told her a lot more, but there were things he still wasn't telling her. There was just so much about him, about who he was, his past, and about being what he was than he was letting her know. She knew it in her gut. But she had to trust him. She just didn't have any other choice.

Kain lay fully clothed on top of the still made up double bed, watching Autumn in the darkness. She slept in her clothes on the other bed, hidden under her blanket and turned away from him. She was finally sleeping. They had driven until after midnight, making their way into Wyoming and stopping in Rock Springs for the night. They still had a ways to go but she needed to rest, and she would want a shower. He also still had a blood debt that needed to be paid for the spell he had used earlier that day. It was beginning to demand his attention, and it wasn't going to be pleasant to deal with.

At least she had talked to him. She had relaxed enough once more to be curious and he had been delighted to scent a trickle of desire from her at one point. It had made her uncomfortable, but it was unmistakable. And that gave him some small hope.

He breathed in deeply, taking in the smell of the hotel room, sifting out her scent among the odors of cleaning supplies, detergent, old food, and old sex. There it was, her unique fragrance, subtly altered now. She smelled like him. The aroma sent a wave of almost maddening possessiveness over him and he swallowed back the growl that tickled in his throat. He still wanted her, badly. Last night hadn't sated him in the least, and had even perversely made him desire her more. He desperately wanted to crawl into the bed with her, to breathe her scent deeply, to lick his mark on her, and make love to her until she screamed his name again.

He groaned and laid back, clenching his eyes shut. He wondered if she would ever allow him to touch her again, knowing more now of what he was. She still feared him; he smelled it on her constantly. She kept a firm distance between them, denied him even her voice for most of the day, and it had tested him thoroughly. He wanted her smile again. He wanted her laugh. He wanted her breath and her body, her temper and her playfulness, her light and her joy. All that he had seen of her the last number of days and more. He wanted her in a way that defied words and logic, and his wolf had chosen her as their mate. His fucking *mate*! He chuckled darkly to himself at the irony of it all as he put his hands behind his head, staring up at the ceiling.

It had always been something he had looked for, even yearned for, ever since Alessia had died over sixty years ago. He lived a solitary life, always traveling, always the vagabond, and for a while, he had enjoyed it. But for all that his kind were solitary creatures, his unusual wolf had never enjoyed being alone. Yet alone he was. He had always chosen to alleviate that loneliness by being with women, lots of women.

Sex helped center him, soothed man and beast alike, and he vastly enjoyed the many different female temptations there were to be had. Yet lately he had felt unsatisfied afterward, restless, and he would be with his chosen partner once, perhaps twice, and then he would leave to look for the next one. With his looks and his charm, they came willingly, easily to his bed. It had started to become boring, and he had been restless with an unnamed need, a scratch he couldn't itch.

Until he had gotten that first glimpse, and that first scent of her. He should have known then. He should have run as fast and as far as he could, but he doubted now that he would've gotten far. He hadn't gotten far, he remembered ruefully, thinking about how strongly his wolf had resisted him leaving her. She had a hold on him unlike any other woman before her, and she had no idea what that meant in his own little world. He had to keep her safe. He would find out why the Eater was after her and stop it, then he would return her to her world somehow.

He rolled onto his side and stared at the indistinct form under the blanket on the bed next to him. Something in him ached just knowing she was right there, yet miles away. When all of this was said and done, he would have to let her go. The thought tore him in two.

He waited for a while longer to make sure she was truly asleep, until her breathing was deep and slow. He hated leaving her for any reason. She was vulnerable, and he feared leaving her alone, but he could not ignore what he had to do any longer. He would have to trust his talisman to keep her concealed and safe. He carefully rose and grabbed his pack, then slipped out carefully and closed the door softly behind him. The blood debt was pounding in his ears by now, and it was late enough that he shouldn't be disturbed in his unpleasant task.

He trotted toward the hills overlooking the town, searching for a place to change. Rock Springs was a small town where most people worked during the day, and everything was quiet and dark as he roamed. He came across a rocky area that contained a thicket of trees and brush, which should conceal him well. It would have to do. He made his way into it then stripped quickly.

Stashing his clothing in his pack, he pulled out the long, wicked looking knife he used for such rituals.

The spell he had used to fight the Eater with was costly, and the blood debt owed for such a spell was high. If he did not balance the books—so to speak—and soon, he could risk madness or a backlash of power that might destroy him. The price demanded for this spell would cost him his hand. Even though it would grow back with his healing abilities, and even though he'd had to do this sort of thing before, it was still going to be extraordinarily unpleasant and painful to do this.

No use crying over it, he needed to just get it done with and get back to Autumn. He knelt and dug a deep hole into a sandy crevasse in a jumble of rocks, making a deep pocket in the earth. Since he was right handed, he would be sacrificing his left hand. He laid his arm along a flat rock and pressed a knee on top of it, taking deep breaths through his nose as he readied his knife. He would have to be fast, and do everything in his power not to scream or make noise. It would disrupt the ritual and would definitely draw attention.

Growling out guttural sounds that were words-not-words he held the knife in front of him and spoke his offering. *Let the blood debt be fulfilled.* He slashed down with all of his strength with the razor-sharp blade and an agonized noise escaped him. Pain exploded through his body as his hand separated from his forearm with a gushing of blood. Wasting no time on his agony, he buried the offering deep into the rock crevasse and buried it back over, all the while growling out more words around his pain. He felt the warmth of the blood debt fulfilled flow through him and away into the earth, power balanced once more.

Kain began transforming instantly, unable to bear the agony of his wound. He concentrated hard, sending energy into his ravaged limb, forcing the flesh to knit and reform his hand. He whimpered through his nose as he continued to change. His pain was exquisite as the stub of his forearm sprouted a bulbous mass of flesh, then small, tender pink digits that pushed outward as bones grew. By the time he'd changed into the black beast his new hand was a misshapen, gnarled paw covered in dark skin, and his new nails were not even thick enough to form claws. It was all he could manage for now.

Hunger roared though his body, and the wolf in him snarled for meat and blood. The sound issued up his throat as a keening moan. He needed to hunt now, to find prey of any kind to replenish himself. He could not risk going back to the room before he did.

He stashed his pack in a deep pile of brush, then turned his senses to his surroundings. He left the cover of the thicket cautiously, scenting and listening for possible threats. Everything was quiet, though, and he set off slowly on all fours. Limping on his bad foot, his nose skimmed the ground for scents. He would find something quickly, sate his need, and get back to Autumn.

Autumn stirred, suddenly realizing she was alone. She rolled over in the darkness of the room and looked around. He wasn't here. He had left. She didn't know why, and probably didn't want to know. She just knew she could finally take a shower now. She hadn't wanted to with him around, even if she had locked the door against him. Not that she expected him to bust the door down, but God only knew. She didn't want to take any chances.

She went into the bathroom and locked the door, then stripped off her clothes and dropped them in a pile. His talisman she left on, not daring to remove the thing. It hung down heavily between her breasts and she picked it up and looked at it again curiously. It was definitely a tooth of some kind, black and fossilized with age. It was a wicked looking thing, capped with an antler tine carved with mystical symbols, suspended by a thick braid of twined leather. There were a couple of carved beads next to it as well, and two moonstones were threaded into the cord. It should freak her out, but instead she only felt an odd comfort as she let it fall back against her skin. She trusted that it really was keeping her safe.

She washed herself thoroughly using the cheap complimentary bar of soap and bottle of shampoo, then stood under the hot spray for a while and allowed it to ease her sore muscles. She would need to talk to him about getting her some clothes and sundries tomorrow. She had spied a Walmart across the freeway, and that would do. She couldn't just keep wearing the same sweats and no underwear or bra. It made her feel dirty, and exposed around him. She needed as many clothes on around the man as she could get.

Feeling better, she got out and dried herself off, then wrapped her hair up in a towel. It would be a wreck with no conditioner, but it would be clean. She really wanted some decent soap, a toothbrush and toothpaste, and some deodorant too. Oh, and some lotion. Dreaming of toiletries, she stood in front of the mirror and wiped at the condensation, then gasped when she saw herself.

It had been hidden by the neck of her hoodie, but now she could see the various little bite bruises on her neck and shoulders, and there on her right shoulder was a half moon of red scabs. In the perfect shape of a set of sharp teeth. She scrubbed the mirror quickly with a dry towel and leaned in close to get a better look at it. It was a bite all right, and from the look of it, he had drawn blood. She had no recollection of when he had done that, somewhere in their throes of passion the other night, but that hardly mattered. He had bitten her! She stared at it in horror, all the fairy tales running through her head. If someone was bitten by a werewolf and survived…she almost became sick and had to sink to the floor, covering the wound with her hand. Eyes wide, her thoughts raced at her discovery of what he'd done.

This couldn't be happening. She couldn't be turning into a…a werewolf. But it would explain her sudden cravings for meat, and the weird wolf dreams. She was beginning to panic again, her heart racing as the implications of it all hit her. She didn't want to be a werewolf. She wanted to go home, run her shop, and tend her garden, not run around chasing and killing things. She didn't want to become a monster!

He did this deliberately! She realized with sudden rage. *That bastard!* She was trembling as she got to her feet and she quickly pulled on her sweatpants and wrapped a towel around her chest. She wanted him to see the wound so he couldn't deny it. Shaking with rage, she stalked from the bathroom to wait for his return, ready to hurt him in any way she could.

His hunt had gone smoothly and successfully. He had managed to find a roaming raccoon fairly quickly and made short work of it, crunching down the last of its bones and fur in under five minutes. He was still hungry and needed more, but it would have to do. He had been gone from her long enough. He limped back to his clothes with his tail waving. By the time he shifted back to human, his left hand was raw and pink, but it looked like a hand again. He hummed a little to himself as he pulled his boots back on. He felt better with fresh blood still in his mouth and he headed quickly back to the motel, eager to get back to her.

He could smell the scent of soap and shampoo as he approached the door to the motel room and he sniffed curiously, but detected no scents of an intruder. Had she woken and taken a shower? He opened the door quietly as he could and curiously poked his head in. The light in the bathroom was on but he didn't see her. Perhaps she was still in there?

Something came hurling at his head from behind the door, and he managed to duck out of the way preternaturally fast. He snarled, darting into the room as she raised the table lamp again with an enraged cry. He lunged at her, grabbing both her hands and pinning her to the wall by them, and kicked the door closed with his foot. She cried out angrily, thrashing against him, kicking at his groin with her feet. He grunted and shifted his hips, avoiding her treacherous feet, then quickly pressed his body the full length against her so she couldn't move. He grabbed the lamp from her and tossed it away, then used both his hands to pin hers to the wall above her head and waited for her to stop struggling. He was much stronger than she was but she fought him wildly and he growled, showing her the wolf in his eyes. She finally stopped fighting with an angry sob.

"Jesus Christ, Autumn, it's me," he said irritably and she met his tingling eyes, hers livid with rage.

"Good!" she spat and struggled again, trying to get free of him and he pressed himself firmly against her with a snarl.

"Stop struggling! What is wrong with you?" he growled, his new hand paining him as he restrained her, and he was dumfounded to see tears in her eyes as she looked at him again.

"You bit me! You made me into what you are, a monster!" she cried defiantly at him and he stared back at her a moment, uncomprehending. He looked her over, belatedly realizing she had only been wearing a towel to cover her chest, and it had fallen away in their struggle. He stared at her for a moment, his thoughts momentarily addled by her. She made an angry noise and twisted against him again, trying to break free from his hold. With a snarl, he tightened his grip and pressed her harder against the wall. He felt himself become aroused for her and he bit back a groan, shaking his head to focus.

"I've done nothing of the sort," he snarled, looking down at her. "I admit I did get carried away, but a real bite, a changing bite, is a little more complicated than that. You aren't turning into a werewolf, Autumn, I promise."

"How do you know?" she asked angrily, scowling at him.

He chuckled darkly and bent to her, looking her in the eyes closely. "Believe me, I would know."

She stared back at him defiantly, her jaw clenched and her brow furrowed.

"Are we done? Can I let you go or are you going to try and hit me again?" he asked and she turned her head away sulkily, then nodded firmly.

He slowly began to ease off her, taking his time. He wanted her to feel what she did to him, and he ached for even this contact with her. Finally, he stepped away and released her hands, then bent and offered her the towel and looked away politely. She snatched it from him and pressed it to herself, backing away from him.

Breathing deeply he gave her space, eyes following her as he raked his good hand through his hair.

"Why in the hell would you think you were turning?" he asked, completely baffled by her temper.

She glared at him. "Oh, only because I've been craving meat and have been dreaming of wolves ever since you showed up. And now I'm dreaming myself *as* a wolf," she said crossly, then moved to the bathroom where she scooped up her hoodie.

Kain stared at her incredulously, unable to process what she had just said. *She what?* He watched then as she threw down the towel and shrugged into the sweatshirt before him, baring her jiggling breasts for a moment as she tugged the fabric down, thoroughly dazing him. He was still gaping at her as her head emerged and she yanked the towel from her head and began to scrub through her wet hair briskly, her face still angry.

"So yeah, I am assuming the worst. I have every right to. And while we're at it, thank you for royally fucking up my life. My life was perfect before you came along. I had a lot going for me. Now my shop will likely be taken away from me, God knows what state my grandmother's home is in, and my friends probably think you kidnapped and killed me. So yeah, I'm a little fucking pissed," she snarled, finishing her toweling with an angry jerk.

Baring her teeth at him she leveled a finger straight at his face. "I need clothes, and I need some basic damned toiletries, so in the morning we're going to the Walmart and I'm shopping, got it?"

He gaped at her, utterly stunned by her fire and her rage. Her wet hair was tousled and tangled around her, her eyes bright with passion, her color high. She was magnificent, and he simply couldn't think of any response save the one his body was having. She growled and stalked into the bathroom, slamming and locking the door behind her.

Her physical presence removed he was able to have a coherent thought again, and her words hit him like a physical blow.

"Wait, you've been dreaming yourself as a wolf?" he demanded, striding to the bathroom door.

"Good night, Kain!" she said forcefully through the door and he blinked, then backed away. She was sleeping in there?

He stood immobilized, at once wanting to break the door down, incensed that there should be any kind of barrier between them, yet not daring to provoke her further tonight. He needed to know more about what she had been dreaming, and why she hadn't told him of this before. He was aware of her sudden change in appetite but to him being vegetarian was foolish, so of course she would eventually want to eat meat. But this?

He clenched and unclenched his hands, his own rage simmering at her words and her removal of herself. The nerve of her to say that *he* and ruined *her* life? With a snarl, he picked up the lamp from off the floor and twisted it in two, snapping it in his hands. Yelling out a curse, he threw the pieces of the lamp and stomped the floor, wanting to smash the wall in, and instead crossed the room and sullenly tossed himself on top of her bed with a snarl. She could lock herself in the bathroom, but that meant her scent was fair game.

He breathed the smell of her in deeply and fumed, his claws sinking into the bunched blankets. Let the little hellion sleep in the bathtub for all he cared. *His* life was a mess now because of her. *His* entire existence was in turmoil over her. Snarling, he burrowed his face into the blankets and cursed her name.

When morning came, Autumn cautiously opened the bathroom and peeked into the room, looking around. She had indeed spent a miserable, sleepless night in the bathtub fuming, then sobbing, then feeling like a bitch, then finally sleeping for perhaps forty minutes before the kink in her neck woke her with a splitting headache. She needed Excedrin and coffee now more than ever, and she was willing to make peace if that meant she could get them.

She found the beds politely made, a crushed and broken lamp on the side writing table, the pieces piled together neatly. The rest of the room looked untouched, unslept in, and, curious, she came out farther, searching for him. She gasped softly when she spied him sitting in the corner next to the door. His arms were propped up on his jeans-clad legs, his torso and feet bare. His eyes glittered at her in the dim light.

"She emerges," he growled softly and she took a step back, wanting to run back into her sanctuary. But the pounding in her head and her guilt at losing her temper won out and she stepped fully into the room, folding her arms across her middle protectively.

"It looks like you had a bad night," she said a little tersely, still somewhat defiant toward him as she glanced at the lamp.

"Does it," he said roughly, and she narrowed her eyes at him.

"What happened to your shirt?" she asked and then blanched a little as he chuckled darkly from his shadow.

"I tore it off myself. It was annoying me."

She eyed him warily as he shifted, rolling to his feet in one smooth motion, then she gasped a little and backed away as he moved slowly toward her. God help her, he was sinfully attractive this morning. His long, unruly mane was wild and tangled around him. His jeans were deliciously slung low around his hips, exposing the dark trail of hair that dipped enticingly below the waistband. His shadow beard was dark along his jaw. His eyes were a luminous light blue in the shadows of his slanting eyebrows, his expression stormy and his face savage as he advanced on her. He moved slowly with predatory grace and she matched him step for step backward. She should be terrified, or at least still pissed, but instead she was getting horribly turned on by him and she couldn't seem to control it.

"How did you sleep?" he asked softly, mockingly, as they rounded the far bed, headed toward the back wall.

"Like shit," she managed to say, her mouth dry. He chuckled, showing her all those long, white teeth.

"Good. Good to hear. It makes me glad."

Her heels bumped up against the wall and she swallowed, pressing back against it as he crowded her and leaned down to sniff her closely. He made a grumbling sound in his throat and pulled his head back, looking down at her with those unnaturally light blue eyes.

"I slept like shit too. On your bed," he said softly. Heat flushed through her entire body and pooled in her groin, her lips parting as his eyes roved all over her face.

She was trying to focus, trying to tell herself that she didn't want this, that he was a werewolf, a monster, a killer, all of the things she had been drilling into her head. But when he bent his head to hers, his lips a kiss away, thought went out the window. With a growl, his lips found hers, and his hands slid into her hair as he pressed his body against her. He rubbed his lips maddeningly against hers, his tongue licking against her lips, asking her to accept him. She made a desperate little noise and opened to him, sighing a little as his tongue slid deep and she tasted him again. Her arms slid up his back as he ravished her mouth, growling with pleasure against her as she returned his kisses.

He thrust into her mouth and withdrew, thrust and withdrew, mimicking what they both ached for with his tongue. Autumn whimpered helplessly. Her body recalled with clarity what his touch would be like, his mouth on her sensitive areas, his hardness filling her to completion. He pressed his erection against her and she dug her nails into his back with the want of him inside of her. Kain snarled against her lips, smiling. He kept one hand in her hair then and slid the other up under her sweatshirt. She gasped against his mouth as his fingers found the hardness of her nipple and pinched it, rolling it between his strong fingers. Fire bloomed in her loins and she arched against him, drowning in sensation, lost in his kiss.

This was dangerous. She had vowed not to sleep with him again. It gave him too much power over her and he held all the cards as it was. But she was sinking, and there was a bed much too close. She had to end this, now. Inhaling a shaky breath, she pulled away from him and he grumbled, his lips seeking hers. With an internal apology to him, she placed her hands against his shoulders and pushed him back from her. Then, with all the force she could muster, she kneed him in the groin.

He groaned and doubled over and she bolted across the room in record time, bounding across the beds until she was up against the door breathing hard. His head whipped around and he snarled inhumanely at her, his eyes glowing in the darkness. She gasped as he began stalking toward her, his bared teeth long in his mouth, but then he stopped, breathing heavily as his eyes bored into her. They stared at one another for a few moments, rage and pain plain on his face, and then he turned and strode into the bathroom, slamming the door shut behind him.

Autumn let her breath out in a huge exhale and slumped against the door. That had been close. She had been seconds away from happily mounting him anywhere in the room he chose, all caution and reason be damned. She had to get control of herself with him. She couldn't afford to let her guard down with him, let alone succumb to her own stupid libido. He was too damned tempting to her. He pressed all her buttons and did so easily. She had to keep her head about her in this or she would never see her home again, and she may not get out of it alive.

No matter how much he tempted or intrigued her she needed to keep her distance. She would not let him bully her either. She would wear her rage like armor if she had to. Determined, yet still miserably aroused, she stood and moved to the chair near the door, listening as the shower turned on and oaths were snarled from the bathroom.

It was nearly forty five minutes later when he emerged from the bathroom, fully dressed, and while the look he gave her was moody he seemed to be calmer and in better control of himself. A traitorous part of her wondered why he had been taking so long in the shower and she kicked herself mentally. Good for him if he had jerked off. At least it made him equable again.

"I'm…sorry for what just happened," he rumbled, inclining his head to her slightly. "The wolf part of me can be…strong sometimes. Hard to manage. I should have been in better control."

Autumn swallowed and nodded, crossing her arms. "And I'm sorry for the cheap shot. I didn't know what else to do."

He grunted but nodded, thanking her wordlessly. She smiled a little, quickly, and got to her feet as he hefted his pack to his shoulder.

"Ready to go?" he asked and she nodded. He left a tip for the maid and they headed to the car again.

"There's a Starbucks right over here. I assume you need your morning kick in the pants?" he asked with a small smile as she got in.

"Oh God, please?" she sighed breathily and Kain chuckled, starting the car.

Maybe she wouldn't have to kill him after all.

CHAPTER FIFTEEN
Recognition

Well, at least I'm dressed for this, Autumn thought with a sigh as they walked through the doors of the Rock Springs Walmart. She felt better for having showered, but she still felt as scuzzy as could be. She didn't even have a comb or anything, and she had done her best to pull her unruly red-gold locks into some sort of ponytail. But she blessedly had coffee in her, and Excedrin was only an aisle or two away as she grabbed a cart and entered the store.

Kain stalked beside her closely, his eyes hidden behind those mirrored sunglasses. She glared up at him in annoyance when he placed a possessive hand on her lower back, sending shivers of awareness through her. He showed her his teeth, his message clear. She would allow his touch or he wouldn't behave himself. The man was strung tight as a bow, and she hadn't mistaken the way he'd had to adjust himself when they got out of the car. Not her problem, she grumbled and sighed to herself, irritated at her own awareness of him.

They moved down the aisles, drawing the glances of every eye at least once. Most of them looked at Kain. Autumn did her best to ignore it as she perused the shampoo, but she was becoming familiar with how people reacted to him by now. There was something about him that drew the eye of every last person: Man, woman, and child. He was simply not your usual man with his height, his predatory grace, his wild hair, and his stunning good looks. Most people looked right away again and kept moving, but many took a second or third glance. They reacted with either nervousness or intrigue, and sometimes even outright awe. Especially the women, who couldn't seem to help looking at him like a piece of candy. All the attention was actually sort of pissing her off, but he acted like he couldn't care less.

"Does it bother you, the staring?" she whispered to him as she tossed toothpaste and a toothbrush into the cart.

He turned his head to her, his expression unreadable behind his glasses and shrugged. "I've gotten used to it over the years. It doesn't bother me…unless they look at you," he said with a small grumble and she snorted.

"They're *not* looking at me, I promise."

He smiled that slow, sexy smile at her and caressed her back briefly. "Oh yes, the men are. Don't worry, they don't look long."

She snapped her gaze up to him, wondering if he had just insulted her but he was looking at her with such surly possession that she swallowed and looked away. They weren't looking because he was making sure they weren't. She felt a little purely feminine thrill go through her at that and coughed, firmly squashing it. He was protecting her, nothing more.

Moving along toward the women's clothes section, she was doggedly determined to ignore everyone and everything else and focus on her shopping. But as she poked through the choices of clothing with a sigh she became aware of a couple that had been following them for a few aisles now. They gaped openly at Kain and talked excitedly with one another. She looked up to see if he had noticed but he was looking at a pair of girly shorty shorts that would barely cover her ass and grinning to himself. She rolled her eyes and went back to the rack of shirts she was sorting through, but kept the couple in her peripheral vision. Perhaps it was nothing. She was sure that if it were a problem Kain would notice and do something about it. But they were certainly acting strange.

After going through the depressing selection of Walmart women's fashions she finally decided that basic was best. She chose three pairs of unadorned jeans, three basic tees, a couple more sweatshirts—since it was still technically winter—a thick sweater that wasn't too horrible, and a pair of flannel pajamas to sleep in. And then it was time to go pick out underclothes.

She took a deep breath and straightened her spine, then wheeled her cart toward the underwear section, looking to get it over with. Kain was right on her heels and she grumbled irritably, deciding to just ignore him. She was going for basic cotton, nothing fancy or flattering. White granny panties and battle bras with huge, wide straps in an unflattering color. She didn't need to be wearing anything that might intrigue him in the least.

She tried her damnedest to ignore him and focus as she looked through the bags of briefs, looking for basic white cotton with a waistband up to her navel. She felt Kain watching her intently, fascinated simply because she was looking at panties. Snatching the bag she'd been looking for, she tossed a couple into her cart and moved out of the aisle quickly, growling under her breath. Men.

Heaving a sigh, she entered the bra aisle and began scanning for the worst, ugliest thing she could find. Of course, he was right behind her and she heard him make a sound of disapproval as she lifted something that looked like what Oma used to wear. Unflatteringly gray with huge, wide straps and tons of hooks and eyes sure to infuriate roving fingers. Perfect. She pawed through the rack of them, looking for her size while Kain leaned in curiously. She turned her head to him and tsked, shoving at him with her hand.

"Will you *stop* being creepy and perverted? Go do something useful," she growled, and he chuckled seductively, sinfully, with that evil grin of his and wandered away while Autumn breathed deeply and tried to focus. She chose two of the ugly things in her size, then moved to the rack of sports bras and got a couple of those, too. Simple, sensible, and hard to remove. She would wear them like armor.

She turned and tossed them in the cart, smirking triumphantly. And there was that strange couple again, staring intently at Kain who had moved to the sleepwear section and was looking at some silky little red thing, apparently oblivious to them. They were a man and a woman, probably a couple, and both had long hair and were covered in tattoos. Though the guy looked like he was in his forties, he had long hair and wore an old denim jacket with the arms ripped off, covered in patches, and a pair of ripped-up jeans. The woman was younger and dressed in black leggings that were too small for her weight and she wore an old cut-up band shirt. Parts of her hair were dyed bright colors, but the rest of it was black. Both wore cuffs and bracelets, rings and necklaces, and the woman wore a studded collar.

They were still having a heated argument with one another it seemed, gesturing at Kain, and she couldn't believe that Kain was either oblivious to their interest (which might well be the case, absorbed as he was in looking at delicate lady clothes), or he was deliberately ignoring them. Not sure what the case was, she decided that either way he had it under control and went to go get some socks.

That done, she decided she needed a bag to keep all her new purchases in so she began heading toward the luggage section. Kain moved up next to her easily and placed his hand on her back again. Instead of snapping at him, she sighed a little in relief. Something about that couple was bothering her, and for once, she wanted Kain close. She couldn't say why. She just wanted to get this shopping done quickly so they could leave.

In the luggage section, she chose a simple wheeled carry-on style suitcase, basic black. No frills, just big enough to put her stuff in. She also got a small toiletries bag to keep her miscellaneous goods in, and she figured that was that. All the basics. It would have to do until she got back home.

"I guess that's it," she said and Kain nodded.

"Good. Let's get out of here," he growled and they began making their way to the registers up front.

They were wheeling their cart to the other end of the store where they had parked when a voice spoke behind them.

"Hey man, wait."

They stopped and turned. It was the couple, approaching them with eager expressions. Autumn took a step back and touched Kain's arm as the guy looked Kain up and down for a moment, and then his face split into a wide grin. "Aw no way man! No way! Holy shit, fuck me if it isn't Derek Wolfsbayne!"

Autumn blinked and looked up at Kain who had a stone cold expression on his face. What the hell was this guy talking about?

The metal head was beaming, practically bouncing on his toes. His girlfriend was giggling like a schoolgirl. "No way, holy shit, man, I never believed the stories! I knew you weren't dead man!" he said enthusiastically and then thrust his shoulder toward them and lifted the torn edge of his jean jacket. There on his skin was a tattoo in harsh, slashing letters that spelled "Wolfyn."

"Check that shit out. I got it done on the *Carnal Thrust* tour, man." He beamed, then worshipfully fisted his hands in front of him, clearly unable to articulate what he was feeling.

Autumn looked up at Kain in utter confusion as to what was happening. Kain's expression was still frosty and a little… pained…behind his glasses, and he waved a hand in front of him.

"I think you're mistaken. You have the wrong man," he said, beginning to turn away from them and the metal head practically jumped up in the air.

"No man I know that voice! I've watched every interview you gave, every video. I own the cassette, CD, *and* vinyl of "'Carnal Thrust.'" I went to like six of your concerts that tour! I had all the merchandise, man! I worshipped you!" he practically pleaded. Kain was utterly stiff next to her, and he growled just a little.

"I told you, you have the wrong man," he said firmly, but the guy shook his head.

"No, I *know* you Derek! I knew you couldn't be dead, no way. Your music was…it was fucking sublime, man! I've never heard shit like it before or since. I lived for it. Shit, it got me out of some tough times back then. It gave me something to live for, you know? You were my hero," he said fervently. His girlfriend was starting to look embarrassed and began tugging on his arm.

"Come on baby, if he says he isn't, he isn't, you know? Let's just go," she said but he shrugged her off and shook his head.

"No way. You look the same, at least in your face, and you're tall, and your voice is the same. No mistaking that. I know it's you. Why won't you admit it? Why'd you fake your death, man?"

Autumn was utterly shocked, looking back and forth between Kain and the metal head, utterly flabbergasted. Was what this guy saying true? She'd never heard of this band Wolfyn before, or Derek Wolfsbayne, but she could tell that this guy really, really believed that Kain was this person. Kain's face was becoming stormy, and she could feel him tense beside her as the guy's girlfriend pulled on him again, harder this time.

"Baby let's go. It's not him. Let's just go," she whined and he shoved her off with a curse, then turned back to Kain.

"Stop fucking around man, admit it's you. Admit that you faked your death," he said, getting angry now.

Kain slowly took off his glasses and even Autumn stepped back from him a little with a small gasp. His eyes were so pale they were almost white, rimmed in red around the edges, and they flashed with suppressed rage. The metal head stumbled back, gripping onto his girlfriend.

"I. Am. Not. Derek. Wolfsbayne. Got it?" Kain growled, and then staring deeply into the other man's eyes his voice changed, becoming…strange somehow. "Forget you saw me today. Derek Wolfsbayne is dead and nothing will bring him back. Go home, make love to your woman, and forget this ever happened. You're a good guy. Live your life and forget about me."

The fan blinked, and blinked again while his girlfriend tugged on his arm. He took a deep breath and shook his head as Kain put his glasses back on.

"Hey babe, I think I might need to lie down," he said unsteadily to his girlfriend. She cooed at him and began pulling him away, muttering apologies and smiling tightly at them as they went.

Autumn looked up at Kain in utter disbelief. "One, what did you just do? And two...seriously?" she asked, incredulous. He grimaced painfully and tried to smile as he continued leading her toward the checkouts at the end.

"Not now. I'll tell you later," he said, clearly uncomfortable. Autumn just gaped at him, almost stumbling over her own feet as they walked away. Just how much did she *not* know about this man? Clearly a lot. Clearly a whole damned lot.

He didn't look at her as he placed the items on the conveyor, bristling with suppressed agitation. She decided not to ask for the moment and just get them out of the store and in the car. He paid for her purchases and they wheeled the cart out to the parking lot in silence while Autumn was practically bursting with questions. She had wanted to get all of her new stuff put away into the suitcase but she knew he wouldn't be able to wait for that now. He tossed everything in the back testily and Autumn ran to put the cart into the corral while he started the car.

She stared at him as he got them on the freeway, and he sped for a while as they left Rock Springs behind them and continued to head east.

"Derek Wolfsbayne?" she asked incredulously, watching as he pursed his lips and continued to stare forward. "Are you even going to bother to deny this?"

He grimaced and glowered at the road, uncomfortable. "It was a long time ago," he grumbled and she gaped at him openmouthed.

"Are you kidding me? So what, you used to be a...a famous rock star? You told me you had never been a professional musician, let alone famous," she said accusingly and he growled, keeping his eyes on the road.

"Yes, I lied, but there is a lot about me that I don't want to talk about. Things that are my own business."

Autumn gave a little sardonic laugh and folded her arms. "Well, isn't that convenient for you. I, for one, would like to know just who I am dealing with here. Besides being a werewolf *and* a rock star, is there anything else mind-blowingly important about you that you feel is none of my business?"

Kain smiled a small, bitter smile, and said, "I'm ninety years old this year, Autumn. That's a long time for a man to live, and there are many things about me I wish to remain buried in the past. My secrets are mine to keep."

She gaped at him, her eyes huge as her mouth worked, trying to form words. "You're...*how*...old?" she breathed softly, unable to look away from him.

He turned to her, his eyes unreadable behind his sunglasses. "Ninety. I was born in 1926."

She made a small noise of dismay and he chuckled, turning back to the road. "All my kind are long lived. Being that we regenerate as we do, we age very, very slowly. But we do age. There are others out there much older than I am."

Autumn was completely blown away by what he just told her, and she stared at him incredulously. He looked no more than in his early to mid-thirties as the most, but if what he was telling her was true, he had lived a lifetime already. She had no words for any of it. She decided she didn't really want to know anything more right now and she sat back in her seat, blinking wide-eyed out the windshield.

Let her chew on that, Kain thought with a small smile then sighed internally. It was just as well she knew about that part of his past, and his real age. She would have found out soon enough once they got to Sturgis.

He hadn't seen Amon since that day he had run from his life with Wolfyn those many years ago, signing over all of his assets to his old ally, and all of the possessions he cared to keep. He wouldn't have cared if Amon had burned it all and spent every cent of his money before now; he cared little for fame and fortune. It had left a bitter taste in his mouth. But he needed those assets now. He couldn't keep using stolen credit cards. One by one, they were being cancelled and his cash was getting low. He had to take care of her now, and he needed access to his own money, and his own belongings. There were things of his that he needed now, things he had entrusted to Amon.

They drove in silence for a while, then Kain asked, "How long have you been dreaming of yourself as a wolf?"

Autumn glanced at him a moment and away again, breathing deeply. "I've been dreaming of a wolf pretty much ever since you showed up. A black wolf with blue eyes," she said with a droll smile. "After...the other night, though, it became two wolves. I was one of them."

Kain glanced over at her. "Describe it to me."

She looked down at her lap and toyed with her fingers. "Well, you know, paws, fur, a tail...running. I am aware that my senses are different, and I have the feeling of being an animal. Like, really being an animal. It's why when I saw the bite mark that I thought..."

"That I had changed you," he said, one corner of his mouth lifting.

They drove in silence for a few uncomfortable moments, neither wanting to talk about last night or this morning.

Finally, Kain asked, "Have you ever had these kinds of dreams before?"

She shook her head slowly. "No, never. Nothing quite like this."

He grunted and nodded, pondering what it could mean, if anything. Dreams were not always simply dreams. Certain kinds of dreams had power to them, but he didn't know what this meant. Maybe nothing, and maybe it had everything to do with what was going on.

"When I'm the wolf it just seems so real, but it's just a dream. Isn't it?" she asked, looking at him.

He looked back at her for a moment and then out the windshield again. "I'm sure they're just dreams, Autumn. But please let me know if they continue or get worse."

She nodded and they lapsed into silence again, both of them lost in thought. They got off the interstate at Rawlins and began to head north on state Route 220. Autumn looked at him then, glancing at the road and back again.

"Where are we going anyway?" she asked finally. Kain leaned back in his seat and propped an arm on the edge of his window.

"We're going to see an old friend of mine in South Dakota. You'll be safe there, and he may know something of what is going on," he said, not looking at her, but he felt her gaze on him for a long moment.

"He's a werewolf too, isn't he."

He glanced over at her and nodded. "He's one of the good guys though. We can trust him."

Autumn breathed in deeply, sitting back in her seat. She was pensive a moment as Kain drove and watched her out of the corner of his eye. Her hand reached up to touch his talisman.

"Back there, in the Walmart," she asked slowly, carefully, "you did something to that…fan of yours. You said things to him and it was like he obeyed you. What was that?"

Kain sighed and pushed his hand into his hair. Might as well tell her that, too. "We have an ability to give…suggestions to others. Depending on how skilled you are with it, and if the person you are using it on is strong willed, it may not work so well, or work at all. Thankfully I was able to use it to calm him down and make him go away."

Autumn looked at him in surprise a moment, then her expression turned aghast as if realizing something unpleasant.

"Did you ever use that on me? Did you somehow coerce me to sleep with you?" she asked petulantly and he looked at her, his expression offended.

"Please. That's a little beneath even me, Autumn. I won you the old fashioned way," he said, then smiled heatedly at her, "Pure, unadulterated seduction. Nothing more."

She blushed, sitting back in her seat with a small, "Oh."

He chuckled to himself and continued driving, heading deeper into the open and empty country of Wyoming.

Autumn chose not to ask any more questions for now and contented herself with looking out the window, chewing on what she had found out about him and his kind so far. She wondered about why such a race even existed, and how. And why all these powers and abilities? She thought about her dream, about feeling like a wolf, and thought of what she knew about them.

Wolves certainly couldn't heal fast, couldn't control people's minds, couldn't do all of those supernatural things he claimed werewolves could do. And they certainly weren't allergic to silver. Any old bullet would do just fine. So why were these "werewolves" so different from wolves? Where had they come from, and what was the point of their existence? Something wasn't adding up to her and she couldn't figure it out. It was all of that information Kain refused to divulge to her, she just knew. There was just too much he wasn't telling her, but she would keep asking her questions. Somehow, she would get all of the truth about what was going on out of him, one way, or another.

They stopped in Casper to get some food and so Autumn could situate her new belongings. She used the bathroom to change into her new clothes, breathing a sigh of relief as she donned new panties and bra, jeans, T-shirt, and one of the new, soft sweatshirts and her sneakers. She brushed her teeth, put on deodorant, and combed her hair, pulling it back into a braid. It was amazing how simple things like clothes and a toothbrush could restore her confidence and she left the bathroom feeling much better about herself.

They ate fast food again, and this time Autumn didn't hesitate to get herself a huge burger. They took it to go and ate in the car, and Kain was obviously pleased that she was really eating for once. She enjoyed every bite.

It was late in the day, the sun hovering low toward the horizon as they neared the dark green of the Black Hills, rising out of the prairie around them.

Autumn didn't know what to expect, what his friend would be like, or what was going to happen from here, but she tried not to be apprehensive as they neared Sturgis. She had only vaguely heard of this town from some of the tourists that stopped in her shop. It had something to do with motorcycles, she knew, but it became clear as they took their exit that this small town lived and breathed biker culture.

Even in the midst of March with snow still on the ground, there were bikes present among the light traffic. It seemed every other establishment was a biker bar or saloon, biker merchandise shop, tattoo parlor, motorcycle garage, or liquor store. Even their town sign said "Welcome to Legendary Sturgis, City of Riders." A lot of the establishments were closed right now due to the off season, but still enough were open and doing business that the whole bike thing seemed to be a year-round staple for the town.

Kain smirked, guiding them through the relatively quiet streets. "You should see this place during the rally. It's insane."

She turned to him, tilting her head "You've been to it?" she asked, and he chuckled.

"Many times. Biggest, wildest party in the wild, wild west."

Autumn rolled her eyes but smiled and looked back at the town. She was just sure he had reveled in his experiences here. There were certainly enough advertisements featuring scantily clad women with barely covered breasts. She could only imagine the mayhem of this place packed with sweaty biker men and the bawdy women who rode with them. Or even rode their own bikes, she supposed.

Her thoughts wandered to what that might be like, to ride a bike of her own as they made their way to the northeastern end of the little town. Nah. She had enjoyed sitting behind Kain too much. She smiled privately to herself. Despite everything, that day would remain a cherished memory.

They drove to a lot at the end of Sherman street, next to the Sturgis cemetery, where a metal sign hung, reading *Amon's Garage*, the words cut out of it with a torch.

Kain drove slowly down a long dirt drive toward a collection of buildings, his mind full of memories. He and Amon went way back, and he was perhaps the one person in the world Kain could call his friend. More than that, his brother. It had been a long time since he had come to Amon that bleak night twenty-seven years ago. Too long.

He drove toward the large garage in back where he was sure to find him. Amon was always tinkering, always fixing something, his clever and complex mind always eager to build up or tear something down just to see how it worked. He also loved craftsmanship, and the art of building machines from scratch. He had some of the sweetest custom rides in the world.

Kain parked while Autumn craned her neck around, looking at the yard with her usual curiosity. He smiled at her as he turned the car off and turned himself toward her.

"Stay in the car until I call for you. He doesn't like to be called on unannounced and I need to make sure of him before you meet him," he said seriously and Autumn looked at him doubtfully.

"I thought you trusted this guy?"

He gave her a reassuring smile. "I do. But he is like me, a werewolf, and he's also a man. We need to…sort some things out first. Stay put," he said. She looked like she was about to argue, but then sat back in her seat with a gusty sigh. Chuckling to himself, he exited the car.

Kain followed the flickering light inside of the garage along with the scent of burning metal. He found Amon toward the back, using the acetylene torch on a piece he had clamped in a vice on a large worktable. He wore a welding helmet as he worked and Kain smiled, staying back as he waited for Amon to sense his presence. Amon lifted his head suddenly and cut the torch. He drew himself up his full height as he lifted the hood of the helmet.

Amon was an impressive black man, standing almost seven feet tall, broad and brawny with thick arms like the trunks of a tree. Like the rest of their kind, he was attractive, with the same exotic, predatory eyes rimmed in dark lashes they all had. Unlike Kain, Amon's human eyes were a light hazel, almost gold in color. He wore his hair tied back in his usual thick collection of well-tended dreadlocks, falling halfway down his back. A blue bandanna was tied around his head. He inhaled a deep breath and grinned as he looked at Kain, exposing strong, white teeth.

"Sonofabitch, if it isn't Kain Ulmer," he rumbled deeply in his rich bass and took off the helmet, striding slowly toward him. Kain held his ground and grinned back, making sure to show all of his teeth as Amon came near. They played out the ritual as their wolves must, circling one another as Amon came close, keeping their distance but breathing in the scent of one another, backs straight and legs stiff, eyes glowing.

"You look good. Better than when I last saw you," Amon commented, as they circled and Kain chuckled.

"I've been busy. Keeping myself out of trouble. You look no worse for the wear," he said back. Amon chuffed, grinning at him, then stopped.

Smiles fading, they looked each other in the eye for a long moment, sizing each other up. Then Amon broke into a huge grin and they both laughed.

"Come here," Amon said and reached out to grab him. They both hugged fiercely, patting each other heartily on the back as they buried their noses in one another's shoulder and got a good, deep smell.

"It's good to see you again, my friend," Kain said as they pulled away, smiling openly with his hands on the larger man's shoulders.

Amon clapped him on the shoulder, eyeing his friend as they stepped back. "What's this I smell on you? Some woman? I thought you said you were keeping yourself out of trouble." He laughed with a touch of curiosity. Kain chuckled but lowered his eyebrows at his friend, looking up at him with his wolf's eyes.

"That serious, huh?" Amon commented, folding his thick arms across his chest and glancing away. "Are you sure that's a good thing? Remember what happened—" he began and Kain growled softly.

"I remember. This is different. And I need your help," Kain said evenly, getting control of his wolf. Amon raised his eyebrows and regarded his old friend.

"What's going on Kain? Are you in trouble?" he asked carefully. Kain sighed, scrubbing his hands on his face.

"You could say that," he said with a small laugh, "and I would like to say it's not my fault this time, but it…well, it is. Sort of."

Amon raised his eyebrow at him in an expression Kain knew well as he waited for him to come out with it.

"I…seem to have…mated…with a woman," Kain said, knowing how it sounded and Amon's face lit up with a big, slow smile.

"Mated? Really? You? You sly dog," he began but Kain cut him off.

"She's human," he said and Amon's expression changed again, falling and becoming incredulous.

"Human? Wait, wait, wait. Wait a damned moment. You just told me that you mated…but with a human? Are you serious?" he asked and Kain, nodded, grimacing.

"No, that's not possible. You must be mistaken. Maybe you only think you mated her."

Kain shook his head."No, Amon, I mate bonded to her… well, my wolf did. Bite and all. You'll see for yourself in a moment when you meet her."

Amon's eyebrows rose almost to his hairline as he blinked at Kain. "Whoa, what? She's here? Are you crazy?"

"Don't worry, she knows," Kain said blandly. Amon tossed his head, his dreads flailing.

"Are you fu…she knows? About our kind?" he asked, his eyes piercing and Kain nodded.

"She caught me shifting," he said, and cut Amon off before the big man blew up completely. "Look, it's a convoluted, fucked up story. The other part of it is that she has an Eater after her and I don't know why."

"A motherfucking *Eater*, Kain?" Amon all but roared and Kain felt his wolf surge forward, lengthening his teeth and changing his eyes.

"Yes, a motherfucking Eater, Amon. I need to get her safe. Will you help us or not?"

Amon breathed heavily through his nostrils, his own eyes icy blue with his wolf as they stared at one another. After a moment, Amon closed his eyes and turned away. Kain breathed a sigh of relief, sending his wolf back.

"You know I will," Amon rumbled, getting control of himself. "She'll be safe here with two of us to guard her. You both are welcome in my territory."

Kain sighed internally with gratitude and clapped Amon on the shoulder. The big man grunted and shook himself, then turned to Kain again with his usual placid, friendly expression.

"Well, then let's go get your little lady and come inside. I just butchered a local deer and I've been slow-cooking a big roast all day. I was gonna have it all to myself, but I guess I can share," he said with an amused smile and Kain chuckled as they started heading out of the garage.

"She does know about us, but I haven't told her everything," Kain warned as they walked. "She doesn't know about the Hunger, and I don't want her to."

Amon looked down at him with raised eyebrows again. "How do you plan to keep that from her? Have you killed yet? We've got less than a week left…"

"I know," Kain growled. "I haven't killed but I'll figure out something. But she is *not* to know about it. I told her only bad werewolves kill humans."

Amon snorted. "Bad werewolves. As in all of us." He laughed darkly and Kain grunted.

"She also doesn't know I've mated her. She thinks I just bit her during sex."

Amon laughed a little in disbelief and stopped, looking at Kain. "Is there anything she *does* know about you? About what we are?"

"Only what I think she needs to know," Kain growled at him and Amon held up his hands in resignation.

"All right. You obviously know what you're doing. Is there anything else I should know before meeting her? What's her name?" he asked and Kain smiled a little ferally.

"The only other thing you need to know is that she is mine, and my wolf is fiercely protective of her. Don't test me with her. And her name is Autumn."

Amon only nodded his understanding as they approached the stolen car and Kain motioned to her.

Autumn had been watching them approach, talking while they came toward her and she was momentarily struck by the sight of them. His friend was huge, a towering and utterly attractive black man wearing a blue T-shirt with rolled up sleeves, showing off his massive, sculpted arms, and a pair of sturdy tan canvas work pants and leather work boots. He was as sinful as Kain was with his strong jaw defined by a neat, close beard, full lips, flaring nostrils, and slanting eyebrows. He had the same kind of bright, exotic eyes as Kain did, some light color she couldn't make out in the fading light.

They both moved with a masculine, animal grace as well, but Kain's stride was lankier than his friend who moved like a big, heavy cat. He reminded her of a tiger, sleek and sensual. Heavens, was this what they all looked like?

She was still gaping when Kain motioned to her and she got out of the car, a little breathless. How could she ever deal with being around two of these men?

Kain strode up to her as she went to them and put a possessive hand to her waist, pulling her toward his friend.

"Autumn this is Amon. Amon, Autumn." He introduced them. Amon kept a polite distance and nodded at her while he looked her over.

"Hi, good to meet you." She smiled politely and held out her hand. He stepped forward and took it, his eyes flicking to Kain as he brought her hand to his lips with a small smile."

Autumn, a pleasure," he said in an utterly sinful bass rumble as he kissed her hand. A growl trickled out of Kain, and Autumn elbowed him to get him to hush. Amon let her hand go and cocked his head, smiling at them both.

"Well, well, fascinating." He chuckled and Autumn looked between the two men. Kain was glaring at his friend who wore an utterly amused expression on his face.

"I just never thought I would see Kain with a woman like you." Amon smiled and Kain grumbled beside her.

"Oh? And what sort of woman do you usually see Kain with?" she asked archly, looking back at him. He rolled his eyes at her in exasperation and shrugged. She leveled him with an *oh really* stare and he growled, pushing a hand into his hair.

Amon suddenly let out a laugh, then erupted into gales of it, roaring as he pounded his thigh. Autumn looked at him in astonishment, then back to Kain who wore a pained expression of long-suffering. She turned back and found Amon trying to control himself, tears in his eyes as he laughed, his fist to his mouth.

"I'm sorry, but this is priceless. Priceless! To think I'd live to see the day…" He sputtered and erupted into guffaws again.

Kain growled beside her and turned on his heel, heading back to the car.

"I'll get our stuff. See if you can get this clown to cool it," he said over his shoulder, and Autumn stared after him, perplexed.

She would never really understand men.

CHAPTER SIXTEEN
Message

Amon's home was a modest split level, and looked like any somewhat older ranch style home in the area. It had four bedrooms, two of which he kept as guest rooms, (*and thank God for that,* Autumn sighed), a pretty standard bathroom with a tub shower, a big living room with a fireplace, a dining room, and a kitchen. His place was tidy, if a little cluttered, and Autumn had been a little disappointed about how…normal it all was. He was a werewolf. Couldn't he at least have some animal heads on the walls or something?

Amon told them to go ahead and choose a room so they could drop their things while he prepared dinner. Kain had tried to argue with her for a moment after she chose a room, following her in and setting his pack down. She had just turned and given him an "*I don't think so*" look. He'd growled, grabbing her arm and pulling her close.

"Amon thinks were a couple," he said, as if that justified him sharing a bed with her.

She had arched an eyebrow at him and jerked her arm from his grasp, then put her hands on her hips "So? It's none of his business, and we're *not* a couple," she pointed out, and she saw his eyes begin to pale as he growled at her.

"I need to be near you to keep you safe," he rumbled, clenching his fists.

She shrugged nonchalantly and said, "Sleep in the hall. But you're not sleeping in here."

And that was that. She had swept past him and into the bathroom with a small smile, feeling proud of herself. She would not allow him to push her around.

After they were settled into separate rooms, Amon invited them to the dinner table where he had prepared a feast. Autumn watched the men happily heaping their plates full of venison roast, mashed potatoes, a lake of mushroom gravy, and chunks of hot, fresh bread. Werewolves certainly did love to eat, and not much of it was vegetables. She sighed as she bit delicately into a bite of the roast. The flavor was different from anything she'd had before, reminding her of something wild, and she found she liked it. She kept her portion small, though, since her appetite nowhere neared what theirs was, and listened as Kain told Amon of their tale so far.

"Strange, why it would target her in such a way," Amon said, leaning back from his cleaned plate while he sipped a beer.

Kain nodded, using a bit of bread to sop up some gravy. "I don't know, it just doesn't add up to me. Why go to such trouble when it could go after an easier target? To be so deliberate, as if it wanted to goad me."

Amon tapped a finger on the table top, considering. "Have you had any run-ins with one before?"

Kain shook his head, sitting back and taking a pull from his own beer. "I've caught their scent on occasion, but I've never met one. They're supposed to be clever hunters, yet I've heard they're all crazier than a shithouse rat. I've always heard that they were extraordinarily hard to kill, even for us. Even with silver."

Kain grimaced and looked up at Amon. "I barely survived it, and I even had to take a potion just to recover. I wounded it enough to deter it, but for how long?"

Autumn listened, chills running up her spine. "Do you think it can find us here?"

Kain looked over at her and dropped his eyes to the talisman. "I'm hoping not. My fang should have concealed your scent, and anything about you that could lead it to you. It could still track me, but even with a strong scent, it would be almost impossible for us to track someone across country, especially via an interstate.

But this thing was like nothing I've come across before. I just don't know enough about them. I was hoping Amon would know something more," he said, and looked back to his friend hopefully.

Amon grunted. "I know probably less than you do. I've only ever scented one once, tracked it to a train station where I lost it. Had no desire to get any closer than that. The rest are just tales we've both heard and no way to know the truth of them. They leave us alone, we leave them alone."

They were all silent a moment, lost in thought about the danger that stalked Autumn. Amon sighed then, running a hand across his short beard. "Wish you could talk to old Bennett. He knows more about them than any of us, but good luck trying to find that tricky bastard."

Kain snorted and shook his head. "Wiley old coot. He'd be the one to talk to, though."

Amon nodded and sighed deeply, then turned to Autumn with a reassuring smile. "Well, you're here now, and we'll keep you safe, I promise."

Kain gazed over at her warmly from across the table, and Autumn felt herself relax some. Surely, between the two of them, and with the talisman she wore, she would be safe here. She hoped.

Kain continued his tale, filling Amon in about their trip and Autumn grew distracted. She excused herself and began looking around Amon's house, strolling around the living room while she allowed the men to talk.

Amon leaned close to Kain then and, keeping his eyes on Autumn, murmured softly enough that she wouldn't hear them. "So you two are mated, but you're not sleeping together? What's going on here?"

Kain heaved a big sigh and took a long pull from his beer.

"I'm mated to her, but she's not to me," he corrected a little bitterly. "She's afraid of me, and doesn't trust me. Not after what happened. She's…difficult, Amon," he said, and Amon eyed his friend.

"So? Compel her or something then. I can smell it on her that she isn't totally unreceptive to you, so work your shit. I can't imagine being mated and not even being able to really touch her. It must be driving you crazy."

Kain shook his head and smiled sardonically, staring at his beer bottle while he toyed with it. "She does, and it makes the wolf in me harder to handle. But no, I won't do it. I don't want to coerce her in any way," he said, lifting his eyes to his friend. "I want her to want me. Me, Amon, not a Compulsion. I've never had this sort of problem before with a woman. Autumn is different. She's stubborn, and willful, and she turns my thoughts all around so I can't even think half the time. She resists me, and it drives me insane." He sighed and began peeling the label off the bottle. Amon sat back, understanding on his face.

"Oooh, man," he said softly, his eyes sympathetic as he leaned toward Kain again. "I don't think you're just mated to her, Kain. I think you're in love."

Kain snorted out a laugh and drank the rest of his beer, rolling his eyes. He didn't fall in love. He thought he had loved Alessia, but he was young then, and that was simple lust and mutual respect. He thought he had loved Carley, but now he understood he had simply wanted to take her under his wing and protect her, perhaps make her into a companion by turning her. But she had died, and while it had enraged him, and he mourned that loss, he hadn't been in love with her. Kain Ulmer didn't fall in love. Period. With anyone. Not even infuriating red heads with a fiery temper and a smile like sunshine.

He chuckled a bit anxiously and began ripping the label of his beer into little pieces carefully.

"I don't think so," he said to Amon and forced himself to meet his friends eyes steadily.

Amon just lifted the corners of his mouth and shook his head, sitting back once more. "OK," he said, finishing his beer as well. "Suit yourself. Deny it all you want, but it isn't going to go away. I know, remember?"

Kain grimaced and nodded at his friend. Amon had been in love with a human woman once, madly in love with her. Kain had saved her from a tragic fate and Amon had sworn an oath to him, a life debt for his true love. But sadly, she was human, and had died from a strange illness a few short years later. No amount of magic could save her; when a life was fated to end, it would end. But Amon had never forgotten her, or his debt to Kain.

Kain leaned over and clapped his friend sympathetically on the shoulder as Autumn came back into the room.

"I think I'm going to go to bed, if you don't mind. It was a long drive." She smiled wanly.

Amon rumbled a good night at her and Kain turned in his chair, giving her a soft, seductive smile. "Sleep well," he rumbled deeply to her. Her lips twitched and her large eyes blinked at him. Then she turned and hurried off down the hall while Kain chuckled in amusement. He loved goading her.

Amon just looked at him with a slow shake of his head.

After listening to make sure Autumn had gone to bed, they settled into Amon's office down the hall. Kain needed information, and Amon had the connections to get him what he wanted. But first, he needed to check his finances.

"So have you spent all my money yet?" Kain chuckled and leaned over to look at the computer screen as Amon accessed his accounts.

"Smart ass." Amon smiled and Kain whistled softly as the portfolio reflecting his money came up.

"Smart investing and trading my friend. I take my cut, but I leave it at five percent. I have my own money. I just manage yours." Amon smiled and Kain gaped at the figures he saw. Amon had been a busy boy over the years.

"Good man," he growled, slapping him on the back and gripping his shoulders. Amon was a whiz at this kind of thing. Kain had always blown through his money without care, and when the success of Wolfyn hit, he'd sated his appetites with abandon, hedonistic and careless in his spending. Amon had cautioned him at the time about his spending, and eventually Kain had capitulated and turned over the handling of his money to him, making Amon his accountant, broker, and beneficiary. Now he knew it was the best thing he could have ever done. He would have all the money he would ever need to take care of what he needed to.

Amon leaned back in his chair while Kain propped his hip on the desk and folded his arms, thinking.

"I need answers, Amon. There's too much going on here even I don't understand. The Eater, my mating to Autumn…and she's changing as well. She was vegetarian when I met her. Now she eats meat…not that I can blame her, but it *is* odd. And she is dreaming of herself as a wolf."

Amon raised his eyebrows at him and folded his hands across his stomach. "Really? That's damned peculiar. What do you think it means?"

Kain pursed his lips and shrugged a little. "I simply don't know. But I need to find out. I need to find my scrying mirror, if you still have it."

Amon nodded, swiveling absently in his chair. "I kept everything. We'll go out to your shed in the morning."

"Good. I also want to find the crystal Larissa gave me those years ago."

Amon stopped moving and gave him a look "What do you want that for?"

"Because if I can't figure out what's going on here, and stop that Eater, I'll have no other choice. I may have no other choice as it is."

Amon sat up in his chair and gave him a look of disbelief. "You'd go to the Queen? Are you crazy? After what she's done to try to capture you?"

Kain looked at his friend and nodded tightly. "I know, but she is the only one that can do a delving. If I can't scry the answers, then she'll at least be able to see what's going on. And she'll be able to keep Autumn safe," he said and Amon shook his head slowly.

"You know what she'll want in return don't you?"

Kain sighed and nodded. "I do, but I am almost willing to do it for the sake of some answers…and for the Partaking. I haven't killed yet, and I honestly don't want to, Amon. I'm tired of it, and if Autumn knew…she would hate me utterly."

Amon regarded him with a sympathetic but disapproving look. "I understand, but you'll be under Larissa's power. She'll make you impart your knowledge to her, and God knows what else."

Kain sighed deeply and put a hand through his hair. "I know, but it will keep Autumn safe, not only from the Eater, but from me."

Amon shook his head and spread his hands. "I don't like it, Kain. I don't trust her. But you're gonna do what you're gonna do. Love is a bitch."

Kain snorted and shook his head. "It isn't love, Amon. I put her in this situation, plain and simple. Until I know what's going on, who is hunting her and why, how to stop it, I'll do what I have to, to keep her safe. Then I'll return her to her life. I owe her that."

"You owe her that," Amon said and shook his head, laughing. "Man, you really think a mating can be undone? You think you can just fix this, send her back home, Compel her memories and then just walk away? Mating can't be undone! You'll carry her with you forever!" he said, and Kain cursed, shoving away from the desk.

"Don't you think I know that?" he growled, pacing the room. "But what choice do I have? She isn't going to mate me back and I don't even know if she can. I will just have to live with what my wolf has done. She won't have to live with it, and she will forget me."

Amon watched him, considering the situation. "You could always try to change her you know. There is a chance…" he began slowly, carefully, but Kain rounded on him in a fury, his wolf sliding over his features.

"Never!" he snarled, clenching his fists, "It's not even an option, Amon! I'll never watch another person die in agony from it, and certainly not her!"

Amon came out of his chair with his wolf in his eyes and it was all Kain could do to keep his own beast from exploding forward, rising to the other male's challenge. They both breathed heavily, barely concealing their teeth from showing. Such a display would have guaranteed the violence that sizzled in the air. After a moment, Amon turned his gaze away, his chest heaving as he struggled for control.

"Easy, old friend. I meant no harm," Amon said softly, his voice calm and smooth as he spoke his Compulsion. Kain stared at him for a long moment, battling his wolf, and finally it subsided and he began to relax. He took several long, deep breaths, shuddering.

"I'm sorry. Just…give me a moment," Kain grumbled, closing his eyes. Amon continued to send soothing energy out into the room, his big form relaxing back into his chair once more. That was close.

When Kain was finally calm, he opened his eyes and moved to slump into a nearby chair, leaning his head on his hand, neither one of them looking at the other.

"I will still attempt to scry this myself before I turn to Larissa. I will only take that step if I absolutely have to," he said wearily and Amon nodded.

"We'll find what you need tomorrow, and we *will* keep her safe. Does Autumn know about Wolfyn?" he asked, changing the subject. Kain smiled sardonically, then told him about the meeting with the fan in Rock Springs.

Amon leaned back in his chair and chuckled, shaking his head. "It still holds on after all these years. You could have really gone far with it."

Kain nodded and ran his hand along his unshaven jaw. "You know why I left. I'll never go back to it. As much as I love the music, I'll never go back."

Amon just nodded at him and they sat in silence for a moment, both of them lost in thought.

After a while, Kain sighed and got to his feet. "For now, I need you to look into a purchase for me."

Kain moved to the desk and wrote down the information on a slip of paper, then slid it to Amon. Amon took it and looked at it, then looked up at Kain.

"What's this?" he asked, and Kain smiled, standing back and folding his arms.

"Don't ask, just see if you can make it happen."

Amon stared up at him suspiciously, then back at the paper again, then made a small sound as understanding hit him. He whistled softly and shook his head at Kain.

"I ain't gonna say it, but you know I'm thinkin' it," he muttered and turned to the screen, beginning his query.

Kain just nodded and motioned to the paper. "Just let me know what you find out."

He left the office and moved down the hall, stopping outside her door. He could hear her rhythmic, soft breathing inside, asleep, and he leaned his head against the door and breathed in the faint scent of her to calm himself further. He fisted his hands and glared at the door, unhappy to be kept from her. He backed away until his back hit the wall, then allowed himself to slide down it until he was sitting, his arms propped up on his legs as he watched her door.

In love, he snorted. Well, Amon could think what he wanted but it was his mate bond, and his attraction to her that drew him constantly to her, a moth to a flame. Folding his arms across his knees, he leaned forward and rested his face against them, glaring at the door.

Tomorrow he would find out what he could. What the spirits would show him. His Hunger was getting stronger, and he would have to hunt very soon. If he went to the Queen, however, she would feed him, she would find out what was happening, and she would keep Autumn safe until the threat could be dealt with. Then she would help him return Autumn to her life. But if he did that, it would cost him everything…

Growling softly he guarded her door, his wolf agitated and his Hunger rising.

Later that evening Kain shifted and ran, binding Amon's land to him with the same spell he had used before, erecting the markers that would warn of any intruders that crossed them.

In her dreams, Autumn dreamed of running in the woods again, and Kain did indeed end up sleeping in the hall.

The next morning, after a large breakfast of waffles and sausages, Amon took them outside to one of his sheds on the property, rifling through his keys as they walked.

"I kept everything for you," he told Kain as he searched for the key. "Saw no reason to get rid of any of it. I knew you'd come back someday, so I figured when you did you could decide what you wanted to take or toss."

Kain clapped him on the back and smiled. "There's not much I want in there, just the mirror and the box."

"Well, it's all here." Amon shrugged as they reached the shed, and after a moment of fiddling with the lock, he raised the rollup door with a loud rattle and exposed a clutter of boxes, bins, and old musical equipment.

Amon stepped back as Kain took a deep breath and headed inside.

Autumn was utterly fascinated and curious as a cat, bouncing on her toes and craning her neck to see what was in there. Kain noticed her after a moment and gave her a small smile, waving at the boxes.

"Knock yourself out. Just let me know if you find a little wooden box or a gold plate."

Beaming, she followed him in, eager to poke into the personal life of Kain Ulmer.

She peeked into boxes of old vinyl records, reached out to lightly touch several old guitars, electric and acoustic, coated in dust, and looked into bins of clothes hastily stuffed into their containers. She pulled out several old band T-shirts from the likes of Led Zeppelin, The Stones, Black Sabbath, Judas Priest, and even Yes and Queen. Bands she had heard of, but growing up as a teen in the 2000s, they were all a bit before her time. Still, good music was good music, and she took note of his tastes.

There was an old motorcycle in here, also covered in dust, and an old looking painting of a lone wolf, eyes glowing as it stood over a pool of water, the moon reflecting on its surface. She opened a box and found a very old copy of The Adventures of Huckleberry Finn. She smiled to herself and grazed the well-worn cover with her fingertips. She wondered about his past, what his life had been. The book was obviously one he cherished and had read many times. Why he had left all his stuff and become a vagabond, dumping them on his friend and hitting the road?

Placing the book back in the box she continued her browsing, sliding in toward the back where some larger boxes were tucked. She unfolded the top of a tall one and saw rolls of glossy paper inside. Curious, she pulled one out and the rubber band that had been around it simply crumbled. Taking it as an invitation she unrolled what was obviously a poster and gaped at the image on it.

It was a poster of Kain...or Derek Wolfsbayne, on stage and screaming into a microphone with the word "Wolfyn" in those slashing letters across the bottom. He had on this get up of skin-tight, ripped-up jeans and a cut-up band T-shirt that barely hung on his sculpted chest. He was adorned with necklaces and bracelets, studded leather, colorful scarves, and black leather cowboy boots trimmed with chains. His hair was wildly different. It was dyed black and though it only fell just past his shoulders it was much...fuller, and he had bangs. Honest-to-God bangs. She stared at the poster and tried not to laugh, but it burst out of her in a snort, and then a full guffaw that had Kain craning his neck around to see what she was laughing at.

"Oh, Christ... Amon why is that crap in here?" he snarled, making his way back to her. Amon stood in the doorway, arms folded across his chest and he shrugged.

"The band sent it to me. I didn't know if it was something you would want so I put it in here," he rumbled. Kain growled as he reached Autumn who was starting to tear up with laughter.

"I'm sorry," she said as he snatched the poster from her hands and began rolling it back up with a growl. "I'm sorry, I shouldn't laugh." She snorted and pressed a hand to her mouth as she tried to control herself.

Kain only grumbled at her and stuffed the poster back in the box, glaring at her as she giggled again, and he maneuvered back to what he had been doing.

"Just...leave it," he growled and she controlled herself with a grin and a sigh, wiping at the corners of her eyes.

She was utterly intrigued now, and she began opening the other boxes back in the corner eagerly. There were all sorts of paraphernalia from patches and buttons to T-shirts and bags. She was tempted to steal one of the band's T-shirts to wear later just to tease him but thought better of it. He seemed to be a bit touchy about the whole thing. She found old magazines from back in the day with Kain's…er…Derek's face blazoned on the covers with captions such as "Rock's Hottest New Playboy" and "Getting Wild with Derek Wolfsbayne." Oh, she would be reading *all* of these, no question. She lifted vinyl and cassette copies of what seemed to be the only record there was and snorted at the title *Carnal Thrust*, recalling what the overzealous fan had said about it.

It had artwork of a scantily clad woman in a red dress, her breasts about to fall out, on her knees with her butt in the air, looking behind her in shock at the shadowed figure behind her. The eyes of the figure glowed red and there was a suggestion of perhaps some pointy ears and claws. That same "Wolfyn" text slashing across the top.

"Really?" She snorted, and turned the album over to read the song titles on the back. The band was pictured there, four other men along with Kain, and all of them had outrageous hair and clothing. She decided there was definitely something primal and sexy about the group, but Kain stood out from all of them. The look in his eyes as he glared at the camera was wickedly sinful.

She read for a moment, biting her lip, then laughed out loud. "Love Pump?" she said, looking over the boxes at Kain who kept going through his things, shaking his head.

"Don't laugh," Amon said from the doorway. "It was number one for three weeks when the album was released."

Autumn stared at the album, turning it over in her hands. Really? She looked at the release date. 1988.

"Wow, I wasn't even born yet," she murmured and she heard Kain drop something with a curse and Amon laughed. She blushed, remembering about their sense of hearing. Well, it was the truth. She was only twenty-six, and compared to their life spans the age difference was enormous.

Not wanting to think about that, she shook her head and put the record down so she could paw through the boxes some more. Something shiny in a glass case drew her eye and she reached for it, lifting up the case and blowing off the dust. It was a silvery metallic record framed with a plaque. Squinting in the dim light she read what it said and gasped aloud.

"Holy shit, this is a platinum record!" she exclaimed, moving so she could show them.

Kain looked up from his searching and stared at what she held. "Platinum?" he asked, and looked around to Amon, who nodded.

"After your disappearance sales went through the roof. I mean, it was already gold to begin with, but with the controversy, everyone had to have it. It went platinum a few months after you left," he said, and Kain looked back at the record Autumn held up for him to see.

"Huh. Interesting," was all he said, and went back to his search.

She gaped at him, looking at the prize again. "Are you kidding me? This is a platinum album and all you can say is 'Interesting'? Your album sold over a million copies!" she exclaimed but Kain just shrugged, sorting through a box.

"That's great. Really happy," he murmured and she blinked at him in disbelief.

She looked at it again in its case with a little awe. A platinum album, and she had never heard of the band before? Sure, her music tastes had always been pretty eclectic, and none of her friends had listened to metal. But by the time she was old enough to have an interest in music as a pre-teen it was the beginning of the 2000s and the whole music scene had drastically changed, and bands like Wolfyn had fallen into obscurity. But even at that, she should have heard something from a platinum album!

She had to listen to it. She wanted to hear what had sold over a million copies to apparently overzealous fans.

"Ah, good," Kain said with a satisfied tone and she craned her head around to see him lift a smallish box out of a crate. Curious, she set the record down and went over to see what he had been looking for. It was a box made of plain wood and unadorned except for an ornate lock, she saw as she looked over his shoulder.

"Do you have the key?" she asked and he just smiled. Putting his finger in his mouth, he nipped himself, then smeared the blood over the lock and uttered a deep animal noise. There was a clicking sound from the box and he opened it with a satisfied smirk.

"Does everything in your world involve blood?" Autumn asked, a little disgusted, but completely fascinated as he took out the bit of purple silk covering the inside.

He grunted at her question as he reached into the small box and pulled out a long chain. Suspended from it was a crystal, capped in a silvery metal, about four inches long and most of it milky white.

"A crystal?" she asked curiously, and Kain slipped the thick chain over his head.

"A message," he said, turning to her and holding up the crystal, looking at it.

"Our kind are not just...shape-shifters. Some of us possess certain knowledge, a very, very old understanding of how the world works on a different level," he said, his eyes shifting to look at Autumn. "Magic, if you will."

She stared at him in fascination. "So after I saw you... change...when you made that mixture in my kitchen, that was magic?" she asked, her eyes wide.

He smiled at her softly and dropped the crystal, letting it rest against his chest. "In a manner of speaking, yes. Some have called it witchcraft, or sorcery. We look at it as an understanding of the basic nature of things. All things in this world have power. The most powerful force of all is flesh and blood, which holds life's essence. It can be used to do many things."

She blinked at him, her mind working. "But isn't that considered…dark magic, or something?" she asked, and Kain smiled at her, reaching out briefly to touch her face.

"When death is not involved, no. There are other means of powering what you are trying to do, but blood is the easiest, quickest, and the surest way to achieve what you want. Our kind heal quickly, so I can use my own blood to power a…spell, for lack of a better word."

Autumn gaped at him, a million questions tumbling through her head. "So all your kind know how to do this? Work magic?" she asked, and he chuckled.

"Thankfully, no. The knowledge is coveted and only a handful know more than a few cheap tricks to get by on. The world would be in a lot of trouble if all of us knew what a few of us do," he said, and put the scrap of silk back in the box and shut it, uttering a command. The lock clicked again and Autumn gave a little gasp.

Autumn turned to Amon who still stood in the doorway watching them. "Do you know how to do this? Work magic?" she asked and he grunted, shaking his head a little.

"I've been taught enough to do what I need to do, but I know nothing compared to Kain," he rumbled, and Autumn turned back to Kain with an incredulous stare. He simply smiled and tapped the side of his head, then put the box back where he had found it and continued looking through his stuff.

It didn't take him long to find what he was looking for, and he grunted in satisfaction as he lifted what looked to be a large, brass plate out from behind a stack of bins. It was highly polished, if a bit dusty. He wiped the dust from its face and the yellow metal reflected his image.

"What's that?" she asked curiously, as Kain tucked it under one arm and began making his way out of the storage shed.

"A scrying mirror. I'll use it to see what I can find about the Eater."

Autumn's eyes widened and she smiled in fascination. That was so cool!

"So how do you know so much?" she asked as she hurried to catch up to him and almost tripped on boxes. He reached out and steadied her with a chuckle.

"My maker Alessia knew these things. When you're bitten, and you survive, a part of the person who bit you is passed on to you. But Alessia was a skilled…well, witch, I suppose. She managed to pass on all her knowledge to me with her bite. Then she taught me to use these things. Thus I know more than the average werewolf." He smirked almost proudly, standing back as Amon closed the shed and locked it again.

Autumn cocked her head, utterly fascinated. "So that pretty much makes you, what, a warlock then?"

The corner of Kain's mouth curled up, showing a hint of teeth. "Our kind don't use such words between one another, but I suppose so."

They turned then and began walking back toward the house, Autumn's mind going a mile a minute. The more she delved into their world the more bizarre and fascinating it became. It was dark, to be sure, but it cast the world around her in a new light. Werewolves were real. Magic was real; she had seen both with her own eyes. Could all the legends and myths be real?

She recalled Oma's stories she had told her growing up. Woods full of elves, goblins, fairies and mystical animals, mountains inhabited by giants and trolls, mischievous kobolds that attended hearth and house, water spirits and sirens that aided men or lured them to their deaths, and characters like the wandering trickster, Till Eulenspiegel, Erlking, the king of the elves, Rübezahl the kindly if mischievous mountain sprite, and the wild huntsman Hackelnberg.

Though she loved the stories and she believed in the mystical to a degree, she had never thought such things were truly, tangibly real. She loved fairies, but she was just too practical to believe that one would actually appear before her face. Now, she wondered if she had just been unable to see such things. How much was she truly blind to? Fascinated and intrigued, she just couldn't help asking more questions.

"So you said that crystal was a message. How? What is the message?"

Kain looked down at her and then at the crystal, picking it up to look at it. "Crystals are natural vessels of energy. They hold information incredibly well, if you know how to do it. This one was given to me a long time ago. As to what it contains is a...map of sorts."

Autumn furrowed her brow at that. "A map? To where?"

His lips fell into a frown then and he clutched the crystal in his hand. "Someplace we may need to go, but I don't want to discuss it right now."

Autumn nodded, still itching with curiosity but willing to let it drop for the moment.

They entered the house and Amon excused himself to check his e-mail. Kain nodded at him and set the plate aside as they sat on the big leather couch. Autumn slipped her shoes off and tucked her feet up under her in one corner, Kain stretched out on the other side.

"There are still a lot of things you aren't telling me," she said after a moment and Kain simply looked at her, his arm stretched across the back of the couch, his long legs stretched out before him on the floor and crossed at the ankle. She was momentarily struck with déjà vu of the night she finally surrendered to him, stretched out similarly on her couch with his eyes full of heated promise of what came later that night. She shuddered a little, flushing with heat, and had to look away.

Kain smiled slowly, knowingly. "Of course, but they are things you don't need to know for now. You just have to trust me."

Amon came back in the room then and shook his head at Kain. "No word yet, but I'll keep checking. Meanwhile…y'all like barbecue?"

Autumn groaned a little and let her head flop back against the couch. More meat? And hadn't they just had breakfast? She was going to gain fifty pounds at this rate.

"Or not?" Amon said, both men looking at her and she sighed.

"Look, I know you boys need to eat, but I'm not a werewolf," she said, shrugging, and Amon nodded while Kain chuckled.

"No problem, I can pick you up something else while I'm out. Anything in particular?"

"Can I just get a salad with no cheese, or bacon, or meat on it? Just vegetables?" she asked, and Amon nodded.

"No problem, if that's what you want. Can't imagine eating that with no cheese at least, but that's fine. Eat what you want." He chuckled, holding up his big hands in defense.

She sighed deeply and thanked him, and Amon left with a promise to be back soon, leaving them alone with one another.

CHAPTER SEVENTEEN
Open Wound

"**So**," Autumn said after Amon left, turning herself toward Kain. "I am, respectfully, asking you…may I listen to your amazing platinum album?"

He chuckled, then sighed and regarded her for a moment. She sat with her legs crossed under her on the other end of the couch, and her hands gripped her socked feet as she leaned toward him. Her face was hopeful and a smile curved her lips as she awaited his answer. She was so damned cute right now in her new jeans and pink hoodie, all open curiosity and good humor. He hadn't seen her like this since their day on the bike, and he groaned inwardly. He could deny her nothing.

"Fine." He sighed, and her face lit up with a huge grin and for a moment, he forgot to breathe.

"Yes!" she said with a little pump of her fist. "I promise not to laugh, I swear," she said as soberly as she could, crossing her heart with her finger and Kain rolled his eyes as he got to his feet.

He looked through Amon's collection for a moment, and finally located the CD. He grimaced a little and sighed again as he opened the case and turned on Amon's system, setting it up for her, then brought Autumn a pair of Bluetooth headphones.

"Knock yourself out," he said and placed them over her ears. She smiled up at him and grazed his fingers with hers as she reached up to adjust the headphones. He stepped away from her as the music began. His heightened sense of hearing allowed him to hear the wail of guitars and the beat of drums even through the noise-cancelling headphones. Autumn listened intently, focused on the music as he sighed and walked away, torn with memories, torn with longing for her, and let her listen in peace.

Autumn listened to the twelve-song, hour-long disc in fascination. Some of the songs were familiar, so she knew she had heard them sometime before, but she simply hadn't known who the band was. As the first song started and Kain's unmistakable baritone began singing a song about a wild-hearted woman, Autumn was entranced. This was not her kind of music, but there was something so electric and primal about the music and Kain's voice that it actually got her heart racing. By the fifth song, she had the absurd urge to get up and dance on the couch, bang her head and let her hair fly.

The band was amazingly talented, working together so well that the music was actually, well, sublime on some level. It was also so well mixed and mastered and put together that the whole album flowed seamlessly, beautifully, even though it was classic eighties heavy metal. The songs themselves were lusty and animal, played with precision, brilliant and almost poetic in their lyrics, and when sung in Kain's throaty roar you wanted to jump up and sing with him. Or jump on him and claim that animal passion for yourself, Autumn thought with her lower lip caught in her teeth during a particularly sensual love ballad.

No wonder the album had made it to platinum. This was pure talent, and while she had never cared for this kind of music before, she knew she would happily listen to it again and again, and it would become a guilty pleasure.

By the time the last song on the album played, a heartbreakingly sung love song, Autumn was completely wound up and breathless with her own wildness. The music had aroused that part of her that appeared in her dreams, the creature that slunk in the shadows and ran through the forest with bright eyes, and she needed to go to him. She removed the headphones and cast about, her eyes searching the room, her nose sniffing for a scent she couldn't hope to smell. She felt invisible ears perk at the sound of an acoustic guitar and she growled softly to herself. She leaped over the couch and followed the sound, licking her lips in anticipation.

He was out on Amon's porch, sitting on a step and expertly plucking and strumming out a complex tune on his six-string. She stepped out onto the porch, intent on him, flushed with her desire, but something about his playing made her stop. It was so different, this playing, than what had been on the album. If that performance was primal, sexual, and seductive, this one was magnificent, and heavenly, speaking deeply of soulful things and she sank down into a crouch, watching him and listening.

Kain had been drawn to the instrument the moment he left the house. Playing had always soothed him when troubled and he yearned for it now. Though he needed to perform the scrying ritual, it was best done at night, especially if there was moonlight. The moon was half full but wouldn't rise until late in the evening. He would bide his time until then and try to rid himself of unwanted memories.

He knew even as he took the guitar out of the case and sat down what he would play. He had always loved improvisational acoustic best, challenging himself with complex fusions of classical, Flamenco, Spanish, Gypsy, and Latin structures. He allowed his fingers to find their own course as he played, tuning in to that place inside of him that was made for music, that lived and breathed it. He lost himself to it, forgetting the pain of his past, the pain of his mate bond, and all of his worries as the music flowed out of him.

Autumn came back to herself slowly as he played, the strange wildness in her receding once again. She was entranced by the music, enthralled by it to the point of transcendence. He was so amazingly gifted, and the world suffered for the lack of his music in it. She rose from her crouch and approached him quietly, not wanting to disturb his playing. He didn't react at all to her as she came up and sat next to him. He was somewhere else, engrossed in his divine playing, with his eyes shut as his fingers flew over the strings.

She allowed his music to entrance her and she pulled her legs up and wrapped her arms around them, then laid her head on her knees. *What a magnificent man.* She could no longer think of him as a monster, as much as an overly cautious and frightened part of her wanted to. He was complex, at once utterly seductive and sexual, yet with depths to him she'd only caught glimpses of. She wondered what his long life had been, if he had ever been in love, and what haunted him so. Why had he given up the music he was so clearly gifted at? Why had he run away from it all?

After a while, his playing came to a natural close seeming of its own accord and Kain opened his eyes and breathed deeply for a moment, then looked over at Autumn.

"You are amazing," she said softly, unable to find the words. She felt so at peace in a way she hadn't felt in days, and in awe of the man who sat next to her. His lips turned up in a small smile and he reached out to touch her, sliding his knuckles along her cheek gently. She closed her eyes and sighed at his touch, butterflies swirling in her stomach. She did not pull away, only lifted her head as he set the guitar aside and slid closer to her, his eyes searching hers. She stared back at him openly, her eyes on his lips, silently begging him to kiss her. It felt like it had been ages since his last, hungry kiss. He leaned toward her, cupping her face, his eyes half-lidded with desire…

Just then, Amon came cruising into the yard, the bass on his huge SUV turned all the way up. Autumn cursed silently as Kain winced and sat back from her with an apologetic expression while Amon pulled around and parked. He stoked her face again, running his thumb briefly along her lower lip and her lashes fanned her cheeks. Damn Amon and his timing!

Amon was singing to himself as he retrieved several plastic bags from his vehicle, then stopped, and raised his eyebrows as he approached them. "I'm not interrupting anything am I?" he asked and Kain sighed. Autumn unfolded herself and stood, shaking her head with a smile.

"No, you're fine. I was just listening to Kain play," she said and Amon nodded, looking back and forth between them. Kain gave him a tight smile as he picked up the guitar and set it inside of its case. Amon sighed and shook his head a little, then raised the bags.

"Sorry it took me so long, I ran some errands and this place is always jam packed. Really good barbecue, at least for these parts," he said and Autumn smiled at him, folding her arms.

"It's OK, we managed to pass the time with some music," she said as Kain closed the case and rose, saying nothing.

Heaving a sigh, Autumn watched Kain head inside, and giving Amon a wan smile they followed him in.

They ate, and Autumn told Amon that she had listened to the album while he was gone.

"Oh? And what did you think?" Amon asked and Kain turned his head to her. She smiled, her mouth open as she tried to describe her impression of it.

"It was…well…it was awesome!" she said, beaming at Kain who chuckled and stabbed at his brisket with a fork.

"No, really! I'm not one for heavy metal or that kind of music, but that was pretty sweet. You were incredible…*are* incredible," she said sincerely. "Why in the world did you ever stop playing?"

A look of pain stole over Kain's face and he poked at his meat, not looking at her.

"I have my reasons," he growled and Autumn stared at him, her mouth open.

"But you're so good, and you clearly love to play. People need to hear your music," she said, perplexed, then gasped as he turned to look at her and stabbed his fork violently into his brisket.

Autumn was shocked, gaping as Kain growled and stalked away from the table. The door to the porch slammed as he left. She looked at Amon questioningly, hurt by Kain's reaction.

"He doesn't like to talk about it. Ever," Amon said sympathetically, and Autumn looked toward the door Kain had just left through.

Amon reached out across the table and laid his big hand on her arm, and Autumn turned to look at him wide-eyed.

"It doesn't mean he *shouldn't* talk about it though," he said, then gave her arm a squeeze with a small smile and went back to his meal.

Autumn smiled softly at the big man, then got up and put on her shoes and ran out the door after him.

She found Kain not far away down Amon's driveway, his back to one of the big Ponderosa pines, leaning his head back against it. He looked at her as she approached slowly, his face betraying nothing. She smiled a little at him, hugging herself.

"I had no idea it would be so painful for you to come here. I'm sorry," she said as she came near to him. He said nothing, just looked away up into the trees. Not knowing what else to do she carefully walked up to him, gently put her arms around him, and laid her head on his chest with a small sigh. He stiffened for a moment, then breathed in a shuddering breath and wrapped his arms around her tightly, holding her close, and buried his nose in her hair. Autumn was a little shocked by the intensity of his reaction to her, and she allowed herself to soothe him, holding him as he trembled against her.

How she knew to come to him, Kain did not know. It was a miracle that she had, and he accepted it gratefully. He'd thought he would be able to handle being faced with that part of his past again, but it had been slowly eating at him. Every reminder of Wolfyn was a reminder of his failure, of the tragedy of that night. Even his music had not soothed away the pain building in him, and he had needed her. Somehow, she'd known it. She hadn't berated him for his outburst, but had simply offered this much of herself to him. He was breathless from it and he held her tightly.

After a few long moments, Kain finally eased a little on her, but still held her close, and nuzzled her hair as he took long, deep breaths. Autumn molded herself against him, stroking his back gently, her touch a balm to his soul.

"In those days I was a fool," he heard himself saying, murmuring against her hair. "I was drunk on power and fame, and thought I was invincible. You don't know what it's like to have thousands of people screaming your name over and over, desperate for any part of you they can get. It makes you feel like a god, like you could do anything. It was heady magic, and I forgot myself."

Autumn simply held him, listening without comment as he reluctantly continued.

"Women were so easy to come by. I didn't have to do a thing, just point at the one I wanted. There was a groupie who followed us for a while, named Carley. I took a liking to her, and she was completely enamored of me. She was young, struggling to make it in L.A., and I was protective of her. I wanted to help her. I thought I might love her," he admitted, and he felt Autumn tense a little against him.

He nuzzled her hair reassuringly and drew in a deep, shuddering breath, remembering that night clearly. "I was arrogant. I thought I could turn her, make her into what I was. I had the knowledge, but not the understanding. Women...don't do as well with the bite that changes. They have to be made of the strongest stuff, their spirits have to be remarkable to survive it. I didn't know. I bit her, sure of myself in all my god-like power," he said with a small, bitter laugh.

He pulled away from Autumn then, tormented as he brushed the hair back from her face. "She died terribly, right there in my arms. It was horrible to watch her go, to know I had done that to her," he said softly, fiercely, and Autumn stared up at him with compassion in her eyes.

He looked away into the distance with his memories. "I walked away from everything that night. I knew fame had ruined me, clouded my judgment, and someone I had cared for had paid the price."

He looked down at Autumn again, sliding his hand into her hair. "I cannot go back to it. I cannot control myself with that power and I know it. I make bad choices and hurt others," he said, then smiled painfully. "Hurting others seems to be the story of my life."

Autumn gazed up at him with such compassion that his heart skipped a beat.

He gazed at her, his need for her clamoring through him after his confession, the old wound lanced open. What he didn't tell her was that after Carley had died he had raged, shifting and running wildly through the streets of L.A. He had been out of control, had denied the Hunger for too long, and Carley's death had broken him. He had gone into a blood frenzy and rampaged, killing a homeless man and his dog, ravaging the old man's body until it had been a gory mess, but even then, he hadn't been sated. He had run on, and happened to come across a woman and her two children as they had walked home after a birthday party. For the longest time he could not suffer the scent of frosting. It had been strong on the children.

He could not tell her that, could not tell her the true tragedy of that night and the reason why he loathed himself for it. Fame had consumed him; his arrogance had made him careless, thinking he could outrun the Hunger. Innocents had died, far too many that night. He had run, fleeing L.A., faking his own death when they later found nothing but charred remains of one of his kills inside the wreckage of his car after he drove it over a cliff.

He looked down at her and desperately wanted sear away his pain with her kiss. And she would allow it. He sensed it. But she was still in danger, and he was still unsure as to why. If he did indeed have to take her to the Queen, the danger to her could possibly be worse. He would lead her deeper into his world than any other human had gone, and she would face new threats. She could get hurt. She could die because of him. She didn't deserve what he might have to bring her into, and he didn't deserve her compassion, her tenderness, or her kisses.

He sucked in a deep, shuddering breath full of self-loathing, and confusion stole over her face as he backed away and let his hands fall away from her. It tore him in two, but he needed to keep the distance between them. If he kissed her now he would bed her again, it was a simple fact. He was a danger to her, his Hunger singing in him even now. He would keep her safe, but he would keep his distance. He simply had to, for both of them.

Autumn didn't understand why he suddenly pulled away, his expression becoming veiled and shuttered again as he stepped back from her. What had she done wrong? Why was he suddenly closing himself off from her? She reached up a hand toward him, her eyes questioning but he just gave her the barest smile.

"I think we should head back," he said, and Autumn stared at him as he turned and began walking back toward the house. What had just happened? She had been open and comforting to him, had let him vent his pain to her, had been willing and eager for his kiss, only to have him completely shut down on her. Had he revealed too much of himself? She trailed after him, confused and bereft.

When he headed away from the house, she stopped and stared after him. His shoulders were rounded, his spine stiff as he stalked away toward the trees. Autumn knew to give him his space and she headed into the house, but it tore her apart.

Amon was putting away the leftovers when she entered the kitchen and he raised his eyebrows at her. She walked over to the table and sat down, her eyes downcast as she toyed with her fingers.

"I take it the discussion didn't go so well," Amon said gently and she sighed, looking up at him dejectedly.

"I don't know. He told me what happened, how he tried to change that girl. Then he just…shut down." She gestured helplessly. "I don't understand him."

Amon frowned and looked toward the door, shaking his head. "Kain has a lot of monsters in his closet. I am glad he at least told you that much; he doesn't talk about his past."

Autumn nodded, folding her hands together. Amon sat down across from her and gave her a gentle smile.

"Have patience with him, Autumn. Kain has his demons, but when it comes down to it, he is a good man despite what he thinks. And I believe he cares for you more than he will say," he said, and Autumn looked up at him with large eyes.

Kain cared for her more than he would say? What did he mean by that?

Amon chuckled at her expression. "You two have a special bond. You'll figure it out soon. I don't think you came across one another by chance." He smiled and Autumn opened her mouth for the barrage of questions on her tongue.

Amon laughed and sat back, holding up his hands. "Don't ask me, woman. I'm not going to say any more than that. This is between the two of you. I just hope I get to hear the ending." He smiled and Autumn sighed, capitulating.

She smiled with her eyes and reached across the table to lay her hand on his. "Thank you, Amon. You're a good man."

Amon grinned, and turned his hand to clasp hers briefly before giving it a light squeeze and letting it go.

"I am glad to call you both my friends. Now, let me get you a beer and show you how to play Oklahoma."

Kain walked away from the house toward the trees, doing his best to rein in his mood. He felt the Hunger in him like a pulse, adding to his aggravation as he prowled out of Amon's property toward the forested ridge nearby. It galled him that he had to keep her at a distance now, but it was the right thing to do. Still, he didn't have to like it, and the wolf in him liked it even less.

He brooded as he climbed until he was overlooking the small town, the hills brown with winter still, dotted with patches of crusted snow. He breathed deeply as his gaze was drawn toward the cemetery adjacent to Amon's property, to the neat and tidy rows of headstones and markers, the small splashes of color from the offerings of the living. He thought of the dead there, how peaceful it must be not to suffer like this. Just the stillness of the grave. Then he thought of all the lives ended in his jaws, the quick surge of power, the jolt of relief and fulfillment as he took it in him, the ensuing rush of soul that nearly maddened.

Hunger surged through him and his eyes burned with change. Saliva shot into his mouth even as he clenched his eyes shut and breathed deeply. He needed to change. He needed to run and to hunt and assuage this maddening craving. He needed to bury himself in her, and find solace in her body and her heat, her tender lips and comforting embrace.

Uttering a roar, he lashed out at a tree, his claws tearing long gouges in the bark. Breathing hard he forced himself to crouch at the edge of the rocky escarpment. Folding his arms over his knees he watched Amon's house far below, keeping his distance from her, waiting for night to fall.

It was dark when Kain walked in the door again, looking around until he saw her. Autumn sat up from where she'd been flipping through a magazine, bored and trying to read though a half-tipsy haze. She had played cards with Amon for hours, enjoying herself thoroughly as he taught her several games.

They'd drunk beers and made wagers with snack food, peanuts being a dollar, and cookies valued at five hundred. She'd ended up winning a tidy sum of five thousand "dollars" and gotten drunk to boot. Finally, Amon had to cut her off and set her in the living room with her winnings and a big tumbler of water. Autumn had protested, wanting to get drunker still. It was more fun that way, and she didn't have to think about Kain.

She was only half-drunk now as she eyed him from across the room.

"Have a nice walk?" she asked, congratulating herself on only slurring just a little.

Kain raised an eyebrow at her as he stepped into the room, his nostrils flaring.

"Are you drunk?"

Autumn's brows knitted together.

"Not as much as I'd like to be, but I'm cool."

Kain frowned and kept his eyes on her as he yelled "Amon!"

Autumn winced, scowling "Jesus, you don't need to yell. He's in his office."

Amon strolled into the room casually, and Kain turned to him with a growl.

"Why is she drunk?"

Amon shrugged, looking over at her. "She's fine. We had some beers and played cards. She needed to get her mind off things so I helped her out."

"By getting her drunk?" Kain seethed, and Autumn saw his eyes flash into pale blue.

Amon crossed his arms over his massive chest, "It was just a few beers. I had no idea she was such a lightweight. It's fine, I'm sobering her up."

"It's not fine! You're supposed to be protecting her, not getting her drunk," Kain snarled, fisting his hands and Autumn frowned.

"I'm not a child, Kain. I can get drunk if I want to. You're not the boss of me."

Kain turned to her, and she felt a jolt of pain at the derision in his eyes. "No, you're not a child, but while I am protecting you I expect you to be on your guard as well. What if the Eater showed up and you were wasted? Would you be able to run from it? Hide? You'd be dead in a heartbeat."

Kain leveled his accusing gaze on Amon again. "I expected better of you, brother."

With a snarl, he strode to where he had set the brass plate against the wall and, snatching it, gave them both scathing looks before walking out the door.

Autumn stared after him, flinching as the door slammed behind him. She was mortified to feel the hot sting of tears in her eyes, and her hands fisted in her lap as she clenched her jaw. She turned to look at Amon who was shaking his head at the door slowly, then he gave her a sympathetic look as he sighed deeply.

"I'm sorry, Autumn," was all he seemed to be able to say.

She sniffed, wiping at her eyes with her fingers as she gathered up her water, magazine, and snacks. "Not your fault. I'm a big girl. I should know better."

Amon gazed at her helplessly, rubbing the back of his neck, "So should I."

"Yeah, well, shame on us both," she said, starting toward the hall, "but your friend is a real asshole."

She hurried past the confused, uncomfortable man, slamming her door for good measure as well.

The half moon rose late in the evening, bathing Kain's bestial form in soft moonlight as it crested the horizon. He had shifted into the black beast as soon as he hit the ridge, ripping of his clothes in his anger and haste. He had run through the nearby hills, pushing his powerful body, punishing himself with exertion. When a lone deer exploded away from him he was on it before he knew what was happening, slamming into the creature with teeth and body. It was dead before they hit the ground. He gorged himself in a mindless frenzy, lost to his beast for a time as he ate, reveling in hot meat and blood. He finally ran from the carcass, full but not sated, the Hunger still gnawing within him.

He didn't know how long he ran, following his own trail, keeping close to Amon's property and the barrier he'd erected. As he sensed the moon's approach, he'd finally loped back to the rocky escarpment, panting hard with his fur crusted with sticky blood as he turned his head toward the rising light. At least he could think clearly again, though rage and pain still needled him. Rage at himself for all of his sins, his most recent the pain he'd seen on her face at his outburst, and pain at his unending need of her, and his insufferable Hunger that his kill had not satisfied.

Ignoring his torment he retrieved his scrying tool from where he had left it and returned to his lookout point. He stood his full height on the rocks and angled the plate until it reflected the rising moon. Nipping himself, he smeared his blood around the outer edge. His claws scraped across the face of it, ringing on the metal when he traced sigils onto the surface, growling and chuffing out ancient words as he did so. Activated, the plate hummed softly in his paw-hands and he stared deeply into the mirror surface, willing to be shown what he sought.

He was pulled in immediately, reeling from the contact. Darkness so deep no light could enter. A hunger so keen that nothing in the world could ever sate it. Death was all around him, death and blood. He saw Amon's face, a death mask of horror. He nearly choked out a cry as he saw Autumn, ravaged and tortured, barely hanging onto life and calling for him. Teeth flashed in the darkness and his own blood sprayed as he reached out a hand toward her. Death was coming, coming for them all.

He shook his head, his wolfish eyes wide with what they beheld and he finally flung the plate away from him into the darkness with a snarl.

He wanted to roar in fury and fear, aghast at what he had seen, and what he had felt in that vision. The cold of that darkness still chilled his blood as he stared blindly out over the lights of the town. He couldn't protect her. Not here, not even with Amon's help. Amon, too, would die if they stayed. He had no other choice.

He found the crystal where he'd stashed it in the bundle of his clothing. He retrieved it and held the milky quartz point between his bestial fingers, trembling slightly as he thought of what it meant.

Larissa had given it to him many years ago; a calling card of sorts after her last attempt to capture him had failed. The werewolf Queen was persistent, anxious for the information he carried in his blood, and his bite. She had tried persuasion and Compulsion, flattery, bribery, and finally threats. But she had never been able to tame him to her hand, or to her bite. It was part of the reason he had been on the run so long. And now he would go right into her lair, and would willingly give her whatever she wanted to keep his mate safe.

He tossed his head, clearing his mind as he gripped the crystal in his massive palm. He felt its cool weight in his hand, and the subtle power that had been ritualistically spelled into it. He rubbed its irregular tip with the pad of his big thumb and bent his head, directing his thoughts toward it, his power into it, and suddenly it gave a small electric jolt and warmed in his hand. Connection.

At once he felt a distant yet irresistible pull north and west of where he stood, compelling him to begin moving toward the far away beacon. His feet moved, claws scraping on stone, and he growled as he willed himself to be still. He concentrated into the crystal, disengaging from it until until it was just a subtle call, a soft reminder instead of a demanding pull.

He opened his eyes and his palm, staring at the crystal that was now clear as ice. He felt the pull of the beacon in his palm as clearly as he felt the pull of Autumn through his bond. He inhaled a shuddering breath and closed his fist around the crystal. Haven. It was somewhere north of here, perhaps in Canada. He couldn't be sure, but now the clock was ticking. The Equinox was a scant few days away, and he could feel the dark thing coming for them now, an unseen menace on their trail. They needed to go as soon as possible.

Shifting back to human as quickly as he could manage, he slipped the chain over his head and was soon making his way back to the house.

It was still the middle of the night but Amon was up, forging new documents for them. He raised his head from his work and looked at Kain with his eyebrows raised, questioning.

"We have to leave, Amon. We can't stay here," Kain began, pacing as he grasped the crystal in his fist. "What I saw…"

"That bad?" Amon asked and Kain shook his head.

"I've never felt anything like it. Darkness, and death…" he said, feeling helpless as he looked at Amon. "This is beyond me, Amon. I've activated the crystal."

Amon nodded slowly, his expression grave. "OK then. I'll finish these documents for you so you have them. You can take the Suburban."

Kain pushed a hand into his hair, nodded and grimaced at his friend. "Thanks, Amon. I need to go wake Autumn. The sooner we leave, the better."

Amon sat back and regarded him soberly. "She's exhausted man, and I know you're raring to go, but I think you'll need these documents. Do we have some time so I can finish?"

Kain paused, considering. He could feel the threat in his bones now, like a gathering storm. It was coming, but it wasn't here yet. Not yet. They had a little time. He nodded at Amon, his lips pressed tightly together, and went to go take a shower.

It was still early in the morning, dawn just touching the sky when Kain entered her room. He breathed in the scent of her greedily as he sat on the bed next to her. She was still deeply asleep, her head turned to the side, her lips slightly parted. She was snoring softly, and he couldn't help the small smile that curved his lips. His smile faltered then, remembering how he had treated her earlier. He had been hard on her when all he wanted to do was find solace in her arms. Yet he had to maintain that wall between them, now more than ever. He was about to bring her fully into his world and he could not afford to lose himself in her now.

Touching her gently despite himself, he brushed his knuckles across her cheek. "Autumn, wake up. We have to go."

She started, snorting as she looked around at him blearily in a haze of sleep. "Whassat?" she asked groggily and Kain withdrew his hand, fisting it to keep from leaning over her and kissing her awake.

"We have to go, we can't stay here. You need to get up, get packed. Amon's making coffee."

She blinked at him for a moment, then nodded slowly, grumbling. "OK. Can I shower first?"

Kain rose to his feet before he reached for her again and nodded. "Sure, but make it quick."

He left her to it, escaping to the kitchen so he wouldn't have to hear her in the shower or imagine her in it.

Autumn got clean and dressed as quickly as she could manage, given her bleary state. She was still hurt by him, tired, and just a little hung over, but the smell of coffee drifting down the hall bolstered her. She didn't know what was going on, but Kain seemed urgent, so despite her mood she forced herself to wakefulness and finished packing her bag. She found the men in the kitchen leaning against the counters, drinking coffee. She was struck again by the sight of them both. Fit, tall, gorgeous men rippling with muscle and dripping with predatory, carnal sensuality as they turned their heads to her. She was taken for a moment by how animal the movement was, and could practically see pricked ears turned her way.

"Morning," she said, concealing the quick, almost instinctual thrill of unease with a cough. Amon rumbled back at her with a small smile, and Kain merely appraised her from behind his mug as he raised it to drink, his expression unreadable. So he was still being moody, huh? Fine, she was in a mood, too.

"So what's going on?" she asked, trying to keep the grump out of her voice as she slid between them to fill the waiting mug with coffee. She was all too aware of both of them, like standing between two male lions.

"I'll tell you in a moment. Get your coffee," Kain said evenly, not budging, close enough for her to feel his intense body heat as she stirred a spoonful of sugar into her mug. She grimaced, annoyed by his curtness, annoyed by her awareness of him. She grabbed her mug and gladly went and sat at the table. She arched an eyebrow at him, waiting.

"I did a scrying last night," he began, eyes fixed on her. "What I saw was not good. I saw death if we stay here, so we're leaving ASAP."

Autumn stared back at him, her mouth falling slightly open.

"Death? Whose death?" she asked, not truly wanting to hear the answer.

"All of ours if we don't go soon." He frowned, and drained his cup with a gulp.

He set the mug aside and Autumn gaped at him with wide eyes.

"Finish your coffee. I'll get our stuff."

Autumn looked to Amon as Kain strode from the room, and he gave her a small, somber smile.

"I'll fix you a couple of breakfast sandwiches to go. There's more coffee if you want it."

Autumn thanked him softly and looked into her mug, stunned. Kain walked past with their things, her one small piece of luggage, and his backpack over his shoulder as he went out the door. Autumn touched his talisman between her breasts, closing her fingers around it. Surely, the Eater couldn't find them, but Kain seemed pretty certain about what he had seen. The talisman felt warm between her fingers, yet not at all reassuring.

Fifteen minutes later, they headed outside to where the SUV was idling, exhaust steaming in the cold morning air. Kain was impatient, his nerves on edge as he placed the last of their things into the vehicle. Amon had given him two new credit cards, driver's licenses for them both, social security cards, birth certificates, passports, and $2,000 cash. All the documents they might need. Then Amon had turned and offered him a hard case, and Kain sensed silver inside of it. He'd looked questioningly at his friend, who unlatched the case and opened it, revealing a black 9mm automatic handgun and two fully loaded clips. The clips were full of silver.

"It's not the most powerful gun in the world, but this will stop any one of us cold," Amon said, snapping the case shut again and latching it. "Whatever you do, don't get caught with it though. The serial number has been filed off, and they'll want to know why you're packing silver slugs." He grinned and Kain chuckled, accepting the case with profound gratitude. Amon had thought of everything.

Once he'd tucked the gun in the SUV, Kain turned to them, standing in the early morning light. He didn't know if he would ever see his friend again as he walked to Amon. Their reunion had been too brief, but he would not put him in danger. They eyed each other for a moment, then with a happy growl, they pulled each other into a big, back-slapping hug with their faces in each other's necks. Then they backed off from one another and grinned, clasping each other's hands.

"Thanks, Amon, for everything," Kain said and Amon grasped his shoulder with his free hand, nodding.

"We have a pact, brother. Anything for my friends." He smiled, including Autumn in the promise.

They let go of one another as Autumn came over and smiled up at the giant man.

"Amon, it was a great pleasure to meet you. I hope to see you again, someday," she said, holding out her hand. Amon enfolded her small hand into his giant palm and brought her hand to his lips. "Autumn, it was my pleasure. I hope for that, too," he rumbled in his deep bass and she smiled prettily, causing Kain to growl in his throat.

"We need to be going," Kain said and Amon let go of her hand with a sigh. Autumn rolled her eyes, chuckling a little.

"Yes, dear," she said, turning to Kain with a little curtsey and flashed a quick smile to Amon as she hurried into the car.

Kain growled audibly and stalked around the big SUV to the driver's side and got in. He rolled down the window as Amon approached, propping his arm up on the edge of the window.

"Stay safe. I expect to get this baby back sometime soon," Amon said, patting the relatively new, sleek black Suburban.

Kain grinned at him mischievously, revving the powerful V8. "I dunno, I might want to keep it. It has that new car smell and everything."

Amon rolled his eyes and chuckled. "Well, then you just might be purchasing it from me, plus ten percent now that I gotta drive my old Bronco."

They laughed and gripped each other's hands and smiled at one another, reluctant to part. They disengaged before anything more could be said and Amon backed away as Kain backed the SUV out of its parking spot. Amon raised a hand at them as they drove down the dirt driveway, and Kain donned his sunglasses to hide his apprehension.

They drove in silence for a bit as they got on the freeway and headed west toward Montana. The morning was bright and clear, the sky an intense blue as they entered the rolling expanses of Wyoming again.

Finally, Autumn turned to him and gave him a quizzical look. "So where are we going now?"

He clenched his jaw for a moment and fingered the crystal, not looking at her. He was taking her into danger, into a dark and treacherous place, banking that he could keep her safe there. Not only from the darkness that pursued them, but also from the denizens of Haven itself.

"The crystal guides me where to go, but it isn't specific. We're headed to Montana I think. Maybe farther. Hard to tell, but you'll be safe where we're going," he said softly, gripping the steering wheel with both hands again

"Oh," she said, looking out the windshield again, then she turned back to him. "But *where* are we going?"

He looked at her, his expression dark. "I'm taking you to a werewolf colony, Autumn," he said, "The only one in existence. No Eater will dare to touch you there."

Autumn gaped at him as he turned back to driving.

"A werewolf colony? Like…a town or something?"

"Not exactly." Kain smiled darkly. "No human has ever been there before." *And lived very long*. Autumn stared at him, her eyes wide as if she'd heard his unspoken thought.

She turned back to the window, saying nothing more as she clutched his talisman.

Kain brooded as they drove, and he finally switched on the Bose speaker system in the SUV and tuned the satellite radio to a hard rock station, the music suiting his grim mood.

CHAPTER EIGHTEEN
Into Darkness

They drove for hours, not talking, just listening to music and avoiding the tension between them. They ate Amon's sandwiches and stopped for gas a couple of times as the Suburban guzzled through it. The day grew cloudy as it waned, and they eventually left Wyoming behind and entered Montana. It was all lovely, beautiful country with huge, open skies and stunning mountainous vistas, but Autumn was apathetic, subdued by Kain's coldness toward her.

The sun was on its descent toward the western sky when they entered Bozeman, and here Kain stopped at an outdoor store he had looked up on the Suburban's GPS. Autumn stared at him quizzically as he parked.

"We're headed north, into the mountains. You need warmer clothes. And boots," was all he said, and they got out and went into the store.

Autumn shopped half-heartedly while Kain stood by, ignoring her as he scanned the store. She got only what she felt she might need. Insulated hiking boots, two pairs of wool socks, a parka with a faux fur hood, a pair of ski pants, gloves, and another sweater that was too cute to pass up. She had no idea where they were going or what to expect, but at least she would be warm.

Once he had paid for her purchases, they hit the road again, traveling into the late afternoon.

Autumn eventually slept as the sun began lowering toward the western horizon. Lulled by despondency, boredom, and the smooth ride of the vehicle, she nodded off and slipped into dreams.

She was running again, but this time she ran through empty darkness, her paws skittering on ice. She stumbled and slid, scrambled to her feet again, her panting breath steaming in the frozen air. Something was chasing her, gaining on her. She ran, unable to see where she was going, only knowing that she needed to run. Run faster. It was almost here. She strained, running as fast as she could but her paws kept slipping, and whatever was chasing her was right behind her. She whined in terror and forced her lupine body to its maximum speed, but it wasn't enough. She slipped, tumbling end over end in the ice and snow until she skidded to a stop.

She lay there, trembling, as her pursuer approached. It was the black wolf, her mate. But instead of helping her, reassuring her, he stood over her with deepest sorrow in his blue eyes. She whined to him and lifted her muzzle to his for comfort. But instead, he drew back his lips from his oversize, long teeth, and lunged for her throat.

Autumn awoke with a gasp, flailing for a moment as the dream retreated. Her trembling fingers flew to her throat, feeling for a wound that wasn't there. Kain looked over at her questioningly but said nothing as she breathed deeply, calming herself. Just a dream. Just another wolf dream. But it had felt so real! She had felt his teeth in her throat, and had felt the burning sting of betrayal. Her heart actually ached with it.

She breathed deeply and looked around her, blinking. They were driving through a blizzard in the dark, and they weren't on the interstate any more. She looked at the time and saw that she had been asleep for almost four hours. Four hours? That couldn't be right.

She looked over at Kain but he was ignoring her. His attention was focused on driving in the perilous conditions. She sat up and saw there were no signs of other vehicles on the road, and the world around them had narrowed to the white of snow flying at them in the headlights with darkness on all sides.

"Where are we?" she asked, looking over at him.

Kain frowned and kept his attention on the road. "I wanted to get to Kalispell or father tonight, but this just came in out of nowhere."

She looked back at the disconcerting sight of snow flying right at them, making it almost impossible to see the road. Kain was driving slowly, but the snow was getting deeper the farther they went, and even the tire tracks of vehicles ahead of them were dwindling.

"How much farther?" she asked, and he switched the vehicle's screen over to GPS.

"Thirty miles to the next town," he said with a grimace and Autumn sat back in her seat, worried. She was glad she at least had put on the snow pants, warm boots and sweater, and the parka was just behind her on the seat. If they did get stuck she wouldn't freeze at least. She hoped.

"We'll get there," he said, and reached over to grasp her arm. She shivered and allowed her hand to find his, gripping him tightly. He looked over at her and gave her a small smile and something in her sighed. She relaxed and felt like she could breathe again, and the tightness around her heart eased a little.

After a moment, he disengaged his hand with a small squeeze and maneuvered the heavy vehicle through the blizzard. Autumn searched the darkness, looking for some lights out there at least, but there was nothing, only the swirling snow.

Without warning, a form darted out in front of the car. There was the fleeting impression of a deer just as they hit it and Autumn yelped as Kain stood on the breaks. They slid, the large SUV lurching around on the icy road to crunch with a jolt off the shoulder and into the snow.

"Autumn, are you all right?" Kain asked urgently after a moment and Autumn looked around at him, a bit dazed.

"I think so," she said, checking over everything just in case. She might have a mild case of whiplash, but otherwise she seemed unharmed.

Suddenly Kain's head snapped up and his nostrils flared at the scent coming through the vents, which still blew warm air. His eyes were wide as he looked out the rear window where the tail lights lit up the dark road behind them softly in red. Autumn turned and could just make out the form of the deer they had hit. It might be suffering. She grabbed her parka to get out and go to it.

"No!" Kain said sternly, and she stopped, looking at him. He darted into the backseat to grab the case that Amon had given him. Autumn's eyes widened as he took out the gun and slapped in a clip, then loaded a round into the chamber.

"Do not leave this car!" he said, and opened his door and jumped into the howling night.

Autumn turned herself to watch him approach the deer with her heart in her throat. She didn't know what he had sensed, but it had to be the Eater. She recalled his words *"It can assume any form, person or animal…"*

The snow swirled around him as he approached cautiously with the gun leveled at the deer's form. It didn't move, and she gripped the seat as he drew close to it. There was a thick swirl of snow and the thing jerked and flew at Kain. There was a sharp bang and a flash, causing Autumn to jump and yelp, and the snow thinned again in time to see the creature of horror slam into Kain, taking them into the darkness, while the gun spun into the road.

The gun!

Without thinking she flew out of the car, donning her parka as she went. Her legs trembled in fear and the wind howled around her as she made her way onto the road. There was no light save for what the headlights and taillights illuminated, otherwise the world was darkness around her. The swirling snow being blown in her face made it impossible to see. She panted heavily in the cold air as she approached the area where she had seen the gun fall, cautiously looking all around her. She heard faint howls and screams around the wailing of the blizzard but they were hard to pinpoint.

She searched around in the snow with her feet, shaking with adrenaline and cold while she shuffled through the powder, muttering frantically under her breath. Finally, her foot struck something and she reached into the snow triumphantly. The gun was heavy and coated in snow and ice and she did her best to clean it off. Would it even work if it was wet? She knew nothing about guns, had never even held a gun let alone used one before. She shook as she cast wildly about her, gripping the gun tightly with both hands, her finger on the trigger.

Besides the howling of the wind, there were no other sounds. She listened, straining to hear anything above the whistling and moaning but there was nothing. And then there it was, an inhuman growl somewhere off to her right. She turned the gun toward it, wide-eyed, and backed away slowly with her heart hammering in her throat.

She whirled around the other way at the sound of an eerie, moaning scream in the distance. Her fingers were white with terror around the gun as she tried to see anything. Then another sound to her right that could have been a grumble, or a snarl. A snapping, breaking sound like something coming through thick brush made her whirl around. The wind made it impossible to know where any of it was coming from, and she couldn't *see* anything!

She turned at the sound of something unmistakably close. An inhuman snarl, the scrape of claws against ice, and she raised the gun, trembling uncontrollably. The snow churned thickly for a moment before her, the wind howling to a fever pitch and she saw the unmistakable glow of eyes out there in the darkness, piercing and violet. She fired, letting out a little scream as the noise blasted around her and the gun kicked back violently in her hands, almost causing her to drop it.

There was a howl of pain and the snow cleared for a moment, revealing a black form that dropped to its knees in the snow and clawed at his side with an inhuman scream. He began to shrink down upon himself, his cries becoming more human as he changed. Autumn stared in utter horror, unable to grasp what she was seeing, what she had just done in her panic and fear.

"Kain!" she screamed, and her fingers loosened on the gun as her knees began to give way. Something struck her and she went skidding across the icy ground, her head spinning with stars and pain. She was still reeling when she was grabbed by the ankle, jerked around, and something began pulling her strongly through the snow. She tried to clear her head but she was still dazed from the blow and she scrabbled feebly at the snow with her hands, whimpering. Her numb fingers caught on something, curled around it. It was a branch, yet it offered her no hold as it was dragged along with her.

Gathering her strength, she pulled up the branch, and with a cry, she swung out at the darkness with all of her might. The branch connected with whatever dragged her along, and suddenly she was staring right into the fangs from her nightmares. It screamed at her, rows and rows of long, pointed, slender teeth and felt its hot, fetid breath on her face. A horrified cry clawed its way out of her throat and she scrambled back from it, weak with terror. It followed her in the darkness, mad eyes glowing like ice. It made a horrible, rasping sound, and she realized it was laughing.

Her death was upon her. It crawled over her quickly, almost like an insect and she felt its horrible weight on her, crushing her into the snow. Claws pricked through her parka as it laved her face with a slimy, hot tongue. Its teeth clicked together above her rapidly as if excited by what it tasted. Wracked with shudders of fear, Autumn sobbed loudly and clenched her eyes shut, waiting for her death.

Λ presence suddenly filled her, and calmness spread through her. She felt herself floating backward, receding as the wildness in her surged, filling her with sharp, calm awareness. The talisman against her breast burned, seeming to ignite against her skin, responding to that which filled her as the Eater opened its jaws and its claws sank into her skin. She felt herself speak words she felt along her nervous system, but did not understand. The talisman seemed to flare without light, chiming without sound, and the Eater let out an inhuman scream and jumped away from her as if burned, hissing and spitting in rage.

"Mother!" it screamed at her, its beady eyes rolling wildly as it gathered itself, ready to attack and rip her to shreds.

Several sharp blasts rang out in the darkness and the Eater jerked back, shrieking in pain as it launched itself at a new target. There was another blast just as it moved and its head whipped backward with a spray of gore. Its body crashed into the snow beside her, its face a rictus as its claws flashed, twitching in death.

All at once, Autumn was released from her stupor as the wildness inside receded again. With a gasp she scrabbled away from the dark creature in the snow, horrified as its form bubbled, then began to melt.

She shuddered violently, watching as it began to flow and shrink, becoming smaller and pinker before her eyes. Its ruined head collapsed on itself as the body tried to become human again, but couldn't quite seem to do it. She sobbed as one baleful, milky eye rolled out of the head and into the snow, and the body continued to contort and melt, pieces falling away from it as it disintegrated. The scent of it was beyond putrid.

Autumn got to her feet weakly, trembling from head to toe. She backed away as the Eater spread out in a noxious pool of quickly freezing black goo and she whimpered, shuddering. It was dead. It had to be dead now. Nothing could come back from being goo, could it?

With a shuddering gasp she turned, horror slamming through her anew as her brain registered everything that had happened.

"Kain!" she screamed, sliding in the snow in her frantic haste to get to him, scrambling toward the lights of the SUV.

He lay curled on the pavement not far from her, pink and naked and human as she threw herself down next to him. Shaking violently, she turned him over. He groaned, blessedly alive. The gun was still in his hand. She gasped when she saw the blood coating his side, dark in the wan light from the SUV not far away.

"Oh no." She sobbed, her hands shaking as she used a handful of snow to wipe at the blood. She managed to clear some away and saw the dark hole of the bullet wound in his side, leaking blood. She shuddered in fear at the sight. His eyes cracked open and he lifted a trembling hand to her, his lips curving into a smile. She took his hand, gripping it numbly as she stared down at him. "Thank God," his lips said, but the screaming wind tore any sound away into the swirling night and he closed his eyes again.

She inhaled a shuddering breath of freezing air as her mind went into emergency mode. She had to think clearly here or he would die. First thing, she had to stop the bleeding. She thought frantically for a moment, then an idea sprang into her mind. Tampons. She had bought a box at Walmart, and they were in her luggage.

She scrambled to her feet, almost falling in her haste as she rushed to the car, and flung the back door open. Her hands were shaking as she forced her frozen fingers to work, clawing at her luggage. She was shaking so hard she fumbled the box of tampons and they went everywhere, but she managed to snatch one and ran back to Kain. She ripped the wrapping off and pulled off the applicator, then brushed the blood away with some snow again until she could see the wound. He screamed as she pushed it inside of him and she sobbed, making sure it was in far enough to staunch the bleeding.

Now she had to move him, get him into the warm car. Sliding her arm under his shoulders and bending her knees, she began trying to lift him. He groaned and tried to get his feet under him as Autumn murmured encouragement, and finally he was standing, panting and leaning on her heavily. He looked down and ran a trembling hand over his wound.

"We…have to get…the bullet out…" Kain shouted as loudly as he could over the wind. Autumn nodded and began to guide him back toward the SUV.

"No," he said, shaking his head. "The gas won't last and you'll freeze to death before anyone comes along. There's a house…just over there…" he yelled, nodding his head into the darkness. "I saw it when…we were fighting. It was dark, looked like it might be seasonal."

He pulled himself off her with a groan and stumbled to the SUV. He leaned back against it, breathing hard. She stayed close to him, looking up at him in the darkness.

"Do you have the gun?" he asked and her eyes widened. She dashed back to where he had lain and, thankfully, it was right there in the snow. She showed it to him as she hurried back.

"Good. Get…the other clip. Grab my pack and only what you need…and turn the car off. We'll leave it here until help arrives," he said, and winced against the pain.

Autumn moved to do as he said, grabbing the ammo and his pack, leaving most of her stuff in the car. She could always make her way back here if she needed it for some reason. She turned off the vehicle and took the keys, locking it out of habit as she moved around the vehicle back to Kain. His breathing was labored and he was beginning to slump again as she gently got her shoulder up under him and put her arm around his back. He gasped and snarled as he lifted himself again, and then began guiding them through the darkness toward the house he had seen.

It was dark as pitch as they stumbled through the blizzard, Kain guiding them. They took it slowly, Autumn trusting his senses to find their way through the dark and blowing snow. She could only just make out vague impressions of trees, fallen logs she helped him over, and tangles of branches they had to find their way around.

At last, she saw the faintest hint of a structure in front of them, dark as the rest of the night. Slowly they worked their way toward it, slogging through the deep drifts while Kain leaned heavily on her. It did appear to be a seasonal cabin, shuttered up for the winter with no visible signs of it being taken care of for months.

They found the closest door to them, apparently the back door, and Kain gave the lock a sharp kick with a small cry of pain. The door cracked, splintering at the lock, and swung inward. Weakened by even such a small effort, Autumn had to practically drag him inside the cabin, his feet stumbling weakly. She laid him on the floor and closed the door as best she could.

It was even darker in the cabin than it was outside, and though they were no longer being punished by the storm, it was still cold as sin. She dropped his pack and fumbled around for a light switch near the door. She found one and flipped it, but nothing happened. The power had been shut off.

"In my pack," Kain said weakly in the darkness. "A lighter…"

She felt her way back over to the pack and fumbled around the pockets of it carefully with numb fingers. He kept a lot of things in the old leather backpack, and she felt around in frustration for a while. Finally her fingers found what felt like the smooth shape of a Zippo lighter and she pulled it out. She was shaking as she flipped the top and struck the wheel of it until a flame caught. The minuscule light was just enough to make out that they were in a kitchen.

She shivered in the cold as she bent over Kain, touching him and feeling that his normally hot skin was cool. He groaned and looked at her, and his eyes caught the dim light of the flame, causing them to glow subtly behind his lashes. He was still conscious, and she breathed out a sigh of gratitude for that. Before anything else, she had to get them warm. She had spotted a wood pile just outside the door, so it stood to reason that there was a wood-burning fireplace or stove nearby.

Getting to her feet she carefully stepped around Kain and saw the outline of a doorway. She lifted the flame high as she entered the next room and made out the shapes of furniture in the darkness, and then there, the rectangle of a fireplace in the wall. The light glinted off something glass on the mantel above it and she saw that it was an oil lantern. She went to it and snatched it off the mantel. She almost sobbed with relief when she saw it was still half full of oil. She removed the glass chimney and lit the lantern, the flame catching slowly. She adjusted it to its full height. Now she could see what she was doing.

She gathered wood from the pile outside and, making sure the flu was open, began making a fire. She spent several frustrating minutes trying to get it started, cursing with fear at Kain's quiet a dozen feet away in the kitchen, but finally the kindling took and she murmured fretfully as she fed the flames, coaxing the fire into life.

Once the fire was going she hurried back to Kain and crouched down next to him, touching his face. He was breathing slowly, but he opened his eyes at her touch and stirred a little, lifting his hand weakly to hers.

"I need to get you into the other room," she said, and he nodded slowly, then began trying to lift himself from the floor with a wince and groan of pain. Autumn pulled him up as much as she could, using all of her strength, and together they got him standing again. He almost blacked out but he kept himself conscious as Autumn supported him and they staggered into the next room.

She laid him on the floor in front of the growing fire and placed the lantern on the other side of him so she could see his injuries. The tampon was utterly soaked and useless now as blood coursed down his side from the wound.

"Need…to get the…bullet…out." He panted, his face contorted in pain. "I n-need to shift…will heal if…if I can do it. Wolf won't come…can't shift until the silver is out."

Autumn nodded, trembling as she looked around the room. She had no idea what was needed or involved, and had only the barest knowledge of what to do in a medical emergency. She didn't know if she could do this, but she had no choice. He was dying slowly.

"Tell me what to do," she said, looking down at him desperately, gripping his hand.

"Look for towels…and a knife. Something to help…grab it with…pliers, or tongs…" he gritted out and she nodded, grabbing up the lantern and hurrying into the kitchen.

She pawed through the drawers and cupboards there desperately, coming up with an armload of dish towels, a kitchen knife, and, thankfully, a small pair of kitchen tongs used for sugar cubes or ice. It would have to do. She tried to get water from the sink in a big bowl but when she turned on the tap nothing came out. The water had been turned off as well.

Cursing, she hurried back to him and set the lantern down next to him, then she placed one of the biggest towels gently behind his head to cushion it. Muttering an apology, she then removed the tampon as gently as possible. Blood gushed from the wound. He hissed in pain as she pressed a towel to it and she looked up at him anxiously.

He panted, focusing his eyes on her. "I can feel it…against my back… God, it burns." He grimaced, writhing for a brief moment before focusing on her again.

"T-thankfully it's near the surface…but you'll have t-to cut me…to get it out…" he gasped, shaking with pain.

Autumn trembled, nodding her understanding, then helped turn him over gently. She probed with her fingers along his back, and felt a hard protrusion several inches lower than where the bullet had entered. He whined in pain as she pressed on it, making sure it was the bullet and not something else.

"That's it. That's it," he wheezed, clutching at her arm and craning his head up to look at her.

"Use the knife. You'll have to cut me, Autumn. Use the tongs to help get it out," he said, sweating now, and Autumn took a deep breath and grabbed the kitchen knife. She had no idea how sharp it was but she didn't have time to find out. Steeling herself, she took several deep breaths, and feeling with her fingers for the bullet again she pressed the knife to his side.

He roared and arched back as she thrust the knife around the edge of the metal, then deeper to get under it. She sobbed as he gritted his teeth, blood pouring from the new wound, and she tossed the knife aside and grabbed the small tongs. She thought it would be easy to grab the small piece of metal but it was slippery inside of his flesh, sliding around as she probed with the tongs as gently as possible. He shook violently, panting between clenched teeth while she searched for the bullet with the tongs but she couldn't get it.

She threw the tongs aside and, whispering an apology to Kain, she used one hand to press against the entry wound, then slipped her finger deep into the cut she had just made. Kain thrashed, crying out in pain. Tears were in her eyes as she held him, probing with her finger inside his warm, slippery flesh. There. The hard object was just under her fingertip, the tongs having pushed it back farther. Closing her eyes and sobbing a little she pressed her finger deeper, sliding around the bullet, and hooked it against her pad. Murmuring a little prayer she began pulling it out slowly. Kain gritted his teeth and snarled in agony.

Finally she pulled the bullet out with a torrent of blood and it clattered against the floor. His blood began to pool under him and she snatched up towels and pressed them to the two wounds, shaking as violently as Kain. Relief flooded her. It was out, but he was now bleeding terribly. Keeping the towels pressed to his wound she rolled him over again. Kain gasped with the movement, and she saw he was visibly pale in the firelight.

"You're bleeding pretty badly," she said anxiously, pulling her hand out from under him to clear her eyes with her sleeve. Both of her hands were coated in his blood.

He stilled for a moment, a look of concentrating on his face as he breathed hard, and then he thrashed his head back and forth. "Silver was in me too long…poisoned the wound. The wolf won't come…" he gasped, his eyes rolling in pain.

Autumn whimpered, tears leaking again as she took his hand in hers and leaned over him. "You can't die," she whispered desperately. He rolled his eyes to her, fever bright.

"Never." He managed to chuckle, wheezed, and clenched his eyes shut in pain.

He kept his eyes closed for a moment, breathing heavily, and then he met her gaze with desperate intensity. "There is something I haven't…told you."

She waited while he seemed to gather himself, turning his head and clenching his eyes again before finding her again with his pained gaze.

"That…bite…I gave you that night, before…I wasn't truthful about it," he said, his voice full of agony. "It wasn't a changing bite…but it is still special. It is a mark, a brand…that shows you are mine."

Autumn stared at him wide-eyed, trying to understand what he was getting at.

"My wolf…" he said feverishly, tossing his head. He seemed reluctant to say it, and she squeezed his hand between hers reassuringly. He met her eyes again, his gaze steady and bright as he gripped her hand back. "You are my mate. I am bound to you, forever. My wolf has marked you. He will respond to you. You must call him out."

Autumn stared at him in disbelief, her eyes searching his face. He wasn't joking. His eyes pleaded with her as he trembled violently, and she nodded slowly, her heart racing. She was his mate? What did that mean?

"What should I do?" she asked weakly.

"Call to him. Howl, and he will answer," Kain said seriously and Autumn blinked at him.

"Howl? Like a…a wolf?" she asked, laughing nervously and Kain's expression became fierce.

"It's not a joke! Do this or I die," he snarled, and Autumn paled. She couldn't lose him, not now. She would strip naked, roll in honey, and cavort with bears right now if it would save him.

She doubtfully sat back from him, and after a moment let out a soft, self-conscious little "Ooooo!"

"No-no-no…" he said, shaking his head and breathing hard. "Take…everything that is inside you. Take all your anger…all your fear…all your…love, and joy, all your passion. Take all that wildness I sense in you and feel it in your gut."

He paused, panting, and grimaced against the pain. Then he opened his eyes and glared at her from under his eyebrows, savage in his agony.

"Feel it inside…down to your toes. Let it…let it become sound. Let it fill you…let it rise."

Autumn did as he said, taking all of her panic, and fear, her anguish at seeing him injured and in pain, and finally the desperate and intense feelings she had for him, feeling it at her core. Yellow eyes blazed within her, and wildness whipped through her soul.

"Now call on that wolf inside of you, dammit, and howl!" he cried out, and Autumn let go.

It came out of her at first as a cry of desperation, a scream of pain, and fear, and lastly rage. And then it lengthened, and as her face turned to the ceiling it became a pure howl, sonorous and lilting, full of humanity and wildness at the same time, and it filled the space around them. She clenched her eyes shut and willed the beast in him to answer her.

Kain roared in agony, his body arching up off the floor as he writhed and screamed inhumanly. Autumn scrambled away from him in fear, snatching the lantern away lest he knock it over, and watched with wide eyes as his skin rippled, and his body contorted weirdly as he shifted with agonizing slowness.

Terror gripped her tightly at the sight of him changing, the sheer otherworldly strangeness of it sending her psyche into a primal reaction of fight or flight. It wasn't right that anything should morph like this. It was unnatural, the way his bones lengthened, the way his muscles writhed under the skin, and the sounds! God help her, that might be the worst part of it. Kain howled and whined, his voice at once animal and human in a way that set her nerves on edge, and his breath whistled through a snout that was beginning to form. There were deep grinding and popping noises to accompany his sounds of pain, and his newly formed claws clicked and scrabbled against the hardwood floor. The wind howled outside and the fire popped and crackled merrily, and Autumn shrank against a nearby piece of furniture, clutching the lantern.

He snapped at the air as his jaws lengthened, the sound like a thunderclap, and his vocalizations became deeper as the change continued. Fur pushed out of his skin with a subtle hiss, his limbs longer now, his claws fearsome. He rolled up into a crouch with his back to her as he continued to grow, and the room filled with the musk of a wild animal.

Autumn watched all of this from mere feet away, her eyes wide and her heart thundering as he rose up now, twisting around and stretching to the ceiling with terrifying jaws open wide. He uttered a moan that turned into a loud roar that shook the house. Autumn whimpered in fear, unable to look away from him or move as his roar died away into a weak rumble and he finally finished shifting. The huge beast that he had become stood panting near the fire, quiet now, and trembling visibly as he lifted an ape-like arm to lean against the mantle in exhaustion.

Kain breathed heavily, weary to the bone, and he cracked an eye open to look at her. She had done it, called his wolf out of him with her song. Saved his life. Yet she was terrified of him all over again. While he had managed to make the shift, it had left him so weak he doubted he would be able to shift back to human for a while. He couldn't run, and she couldn't look away from the beast that he was. She would see him now, fully, and the scent of fear spreading from her was his condemnation. Mate bond or no, she would never be his again. He hung his head weakly and trembled, unable to do anything else.

Autumn waited for what would come next, staring wide-eyed at the beast slumped against the fireplace. But he did not come for her, did not threaten or menace, only braced himself and hung his head. He breathed heavily, his sides heaving from the exertion of changing. Minutes passed, and nothing else happened. There was only the sound of his breath and the crackling of the dying fire, the wind moaning occasionally outside. He didn't look at her again, just breathed, his pointed ears laid back against his skull.

Curiosity slowly overcame her fear as the minutes ticked by, her panic receding as no other threat from him presented itself. This was still Kain, she reminded herself. Somewhere in there it was still Kain. He had said his wolf had…bonded to her. Mated to her. If that was so, would he harm her? Could he? She held her breath but the beast didn't move. She slowly got to her feet, the lantern in her hand.

Slowly, ever so slowly and cautiously she approached the werewolf Kain had become, waiting for some sign of aggression from him. He didn't move, only turned his head toward the wall as she came within touching distance. He was a massive creature, possibly taller than the ceiling at his full height, and his bulk seemed to fill the room. He was covered in a thick pelt of the blackest fur, and he stood upright and had the torso of a man. His long and thickly muscled arms were a little more ape-like than human. His legs were like that of a wolf, but much thicker, bulkier to hold his massive weight upright. His feet were gigantic paws, tipped with deadly looking black claws and those big toes spread as he shifted his weight subtly. She looked up at him but he still had his big head turned away.

She reached out slowly, tentatively, toward him, hesitating briefly at the heat being radiated by him. But he stayed stock still, and she touched his strange arm. He was incredibly warm, and his arm was corded with muscle and rock solid beneath the thick, hair-like fur that cascaded down it. She ran her hand down his arm and lifted his heavy hand. A trickle of fear threaded through her as she turned his hand over and those long, dagger-like black claws thrust up. She swallowed her fear, though, and examined it. It was like a human hand with an opposable thumb and four fingers, and on each was a big, thick paw pad, with three larger pads on the palm. He even had that little wrist ball like dogs did. She ran her fingers across the dry, pebbly skin curiously and she felt him tremble. She looked up and caught her breath to see those icy blue eyes, ringed in red, looking down at her, but she forced herself not to look away.

His head was wolf-like, with a broad muzzle, small, intensely bright eyes limned in black, dense cheek fur and thickly-furred, pointed ears. But there was a savageness to his face that she had never seen on a wolf, even when he was clearly being placid and calm. As if rage were always just below the surface. He looked away from her again and she saw the tips of massive fangs poking out below his upper lip.

She took a deep breath and let go of his hand gently to continue her exploration of him. She stepped around to his back. His shoulders were broad, human, and they tapered to a very human-looking waist and buttocks. She was fascinated to find a tail hanging down. She lifted it and ran her hand along it, wondering at how wolf-like the fur was. She reached up and stroked the thick ridge of hackles down his back. The black fur was stiff and almost hair-like, and he had a mane of longer hair falling in layers from his neck like extra-long hackles. She stroked these, lifting them and thinking of Kain's human hair. These were stiffer than human hair, but gave him the same wild effect.

She stroked his arm again, noting the longer feathering of hair at the outer edges, and made her way around to his front. His chest was broad, his abdomen thickly muscled, and when she laid her hand against his stomach she found his body was rock hard. She looked up and saw his fur was thickest around his neck, creating a dense ruff. She ran her hands up into it, admiring the soft, deep fur there.

It was like being able to get up close and personal with a wild lion, or bear, or other large predator and she was awed by it, by being able to touch such a creature. Her fear melted away completely then and she stood on tiptoe, stretching to reach her hand to his stiff cheek fur, petting him. He looked down at her again, his pink tongue flicking out to lick his nose uncertainly. The action was so dog like that she laughed a little, and stroked her hand along his muzzle, feeling his black whiskers. He stared at her with those bright, intense eyes and his ears were still laid back against his skull. His look was full of apprehension, like a bad dog that was afraid of being kicked by the person it loved.

She stared up at him in awe and shook her head, smiling a little. "You are magnificent. Such a beautiful creature you are," she said softly, and a long, high whine issued slowly from his muzzle.

He stared at her in shock, unable to believe what she had just said. What her scent was telling him, and what her eyes told him now. She didn't hate him, and her fear was gone. She was looking up at him with calm, trusting eyes, and her hands were on him, petting him soothingly. Accepting of the beast he was. Trusting of his wolf. He whined, full of disbelief and hope, full of emotion that was crashing down on him like the sweeping rush of the tide. He didn't quite know how, but he began to change before he knew what he was doing. He needed her like nothing he'd ever had before, and the wolf stepped aside without a fight as the man surged forward powerfully.

He sank to his knees and clung to her waist as his body shrank quickly. Autumn gasped as the energy leaving his body rushed over her, and he resumed his human form within a few moments. He trembled against her, clinging to her desperately, and didn't say a word. Autumn stroked his head that was pressed against her ribs, and his arms wrapped tightly around her waist. She felt tears in her eyes, her own heart too full of things she couldn't say.

She had misjudged this man, labeling him a monster when she saw, now, that he was anything but. Strange perhaps, powerful, certainly deadly, and definitely otherworldly, but she saw no evil in him. In fact these last few days she had seen that he was deeply caring, burning with passion and emotion, and he had a deep affection for those he cared for. Perhaps he wasn't all that honest at times, but he had honor. Yet he was full of hurt and self-loathing and deep, deep pain. He was breathtaking in his talent and in his passion, and he was stunning in his beauty that was far more than skin deep. He was magic, and made of wild darkness and savage fire.

He had saved her life.

He had marked her. Called her his mate. Said he was bound to her…forever. It made her feel weak in the knees.

She had almost lost him tonight, by her own hand. Her mistake. She had made a lot of mistakes. It was time to stop listening to her fear, and to her own doubts and uncertainty. It was time to listen to what her heart had been telling her all along.

She was in love with Kain Ulmer. Deeply, desperately, pathetically in love, and she had been from the moment he had sat down with her on the porch at Dragonfly, seemingly centuries ago. She knew that now, and there was simply no denying it.

She inhaled a deep, shuddering breath with the knowledge and closed her eyes, trembling as she held him close to her. He leaned into her, trembling as much as she was, and she blinked back tears. He was still weak, she could tell, and while his transformation had healed him, he still shivered against her. She needed to get him warm, and he needed to rest.

It was time to heal on all levels.

CHAPTER NINETEEN
Love Touch

Kain refused to acknowledge what raged through him, threatening to consume him whole. The force of it was potent, and he clung to her, shaking as he resisted naming the overwhelming emotion. If he did he would be lost to it, and who he was would cease to be. It terrified him, so he denied it, refused to accept it, refused to admit to just what had brought him to his knees. He buried his face against her as he fought to regain control of himself.

He needed to keep his distance from her, for both of their sakes. He needed to pull away from her. He needed to remove himself and make himself become detached from her again. He had to get her to Haven, and putting distance between them would make what he had to do so much easier. He *had* to let her go. It only made him cling to her tighter.

He was drowning in the force of what gripped him, trembling fiercely as he tried to deny it. Thankfully she pulled away from him a little, stroking his head.

"I think you need to rest," she said softly and he breathed deeply as he fought for control. He felt bone weary. The oblivion of sleep would be welcome. Perhaps there he could escape, could gain control of himself again. He nodded and did not look at her as he reluctantly let her go. Her hand caressed his head one more time as she took the lantern and went down the hall. He sagged against the floor, too tired to do anything but sit there bleakly while his mind raced like a caged animal.

She came back a few moments later dragging several blankets and quilts she had managed to find. He watched as she began arranging a bed on the floor in front of the fire, piled with every blanket and pillow she could find in the place, then left again. She came back in a moment later with a pot full of snow. Tossing more logs onto the fire she set the pot next to it so the snow could begin melting, then cleaned up the mess of bloody rags.

Belatedly he ran his hand down over his naked torso. His blood was sticky on his skin still, but the wound was gone, sealed over now and completely healed. It would leave a puckered scar that he would bear for the rest of his life. The shift had done the trick. He sighed, closing his eyes as he beat back his emotions again. He did not want to think about what she had just done for him. How she had saved his life. He only prayed that they were safe for the moment. The scent of this Eater had been different than the first. A second one, which he didn't want to contemplate at all. He hung his head, too weak to think about it for now. He just uttered a little prayer that for tonight she would be safe so he could heal.

She came back in the room with a few more towels, and checking the pot she saw the snow had mostly melted. She brought it over and crouched down next to him.

"I'm sorry this will be cold, but I need to get you cleaned up and into bed," she said gently, and he winced a little as she laid the cold, wet towel against him and began wiping the blood away carefully. He turned his head from her and clenched his eyes shut as the emotional force that he refused to name came back for him again at her touch, insistent, demanding he acknowledge it, but he refused. He was on the verge of shattering when she finally stopped and set the pot aside, then rose and went to the makeshift bed and turned the covers back.

"In you go," she said, motioning. He obeyed with a sigh, crawling over to her and laid down with his body turned toward the fire. She laid the pile of blankets over him.

She didn't say anything as she walked away, and he could hear her washing her hands with water from the pot. He was weak, and he was hungry. Terribly hungry. His body and the beast inside of him needed the energy of a kill now more than ever. But he denied it as he denied her, curling into himself while he listened to her shuffling around, taking care of things.

Autumn tossed the bloody water out into the snow, then scrubbed her hands as best she could with fresh snow until they were as clean as she could get them. After that she brought in more wood, creating a tidy stack next to the hearth, and set a fresh, clean pot of snow close to the fire to melt. She hoped the snow would be safe enough to drink. That done, she stoked the fire until it was roaring.

Finally satisfied that everything was taken care of she placed the gun and his pack within his easy reach and began pulling off her shoes, laying her soaked socks nearby the fire to dry. She doffed her parka, tossing it on a piece of furniture, and shoved down her wet snow pants, then pulled her sweater over her head. She watched Kain's still form as she stripped her bra and panties off. She shivered, the chill air and anticipation giving her gooseflesh.

No more denying. No more running from him, or from her fate. Her heart would not be denied what it had felt all along for this man. Whatever he might feel for her in return, if anything… time would tell. Right now she had to heal this rift between them, and she had a pretty good idea about how to do that.

She took a deep breath and went to him. She slid under the blankets and found his warming body, then molded herself to his backside with a shuddering breath at the contact of skin to skin. He jumped and stiffened, and lifted and turned his head to her with questioning eyes.

"Autumn?" He sucked in a breath as she slipped her hand down across his belly and up to his chest, holding him close as she kissed his shoulder.

"Shh," she said, nuzzling into his neck and hair. "You need to rest. Just be still and let me feel you."

He shuddered violently and turned his head away, yet remained tense as she touched him. She stroked across his chest and gently let her fingers trail through his chest hair, her fingers tracing his curves and hollows. She followed the line of hair down to his navel, then slid her hand over to caress the scar left by the bullet. He held his breath as her hand trailed to his hip bone, caressing the sensitive area before sliding down his thigh, then back up to gently palm the curve of one taught cheek. She moved on, trailing her fingertips up his side as he trembled, all the while kissing his shoulder and neck tenderly. She bit him gently on the shoulder as she fanned her fingers against his belly and he groaned a little. She was reaching him.

Kain couldn't believe what was happening. He had expected her to sleep on the floor next to him of course, but fully clothed and in her own blankets. He expected her to be wary of him even after her encounter with his beast, but instead here she was, naked and pressed against him. She was touching him gently, maddeningly, with soft caresses and even softer kisses. This, after she had watched him shift. After she had seen the beast up close. He vaguely wondered if he was dreaming, or if he was perhaps dead and this was heaven. Yet he still resisted her, resisted the emotion that came slamming at him, harder this time, demanding he acknowledge it. He trembled a little in fear at the power it had over him, terrified to open himself to it, to her. Perhaps she and the feeling were one and the same. Her teeth grazed him and he nearly swooned, closing his eyes.

He should stop her. He should turn her away and make her leave him alone. But he could sooner move a mountain right now, or stop a raging river with his bare hands. She was simply a natural force in his world, and her smallest touch, her barest smile worked on him like the rain or wind, gently and inexorably changing him.

He had never in his life felt so vulnerable with a woman, but Autumn was no mere woman to him. She was strong, and brave, and she awed him with her quick wit and her fiery passion. She was smart, and he adored her curiosity, her humor, and her tender heart. She was deliciously feminine, and she made him feel utterly like a man. He couldn't get enough of being around her, and it was laughable that he even tried resisting her. She was a siren, drawing him out of himself, making him live again. She opened his deepest wounds and healed them with her gentle compassion. She reminded him of what was still good in himself, that he was a man and not a monster, and that his soul was worth redemption. *She* was his redemption, his salvation, and his heart leaped at her tender touch.

Her hand trailed down and cupped his throbbing groin and he sucked in a hissing breath. She caressed him gently a moment, then curled her fingers around his aching shaft for a long, slow stroke. He uncurled himself to give her better access, and his hand drifted down to touch her hand lightly as she stroked him again. He tried to make himself remove her hand, tried to deny her one last time, but instead his fingers curled over hers and he squeezed her fist in his to grip him tighter. He groaned as she began stroking him firmly, guided by his hand. Her breath was hot against his ear for a moment before she sucked his earlobe into her mouth. His earrings clicked against her teeth as she nibbled on the tender flesh. He turned his head slightly to her, breathless with desire for her. She nuzzled against his stubbled jaw as their hands worked up and down on his erection.

She licked his neck and glided her tongue to his shoulder, then she released her grip on him and slid her leg over his hip. She turned him then with her body and he let her, allowing her control over him, and wondered what she would do next. She moved over him and nudged his knees apart to position herself between his legs, then she kissed his chest and flicked her tongue over his nipple. He growled a little in his throat, watching her and caressing her hair while she continued to nuzzle, lick, and kiss her way down to his stomach.

Autumn took her time worshipping him with her mouth, swirling her tongue around his navel, nuzzling the hair on his flat belly and savoring the heady, masculine scent of him. She had almost lost him tonight. She began following the darker, silky trail of hair from his navel downward with her tongue. She had made a mistake, and it had nearly cost him his life. The knowledge made her nearly frantic for him, to taste every inch of him, to do all she could to pleasure him thoroughly. She apologized with her hands and her mouth, kissing down to his hip and laving him with her tongue there. He shifted and let out a breath as she swirled her tongue around the sensitive skin, inching closer to his nest of dark hair, and his erection that brushed against her cheek.

She looked up at him while she slid her hand up his thigh, lightly scratching the underside of his scrotum with her nails before she curled her fingers around his thick base. His eyes glittered down at her, his mouth partly open, breathing heavily as he waited in anticipation. He sucked in a hiss of breath and then moaned aloud as she slid her mouth down over him. She took him in as much as she was able and worked him with her tongue, sucking him hard as she pulled her lips up his shaft. She went for another pass and his hands found her head, sinking into her hair. Her eyes flicked up to his again, watching his face tighten with lust as he watched her suck him, her hot mouth taking him in again and again. His eyes rolled back and he tossed his head as she swirled her tongue around his taut and darkened crown, suckling him there for a moment before plunging down again.

His hips began to move with her rhythmically, and Kain uttered a soft grunt as he looked down at her again and thrust up into her mouth. They kept their gaze on one another as she worked him with her tongue. Autumn savored his expressions, his sounds, the musky salt of him in her wet mouth as she drew on him. She lapped the underside of his glans and saw his eyes shift, swirling from the dark blue of a moody ocean to the pale blue of a winter sky, ringed in red.

Autumn felt his thighs begin to tremble next to her ears as he thrust into her mouth, his breath hissing as he gripped her head. His whole face was tight with lust, his teeth slightly bared while he watched her. She smiled around his cock and worked him faster. She bobbed up and down quickly, gripping his lower half in her fist as his thighs and belly tightened. He bucked against her, thrusting harder into her mouth now as he panted through his teeth. She gripped his hips, digging in her nails and she took him as deeply into her mouth as she could, frantic now with her own need. He trembled all over, snarling as he bucked against her mouth and she took it, growling back at him as she sucked him hard. *Her* prize, she growled possessively as her wildness whipped through her.

His growling rose, becoming louder as he pumped his hips. His growls turned into a groaning roar and he clamped down on her head as his hot seed shot into her mouth. Autumn practically purred and she swallowed greedily, suckling him and swallowing down the hot, salty prize of his climax as he cried out with his orgasm. The taste of him was exquisite, and she was loath to give him up as he finally went limp around her, spent. She licked him lazily, making sure she got every delicious drop of him.

Kain lay there, dazed by her as she licked him with his legs limply spread around her. He didn't know if it were because she was his mate, or if she truly was that good, but he couldn't remember when he had been given such exquisite head. He still throbbed with his release, shuddering subtly as she finished her ministrations with a final, soft suck and looked up at him from under her lashes with smoldering eyes. She licked her lips and his breath shuddered as she crawled up him then, brushing her naked body along his. Her lips brushed his gently and he gripped her ass in his hands and pressed her against him. She pulled away and he growled in his throat, her eyes searching his for a moment before she met his lips again, teasing him with light kisses. He felt himself growing hard for her once more.

Snarling, unable to bear her teasing, he stroked his hands up her body and pushed them into her hair, gripping her head, and crushed his lips to hers. She smiled against his mouth and parted her lips for him. His tongue slid deep, taking her mouth desperately. Their tongues danced with one another for a moment and then he was slowing the kiss down, still desperate yet deeper, kissing her like he was afraid she might disappear at any moment. She returned his kisses with deep and tender ones of her own, sighing against his lips as he savored her.

After a few more moments he pulled away and leaned his forehead against hers, sharing his breath with her. They were both trembling, and when he pulled away from her slightly and opened his eyes he stilled at her expression. Her eyes were languid yet intense, full of vulnerable emotion that made him want to weep. To see such a look in her eyes… He rolled her over with a growl and pinned her beneath him as he bent to her lips again. She moaned against his mouth and wrapped her arms and legs around him, burying her hands into his long hair. He kissed her deeply for a while, savoring her, cinching his cock into her wet folds and grinding against her gently with a hungry sound in his throat. She sighed and wrapped her arms around his neck as he moved to her throat, nibbling with his teeth and licking her with long sweeps of his tongue.

Kain lifted his head and took her lips again, passion and the emotional intensity roaring through him so hotly he could hardly contain it. He pulled back from her a little and, gripping his cock, guided himself to her opening. He held her eyes and pushed himself into her body, joining their flesh together once more. She cried out with it, her tight sheath yielding to him and he groaned as he slowly filled her to the hilt. Electric heat rocked him from head to toe and he tossed his head back in ecstasy. Christ, he was mating her again, something he never dared hope for, and it was beyond exquisite.

He began thrusting deeply, slowly into her with soft growls. His wild hair curtained them, swinging gently with his movements. Autumn writhed beneath him, her face taut with lust and something deeper as he moved within her. She made him delirious with her small sounds of passion, her sensuous pout glossed from his kisses, and he reached out a hand to caress her face. Her lashes fanned her cheeks and she laid her hand against his, breathing out a deep sigh as his fingers brushed her lips. She opened her eyes and he groaned when she guided his index finger into her mouth. She sucked on his finger, her vulnerable gaze never leaving his as her clever tongue stroked his fingertip and his balls tightened painfully.

He cursed and began thrusting faster while she suckled his digit, miming what he was doing to her with his own finger. It was too much, the sight of her lips wrapped around something so innocuous. His orgasm was almost upon him when he made himself stop with a snarl and removed his finger from her mouth. She made a sound of dismay, her sheath clutching at him as he pulled out of her with a groan. He silenced her protests with a deep kiss and turned her to face the fire, then positioned himself at her back. He dragged her back against him and propped himself on one arm, then pulled her leg over his thigh, exposing her to him. She moaned as he filled her again with a satisfied rumble.

She gasped breathlessly as he thrust into her slowly from a spooning position, taking his time. He slipped the fingers of his free hand into her silken folds, finding where they joined together, and then slicked her creamy wetness up over her sensitive clit. Circling her pearl expertly and thrusting with exquisite slowness, he bent to her shoulder and licked his mark upon her. His teeth grazed it once more with intense possessiveness, mimicking the original bite. She shuddered and made an utterly female sound of pleasure that caused him to smile smugly against her skin. He growled, scattering small bites across her neck and shoulder, and bent his free arm around her to roll one of her nipples between his fingers.

She gave a lusty moan as Kain did the same to her clit, pinching the hard nub delicately before releasing it again. She whimpered, gasping as he began upping his tempo, fighting against his impending orgasm as she writhed against him. He wanted to slow down time, savor her every reaction, every sensation as he brought her closer to her release. He wanted this to never end, to stay locked within her, timeless, suspending their ecstasy and spinning it out through centuries. He wanted to keep her on the edge, always hungering for him, never sated as he was never sated for her. He never wanted to let her go.

He murmured her name against her neck as he pumped harder into her, his fingers matching his rhythm, tapping against her clit quickly as her thighs trembled against his. They tightened, clenching together as she neared her orgasm. He growled and kept his hand where it was, pumping his hips against her as she gasped out her moans. She was on the brink, ready to shatter, and he would send her over the edge.

"You're mine, Autumn. *Mine*," he growled breathlessly in her ear. *And I am yours.*

She howled as she came, arching against him and clamping her knees shut around his hand. He relinquished her wetness and pried her thighs apart, holding her open as he drove into her with a mindless, animal frenzy. Her sheath gripped him hard, squeezing him convulsively with her orgasm. The scent that marked her as his mate wafted over him, stronger with her climax, and he bucked against her, maddened with his need for her. He bit down on his mark and held on as she shuddered, never breaking her delicate skin as his balls drew tight and he panted quickly through his teeth.

When he came he flung back his head and roared her name, thrusting into her with hot spurts, bucking against her wildly as his orgasm went on and on. Autumn cried out with him, climaxing again with the strength of his release. It was like being reborn, exploding into existence with a burst of stars as she came with him. Spiraling down he thrust inside of her one last time with a final jerk.

He dimly realized that his fangs were out as they lay together a moment, panting, too exhausted to move. He was stuck in her again, tied with her by his swollen cock. His eyes rolled back as they were both rocked with a smaller orgasm, and Autumn shuddered sweetly against him. He half turned her in his arms and gazed down at her face. She stared at him in languid wonder, reaching up to slide her hand against his jaw, and her thumb brushed a fang.

He bent and kissed her lips tenderly, relishing her as they shuddered with another tiny orgasm.

"Kain…" she breathed softly against his lips. "What is this?"

He lifted his head and looked down at her a moment, then bent and covered her face with small kisses. "My wolf is a little over zealous. Call it a gift from him." he chuckled softly and she stared up at him with large eyes. They pulsed together, shuddering with pleasure once more. He pressed his forehead to hers, breathing with her. It was utterly amazing, magical even as the waves of sensation poured through them both.

They stayed that way a little while longer, Kain kissing her lazily and stroking her with the tips of his claws as the small pulses began to become less and less, until they finally stopped altogether. By then his teeth and eyes were back to normal and his claws had retreated as well. He pulled out from her with a small tug and a last, lingering kiss.

By now the fire had died down considerably and the chill was seeping into the room. Kissing her shoulder with a smile he rose, covering her with the blankets while he got the fire going again.

She watched him from their makeshift bed, exhausted and full of a sated bliss she had never known before. So he was a werewolf. She kind of liked it, and the new wildness inside of her liked it even more. She hadn't imagined some of those looks he gave her, and what his passion had told her. She had reached him again, perhaps deeper than ever before. She bit her lip as she watched him, the taste of him still on her tongue. There was no hint as to what tomorrow held, no words exchanged between them. No promises made. He had said that she was his. He had said his wolf had mated her. What did that mean, exactly? What about the man? Would he leave her once he had her safe? Did he feel the same for her at all? Was there any hope for them here?

He stood next to the fire, bathed in light as he took up the pot and drank the melted snow from it. Water trickled down his naked abdomen and the firelight limned his body. She breathed at the perfection of him. He was sinfully gorgeous, and she was so in love with him. Whether he could ever return her feelings…she tossed her head and banished her thoughts. It didn't matter right now. Now, he was here. Now, he was hers, and she would take all of him she could get.

He wiped his mouth on his arm and looked down on her, barring his teeth in a sensual grin. He knelt and handed her the pot to drink. She did so, then handed it back and tossed the blankets aside, holding her arms out to him. He set the pot down and grinned, growling softly as he came to her. He covered her and took her lips passionately as she drew the blankets over them and pulled him down.

Tomorrow they would figure out what to do about their situation, but tonight, tonight was for them alone.

Kain awoke slowly in the dim light of morning to find Autumn's lovely body draped across him. She was snoring softly and he smiled to himself, stretching a little. Though they were both exhausted, they had loved each other repeatedly through the night, and he doubted he could have outlasted her even if he still weren't weakened by silver. She had a passionate appetite that he found was a match for his own. They had sated themselves on one another until exhaustion claimed them completely.

He stroked a hand lazily down her body, unable to help himself. She murmured a little and shifted some but didn't wake and he wrapped his arms around her. He wanted this to last forever. He wanted to just stay right here in this lonely little cabin with her while the world passed them by. No Hunger, no danger, no day and no night. Just her, and him, suspended in this moment.

The crystal had come off last night in the battle; he could feel the pull of it outside in the snow. Its subtle call northward was a reminder of the danger she was in and he frowned. He didn't want to bring her to Haven. He wanted to keep her safe from his world forever, and live with her in her bright cottage in her emerald forest like the happy ending to a fairy tale. But there were no happy endings in his world. The Hunger lay between them, and soon she would know of it. She would understand his sins, and his darkness. She would never be able to forgive him then.

She was still being hunted, and not just by one Eater, but two. By some stroke of luck he thanked every god for, he had managed to kill the second, but first was still out there. And if there were two there could be more.

He didn't understand it, couldn't see why they were after her. He didn't know the spells to delve deep and find out what was behind this, but Larissa did, and she would need Autumn there to enact them. It was dangerous to bring her there, especially now with the Equinox so near. The Hunger would be on everyone.

Larissa would not perform the Partaking until the night of the Equinox when its effects would be strongest. A human would die, but it would be just one, and all would be sated by it. It was the queen's greatest gift, and many sought to be a part of her colony for it. They were hers, under her control, but they no longer needed to kill.

It was dangerous to bring Autumn there, and he was betting on the biggest gamble of his life that he would win. She would be safe, not only from what hunted her, but from him as well. And he would do what he had to.

He would give her back her life again.

He tightened his arms around her, frowning, his thoughts darkening with what lay before them.

Autumn stretched against him and smiled, making soft sounds of waking as she nuzzled against his chest. He smiled again and ran his hand down her once more, relishing the feel of her against him. The darkness of his world would descend soon enough. Until then he would savor every moment with her.

Autumn came to slow, delicious wakefulness at his caress, smiling against his skin and breathing in the warm, masculine scent of him. Surely if there was a heaven, this was it, waking on top of this man, feeling his morning erection trapped between them. The hardness of it pressed against her belly. She shivered deliciously, surprised that, tired as she was, she was ready again for him. She had never had such amazing marathon sex, and sex with this man, *her* man, was intoxicating. He was literally like some drug she had taken that she couldn't get enough of. Being in love did that to a woman.

He lazily ran his hands up and down her body now, making her squirm and she looked up at him bleary-eyed through a tangle of her sleep and sex-mussed hair with a smile.

"Good morning," he rumbled at her, chuckling a little at all the hair across her face. She giggled and puffed at it, and he groaned softly as he brushed the fire-gold strands from her eyes with a smile.

"I hope I didn't hurt you at all last night," he said, still stroking and smoothing her hair. She blushed and shook her head, catching her lower lip in her teeth. She felt his erection pulse against her and she giggled, squirming against him.

"Dammit, Autumn, you tempt me like no other," he murmured, and she caught her breath, looking at him. She felt her cheeks heat slowly and she gave him a coy grin.

"I bet you say that to all the girls." She smiled sleepily, playfully spreading her fingers across his chest where she lightly toyed with his nipple. She was enjoying this, flirting and teasing with him. She loved seeing his reactions to what she did to him, because she knew well what he did to her. He had to be teasing her now as he looked down at her, his bottomless blue eyes sparkling.

"I've said a lot of things to women over the years, but never that. You are magnificent," he growled, his expression sincere as he ran his fingers over her face. "I've never wanted a woman more."

Autumn looked at him, trying to decide if he was joking. The look he was giving her certainly didn't look like he was joking. In fact, he was giving her a level look, a small smile on his lips as he stroked her face tenderly while his eyes searched hers. He was serious. Of all the women he had slept with—and the number was likely staggering—she was the one he had "never wanted more"? It wasn't an "I love you" or anything, but it was the best she was likely to get from Kain Ulmer. She'd take it.

Smiling wide, she pushed herself up his body and pressed her lips against his grin. She became entangled once more in his divine, heated kiss, her senses filled with him completely. They kissed passionately for several long, searing moments, breathing each other's breath, lost in one another. Autumn was just about to rise and take him inside of her once again when there was a small sound from the darkened doorway of the kitchen, barely registering in Autumn's desire-clouded brain.

Kain, however, reacted instantly to the sound, immediately lifting and turning Autumn to place her behind him before he jumped into a crouch with a snarl. The tall silhouette of a man stood in the darkened doorway, cupping the flame of a lighter to his lips.

"Jesus Christ, are you two about done yet?" the stranger grumbled around the cigarette, taking a long drag and raising his gray eyes to them. The crystal Kain had been wearing and lost in the snow last night fell from the stranger's fingers, swinging on its chain, filling Autumn with an unexplainable sense of foreboding.

"The Queen is waiting to see you."

To be continued...

THE STORY CONTINUES...

HEAT

CHRISTIE GOLDENWULFE

COMING SOON FROM

SISTER MOON PUBLISHING

www.sistermoonpublishing.com

About The Author

Christie Goldenwulfe is a full-time professional artist and werewolf nerd. Hunger is her first novel. She currently lives near Albuquerque, New Mexico.

To find out more about Christie and her werewolves, visit her website at:

www.christiegoldenwulfe.com

Made in the USA
San Bernardino, CA
25 January 2018